POISON TOUCH

MONARCH VIPERS

VENGEANCE
BOOK ONE

KELA MARQ

Edited by: Telltail Editing
Cover by: Christian Bentulan / Covers by Christian

Poison Touch / Kela Marq.—1st Edition
ISBN 978-1-964943-00-8

ABOUT THIS BOOK

I made three crucial mistakes on my first day at Monarch University:

1. I thought my plan for revenge would be simple.
2. Underestimating Ledger Hunt—the ruthless king of Monarch.
3. Believing I could control my desires around him.

Ledger Hunt is everything I should hate: dangerous, manipulative, and the key to uncovering the truth I've been chasing. But every time our paths cross, something shifts. His stormy eyes watch my every move, daring me to get closer, tempting me to trust him when I know I shouldn't. He's after something —something more than my secrets—and I can feel his pull, like gravity dragging me toward a collision I'm not ready for.

He plays the part of the predator, but there's a war behind those eyes, a hunger that goes beyond power. He wants me. But if I fall into his arms, I risk losing everything. I have to make him pay for what he took from me before he takes my heart, too.

Author's note: *Poison Touch* is the first book of a trilogy and ends on a cliffhanger.

This book contains the following topics which may be sensitive for some readers: violence, suicide (description of past event), rape (vague description of past event), attempted rape, murder, bullying, explicit sex scenes, and marijuana use.

If none of these topics are triggering for you, then welcome to Monarch University.

To all the reckless girls.

PROLOGUE

KINSLEY

I've always been drawn to recklessness. Tonight is no different.

Faceless, restless men surround me. Masks hide their manic expressions and salivating mouths. It's like being in a fucked-up funhouse. Clowns and ghastly faces are everywhere I look. The energy in the air is a cocktail of rabid savagery and unrelenting greed. On the brink of climax, their desperate need to fall into its grasp escalates as they scream at the two fighters in the octagon cage.

My father is one of those fighters. He has no idea I followed him here and snuck into the illegal underground fight, as I do every time he fights.

Every few weeks, you can find me here.

Every few weeks, thousands of dollars slide through greedy hands.

Every few weeks, a fighter is dragged away, bloodied and bruised.

I was five when I started training to fight. Since then, my father has repeatedly said, "Never put yourself in a position where you have to fight for your life."

The exact moment I know his words are the absolute truth is

the second his opponent sends a hard strike to his temple, and my dad's body crumples to the mat. My hands fly to my covered mouth as his words echo like a bass drum in my head. The constant thrumming of syllables reverberates with a fierce warning as the masked figure descends over his unmoving form. He lies on his back with his arms limp at his sides. As I stare at his body, willing him to get up, I'm terrified as hell that my dad didn't take his own advice.

Blood splatters the dragon tattoo on his forearm. Unnecessarily, the fighter, who calls himself Python, pins my father's wilted body to the ground. He looks up into the crowd, scanning the masked faces of the audience. His eyes are wild and unsettled, like a rabid dog as he searches for someone specific. It's all too easy to lose your sense of surroundings in the octagon. His amped-up fans are too hyped with the scent of blood and sweat in the rancid air to notice. They roar for him to finish off his prey as I silently beg him to have mercy.

I scan the crowd to see who or what he's searching for. The fighter's gaze finally settles on a group of men in the far corner. Venom.

Tonight's illegal event is being hosted in an abandoned warehouse. Anyone invited or involved in the festivities is required to hide their identity behind a mask. The suited men in the corner are no different. What makes them stand out is that they all wear the same mask, featuring a green striking viper.

I drop back into the shadows. My attention ping-pongs from the fighter in the ring to my dad to Venom. The man heading the group, with his arms crossed over his chest, nods slightly to Python. The nod is all for show, a way to hype the fans, increase the bets, up the odds, and raise the stakes. It's only a savage game, after all. May the best man win. Fighters get the shit beaten out of them, their faces swollen beyond recognition, and some even end up unconscious. That's the risk they take as soon as they step inside the cage. But no one has ever been killed—at least that I know of.

Tonight feels different. There's an intensity building that leaves chills snaking across my heated skin. I rub my arms through the sleeves of my hoodie. Nothing in that cage is staged or an accident. Nor would my father act as if he were unconscious just to put on a show. It's clear Python has already won, so why not announce him as the winner? Something's off, and it isn't good. The air becomes heavier with each breath I drag into my lungs.

The fighter in the cage returns the simple gesture to the suited man with a slight nod. That one silent command is anything but good for my dad. The tattooed snake slinks down the side of the man's torso, its open mouth revealing large fangs and a forked tongue—very similar to the ones on Venom's masks. The fierceness in its inked eyes echoes that of the fighter.

I stifle the scream on the verge of freeing itself, threatening to expose my presence. Furious tears spill over the rims of my eyes, soaking the edges of my black mask.

The eyes of the six men of Venom flash with determination and dollar signs. Even the hosts of the event know it's safer to remain anonymous behind their masks—especially when the ringleaders are playing dirty games and making indecent deals. It's as if they decided to use my father as a pawn in their sick game tonight.

As stupid and dangerous as it is, I can't stand back for another second. I push my way through the crowd. All of them scream for blood, for my father's life to be snuffed out for sport and extra cash in their pockets. The fighter raises his arm and pumps his fist into the air, giving his fans their money's worth.

The onlookers chant his name. "Python! Python! Python! Python!" The long, drawn-out pause between the Y and the T makes the single word sound like two separate words.

Streams of sweat run down the fighter's face through splatters of blood, turning it pink. Python takes one last look around, soaking up the energy of the uproar in the overcrowded, stuffy room. Any second, his fist will come down onto my father like a sledgehammer.

Body odor and blood fill my nostrils. Ignoring the nauseating scent, I grasp the chain-link cage and call out to my dad by his stage name. "Slayer! Get up! Slayer! Slayer!"

The metal bites into my palms, but I hardly feel the rough edges slicing into my skin. The only hurt is the aching in my chest, the heaviness of guilt and helplessness weighing me down like a massive anchor.

Nothing. There's no response from my dad. I'm shoved to my left, then into the wall of the cage. The side of my face smashes against the fence. The jarring pushes my mask out of place. Pain bursts along my cheek. The corner of my lip snags along the rough edges of the metal. I lick away the wetness along the scratch. Holding on to the fence for my life, I refuse to move as a fight breaks out behind me in the crowd. Their hollering saturates my own as I continue to call out to my dad.

Finally, his eyes flutter open as though he's waking from a deep sleep. Blood from the gash along his brow seeps into his unfocused gaze.

"Stay with me!" I scream. "Slayer!"

He doesn't—or can't—hear me. I can barely hear myself. Over and over, I call out to him. My throat feels like it's on fire, but I don't stop. His head lolls to the side, facing me. I can save him if I can get him out now. His right eye is swollen shut. His split lips slowly part as he finds the strength to open his one good eye. God only knows how badly he's bleeding on the inside.

With no other option, I raise my leg, bracing the toe of my boot through the fence, and pull myself up. I begin to climb up the side of the octagon cage. I'm only a few feet from the top when someone grabs my ankle and yanks me down. I try to kick the asshole loose, but his grip only tightens.

"Where the fuck are you going? Get down. Let Python finish the loser!"

The second he jerks me away from the cage, my feet hit the ground, and I stumble. Catching myself before I fall, I round on the guy who pulled me away from getting to my father. He's already disappeared within the messy brawl, leaving a hundred other crazed fans who look just like him, their faces hidden behind a mask and their eyes possessing the same heated hunger and rage.

Movement in the center of the ring grips my attention. Python's balled fist is cocked and ready. It's too late.

I'm too late.

I scream as his fist slams into my dad's face. Again and again, he repeats the drone-like beating while the ref stands over them and does nothing. I scream until my throat is raw and the taste of metal coats the inside of my mouth. No one hears them, though. Nothing can be heard over the crowd chanting, "Finish him!"

The collective demand shoots straight to the center of my chest. I press my hand over my heart, trying to calm its fierce pounding. It's no use. Caught up in the glorified frenzy, they have no idea what they're begging for. To them, my father is a plaything, an actor in their game. He's not a man with a daughter and a wife, someone who has an actual life. Begging for death would be the last thing they would be doing if it were someone they loved under the hammer of Python's fist.

A gunshot goes off in the warehouse, the sound ricocheting off the concrete walls. Panic becomes a living thing as everyone crouches, waiting for another shot. Heavy breathing and panting are the only noises for several seconds. Then, as if the entire warehouse counted to five to move, all hell breaks loose. The room begins to spin.

In a whirlwind, I'm swept away with the mob. I try to fight against them, but it's useless. Seconds ago, these same crazed spectators were chanting for death. Now, all of them race toward the exit to save their own ass.

Like salmon going upstream, I fight my way in the opposite direction, back to the cage. I shove and push as if I'm not even there. I slowly make my way through the crowd until I'm in a small clearing. I jump up to see over the heads of the crowd and into the octagon. No one is standing in the cage. Python and the ref are gone. Only my father's body lies in a bloody heap on the mat.

Before I reach the cage, another fight breaks out, and I'm shoved toward the same dark corner from where I began watching this hellish nightmare. I need to get back to my dad. Tears blur my vision as I try to fight my way through the stragglers. A white-hot pain like I've never felt before splinters through my side just above my hip.

I grab the area, and wetness coats my hand. "What the—?"

I double over. My breaths become short gasps as I try to remember to breathe through the piercing pain. The only thing I can concentrate on is the searing throb. I close my eyes, tuning out the surrounding chaos. When I catch my breath, I stand. Even in the dingy light of the warehouse, I can see blood coating my hand. My father isn't the only one in trouble.

"Get out of here," a deep voice rumbles next to me.

A masked figure stands before me. The snake's fangs on his mask are only inches from my face. Venom. His dark, arresting eyes are his only visible feature. Like me, the rest of him is shrouded by a dark hoodie pulled low over his brow.

I'm unable to focus on him, too overcome with the chaos around me and the unbearable pain shooting through my side. My entire existence feels taken out of context, as if I slipped into another realm and I'm watching a different version of myself, a version of me who's helpless and frail. She's so unfamiliar because I've never been either of those things.

The masked man stands at least a head taller than I do. I catch sight of his hands to see what he stabbed me with, but they're empty. Confused and reeling with pain, anger, fear, and grief, I do the only thing I know how to do. I lash out. He quickly catches my wrist before I'm able to strike him.

His gaze is drawn to my hand, covered with blood. "What the fuck?"

Shock or concern causes him to reach for me, then he jerks back and stares at me as if I'm some new species. Too confused and scared for my dad, and now for myself, to decipher what's going on, I yank my arm free. He reaches up to tug my hood down. I move to stop him with my free hand, but it's too late. My blonde hair spills out. Several people, their masks a blur, run past us to their freedom, back to their safe, sheltered lives.

As he takes me in, the stranger's eyes darken to a deeper shade of night. I should be scared by the fury igniting in them. I'm not. If my dad weren't on the verge of death, then there might be a slight possibility I would be, but not tonight.

"I need to get Slayer out of here," I rasp. I'm losing blood and precious time standing here with this greedy killer.

"It's too late for him. He's already gone. But *you* need to get out of here. If they get a hold of you"—he jerks his head toward the rapidly approaching sirens—"you're done for."

By his low, heated growl and the uneasy way he looks around, I don't think the cops are the only ones he's warning me against. When he faces me again, the gaping mouth of the viper on his mask sparks a renewed, vibrant anger deep in my core.

"No! You're the reason he's— I won't leave him."

"Let's go. Now!" someone yells over the surrounding chaos to the masked figure standing with me.

"I won't leave him!" I shout again as a thunderstorm of hysteria overtakes me. None of this was supposed to happen.

He grips my shoulders. "You don't have a choice. Leave now and disappear," he hisses.

Why is this stranger so hell-bent on my escaping the danger on its way? I'm no one but the daughter of the man who lies dying only twenty feet away from me. I try to fight against him to get back to my father. He's the only one who matters right now.

The moment the stranger's grip loosens, I take advantage of the split second I have, spinning around and escaping his hold. I turn to run back to my dad. Something slams into the back of my head before I take two full strides. An explosion of pain erupts inside my skull. The room tilts. My body sways on its own accord. As if I'm walking into a tunnel, darkness closes in around me.

Dad... He's the only thought I have before the black hole of defeat drags me under in its unbreakable embrace. Yet, somehow, I know this is only the beginning of the hell that's coming for me.

1

KINSLEY

I T ' S BEEN three months since my dad was brutally killed and I was stabbed. My sliced flesh has healed a lot faster than the hole left in my chest.

No one says cage fighting is for the faint of heart, but it rarely ends in death. Nothing about that fight was fair. Why him? There were six other fights that night. His fight was the last of the night. The fight everyone showed up to see was the one with the highest bets. He was no doubt one of the best fighters.

I've run the scene over in my mind a thousand times, and none of it makes sense. He brought in a lot of money, but that was what the Underground, the UG, was about: paying to watch the brutal entertainment to make some extra cash with a good bet.

I don't believe my dad was in for the money. He was all about the thrill of the challenge. It was his way of balancing the exquisitely sharp edge of fighting. One side of the blade seeks the high of the winning, while the other side bleeds the honor and respect for the art. It seemed his competitive side fought harder for the high than the honor. His death is proof of that.

The last months of my senior year were supposed to be filled with parties, prom, and prepping for college, not mourning.

Taking a deep breath, I toss another pair of sneakers into the box labeled *Shoes*. Cardboard boxes line the walls of my bedroom. Most of them are filled with stuff that used to have much more meaning. But after you lose someone who means the world to you, most things are just that, worthless things.

"No one needs this many damn shoes," I mutter.

Of all the stacked boxes packed with clothes, books, and mostly nonsense, only a few are going with me to my uncle's house, my new home. For the past few hours, I've been dragging ass to avoid saying goodbye to this house and my mom. But time is closing in on me. I knew moving and starting a new life would be difficult, but is it supposed to be this hard? I'm not ready for the change, the move, or for tomorrow, my first day at Monarch University. The only thing I am prepared for is revenge.

I was supposed to attend college with my best friend, Luca. We had it all planned out. But everything changed the night of that horrific fight.

With dread, I step onto my balcony and stare at the vast front yard with its perfectly cut green lawn and pruned shrubs. A limo, a moving truck, and a blacked-out Kawasaki Ninja motorcycle are lined up around the circular driveway near the fountain. It sounds like the beginning of a bad joke. Hell, the reality of it is a joke—a sick one.

A red Tesla comes up the driveway and parks behind my motorcycle. Some upbeat pop song blares from the speakers before the windows roll up. My best friend steps out from the driver's side. As usual, Luca is dressed to perfection. He strides up the wide stone steps, his lean, muscular body evident through his tight white shirt and black dress pants. He doesn't pause to knock on the front door like a visitor. Luca hasn't needed a reason to knock since we were kids. He disappears through the front entrance. He'll be at my door in a few moments, and there's no one else I want or need to see more.

If it weren't for him, I'd be lying in a grave next to my dad. He found me that night at the warehouse using the tracking app on his phone. According to him, his timing was perfect. He arrived just before the cops stormed the place and was able to get me out. If he hadn't, I would have been arrested and questioned about what happened. And as much as I wanted to call the cops myself and tell them everything, that would only get me killed.

When I woke in the hospital, I was stitched up, told I had a concussion, and hooked to enough tubes and wires to make my mother nearly have a heart attack. Luca told them some bullshit story about us practicing our weapons technique, and whoops, Kinsley accidentally got stabbed and knocked out. No one believed him, but everyone let it go when I told the same story after he briefed me.

There's a brief knock before Luca opens the door. "Hey, baby Kins."

He doesn't bother to ask how I'm doing. He already knows. Before I can say anything, he's across the room, taking me into his arms. Luca knows precisely what to say or do, especially when no words are needed. Unlike me, who's the complete opposite. I usually say the first thing that jumps into my head and then suffer the backlash as it immediately nosedives off my tongue. It's most likely the reason I have very few friends.

Luca does his best to keep me out of trouble. And most of the time, he does a great job. If only he were with me at the UG. Not only is his level of self-control a thousand times greater than mine but he also has enough balls to verbally bitch slap me when I need to be reined in. Because he's an almost perfect being inside and out, most people drop to their knees to please him. So, I like to think of myself as his breath of fresh air. I don't fall to my knees for anyone. And I'm convinced this is the reason he loves me.

If I had my way, I'd pounce on his fine brown ass, tie him up, and beat the shit out of any girl who got near him. But there's one teeny issue that I can't change about him. Luca's sexual preference puts somewhat of a damper on my interests and needs. It's frustrating as hell, but there's not much I can do about it—no matter how short I wear my skirts.

He pulls back and stares down at me. In my already fragile state, I can barely look into his sad, mocha eyes. His pain is just as palpable as mine since he was almost as close to my dad as I was.

"It's okay to feel vulnerable. He was your whole world."

I nod. "Yeah, he was."

The fist gripping my heart squeezes again. It has never completely let go. The tightness is a constant agonizing reminder that my life will never be the same again. My dad was my rock and superhero. He was the one who brought me to karate class and taught me to love martial arts. The one I went to when a boy broke my heart. He was my everything.

"I don't know how to live without him," I admit. "I'll never hear him tell me my kick was off or perfect or feel his arms around me." The wall holding the torrent of tears breaks. "He gave the best hugs." I grip the sleeves of Luca's shirt.

Luca sniffs. "I know they're not the same, but you can have these arms around you whenever you want."

I bury myself deeper into his hold. That's the most painful thought. There are so many things I'll never get to experience with my dad, a thousand moments stolen from me. That's also the thought that keeps me strong, reminding me what I need to do. It won't resurrect my dad, but it'll reward my selfish vengeance.

Luca just holds me until I ease out of our embrace.

"Thanks, I needed that." I take a deep breath to collect myself.

"I know." He wipes away a tear on my cheek with the pad of his thumb.

I glance around my room. "What now?"

He tilts his head, then jackknifes his finger at me. "Now we talk about this horrible idea of yours. You're leaving me," he says, crossing his arms over his chest.

Guilt washes over me. But I didn't give myself another choice. Luca doesn't understand now, but one day, he will—just not today. As corrupt as they are, I have reasons for attending Monarch, but I'm not ready to share those yet, not even with my best friend.

"I know."

"We've always planned that we would go to Maylen, join a dojo, and kick ass—together. And now you're going to Monarch. I just don't get it." He throws his hands in the air. "You hate all that bureaucratic bullshit and the dirty money that follows it."

I couldn't argue with him. Even though his family and mine are rich as hell, we don't flaunt it or use it to up our game like most we went to school with.

"You know that college has a freaking uniform for undergrads, right? You hate uniforms."

He isn't wrong. It's ridiculous. "It's just for a year."

"And that college is notorious for only accepting spoiled, rich assholes whose families want them to follow in their corrupt corporations? I'd hate to see you get caught in any bad shit."

"I'm sure I'll have no problem handling myself."

He turns me so that my back is against his chest. I lean back into his warm body. His arms wrap around me, and he rests his chin on my shoulder. I'm glad he can't see my face as I let the lie slide so easily from my lips. "I promised my mom I'd stay close."

"I know. I'm being selfish." Luca pulls back a little and twists me slightly so I can look at him. His full lips quirk into a lopsided grin. "Selfish or not, my last argument for you not to attend Monarch is that you've missed the first two weeks of the semester. It's going to be a bitch to catch up. And I'm going to bet you got shitty classes."

I shake my head and laugh. "Again, you're not wrong."

He's right on target with that one. I'm with the leftover classes. It'll suck, but the small sacrifice will be worth it.

"That's all I got, and it seems that isn't enough for you to change your mind."

"We have next year," I say without knowing where this year will leave me.

"Fine." He spins me around to face him. "So, you want to fight today? I bet we can kick this shitty day's ass."

Being Luca's best friend not only comes with all the standard best friend perks but we also enjoy the benefit of kicking the shit out of each other. We've studied jiu-jitsu, karate, and other martial arts for most of our lives. We're a good match most days, but I can usually take him down if weapons are involved. And I never let him forget it.

I plop down on the bed. "As much as I'd like to, I still have a ton to do. Besides, I'm still on the mend." Subconsciously, I touch my side where my stitches were.

"Nice try. I'll buy the excuse of a lot to do but not the 'on the mend' one. You and I both know you're ready to get back on the mat."

I grin. "Jeez. Let me have a little more time before you hand me my butt again."

"I did get you good in our last match." He laughs and sits beside me, tracing the lines of the dragon tattoo that runs the length of my forearm. "I still can't believe you're leaving me."

I lay my head on his shoulder. "It's not like I'm moving to Alaska. I'm only a couple of hours away from Maylen."

"I know," he grumbles. "How's your mom holding up?"

My mom hasn't taken my dad's death well at all. To say they were in love is like saying you might get burned if you touch fire. The pills have helped numb some of the pain, but I'm not sure the thousands of shattered pieces of her heart can ever be put back together.

I shrug. "The same. It's like she's turned into an empty shell. It's horrible to watch."

I swipe at the wetness pooling in my eyes. I know she loves me, but I feel like I lost her too when my dad died.

Lifting my head, I knock his shoulder with mine. "Hey, I thought you came over to cheer me up?"

"You're right. I'm sorry." Luca jumps up, pulling me with him. He looks around the room of boxes and half-emptied bookshelves. "Why don't we order pizza while we finish packing?"

And that's exactly what we do until Silvia, our housekeeper, gently raps on my open door, a man in a dark blue jumpsuit standing next to her. The label on his breast pocket reads Alex. "Are you ready, dear?" she asks.

With the sting of anguish, I answer reluctantly, "As ready as I'll ever be." I point to a stack of boxes near the closet. "Those are the ones to be delivered this afternoon."

The mover in the jumpsuit nods, pulling the tape gun from his belt.

Luca glances at the three boxes. "That's all you're bringing?"

I look at the boxes. "What? I packed clothes, toiletries, and a box of miscellaneous crap. My school uniforms were delivered to my uncle's. What else do I need?"

"There better be a picture of me in one of those boxes."

I laugh. "You think you're that important, huh?"

"Hell, yes!" He pulls me into his arms. "I'm going to miss the shit out of you, Kins."

His words settle with an ache deep in my chest. The thought

kills me more than it should. Not seeing Luca every day will be the hardest part. It makes it slightly easier knowing he's only a call or text away. Only slightly.

Unable to hold back the tears, I let them fall. "Me, too."

He kisses the top of my head, releases me, and then heads for the door. I grab my jacket and backpack from the back of the desk chair. As Luca goes on ahead, I tap Alex on his shoulder. He pulls the tape across the box, sealing it.

I lower my voice to a whisper. "Can you also bring that small one over there?"

He looks to where I'm pointing. "Sure, miss."

"Thanks."

My mom is in the kitchen. She throws back her head, then takes a sip of water. It doesn't take a genius to know she's trying to numb the pain of the loss of her husband.

"Mom." The cautiousness in my voice is new when I speak to her now. Before, she was so lively and fun. Now, she's more like a zombie, just trying to make it to the next day.

She sets down the glass. "Hi, sweetie."

Luca leans against the counter and looks from me to my mom. I don't miss his prefab, easygoing expression. Like me, he also notices the change in her.

"Where are you guys off to?" she asks.

I wonder if she remembers that I'm moving to her brother's house today, where I'll be staying while she visits her sister. "I'm all packed and ready to leave for Uncle Trey's."

A hesitant smile plays on her face, then falls pleasantly into place. "Yes, Trey is looking forward to having you there. It's perfect that he lives so close to Monarch."

"Yeah, it is. We talked yesterday. He's got my room all ready."

Her fingers play with the ends of her ponytail. She managed to get dressed in a simple flowing sundress and sandals. It's a step up from her usual attire. The roots of her hair have grown out, and her skin looks pale and chalky. It breaks my heart to see her look so lost without my dad.

"It's been a while since he's had someone else living with him, so try to be patient. Help him when you can. Make sure you clean up after yourself."

I know all of this, but I let her talk it out—do the mom thing. "I will."

As she opens her arms to me, I go into them with all the sadness, longing, and pain she feels. I swore to myself that when this moment came, I wouldn't cry, but I'm unable to keep that promise. A tear slips free, falling onto her bare shoulder.

She pulls back and cups my cheeks. "Oh, sweetie, this is for the best. We'll both take some time away from here, restore our strength, and find our happiness again." The forced smile on her lips does nothing to sugarcoat the words she desperately wants to believe.

There's so much I could say to her. Living in the house they built together has been hard for her. Memories of him are on every wall: family pictures, the art they bought together, and even the light, feather-gray paint they chose from a hundred different swatches. I want to tell her that being apart isn't for the best, that we need each other and this is the easy way out, but I don't say any of those things. As much as it hurts to admit, she feels she needs time to heal in her way, without me, and I need to respect that.

She continues. "Listen, I've had the accountant set up accounts for anything you need." She hands me an envelope. "Here are debit and credit cards and some cash."

"Thanks." I stuff it into my backpack. "I'll text you when I get there."

She nods. "I don't know how long I'm staying with your aunt, but I'm just a phone call away."

I wish she weren't leaving at all. But it isn't fair to ask her to stay. Luca wants me to go with him, but I also have to do certain things to heal. And like me, my mom is doing the best she can. We all are.

I give her one final hug. "I love you."

"I love you, too, so much, my beautiful girl." She walks me to the door.

I try so hard not to look over my shoulder, but I take one last glance at her. Mom has already disappeared back inside. There's hurt stacked upon hurt as I stare at the closed door. Her pain is masked with pills, while mine is raw and without. The only thing I'm grateful for is that she didn't see the brutal way Dad was killed.

Luca patiently waits for me next to my motorcycle. We hug each other like we may never see each other again. Before I give a chance for more tears to fall, I climb onto my bike and don't look back as I drive through the iron gates. If I do, I'm not sure I'll have the strength to follow through on what I have planned.

It's almost five when I turn down my uncle's quiet, picturesque street lined with canopied ficus trees. His home is nestled in a small neighborhood, a block from the beach, with a few other Key West-style homes. The driveway of his light blue house is empty when I pull in. Waves breaking against the shore replace the humming of my motorcycle engine when I turn the engine off. The sound immediately soothes the tension in my chest. The tightness in my arms and legs eases as I stretch them after the hour ride. The key is right where he said it would be, under the small stone statue of happy Buddha.

Natural light floods the entry and living room. Everything is like it's always been: pastel blue, turquoise, and white are the backdrop to the beachy, nautical décor. The driftwood table, the antique ore propped in the corner, the picture of me winning my first tournament next to the silver octopus lamp, all of it is the same. And although I've been here a thousand times, today feels different, more permanent. The house hasn't changed, but I have. I'm not visiting for a BBQ or watching a martial arts tournament. This time, I'm here to stay, at least for the next several months.

The note on the kitchen counter reads: *At the dojo. Be home around 8. Uncle T.*

I already know which bedroom is mine. I used to sleep here when my parents went on vacation or when Silvia took time off for her vacations. I make my way down the short hall and push open the door. The queen bed, covered with a light pink comforter, is in the center of the room. A nightstand is to its left, and an armoire is in the corner. A new desk with a chair sits against the opposite wall.

I press the switch to turn on the closet light, then throw my backpack on the floor next to the desk. My uniforms are hanging on the wooden rod just as expected. Black and green are the colors that represent Monarch University, the Vipers.

I hate green.

Heading toward the kitchen, I glance into the family and dining rooms. The house is small but quaint and comfortable. I grab a bottle of water from the fridge. After taking a drink, I roll the cool bottle over my forehead.

"This is my life now," I mutter and open the French doors. The sound of waves crashing against the shore fills the silence. The soothing noise and salty air immediately begin to calm my jumping nerves.

The movers arrive thirty minutes later with my boxes. It doesn't take long to put away the few things I brought from home. I set the picture of Mom, Dad, and me on the nightstand, and then the other one with me and Luca winning our first competition. It's only been three months since that dreadful night. It feels like it happened yesterday and also like it was a lifetime ago. Neither lessens the relentless hurt. I miss him so damn much. The mess of feelings tangled in my heart is in a constant battle: anger, remorse, regret, frustration, loss, emptiness, and sadness, all vying to be at the forefront. None of them win for very long before another takes its place.

The small box I asked the mover to bring sits on the floor under the windowsill. It holds a collection of things left by my father. I haven't had the courage to open it yet. Maybe it's fear of what I'll find that keeps me from being brave enough to lift the lid. Or possibly I don't open it because when I finally do, I'll no longer have his treasures to look forward to.

I don't have the energy to open it today, so I leave it under the sill where the sunshine, the rain, the moon, and the stars can watch over it until I can gather enough courage to lift its lid. I lie back on the bed and watch the ceiling fan spin in lazy circles. It's crazy how you think your life is untouchable, then BAM! It's turned upside down in one night. And it will never be the same again.

"Kins, I'm home, and I brought dinner."

I wake to the sound of my uncle's voice. Damn, I must have dozed off. Through the curtains, darkness has replaced the light. I glance at my phone. Eight thirty. After pulling on a pair of sweats, I head into the kitchen.

Uncle Trey sets the cardboard box of white paper containers on the island. The smile on his face is as welcoming as it is sad. His short, light brown hair is starting to gray at his sides. With his board shorts and flip-flops, he still looks younger than his forty-two years.

"Come here, kiddo." He embraces me in a warm hug.

"Thanks, Uncle Trey."

He rests his chin on the top of my head. "Anything you need, I'm here."

"Thank you." For the third time today, I cry.

We make small talk as we eat. After our bellies are full of lo mein, cashew chicken, fried rice, and egg rolls, I fold the tops of the half-eaten boxes and place the leftovers in the fridge.

When I turn, my uncle says, "Here," and tosses me a fortune cookie.

I catch it and smile. After ripping open the cellophane, I break the cookie in two. The small piece of paper blossoms from its center.

A stranger will teach you true sacrifice.

"Whatever the hell that means," I mutter as I toss the shred of nonsense into the trash.

Besides getting my uniform ready for tomorrow, there's one thing I have to do. I tell Uncle Trey good night and head for my room.

He glances at his watch. "Just so I'm not crazy, most college students don't usually go to bed before ten, right?"

I chuckle. "I'm just tired."

"Completely understandable. And have no fear, I'll get the hang of this..." He wags his hand between us. "Just give me a couple of weeks."

"You got it." I smile, then head for my room.

In the en suite bathroom, I stare at myself in the mirror as I pull the band from my hair. Light glints off my double eyebrow piercings, one a ring, the other a small, curved barbell. Blonde hair cascades down my back. I'll miss it a lot, but what I need to do is necessary for what's to come. I set the box of dye on the edge of the sink.

An hour later, as I look at myself in the mirror, I barely recognize the girl with bright blue eyes and dyed black hair staring back at me. It's amazing that with one little box that costs less than ten bucks, I can transform into a different person, a person who will be recognized by fewer than a handful of people as once being a blonde.

I don't know who confronted me the night my father was killed. I only know he's a part of Venom, and I can't risk being recognized tomorrow when I step onto Monarch's campus, otherwise known as Venom's den.

Murder isn't exactly on my list, but hell, who knows what I'll be capable of when I come face to face with the snake responsible for killing my father. There are only three things I know for certain: his death wasn't an accident, Venom was behind it, and they will pay for what they've taken from me, one way or another.

2

KINSLEY

As I LOOK DOWN at my outfit, I want to vomit all over my Dr. Martens. No one informed Monarch University that uniforms in college haven't been a thing in decades. I feel like I'm wearing a costume in the green and black uniform. The black tie sporting Monarch's green viper mascot wraps around my neck like a noose. I consider tying the black blazer around my waist to hide the hideous plaid skirt, then dismiss the idea. Instead, I hike up the skirt so I won't be confused for the librarian.

My phone dings with a text from Luca:

Good luck today!

Thanks, I'm going to need it

I type back and follow the scent of fresh-brewed coffee into the kitchen. Uncle Trey sits at the high top.

"Good morning," I mutter. I toss my backpack on the chair. From the fridge, I grab the orange juice.

His steaming mug of coffee is halfway to his lips when he pauses mid-air. "Hey, you— Whoa!" He slowly sets his mug on the counter. "When you said good night last night, you *did* have blonde hair, right?"

"Yeah, you're not going crazy," I tease.

"Good to know." He wipes his brow. "Don't get me wrong, I like the black and all, but what happened to the blonde girl I've known since the day she came into this world?"

I comb my fingers through my hair, still in awe of the long, dark waves around my shoulders. "I just wanted a change," I say, offering a quick shrug.

"It's a change all right and a bit of a shock." He smiles. "One I'll have to get used to."

"Yeah, you and me both," I mumble as I fill a glass with orange juice. "I'm going to get going."

"Don't you want something to eat before your big day?"

The toast smeared with avocado on his plate looks delicious, but I don't have the stomach for it. On any other day, I'd have sat down and eaten. Today, my nerves have climbed to new heights. I'm not nervous. It's more of an anxious, get-this-over-with feeling.

"Nah, I'm not hungry. I'll grab something at school. From what I read on their site, I'll be eating like a queen."

He must hear my sarcasm because he says, "Monarch is a great school. Give it a chance."

Monarch is a legacy school. Students attend because it's their birthright to shadow their parents, and most of them don't have a choice. They begin their education at Monarch Preparatory, then flow into the university. Rarely does anyone apply or transfer to Monarch University. The moral of the story is that everyone knows everyone, and the hierarchy and cliques usually don't change. It doesn't help that I'm starting the semester two weeks later than everyone else.

Monarch accepted me because my mom agreed to pay double the yearly tuition. The cost could probably buy a modest-sized home. She doesn't know my true reasons for wanting to go to Monarch. And she didn't care, so long as it made me happy. Since my dad died, there's nothing she wouldn't do to see even a sliver of a smile on my face.

The school is known to be overflowing with assholes who think they're entitled to anyone and everything because of Daddy's money. Yeah, not my scene. Besides, I won't be here long enough to give it a chance. Monarch serves one purpose: my gateway to Venom. And since they're the elite who overshadow everyone and everything on campus, they shouldn't be too hard to find. Then I'll zero in on which one delivered the fatal blow that set my life on a new course.

Uncle Trey slides off the stool to stand. "I'll be at the dojo when you get out of school. If you want to come by, we can get some kicks in. Maybe do a little weapons training."

My head isn't anywhere close to making plans for after school. I have three goals today—navigate my way around campus, find my dad's killer, and try to stay invisible.

I grab an apple from the fruit basket on the counter and toss it into my backpack. "Yeah, sounds good."

"All right, have a good day, and kick some ass."

"Thanks, sensei. You too."

Uncle Trey laughs as he closes the door behind me.

By design, it's still relatively early when I arrive at Monarch. Only a few people are in the parking lot. Fewer people equals fewer stares. Most students reside in the dorms or off-campus apartments. I pull into the spot just outside the entrance and then shut off the engine of my Ninja motorcycle. I hoped the ride here would calm me, but my nerves still vibrate with tension.

"Get a grip." As much as I want to believe this year and my plan will be a piece of cake, I'm not banking on it. As I recently learned, very few things go as planned. And for something as big as what I have in store, shit is bound to happen and screw things up.

Taking a few deep breaths behind the protection of my helmet, I fold my arms over the gas tank and close my eyes. The most important thing I need to remember at this school is that I'm here for one purpose and one purpose only—revenge. Don't get me wrong, leaving with my life would be beneficial. But revenge first.

In a whisper, I repeat, "Revenge. Revenge. Revenge."

While I try to etch this vital info into my brain, a deep voice crashes into me, knocking me off-kilter. "You lost?"

Opening my eyes, I glance over my shoulder. Through the tinted face shield of my helmet, I see four guys in a black, muddied Jeep. All of their stares are locked on me. The Jeep blocks any cars wanting to pass. Either they aren't bothered or are too busy glaring at me to notice anything or anyone else.

My guess is the latter. As if there's a giant target on me, the driver's piercing eyes shoot darts of annoyance and curiosity directly at me. So much for staying invisible. Any remnants of calm I just achieved dissolve into unease. It's difficult to look away from his compelling gaze until movement to his left catches my eye. The guy in the passenger seat peers around him to get a look at me. His full lips are slightly open as if he's about to speak, but he says nothing. Instead, a stream of smoke seeps out of his mouth.

Shifting my attention to the right, I'm met with the faces of the occupants in the back seat. They're identical replicas of the same beautiful mold. Only their hair makes it easy to tell them apart. One is short and intentionally messy, while the other is longer and so unruly that it has the potential to become dread-locks. Both of them are grinning like fools.

I turn away from them, giving them a view of my back. I think about staying on my bike and ignoring them. Or better yet, turning the engine back on, kicking it into gear, and high-tailing it out of there.

Heaving a sigh of defeat, I remind myself why I'm here. I

press down on the kickstand. The bike leans and steadies. I want nothing more than to turn around and see the space behind me Jeep free, but I know better. I slowly ease my leg over the seat and stand. After taking off my helmet, I set it on the motorcycle seat. The fresh black waves fall to my lower back.

"Fuuuck... me... now," the guy with the wild hair drawls through the open window.

His twin opens the back door, hops out, and then heads toward a girl waiting on the sidewalk.

"Did you hear me? Are you lost?" the asshole driver repeats.

Ignoring Asshole's and Crazy Hair's comments, I look around and pay particular attention to the oversized viper statue in the center of the fountain near the entrance. The sight of it shoots determination down my spine. Water cascades down its coiled body and around the sign at its base, *Monarch University, Home of the Vipers.*

I focus my attention back on the driver. "Nope, definitely not lost."

His straight, dark hair falls forward, landing on the peak of his defined cheekbone. He narrows his eyes. His stern gaze adds to his undeniably gorgeous face. "I'll be more direct. You're in my parking spot."

Needing a moment to catch my breath while I force out the images and heated sensations this jerk has spontaneously inspired, I bend over and adjust my black knee socks. After a few short breaths, I feel confident enough to face him with renewed control. His lethal expression remains in place. Acting like a bitch probably isn't the best way to make friends on my first day, but I refuse to let them think they can bully me.

"Well, it doesn't look like it's your spot today."

The twin scoffs out a laugh and slaps the driver on the shoulder. "Damn, Edge, she ain't taking your shit."

The driver—Edge—doesn't flinch. His cold, slate eyes never stray from mine.

I sweep my hair to the side, drape it over my right shoulder, and then hang my backpack off the other. With a mocking, sympathetic expression, I take a few steps toward the Jeep. The scent of men's cologne, weed, and exhaust fumes mingle in the air around me. Edge is even more striking up close. His face is smooth and flawless, except for the scar that cuts across the right side of his chin. Some of the dirty, heated images surface again before I can suppress them.

Jesus, Kins, you've been here five minutes, and already you're losing focus. I mentally slap myself back into submission.

When I'm only a few feet away from his window, I say in a sickly sweet voice, "Aw, don't be offended. It's not just you. I don't take shit from anybody."

Without waiting for a response, I turn and take off toward the enormous wooden doors of Monarch University.

Still feeling those storm-clouded eyes burning into me, relief begins to surface the farther away I get from him. Sucking in a huge breath, I step into the viper's den. Just as the doors shut, the Jeep's engine grunts and roars as it takes off.

The halls are still relatively empty due to the time of day. But my plan to arrive early and potentially avoid any drama backfired. The campus isn't that large, but I have no idea where I'm going. I may have seemed confident as I walked through those enormous doors, but no. I've never stepped foot on this campus. I bring up the map on my phone. My first class is fine arts, painting. The map on my phone says I'm not even close to the arts building. While navigating the halls, an arm wraps around my shoulder, and I'm tugged hard against a slim body. My captor laughs as he pulls me down a side hallway.

"Girl, you're either crazy or stupid. Either way, I want to be best friends."

What in the actual...?

I duck out from under the stranger's arm. With confusion, I turn to see a handsome enough guy, clearly on the nerd spectrum, who knows fashion better than I ever have or ever will, even in a uniform.

Noticing someone else has joined us, I turn. A girl with faded, cropped blue hair takes a swing at my captor's head. Her flimsy canvas bag makes contact, causing him to yelp.

"Ow! What was that for?"

She yanks on his plaid scarf, lowering him to her height. "You already have a best friend!"

Apparently, I just unintentionally stepped into a pile of BFF crap. My agenda for the day is already going to shit.

The guy who wants to be my new bestie pulls himself free. "Damn, girl! You know I'm not replacing you, but this diva just told off Venom. And not just any viper of Venom— but *the* Viper."

Well, shit me. Knowing I truly and ultimately fucked up, I want to cave in on myself. In the span of five minutes on campus, I managed to become prime prey for the ones I intended to stake out and take down. I really suck at staying invisible. The slight unease that ate up my calm from earlier is now pleasantly feasting on the fraying ends of my nerves.

Still gushing over my lapse in judgment, the guy says, "Eden, you should have seen it. It was the most epic thing to happen in this place in, like, forever."

"I didn't have to see it. She's the topic of every conversation I pass." She turns to look at me. "If I were you, I'd keep your head down and don't talk to a soul as you head to class as quickly as your Docs can carry you."

"I'm Bryce, by the way," the guy says. He nods toward his so-called bestie. Dropping his voice, he whispers, "That's Eden. She comes off as a rather bitchy nerd, but she's cool."

I stifle a chuckle. "Thanks for the heads-up."

Eden goes to slap him again but pauses, hand in mid-air, as a small woman approaches. "Ah, Ms. Bass."

"Eden," the woman with a silver high-set bun says. With the

added frown on her thin red lips, she clearly didn't miss Eden's intention of assault.

"Yes, ma'am."

The way in which Eden and Bryce back down, the no more than five-foot woman, is packed with intimidation. She turns to me. With a soft voice, she says, "Have a good day, dear." Then, she shuffles away.

"Thank you," I mutter.

"I'm out, too," Bryce says. "See ya later, new girl." He hands a paper bag to Eden. "Breakfast. It's your favorite, a blueberry muffin. And not that I should have to say it, but you'll always be my first bestie."

A thin smile cracks along Eden's mouth as she takes the bag. To me, she asks, "Where are you headed?"

During my short run-in with Bryce and Eden, the halls had come alive. Most everyone is too caught up in their own circle of friends and passing around the gossip about the girl in the parking lot to take notice of me. "Fine arts building."

Eden nods. She's more guarded than Bryce. That's probably why they get along. They balance each other out, like Luca and me. However, Bryce seems to be a fan of my untamed mouth.

"Your class is on the way to mine. I'll show you where it is." She doesn't look upset, so I consider this a good sign. "I'm Eden," she offers.

"I kind of caught on to that from your BFF."

She gives a small laugh. "Bryce is a great guy, a bit eccentric, but great. We've been friends since third grade."

"Anyone who brings you breakfast is golden in my book." I grab the pack of gum from the front pocket of my backpack. Unwrapping a piece, I put it in my mouth, then offer the pack to her.

"No thanks." Eden tucks strands of blue hair behind her ear, which is lined with studs, and holds up the paper bag. "I'm going to eat—"

Her words are cut short when an already familiar voice sounds behind us. "Hey, Ninja."

I slow my pace and turn to see the Venom crew heading right toward us.

Ninja... cute nickname. He has no idea how perfectly it fits me.

3

EDGE

THE NEW GIRL HAS BALLS. Unlike most girls here at Monarch who fall at my feet and will do *anything*, anywhere for me, she basically told me to fuck off to my face, then simply walked away. Not only did she get my attention but she snagged the rest of the school's as well with that stunt.

Gunner, one of the twins, props his arm on my shoulder as we walk down the hall. "So, what are you going to do with the new hot little heathen?"

She is hot as fuck, and I have a thousand ideas of what I want to do with her, none of which I want anyone in this hallway to witness. "Kindly let her know who's in charge," I answer.

He huffs out a laugh. "Good luck with that, bro. That chick right there..." He points down the hall to the girl with long black hair. Her back is to us, but there's no mistaking that it's Ninja with her high socks and black boots. "She just might be your ultimate match."

Levi, Gunner's brother, says, "Whatever the fuck happens, I want a front-row seat." He rubs his hands together as if he's getting ready for a showdown.

"I don't even know this girl, and I already like her," Estelle, Levi's girlfriend, says.

As expected, Kade says nothing. His silence alone says all I need to know. If I have my way, I'll say my peace, the little ninja will nod in agreement, and we'll both go our separate ways. But something tells me dealing with this firecracker won't be that easy.

The crowd in the hall parts as we approach the little ninja. When we're halfway to our target, I call out to her. She slows but doesn't turn around until the daughter of Monarch's chancellor looks over her shoulder and says something to her. Only then does she stop and unhurriedly turn in our direction. Seeing us come toward her, she crosses her arms over her chest. Usually, that's a defensive posture, but she uses the gesture to signify pure boredom.

The blue-haired girl, Eden, I think her name is, tucks herself in behind the new girl. At least someone has their fucking head on straight.

Ninja blows out a small bubble, pops it, then sucks the thin layer of gum back into her mouth. She's the poster child for bad schoolgirls, especially in Monarch's uniform. She wears the standard white shirt, unbuttoned to reveal just enough skin to have my gaze traveling down the line of her delicate throat to the tight knot of the necktie lying over the inviting crease of perfect breasts. My eyes continue to drag down the length of her body over the plaid short skirt to several inches of her smooth, slightly parted thighs, then black over-the-knee socks with chunky boots.

I've seen hundreds of girls in that uniform, and I've never seen any of them make the uniform look as hot as she does.

The closer I move in on Monarch's new troublemaker, the more I think I may have made a mistake I can't back out of. She sets her sights on me and juts her full, pouty lips. As I close the distance between us, the shuffling and murmurs of everyone around us fall away. It's only her and me.

I stop a few inches from her. She doesn't step back but holds her ground. Her sweet, minty breath tickles my nose. My senses run wild, imagining that mouth, how it tastes and all of its capabilities. Fuck. Who am I kidding? I want to know how she tastes everywhere.

Tilting her head slightly to the left and smirking, she makes it clear she doesn't miss how my gaze is glued to her lips. There's a hint of humor in those blue eyes, as if she gets off on encounters like this. When the corner of her mouth lifts a fraction, the slight shift is her tell. This dark-haired beauty clearly enjoys the challenge of being called out front and center to defend. I wonder if she knows what she's giving away.

I almost run with it, letting her know she's not as slick as she thinks before I notice her eyes... and fuck me to the corner of the earth. Those clear oceans of bright blue are as striking and unyielding as the first time I saw them. My heart stammers and then picks up its pace. The change is sudden and subtle to the naked eye. But as close as our bodies are, I hope she doesn't notice.

In the parking lot, I was paying more attention to the overall scene of the hot new girl on the badass motorcycle than the details.

Now that I'm standing directly in front of her, the realization of who she is hits me like a meteor falling right out of the fucking sky, and it's like I'm staring at a fucking ghost.

4

KINSLEY

Eden slips in behind me. "Oh, shit. It's Edge."

Edge? What kind of name is that?

Front and center, Edge must be the guy everyone either fears or fawns over. His rolled sleeves expose tanned, defined forearms. The first button of his white dress shirt is unfastened, offering only a hint of what's underneath. Otherwise known as a trap, guiding you in only to devour you in one swift go.

None of that is what sets my core aflame. For some unknown and morbid reason, it's the black Monarch necktie wrapped around his fist. My imagination morphs into dirty thoughts before the vehement look on his face comes into focus, as though he's picturing how to use that same tie as a noose to strangle me.

The rest of his friends have the same expression. Intimidation bleeds from every one of them as they glide through the now-divided hall. Everyone stares at the scene before them like they're the four horsemen riding into town to burn it to the ground. Several people take out their phones. What do they think is going to happen—a sacrifice right here in the hall for stealing a parking spot? I don't have the chance to ask Eden about her weird, nervous reaction before Jeep guy fills my personal space. The combination of cinnamon and weed lingers in the small space between us.

From years of training to fight with guys like him, backing down or away isn't an option, even when the toe of his boot bumps the tip of mine. I've been confronted by more than my share of guys who think they're tougher than me on the mat and off, and this guy is no different. The only difference here is that the mat is a place of safety. Not to say I haven't had my share of broken bones, but an official oversees those encounters. Here, I get the feeling the referee and these guys are one and the same.

I don't say anything. Instead, I meet his steely gray eyes. He's quiet for longer than necessary since he's the one calling me out for some stupid reason.

When the silence remains for far too long, I finally ask, "What? Did you forget why you decided to invade my personal bubble?" My voice comes out low and sounds more uncertain than I'd like.

I also don't like the fact that I have to look up at him. I feel small in my five-seven frame compared to his defined muscular build and standing at six-two or taller.

He narrows his eyes. After a long moment of him staring at me, a grin slowly thins his full lips, a sign of control, his way of letting me know who's in charge. He's obviously the one who calls the shots around here, so I assume he's not used to being questioned.

He runs his fingers through his hair, pushing it back from his forehead. I wonder if he's the one who killed my father. His build is the same as Python's, but then again, all four of the guys standing in front of me have almost the same muscular body— bodies that no doubt get their fair share of whatever they desire.

When he still says nothing, I turn to leave. He reaches out and grips my upper arm before I turn entirely away. I don't demand or even ask him to release me. This is his way of pissing on what's his, this school and his measly parking spot. By the way the entire campus seems to bow down to these fuckers, I need the spotlight off me if I'm to get what I came here for, so I give him this single moment of power over me. I'll let him believe he's the one taking it, and I'm not handing it over on a silver platter.

The strands of hair fall again along his face as he tilts his head to the side. There's a slight tick to his smooth, square jawline. Fuck if he's not a gorgeous specimen. Why are the assholes always hot? He could make almost any girl drop to her knees. The perfect hair, his tall, muscular body, penetrating smoke-gray eyes framed with thick lashes, lips I can only imagine being well-versed in the art of kissing and other things, and above all, a don't-fuck-with-me attitude. He has all of the ingredients of what a bad boy symbolizes—the exact kind of guy parents never want to see their little girl bring home.

I want to believe I'm immune to his hypnotic allure, but the stirring low in my core proves otherwise. Focusing on his brazen glare, I wrangle in my racing hormones. I refuse to squirm or let my guard down—any more than I already have when dealing with this asshole. I glance down at his fingers wrapped around my arm, then back to his face. I tried to stroke his ego, even though he clearly doesn't need it. But this fucked-up stand-off is taking way too long for my level of patience.

"Do you plan to hold me here like a caveman all fucking day, or did you forget it's your turn to speak? Or both?"

The fire in his eyes blazes brighter. I'm getting to him in a very bad way. This probably isn't the most intelligent way to handle this interaction, but I'll be damned if he thinks he can manhandle me like one of his playthings. If Luca were here, this would be one of those situations where he would kick my boot and let me know I'm taking things too far.

I start to pull my arm free. He, in turn, only grips it tighter.

For some fucked-up reason, I smile, knowing he's enjoying this interaction. Acknowledging the challenge in my defiance, he furrows his brow, studying me to see if I have the balls to challenge him. I would have missed the tiniest twitch of his full mouth if I weren't standing so close to him. The show of his dominance is only a small part of what's happening between us.

"Since it's your first day"—he pauses to peer around to my backside—"and you have a nice ass, I'll let your attitude, and taking my parking spot, slide—but just for today."

Clutching my free hand to my chest, I say, "Well, aren't you a gracious guy?"

He draws me in even closer. Our bodies are so close that heat radiates through his clothes. He would have to have nerve damage not to feel my heart racing in overdrive.

"Don't ever believe that I am anything but your new nightmare," he warns as his eyes drop to my mouth.

I bite the corner of my bottom lip, slowly dragging the soft flesh through my teeth. His gaze feasts on the slight movement, and his eyes again find mine. "Good thing I'm not afraid of the dark," I whisper.

His menacing grin spreads. "I don't need the dark to do nasty deeds." His low, deep voice draws out his threat as if he's asking me to have wild, uninhibited sex for days on end.

Yes, please. Sign me up!

Wait. NO!

I pray he doesn't notice how I tighten my thighs or realize how he's penetrating my exterior like a laser cutting through iron. My prayer goes unanswered as his mouth curves up.

"Is this all it takes?" His fingers press tighter against my arm. His eyes are like silver flames as they return to mine. He leans into me until his mouth brushes the tip of my ear. His breaths are like feathers brushing lightly against my skin. "Imagine if my hands were gripping something else."

Shivers of heat spread like whispers down my spine. With

his broad, imposing body demanding all the space between us, it's like we're the only two people in an empty hall.

Denying my body any delight in the thoughts those cocksure words conjure, I quickly regain my composure after feeling like his savage spell has just sideswiped me. I back away from him, forging space between us. With our glares still locked, I say, "I suggest you get here a little earlier if you like that parking spot so much." I jerk my arm free of his grasp.

His shadows peer over his shoulder. By the look on their faces, they're clearly entertained and fascinated by the defiant new girl. Buzz-cut from the front seat rolls his tongue, tapping his metal bar against his teeth. He's definitely the serious one in the group. He's also the scariest, despite his overpowering, douchebag leader standing only inches from my face. Lucky me has managed to make it onto the arrogant asshole's shit list before I even have a chance to whisper "Venom." *Perfect.*

Phase one... complete.

Not done with me yet, Edge leans into me. "Don't let there be a next time."

He doesn't attempt to move, nor do his piercing eyes stray from mine. As hard as he tries to hide behind his irritation, treating me as if I just splattered onto his windshield, his darkening eyes betray him. He can't help but be as curious as everyone else watching our exchange.

I press my hand firmly against his chest in an effort to push him back. His skin is heated, as if he spent the morning in the fires of hell before coming to school. He doesn't budge, but I don't let it dissuade me from making a stand.

"Don't ever touch me again."

"Is that a threat?" he challenges.

I shake my head. "No. But this is. If you do, I promise you'll regret it."

The smile sliding over his mouth is undoubtedly one on loan

from the devil himself. "Looks like you're going to be harder to tame than the others, but don't worry, I have my ways."

"Give it your best try." I move around him without taking looking away from him. "I dare you."

"Be careful, little Ninja." His smirk only grows until Eden clears her throat. He tilts his head and moves his stare over to her like a snake slithering through the grass. Disappointed in his subject, he purses his lips. "You should know better, Blue. You better work on keeping this one leashed."

I feel like I've just been slapped. Eden visibly swallows. Her mouth is open to respond—to agree or bow down—when I lay my hand on her arm, stopping her.

The asshole might be hot as hell, but his deplorable personality could use a major overhaul.

I step right into his personal space, a place the two of us are all too familiar with in such a short time. "Don't go there, asshole. Just don't."

I don't know if I'm speaking up for her or reacting to the leash comment. Both piss me the fuck off.

Without giving Edge a chance to respond, I burrow past him and through the gawking crowd. My nerves buzz as I fake my cool. I walk down the hall without knowing where I'm going, hoping Eden follows me. But after seeing the way she cowered back there, I'm probably on my own.

Chatter resumes as I pass. It was probably there all along. I just didn't notice during my encounter with my new enemy. It's all nonsense and barely audible until I hear phrases like "There she is..." and "She's the one..."

I try to ignore them like they're not talking about me, but I know better. I get to the end of the hall and can turn left or right. The left is lined with doors, and the right has an exit to the outside. Yep, this school is way more challenging to navigate than I thought, in more ways than one. I've entered the den of vipers and have officially become their prey.

Eden catches up to me. She's silent for a beat, then says, "You shouldn't have done that." She turns left, and I follow.

I hike up my backpack. "Done what? Stick up for myself?" Or you? I want to tell her she should have stood up for herself, but she's obviously still shaken and unable to listen to that sound advice right now.

"Listen, I know it's your first day and all, but those guys, Venom—*the* Vipers—"

"Aren't we all Vipers since that's the school's mascot?" I question.

"Yeah, but they're *the* Vipers. Like you don't want to mess with them."

That's exactly what I plan on doing until I bring justice down on them. "Or else what?"

"They will find a way to make your life a living hell."

She has no idea that they already have. I push away the unwanted feelings of remorse and pain slithering just under the surface of my unfazed facade.

Shrugging, I say, "So, I'll park somewhere else tomorrow, no big deal."

By the look on her face, she's not convinced that will fix the damage I caused in less than fifteen minutes. Man, I work fast. Fuck, it would be impressive if the circumstances weren't so dire.

"You know it's not that simple, right? You challenged them in front of everyone. Edge, the one all up in your face, won't let this go that easily. The others won't go as hard, but you still need to watch your back."

There were a ton of rumors in my high school about the Vipers, but I thought it was just a bunch of bullshit or at least about Monarch as a whole—newsflash to me. All I know is I may have found precisely who I've set out to destroy, and all before my first class.

I glance at my schedule to find the room number. I'm not

even close when I realize the class numbers we're passing. I stop and turn to face Eden. "Look, I know you're trying to give me some great advice, but I just want to get to art right now. Will you help me or not?" I expect her to say no.

Surprisingly, she sighs out a defeated breath. "It's this way."

We take another left in the next hallway and out of the building through double doors. The uneven stone path, lined with tiny purple flowers, has got to be hell to walk on in heels. Thank God for Docs. At the end of the walkway is a building older than the one we just came from. Vines crawl up its walls like thick green webs surrounding tall wooden doors.

"This is the arts and music building," Eden says.

"What class do you have?" Since she came after me, even if it was to warn me, I should show some interest if she has a class near here.

"Photography."

With genuine curiosity, I ask, "Cool. What do you like to shoot?"

She tucks her hair behind her ear. "People mostly, candid, natural shots, or sometimes, the complete opposite, when the subject looks directly into the lens. I like those kinds of pictures. You can't hide anything. They're real, every freckle, every flaw, every scar, all of it. I get to see that person exactly how they look, feel… Sorry, I get carried away."

"Hey, no, it's all good. It's awesome to be that passionate about something."

"Yeah, I guess you could say that." She fidgets with one of the studs lining her ear.

I follow her down another corridor, finally reaching a class-room with room number S24. Jesus, will I be able to find this place on my own?

Eden stops just outside the open door and touches my arm. I can tell it's entirely out of character.

I narrow my eyes on her. "Why do you look like you have something to say and I'm going to hate hearing whatever it is?"

Her face scrunches before she blurts, "Gunner is in this class."

I have no idea what that means or why it's relevant to me. "Who is that and why do I care?"

She sighs. I'm sure she's internally cursing herself for ever getting involved with me. It doesn't help that my bitchy personality is in high gear right now. I'm not here to make friends, but I also don't want to push away the only person who's been nice, or at least has tolerated me so far. At some point today, I need to apologize to her. And just maybe she'll share more about what goes on in this school and more about Venom, which is someone I could use in my corner right now.

"The guy with Edge, the one with the crazy hair," she explains.

As the words leave her mouth, I know exactly who she's talking about. Dread pools at the base of my spine. I'm always ready for a confrontation, but hell, I just came face to face with the bad guys. It never occurred to me that any of them would be in art class—or any of my classes, for that matter.

"He's part of Venom," she unnecessarily adds.

I purse my lips and nod. Shrug off the news like she just told me it would rain later and not that my new nemesis and I would be confined to a room together for the two hours. "Thanks for the heads-up and for walking me here. I guess I'll see you later."

Eden points down the hall from the direction we came in. "Your next class is in the Armstrong Building. Go out the way we came in, and it's just on the other side of the courtyard."

"Thanks." The courtyard? Did we pass that? Fuck, with my head so full of Venom and Edge, I noticed little on the way here except purple flowers and clinging vines.

Without another word, she takes off down the hall to her class. Taking a deep breath, I walk into art class, more specifically, painting. There's no doubt I'm in the right class with all of the easels propped up around the room and a platform in the center of the large space.

Painting isn't one of my strong suits, but since I applied so late, I wasn't left with many open options. Plus, how hard can painting be?

"Hi! Welcome to painting," a smiling woman with a bright purple and pink braid says.

"Thanks."

She wipes her fingers on her apron, which is splattered with a palette of every color. "Sorry, breakfast." The other half of the hard-boiled egg lies on a napkin. I'm Chelsea Bray. Call me Chelsea. And you must be Kinsley West."

"Yeah, how did you know that?"

She drops her head to look peer over the rims of her turquoise glasses. "Because you are the first new student I've had in..." She bobs her head from side to side. "Since forever. Monarch doesn't get a lot of new faces." Picking up her egg, she says, "Anyway, there are a couple of empty seats in the back. You can take one of those. Once class starts, I'll call you back to discuss a few things with you."

"Thanks." I weave my way through easels, stools, small tables topped with cleaned pallets, tubes of paints, and brushes until I find an available seat. Sliding off my backpack, I set it on the floor in relief, then plant my butt on the stool. For the next hour, I plan to stay in this little corner of the world and just breathe.

"Damn, girl, you have a way of sliding into places that have already been claimed."

I'm not shocked that the husky voice belongs to Wild Hair from the back seat of the Jeep. This must be Gunner. The sly, know-it-all grin splayed across his tanned face should be put on a warning label. *Danger! This smile may induce you to make stupid decisions.*

"Sorry, love, that seat is mine."

Groaning, I pick up my backpack. As I study him a little harder, I realize there's an actual style to his sun-bleached, unruly locks. A small wave is tattooed on the side of his neck, peeking out just above his shirt collar. I try to remember the details of Python and the tattoos on his body—if he had any on his neck. Frustration blooms. I was too frantic that night to notice anything more than the snake tattoo on the side of the killer's torso.

Gunner's chest skims the front of my blazer as he passes. Without breaking eye contact or the curve of his dangerous smile, he plops down on the stool. Patting his thigh, he says, "This seat is available."

His chuckle follows me as I ignore him and head to the opposite side of the room. An easel propped against the far wall, a small rickety table, and a too-short chair are calling my name. Without the skills to paint even a stick figure, this setup fits my level of experience perfectly. The big bonus is that it's as far as I can be from Gunner without leaving the classroom.

I toss my backpack on the floor. Falling into the squatty chair, I let out a long sigh. It's not even eight in the morning, and I feel like I've been handed my ass, tossed to the wolves, and eye-fucked. I just want to collapse onto my bed and sleep away the rest of the day.

"No need to wait for an invitation. If you're here, get your canvas," Chelsea announces.

Unbeknownst to me, my seat is right in front of the closet where everyone needs to go. I fumble to get up and out of the way to avoid getting trampled. When the last of the crowd leaves, I sit back down. Then, before I can take in the whole situation, it's too late to move out of the way before Gunner looms over me. He's way too close. If I were to take my gaze off him and look straight ahead, I'd be eye to eye with his—

"Kinsley?" Chelsea calls for me to approach her desk when most of the students are settled.

Saved.

Jerking my head away from the surfer's zipper, I say, "Coming."

Shit! I realize too late that's the wrong word to use.

Gunner offers me a lopsided grin like he knows exactly where my mind just strayed. "Dirty girl. I like it."

There's no way I'm even going to respond to that comment.

"You know, if you had taken *my* available seat, you wouldn't have been in the way." Reaching around me, he withdraws a large canvas, then swaggers back to his seat.

"If I had taken your so-called available seat, you'd be dickless right now." I head to the front of the class before he can get a word out.

Chelsea turns so that her back is to the class. "Listen, Kinsley," she starts, lowering her voice, "I just want to let you know that if you need someone to talk to or anything, I'm here. Sometimes this school can be a little challenging."

"Thank you." I doubt I'd go to a professor for anything I'm dealing with, but the offer is nice. However, it's the last part of her speech that catches my attention. "What do you mean by *challenging?*"

She looks like she may regret saying that. But she doesn't dismiss my question. Her voice drops to a whisper. "The students here are used to getting what they want. And that's all I'll say on that," she says, then drags her hands down her apron like we didn't just have a cryptic conversation.

I nod like she just spilled top-secret intel. Of course, they do. They've been raised that way since birth. I can only hope there's not much more to deal with at Monarch than wealthy, bullying murderers.

"Okay, on to the stuff I get paid for." She tucks loose purple strands behind her ear and smiles. "The assignment we're working on is about self-expression. So, since you're a little behind the rest of the class, why don't you walk around the room to get an idea of what others are doing? Have the supplies listed on here by the end of the week." She hands me a syllabus. "That gives you a few days to think of an idea for your canvas."

Oh, joy...not. It's more like a dilemma. Dilemma. Dilemma. And here, I thought art would be an easy A.

As I turn to leave, two girls, giggling and whispering, prance through the open door. The stench of their expensive perfume fills the air like an invisible fog.

"I know we're late, Chelsea, but don't get uptight. We had to help Mikayla with her lashes. Her mascara was—"

"I don't care, Brielle, you're late. As are you, Peyton," Chelsea says. "Get your canvas, then get to work."

With a huff, the girl with bleached blond hair, Brielle, abruptly turns and stops dead in her tracks when she sets her sights on me. The other girl, Peyton, runs into the back of her, a gold pen and lip gloss falling out of her sequin mini purse that can't hold much more.

"Brielle, what the—"

Brielle stands stone-still. Her hand tightens on the strap of her red designer bag. "You must be *her*."

5

KINSLEY

I DIDN'T THINK college had mean girls, but I believe I just met the self-appointed bitch of Monarch University. Damn, I'm on a fucking roll.

Brielle sneers as she bumps my shoulder on the way to her desk. Her four-inch heels clack on the tile floor as she walks through the mass of easels toward the back of the room. In the short twenty or so seconds of my meeting the bitch, I assumed she would sit next to Gunner. And I'm right.

As I follow her toward the back of the room, I pretend to look at some of the artwork I'll be expected to create. Some are serious masterpieces, while others are mediocre. With my lack of artistic skills, mine will definitely be on the mediocre end of the spectrum. Even with the bar so low, I'm still way over my head.

An irritating whine scrapes along my eardrums as I slide into my seat.

"I don't know what all the hype is about," Brielle says. "She's just another dirty whore—which I could totally deal with—but this one is also a complete bitch."

"Bri, you don't even know her. Why don't you give her a

chance? Who knows, she may fit nicely into your little group of hot hoes." Gunner adjusts his crotch. "In fact, I'm hoping she does. I bet having a piece of that would be more than sweet."

My mouth drops open. As if there would be a chance in hell of either of those things ever happening. It takes every ounce of control I have to force myself to stay planted on this rickety stool and listen to their bullshit. I thought I was far enough away from their corner, but apparently, not far enough.

I reach for my phone in my bag while I try not to pay attention to them, but it's so damn hard, especially when they're talking about me. They have to realize I can hear every word they're saying. Not that they should care, but wouldn't they want to plan their attack on me privately?

"You don't know her either," she retorts. "What'd you have, like a three-word conversation before I got here? Besides, I don't need to get to know her. If what's going around is true—which I'm pissed I wasn't there to see it for myself—then she's just a piece of trash who needs to be taught a lesson. She can't challenge Edge in front of the entire school. So, the only thing that bitch will get from me is a lesson she won't forget." Brielle looks down at her chest, reaches into her bra, and adjusts her boobs so her cleavage is on full display.

I roll my eyes and stifle a laugh. I would bet my life that her chief weapon is her tube of mascara.

"Trust me, Edge had it handled," he says, chuckling.

Brielle meticulously lays her tie over the fake mounds of silicone as if there's no chance it will move all day. "That's not what I heard."

With a glance in their direction, I notice Brielle's sidekick. I think her name is Peyton. A pink bubble expands from her lips, then pops over her mouth. She peels off the sticky wad and shoves it back into her mouth. "Maybe she just needs a friend."

Brielle takes out a compact mirror and adjusts her lip gloss. "What has gotten into both of you? Since when the fuck do you care if a new girl fits in or not?" It's obvious she doesn't expect either of them to answer, nor does she care. She's already made up her mind about me. "Besides, someone needs to tell her that those hideous, bulky boots and high socks look like she's just walked off a zombie set."

Gunner grunts. "I think they look fucking hot as shit."

"You would, you beast."

Trying my best to ignore them, I look anywhere but at them. This is going to be a long-ass semester if this is any indication of how the next couple of months are going to go. Now that I think about it, I wouldn't have pegged them for the art class type, either. So, maybe this class is easier than I think.

In my determination to ignore the shit show in the corner, I don't notice Chelsea coming right toward me until she's standing over my desk. The scent of the egg she ate for breakfast comes right along with her.

"Kinsley, here's some drawing paper. Why don't you work out a small sketch of what you think you'd like to do, then you can transfer it to your canvas when you bring it in?"

"Thanks."

I dig a pencil out of my bag. Staring at the blank sheet, I'm left to imagine what a self-expression drawing of myself looks like. Eventually, I put the lead on paper and force lines around the white page. It doesn't look like a stick figure, but it doesn't look like a drawing of me, either, or anyone, for that matter.

The whispers start up again. "Where'd she come from anyway?"

Brielle's voice grinds on my nerves. I swear she learned to whine from an orgy of goats. The thought of stabbing the tip of the pencil into her larynx sounds way more appealing than wasting it on a useless drawing. At least then I'd be making an impression.

"I don't know, but I'm still thanking the gods for sending her fine ass here," Gunner says. "And I know I'm not just speaking for myself."

"You're a walking boner," Brielle spits.

Gunner's naughty chuckle draws a few stares from around the room.

He may feel like that now, but if he had anything to do with my dad's murder, he's going to regret ever saying that.

I turn the paper over and draw a circle for my head, two smaller circles for my eyes, then wavy lines off the head that could be hair. I completely suck at this.

My pencil tears through the paper when my stool jerks hard from the back. "Move. You're in the way, trash."

Brielle's too-sweet perfume envelops me like a cocoon. I hold my breath and try to ignore her, knowing she wants to get her canvas from the closet behind me.

"Are you like stupid, or deaf, or something?" She bends down close to my ear and speaks louder. "Can you hear me? Move!"

I set down my pencil and rise at a snail's pace to stand face to face with her. She needs those four-inch heels to reach my height. Smiling, I say, "Trust me, everyone in this class, and most likely the classes across the hall, can hear your annoying voice. You haven't shut up since you walked into class. And no, I'm not deaf or stupid. The only thing I am is sick of listening to you talk shit all morning."

"Ladies, do we have a problem back there?" Chelsea calls out.

"No," Brielle and I respond in unison.

Brielle scowls. The angry look molds into the lines of her face perfectly, falling right into place like I'm sure they've done a thousand times before. She's going to need Botox by the time she's twenty.

She lowers her voice. "Move the fuck out of my way."

She bumps into me as I back up a little. Reaching just inside the door, she grabs the last canvas. Curious, I glance at her piece. It's just okay at best. Nothing exceptional. For some reason, it makes me feel better that she's not a Picasso disguised as a bitch.

Then I find I can't help myself with my next comment. "Nice expression, but isn't it supposed to be a self-portrait? Shouldn't you have painted a wildebeest or rabid hyena?"

Whispers and shocked "oohs" and "oh shits" erupt from around us.

A low growl emanates from her chest. "You're digging your own grave, trash."

A tiny laugh bubbles up in my throat. "Whatever you say, swine."

Brielle spins on her heels and heads back to her seat. "I'm going to fucking kill her," she says to Gunner as she places her canvas on her easel. "And now that I've looked closer, she's as ugly as they come."

"You're just jealous 'cause you know she's hot as shit. Your problem is you want Edge's dick all to yourself, and you're afraid you might have to share."

Peyton chimes in. "Yeah, she does."

"Shut up, Peyton," Brielle snarls.

Continuing to draw the effed-up sketch of myself, I listen to their conversation. I can't deny Edge is hotter than any guy I've ever seen, with his intense storm-cloud eyes and perfect mouth. But even with the little I know about him, I'm more than happy to let her have his dick all to herself.

Ten minutes before class ends, the art professor tells everyone to clean up and put away the supplies. The past hour dragged out into eternity, leaving me completely convinced of the relativity of time.

Still wondering what I did to deserve the past hour of hell, I fold the horrible drawing in half, already planning its funeral in the garbage can near the door. I toss my pencil into my backpack and move out of the way to avoid the herd coming my way to put their paintings into the storage closet. Next time, I need to find a better place to sit.

Gunner catches sight of the paper and unfolds it to reveal my pathetic attempts at drawing. "Hey, little Ninja, not really the artist, are you?" He winces, then drops it back onto my desk. Leaning down, he says, "I bet you make up for that in other ways," and then the fucker winks.

Silently agreeing with him, I don't bother with a response as class ends. Balling up my paper, I throw it in the garbage on my way out of class. Miraculously, I find my way to my next class with only a few wrong turns. Eden is next to the professor's desk in the back of the room.

I walk down the center aisle toward them. "Hey, Eden."

"Hi." She doesn't sound thrilled to see me, but she also doesn't ignore me—so there's that.

The biology professor glances at me and then arranges a few random papers on her desk into a neat pile. "Welcome, Ms. West."

"Thanks." It's so weird that the professors know my name just by looking at me. It proves how elite and small this institution is.

I follow Eden up the left side of the room, stopping at a lab table near the front.

"You can sit there," Eden says. She takes out her notebook and then hangs her backpack on a peg nailed to the table. I follow suit. "So, how was art?"

I scoff. "Interesting. Along with Gunner, Brielle, and Peyton are also in my class."

She winces. "I forgot to mention them. I think our—your encounter with Edge threw me a bit."

Shrugging, I sit on the stool in biology. "No worries. She's just another bitch who thinks she's entitled to the world."

Eden gasps. "You didn't say that to her face, did you?"

"No, not in so many words."

Eden scoots a little farther to the edge of her side of the table. "You are going to go down in flames, and you haven't even been here a day yet."

She doesn't say anything to me for the rest of class. We sit in silence, taking notes until Professor Lennon releases us.

Eden shoves her notebook into her messenger bag. "Listen, but I'm not looking for trouble. I keep to myself and stay out of the way. So, if you can try to stay invisible, why don't you join Bryce and me for lunch? We sit in the courtyard near the big oak. We're usually there from noon until one." Without waiting for a reply, she grabs her bag and darts out of class.

I'm not sure what to make of that. "Thanks for the invite," I mutter.

But it's bullshit if she expects me to back down from a possible murderer and a bully bitch just to have someone to hang out with. I'd rather be on my own.

Before leaving class, I ask the professor where the library is. She says it's the building that looks like a castle in the center of campus, then gives me directions. How hard can that be to find? As I reach the massive structure, I realize the library *is* in the center of everything. All the other buildings fan out from it.

During the short walk, I dodge a lot of whispers and stares. Nothing I haven't seen or heard before, but this time, they're all directed at me. At my other school, I wasn't a complete bitch, but I had my moments of sizing up the new student, deciding whether I would give them the time of day or not... usually not. My decision wasn't based on looks or financial status. It was based on how time-consuming they would be and how much maintenance and patience I would have to put forth. But that was high school. I thought college would be different, easier. But not Monarch. Learning how these people stick together, and still bow down to the bullies, I'd make no effort to be my friend—too much rebellion, not enough conformity. So, I understand Eden's attitude toward me.

The library is sparse with students. I have my pick of tables, so I choose one near the back, near the first aisle of books. I take out my laptop to start my biology homework. Being already behind sucks. For the next hour, no one bothers me or says a word in my direction. Maybe I've mastered this whole invisible thing.

Just as I'm ready to pack up, I dig in the front pocket of my backpack and touch cool metal. Sliding it out, I cradle the bracelet in my palm. My dad gave it to me the last time he came home from one of his business trips. The rose quartz heart stone is set in the center of a thin silver chain. I drape it over my left wrist, and with only a little trouble, I clasp it.

Soon, Dad. Soon.

I have a break until my next class. I almost decide to stay here, but for the sake of the cause, I pack up my things and follow a small crowd into the courtyard. It's easy to guess where the cafeteria is, as most people funnel into the building. I meet Bryce and Eden under the oak instead of trying to battle my way into the lunchroom. And after having two confrontations with the most popular people on campus, I think I'll stay clear of welcoming any more drama today.

"Kinsley!" Bryce sits under the big oak, just like Eden said. She's not there yet. I'm not sure how I feel about that. However, Bryce was friendlier than she was. I make my way over to him. "Hey, girl. How's your first day going so far?"

"Peachy," I say, tossing my bag on the ground. "Where's Eden?"

He lifts the lid off his container, exposing a sushi roll, a dollop of wasabi, and a packet of soy sauce. "She'll be here. She takes a few extra minutes to get here because she comes from across campus, where the dorms are."

"Does she live in the dorms?"

He shakes his head. "No, but her class is in the building next to them."

Reaching into my backpack, I pull out the apple I tossed in this morning. Jeez, that seems like a lifetime ago.

Bryce's hand pauses mid-air with chopsticks, a piece of sushi balancing between the sticks. "That's all you're eating?"

"Yeah, I'm not that hungry." In truth, having skipped breakfast, I'm starving, but I'm in no mood to eat.

Bryce's gaze catches on something over my shoulder. "There she is." He moves the piece of sushi to his mouth, then stops mid-bite. "Oh shit," he says. Poor kid can't catch a break to eat his fancy lunch.

I assume he's talking about Eden until I turn to see who has him fumbling with his chopsticks. Brielle is on a direct path to us, accompanied by two other girls. One is Peyton from my art class. The other, I assume, is the girl with the eyelash issue, since they're almost an inch long and look as though they may help her take flight any second. Mikayla, I think her name is.

"Of course, she's sitting with the fucking nerds. Suits her well, don't you think?" She stops a few feet away from us. "So, trash girl, this is your new friend?" Brielle looks around. "No doubt the blue freak will be joining you. What a crew the three of you make." She props her hands on her narrow waist. "You guys are a joke."

Who the hell does this bitch think she is? "Don't you have anything better to do, beast, like blow some asshole in the janitor's closet or something?"

Bryce's sushi slips from the vice of his chopsticks. His mouth goes slack before slowly easing into a smile. "This is going to be good," he whispers.

"Look, you skank whore, if you think you can just walk right into the viper's den and—"

I hold up my hand. "Don't. You sound ridiculous, and you're starting to whine."

Blue hair catches my attention in my peripheral vision. Eden pauses, watching my exchange with the three girls before chancing it and walking into a possible fight.

I stand and face off with Monarch's self-elected bitch. Her face is tight with fury. "The only thing you need to know about me is I don't back down to anyone. And trust me, I know my place. So, if this is the lesson you think I need, consider it given."

"You're digging your own grave," she warns.

"So you've said. Now, if you're done, you better hurry along. Wouldn't want those spike heels getting stuck in the dirt." I swish my wrist toward them, dismissing the trio. I turn my back on her, finished with the conversation—if one could even call it that.

"This isn't the end," she spits.

Still not facing her, I sit down. "Yeah, yeah, I can't wait." I fold my hand in a wave over my shoulder. "Bye now."

She rants out a slew of profanities as she turns, her friends following in her wake as they make their way back to the cafeteria.

Eden steps out of the shadows. "What was that about?"

Bryce is huffing out gasps of breath mixed with laughter. Pointing at me, he says, "This chick has balls the size of Jupiter. Seriously, I mean—shit." He grabs a handful of his hair. "I can't believe it... This is awesome! You're like the golden egg on Easter morning."

Eden doesn't look so impressed. "Simmer down, Bryce. If she keeps it up, she's going to get her ass kicked and take us down with her."

"I don't care. I'm all in. This is way too fun to pass up."

Eden's eyes pop open, and she studies her best friend as if she just watched him grow another head. "Who are you?"

He sets down his container of food. "Eden, this year could be epic. We could watch Kinsley tear down the hierarchy of this forsaken institution. And being her new besties, we get front-row seats and maybe even a little recognition."

Besties? If he keeps on with that, he's going to get another smack in the head from Eden.

She leans toward him and tilts her head, studying his eyes. "You said you were going to lay off the weed."

He holds up his hands. "I did. I swear!"

Backing down, Eden takes a lunch bag out of her backpack. The hummus and veggies aren't nearly as fancy as Bryce's sushi but seem fitting enough for her personality, bland and adequately healthy.

"What?" she asks me.

I didn't realize I was staring, but I guess I am. "Nothing. It looks good... and healthy." I take a bite of my apple to fill my mouth.

She pulls apart the baggie of celery and carrots. "Listen, you could have a lot going for you. You're the type to fit in with the mean girls and Venom if you want to."

She could have told me I was the biggest piece of shit she ever laid eyes on and that would have been better than what she just verbally threw at me. My face must say as much because she tries to defend herself.

"What I mean is, you're beautiful, you have a chip on your shoulder, and you've managed to gain the attention of everyone and their cousin at this school in less time than it takes me to put on my makeup."

"You don't wear makeup," Bryce pipes up.

"Exactly," Eden growls. Focusing her attention back on me, she asks. "Why are you choosing to get on their bad side on your first day?"

I swallow the mushed mess in my mouth. "First of all, that's not me. In case you haven't noticed, I don't want to fit in with the rest of the assholes around here. That's not who I am. I just want to be left alone, get through this year, and get my rev—" I cut myself off. Revenge. Shit! I almost blew my cover. Hopefully, I haven't let too much spill. I'm letting my pride override my need for revenge, and I need to back off. Reeling from my hostility, I ask, "Why does this feel like high school all over again? Didn't these people grow up?"

They're quiet for a long beat. Eden is the one who answers. "To them, it's all the same. Same friends, same hierarchy, same family money. The only thing that's changed is the campus—"

"Yeah, now we're on the west side. Monarch Prep is on the east, just over there." Bryce points over his shoulder with his thumb.

"Well, that makes things a little bit clearer." I reach over my head to stretch out the tension building in every muscle in my back. It would probably help me to gain access to Venom and their ~~whores~~ inner circle more quickly. Then I can put all this to rest. But like I told Eden, that's not who I am. Plus, I have no idea who or what I'm dealing with exactly. All I know is that Venom is here, and this is where I need to be.

"You're not like the other girls at Monarch. Tattoos and face piercings are out of the norm here."

I've never been like other girls anywhere. "Nope. It's too exhausting to try to measure up. Besides, this is college. Aren't we supposed to figure out who we are?"

Eden shakes her head. "No, not here. Not at Monarch. We fall into place, just like we're meant to. We've known our places since grade school."

"Can't do it," I say as I roll up my sleeve to reveal the ink. "This is who I am. I like them, and I'm owning it. So if anyone has a problem with it, they can f—" I shut my mouth before I finish. Whether or not I like it, I've done enough damage today with my words. I don't need to say anything I'll regret.

"Well, I, for one, love it!" Bryce's voice is filled with rebellion.

I can tell Eden wants to say more. "What now?"

She dips another carrot into her hummus. "Listen, I know you're having a rough first day and all, and I hate to be the one to tell you, but I saw strength training on your schedule, and Venom is in your class—all of them."

I purse my lips and nod. "Of course they are."

Any rest for the wicked? Not a chance.

6

KINSLEY

Dammit! I forgot to ask Eden how to get to the gym. A girl near the window is still packing up, so I decide to test my luck. "Hey, can you tell me how to get to the gym?"

Just then, Brielle, Peyton, and Mikayla come into the room. "If you tell her, Marissa, then consider yourself an outcast added to my list," Brielle warns as she gestures to write on an invisible paper.

Marissa looks ashamed as her gaze falls away from me and lands on the book on her desk. Without a word, she picks it up and then takes off out of the room. Brielle's smug face of triumph nauseates me.

"I'll find it on my own," I say and start toward the door.

"Not so fast, new girl."

I release an aggravated breath. It would take all of ten seconds to slay the three of them, but I can't, and it's frustrating as hell. Lashes—Mikayla steps in front of me. With a dazed expression, Peyton snaps a bubble. I swear the girl's head is full of helium. I imagine grabbing the wad of pink goo and smearing it in her hair. Instead, I scrunch my nose in response to the flowery scent wafting off her and move to the side to go around her. She steps out again. My hip bumps into the desk.

Brielle takes a step closer to me. "Listen up, I have one piece of advice for you. Stay away from me, and stay away from Venom. Keep to your little corner of nobodies, and all will be right in the world again." Her fake fiery-red smile is perfectly in place. I got to hand that to her. She's mastered that small feat.

Giving her a dramatic bored eye roll, I barrel past them and turn back to face them when I reach the doorway. "In case you're a little confused, each time I've tried to keep to my little corner of the world, you've come to find me to give me your words of wisdom. So, if you leave me the fuck alone, I'll leave you the fuck alone. Deal?"

Brielle crosses her arms over her ample chest. "I don't trust you."

One side of my mouth quirks up into a nasty half-ass grin. "Maybe there's a brain cell in there after all," I quip. Then I turn to leave.

I ask a guy in the hall where the gym is, and he kindly gives me directions. At least not everyone seems to be an asshole here.

Fuck! I forgot to bring a pair of sneakers. Oh well, my boots will have to do. A few more girls file in. I wish I had been quicker to change. Not because I'm embarrassed, but I could do it without the extra sets of eyes sizing me up.

I would generally complain about gym class, but I could use the physical release today. Leaving my boots on, I roll down my socks and slide off my skirt. Because I drive a motorcycle, I'm wearing boy shorts instead of a thong. Before I take off my shirt, the pink jagged scar on my stomach gives me pause. I hate that I'm concerned about the possibility that someone will ask where and how I got it.

"Be on the courts in two minutes," a deep voice calls from the speakers.

No one speaks to me as we file into the gymnasium. The several sneers and glances at my forearm don't go unnoticed. I'm over trying to hide it. I don't owe any of these people anything. The only person I owe is my dad. And speaking of—as soon as I step out onto the glazed wooden floors, I recognize the tall, broad frames of the four assholes I met earlier on the far side of the gym. Venom. I have two choices, both of which are risky. I can either play nice at their game, which may bring me closer to their inner circle and possibly the truth, or I can play hard to get and hope they snag on my line.

Their presence sucks all the attention from everyone else in the rest of the gym. This is hardly the place to practice their fighting techniques, but that's precisely what they're doing. Gunner Crazy Hair grabs his twin around the neck, then locks his hand around his own wrist, securing his brother in a guillotine chokehold. Edge taps on Gunner's hand. Gunner slightly releases his grip as Edge repositions his arms to show him how to entrap his brother better.

Just as Edge maneuvers Gunner's arm, he raises his head. His eyes darken when he sets his sights on me. As if tethered together by some unseen force, the other three follow his lead. Their four hardened glares feel like an invisible weight fixing me in place. But there's something else, a unique cord of shared familiarity drawing me to them... domination, savagery, ferocity, the thrill of fighting. I couldn't turn away if the room went up in flames around me.

Long seconds pass before someone calls out my name behind me. Abruptly, I'm shaken from their visual grasp.

"Kinsley West, I presume." A large, balding man, holding a clipboard, approaches me.

I swiftly nod. "Yes, that's me."

Coach inspects my footwear. "You're out of uniform. Make sure you bring proper shoes to the next class." He makes a check next to my name on his roster, then moves toward the front of the group.

I take a chance to glance over my shoulder. Venom walks toward my class, and I internally groan. Eden gave me a fair warning that *all* of them are in my gym class. Giving me a heads-up surprises me, considering she's not as huge a fan of me as her sidekick, Bryce. A few feet away from everyone else, the four stop as if they are a single unit moving as one.

"Well, well, well, look who we have here," Gunner says as he looks me up and down. "I get to have you twice in one day." He rubs his hands together as if readying for a meal. "This has got to be my lucky day."

Finding it difficult to ignore Venom completely, I play nice for now. That may change within the next five minutes, but for now, nice seems the way to go, especially after seeing them practice their fighting skills.

"Maybe. Or it might be karma catching up to you," I say teasingly.

Gunner almost smiles, then falters as he contemplates what he's done to have such bad fortune. If only I could share my secrets about what I know. Even though I'm ninety-nine percent sure they were at the fight that night, those secrets will have to wait until I know one hundred percent.

Gunner throws his arm over his identical brother. "Anyway, this is Levi. He's taken, so don't get any ideas."

Levi's smile isn't as playful as Gunner's, but it's just as panty-dropping. Their parents must be gorgeous to have produced these two.

Gunner continues. "You already know Ledger, known as Edge, and that there"—he points to the one from the passenger seat in the Jeep—"is Ashton Kade, a.k.a. Kade." Gunner shrugs. "He's a bit of a loner and quiet as hell, but makes up for it in kicking and getting ass."

Edge doesn't say a word during his friend's verbal vomiting

on all his BFFs. His damp hair has fallen to one side over his face. Dear Lord, why is the jerk so fucking hot? I try not to stare, even though it's exactly what I want to do. In fact, I could prop him in the corner of a room and just stare for days on end. For fuck's sake, what the hell has gotten into me?

"So, you guys are into submissions, huh?" I ask. I don't mean for the words to come out, and I wish I could grab them out of thin air and make them disappear. But it's too late. Three out of the four of them seemed taken aback by my question, as if I just spewed Japanese. Each one of them is silent, even Gunner, surprisingly. I seem to fall right back into the depths of Edge's glare when my gaze settles on him. Unlike his friends, Edge's demeanor is unchanged, guarded.

"And what do you know about fighting?" Levi asks.

Tearing away from Edge's invisible clutches, I focus on Levi and shrug. "Some."

Common sense kicks me in the ass as the urge to straight up ask them about UG fighting sticks in the back of my throat. Thankfully, I have some restraint. I don't want to scare them off. I doubt they would tell me anything anyway.

With a hungry grin, Gunner wraps his arm around my shoulder. In a sultry voice he probably practices in front of the mirror, he says, "I could show you a few moves if you want."

I have a feeling the moves I'm envisioning are very different than the ones he's talking about.

"Everyone ready for a little rope climbing?" the coach hollers. The class groans like they've just been told to climb Mount Everest.

Gunner drops his arm from around me. "Maybe some other time."

"Rope climbing? What, are we in boot camp?" I mutter.

The girl standing next to me, and the only other one in this class, leans in and whispers, "Kinda. Coach was in the Army, and he gets off on torturing us with drills like this."

"Hmm... that sucks."

"A lot," she agrees.

On the opposite side of the gym is a group of girls, the cheerleaders. That must be where all of the other girls in the locker room went. Because it certainly wasn't to strength training.

Kade nudges Edge's arm and juts out his chin to me. I look down at my shirt and wonder what other ammo I've given them to fire back at me.

"What is that?" Edge asks, his voice low and menacing.

Nothing is on my shirt, so I have no idea what they're talking about. "What's what?"

Edge slightly shakes his head, giving his friends some kind of silent command. Gunner's eyes pop, and Levi's mouth creases. All of them are studying the tattoo on my forearm. Edge says nothing, nor does he make a sound as his jaw ticks in annoyance.

Not sure how to react to their bizarre behavior, I say, "It's just a tattoo. Get over it." I turn away from them and follow the others to the dangling rope on the far side of the gym.

The heaviness of their scrutiny falling against my back is enough to weigh a girl down. Standing with the rest of the group, I switch gears and do my best to ignore them. I play with the clasp on my bracelet. Realizing it's a nervous gesture, I consciously stop and fold my arms over my chest.

"All right, class, we're going to start with the end of the alphabet." There's a mix of more groans with added cheers.

"Zepher, you're up first."

A guy with tousled light brown hair who looks like he should be the head of the chess club walks up to the rope. I've learned enough during my martial arts training never to judge someone by their appearance. You never know what they're capable of. I did that only once at a tournament. As soon as the ref lowered his arm for the fight to begin, I was on my ass. But in this case, by the sweat already beading on Zepher's brow, I'd bet I'm correct with my assumption of him.

Zepher turns out not to be a surprise. He twists his fingers with nervous energy, as though the coach asked him to gather the arrows during the middle of an archery competition and not climb a harmless rope. He wipes his palms on his gym shorts before grabbing the rope. The coach blows the whistle. Zepher barely pulls himself up. His arms strain as he tries to lift off the ground. His sneakers slip as he tries to brace himself for another upward pull. It's a no-go. The poor guy can only get a few feet off the ground before sliding back down. I hate to be the one to break it to him, but if the zombie apocalypse ever happens, this guy is for sure a goner. His major must require fitness, or else I bet he would save himself from this torture.

The coach marks something on his clipboard before calling my name. "Next up, West."

My head snaps from Zepher to the coach. Here we go. I tie the laces of my boots before striding to the center of the group. Everyone stares at me as I take my place at the foot of the rope.

I wipe my hands on my shorts before I grip it just above the knot. For some unknown reason, I glance over my shoulder. Edge's granite-hard glare is aimed right at me. My heart pounds more for all the unwanted attention than for the task.

The whistle sounds loud and shrill. I pull up with my arms as my legs wrap around the rope and push my body upward as I continue to pull with my arms. My arms begin to burn a little just over the halfway mark. But there's no way I'm going to fail at this. I focus on moving up as fast as I can and try to ignore the tug low in my side from where the knife's blade sliced through my flesh, concentrating only on the golden bell above me. Cheers from below me fade as I tune them out. I use my legs with as much leverage as I can to heave myself up.

A few seconds later, I ring the bell at the top as the whistle sounds. I take a deep breath and let it out slowly as I slide down the rope. When my boots touch the floor, I'm able to relax a bit, even though my heart is still racing. I place my hand over my side and cradle the still-tender wound.

"Holy shit," someone says.

"She's like Spider-Woman."

"That's got to beat Edge's time."

"Don't count on it," a deep voice says behind me.

Edge's thick arms are crossed over his impressive chest as his slate eyes narrow and zero in on me. I should probably get used to that look—the one with the tsunami constantly stirring in them whenever he has them focused on me. Having had enough of Venom for now, I maneuver to the opposite side of the class.

"Hey, you're new, right?" The guy is a couple of inches taller than me, with light brown hair and soft hazel eyes.

"Yep, how'd ya guess?"

He's the type of guy most moms would be happy for their daughter to bring home—hence, the complete opposite of the Venom guys hovering on the other side of the group.

He chuckles. "Sorry, that was lame."

"Yeah," I agree.

"Hey, listen, you were amazing. I mean, no one has ever climbed the rope that fast. Well, except for those guys over there."

I know who he's talking about without looking in Venom's direction. What are they, like gods at this school? "Yeah, it was no big thing."

"Actually, it is. If you beat Edge's time, you're not only a real badass, you've set a new record."

"If you say so." The feat might be big to some, but as long as it got me an A, I'd be happy.

He chuckles. "I'm Josh, by the way."

"Kinsley."

He plays with a loose string from the hem of his shirt. "This school isn't one for making newcomers feel very welcome—we actually never get any."

I scoff. "Thanks for the heads-up, but I got that the instant I stepped on campus."

"It isn't their fault. They've— Well, we've all known each other since grade school."

I know what he's trying to say. It was the same at my last school. We all stuck together. Even if we hated each other, it was better than letting some newbie into our pack. "Yeah, I get it."

Another student is called to the rope. She gets farther than Zepher but doesn't make it to the top.

"Listen, maybe if people see you out, not on campus—"

"You're joking, right?" What would make him think I would voluntarily hang out with people who don't like me?

He jumps in to explain when he sees the what-the-hell expression on my face. "No, I'm serious. Just hear me out."

Each student is called to the rope one by one. Only a few come close to reaching the top. Of those, even fewer can reach high enough to ring the bell. Most of them probably haven't had nearly the training that I've had or the abuse I've sometimes put my body through to be better than my opponents.

Josh continues to talk endlessly. Although it's not as irritating as it should be. His droning prevents my attention from navigating toward Venom. I play with the ends of my hair to do something useless with my hands.

The coach calls his next victim in a loud voice that booms across the gymnasium. "Hunt."

Everyone goes quiet. My attention falters from Josh to Edge, who purposely makes a point to walk around the back of the crowd and come up alongside me before heading to the rope. As he peers down at me, a secret smirk touches the corner of his mouth. Neither of us moves. Deep in his heated stare is something raw and primal, a reckless need snaring more than my curiosity. It only lasts for a brief moment, but it's long enough to awaken the interests I felt earlier. Fuck! The second the connection breaks, I blink a few times to dissolve whatever just transpired. I swear the guy's got to be into voodoo or some shit to make me feel that tug to him whenever he looks at me like that.

"Watch out, little girl." His voice is gruff and threatening.

"So now I'm little girl, not Ninja?"

His mouth settles into a cruel grin. "I haven't decided yet."

He makes his way to the rope and grips the length of it. His eyes never leave mine until the whistle blows. His muscles bulge as he scales the rope with graceful speed. He's in a different dimension altogether from the other students. His legs grip around the rope, pushing him upward. It's more than impressive to watch. I hate to admit that I wish the rope were higher so I can continue to watch the muscles in his sculpted body contract and define with each movement.

He rings the bell.

I can't help the satisfied smirk spreading over my lips as his feet touch the floor. He knows I beat him. And any second, the entire class will know, too.

The coach announces his time, then adds, "Hunt, it's a new record for you, but you were just shy of West. She took you this time. She beat you by seven-tenths of a second." He jots the time on his clipboard. "You better watch out for her."

I couldn't have said it better myself.

With less than one freaking second, I have officially gained bragging rights against the big bad Viper himself. Not wanting to draw too much attention, I hold my smile inward.

After a few more people are called to participate in the drill, the coach dismisses the class for the day.

Just when I think I'm done with the drama, Edge steps into my path. "Not so fast."

I'm still too far down the confining hall from the ladies'

locker room to ignore him and duck into its safety. On their way to the locker room, the group of girls slows their pace. Edge waits for them to pass, then uses his broad body to inch me closer to the wall. With my back against the bricks, he leans in and props his hands against the wall behind me, caging me in.

I tilt my head up. Playing the sassy girl card, I say, "Oh wait! You're not one of those burly sexist assholes who have their one feeling hurt if a *little girl* beats them, are you?"

"Hardly."

"Well, it's like I said this morning, don't take it personally." I duck under his arm. "If you play nice, maybe I'll let you win next time."

A hint of a smile plays on his full lips before he quickly shuts it down. "I want a rematch."

"Yeah, well, I want a lot of things, too, but a rematch isn't one of them."

"Are you afraid you won't beat me a second time?"

I throw up my hands and walk backward. "Nah, that's not it. I don't want to have anything to do with helping you stroke that already too-big ego of yours."

His friends snicker behind him.

Catching me off guard, he asks, "What does that dragon stand for?" He nods at my forearm.

"It's personal. And I don't think a day will come when we'll ever be that close."

"Are you saying we won't be friends?" His deep voice displays a hint of teasing. I didn't think he was capable, but there it is.

"That's precisely what I'm saying. You made that perfectly clear this morning." I wink. "Maybe in the next life."

I turn away from him, keeping my eyes downcast to avoid getting lured back into his visual trap again. Walking the short distance to the locker room, I'm surprised and happy when the big man doesn't follow me. Without showering, I change back into my uniform and stuff my gym clothes into my bag to take them home to wash.

"Nice job out there." The girl who told me about the coach running gym class like a boot camp brushes out her ginger hair and offers me a hesitant smile. I realize now that she's the same girl I asked how to get here before Brielle showed up. Her face falls a fraction. "Listen, I'm sorry about earlier. Brielle can make things difficult."

I nod. "I get it." And I did. "No worries."

"I'm Marissa, by the way."

"I'm Kinsley."

She closes her locker. "The only ones who have ever come close to Edge's time are the rest of the Venom. So, I must say that it's bad that a girl could take him down—even with all those skills… and rock-hard muscles." Her smile goes dreamy as she describes my archenemy.

"Yeah," I say, grabbing my backpack to head out.

Josh is waiting for me outside the locker room.

I raise an eyebrow. "This isn't creepy."

He shrugs. "Maybe a little. Anyway, like I was suggesting earlier, about you hanging out. I wanted to invite you to a party that's happening this Saturday. It's at Tristan's beach house. It'll go all day, so you can get there whenever you want."

"Who's Tristan?" Knowing how these kinds of parties work, having been to a ton of them, I don't care who Tristan is. These parties are an excuse to hook up and get drunk. Which really isn't my scene.

"All you need to know is he's a guy who throws awesome parties." He forces a laugh.

I shrug one shoulder. "Sure," I say, having no intention of going.

Josh's face lights up. "Yeah, all right. Cool. Bring your bathing suit… and yeah, we'll chill out, drink, party, and you can get to know everybody."

"Sounds fun," I lie.

"All right, see you later." He smiles like he just won the giant teddy bear at the fair and walks away, holding the biggest prize.

Turning the corner, I come face to face with Venom. I swear to fuck I must have a giant snake magnet on my ass.

Edge does his usual and blocks my path. "Where ya headed?"

"Why do you care?" I try to move around him. With his body being the size of a small country, I make no progress. Giving in, I say, "psychology."

Edge slides his eyes to Kade, then back to me. "We'll see you there, little Ninja."

Are you effing kidding me? "Sports medicine?" I say, unable to hide my disdain, and praying that I'm wrong and we don't have the same major.

His grin widens in response. And I wish he wouldn't smile like that, consciously or unconsciously trying to drown me under his hellish spell. "Well, isn't that a coincidence?" I scoff.

"It is. And I look forward to making your life hell."

Even as he delivers his threat, his deep, throaty chuckle is as menacing as it is sexy. I wonder if he knows it. By the way his slate eyes glimmer, he definitely knows it. "Lucky me."

I swear to the gods. Tonight, I'm getting on my knees and praying, asking them what the fuck I did to deserve this.

7

EDGE

NINJA IS ALREADY in class when Kade and I arrive. With the guidance of Professor Hansley, I bet he told her to sit in the only empty chair—the one directly in front of mine, in the last row in the far corner. There's no assigned seats, but since class started a few weeks ago, we gravitate to the same ones.

Welcome to psychology, little Ninja.

Her hair is up in a sloppy bun on top of her head. Thin dark strands fall around her flawless face. From the second she took off her helmet in the parking lot, she's been the only thing on my mind the entire fucking day. She's hot as fuck without riding a motorcycle, but the blacked-out Ninja between her legs is certainly a nice bonus.

Her blazer is draped over the back of her chair. She rolled the cuffs of her shirt just enough to see the tail of the inked dragon. *A dragon.* Any doubt I had about who she was this morning vanished the moment I saw her tattoo and her questions about submissions in the gym.

Her posture is tense as she doodles in her notebook and does her best to ignore everyone coming into class. But she's not getting off that easy with me. I haven't decided what to do with her yet, but there's time.

"This should be interesting," I say, sliding into my seat behind her. Kade sits in the seat next to mine.

Without turning around, she lets out a frustrated breath.

"What's got you jacked? I did tell you we would see you here."

She turns around to glare at me. "You've got to be kidding." The brisk movement sends a light breeze my way. It's a mix of sweat from gym class and a light, sweet scent reminiscent of honey and whiskey. A few more strands of her hair fall to frame her scowl. Her heated blue eyes are striking and severe. A quick image crosses my mind, and the thought of her fighting in the ring has my dick twitching in my pants. Fuck, this girl has no idea what she's doing to me. Without even trying, she's managed to consume every damn one of my senses. The sleeves of her shirt ride up her forearms, exposing shaded cherry blossoms wrapping around the dragon.

"I assume you're talking about the seating arrangements." Almost on its own accord, my hand goes to tuck the loose strands behind her ear. My brain kicks into gear before I go too far, and I think about what I was getting ready to do. Thank fuck, I stopped myself.

"Aren't you a genius?" she grumbles.

"Well, little Ninja, I hate to break it to you, but we were here first." She can hardly argue with that.

Her back stiffens, probably because she knows I'm right. "By the way, my name is Kinsley."

"I know your name. The whole damn campus knows your name. But no, I'm going to stick with little Ninja. It fits you."

"It's better than little girl," she mumbles.

I scoff. "Maybe, maybe not."

Over her shoulder, I follow the clean lines of her tattoo. The dragon is as delicate and graceful as it is menacing. I don't think its personality is too far from the little Ninja herself.

I've got the next hour to torment her. I don't have a reason to, except that she challenged me this morning and then again in the gym. And if there's anything I hate more, it's being challenged. I still can't believe she beat my fucking time. Not that I'll let her know, but it's impressive as shit and only adds points to her already high tally card. How the hell she did that, I have no idea. No one has ever come close to my time except my boys, and then here comes this girl who does it on her first day.

That's not the thing that fucks with my head, though. What pisses me off the most is that she doesn't care. She's not trying to impress anyone here, yet she keeps doing it with her don't-give-a-shit attitude, an attitude that's packaged up in a tight, hot ass.

Professor Hansley jumps right into today's lecture. Ninja's hand moves at a feverish pace over the page as she takes notes.

Kade elbows me. "I wonder if she has anything else pierced."

My imagination is excited about where this is going. "You mean besides her eyebrow? Like maybe places that need to have clothes removed to see them?"

Kade nods. He's usually quiet and keeps to himself, but this girl has even piqued his interest, or my asshole-ish demeanor is finally rubbing off on him. If I had to guess, though, I'd choose the former. Ninja seems to have that effect on people, even my best friend. She makes people curious. At first glance, the guys want to fuck her, and the girls want to hate her. But after she pulls a stunt like she did this morning, curiosity wins. You want to know everything about her—and still want to fuck her.

She stretches her neck from side to side. I know she heard our conversation. How could she not? It gives me more satisfaction than it should. I lean back in my chair, stretching out my legs, my boots landing on either side of her desk.

Her gaze drops from Professor Hansley to the floor. Her profile is the only glimpse I get of her before she faces forward.

"Feeling a little caged in?" I tease.

"Since the moment I stepped foot on campus," she returns.

I chuckle. "You haven't seen anything yet."

"Ms. West, Mr. Hunt, is there a problem?" Mr. Hansley interrupts our conversation.

Her head pops up to look at the front of the room. Almost the entire class whips around in their seats to see what they may have missed. Fucking pathetic. Since they can't find a thread of entertainment in their own miserable lives, they latch on to anything they can. I imagine Ninja's face reddening, but then again, maybe not. She's proven she's not easily flustered.

"No, we're fine," she answers for both of us.

Disappointed they have nothing worth spreading around campus, the class faces the professor again.

I draw my legs in and lean toward her. Her sweet scent, mixed with her musky perfume, clashes with the rebellious attitude radiating from her. That alone should be a warning enough to keep my distance. But I'm more than intrigued and way too curious to stay away.

"Are we fine now?" I whisper into the back of her hair.

The sound of paper being ripped scratches in the quiet room right before the crumpled ball is flung over her shoulder. It lands on my desk.

"A love note, I'm guessing."

"In your dreams," she whispers over her shoulder.

Unfolding the bundled mass, I'm again floored at her boldness... or stupidity. As hot as her sassy ass is, I haven't decided yet which better suits her.

Small, block, precise letters spell out, *LEAVE ME THE FUCK ALONE!*

"Not a chance in hell." I scoff. Sitting back, I fold the torn piece of paper and tuck it into my pocket.

Catching the last few words from Professor Hansley about an upcoming test, I can't help the wicked smile playing over my lips. This is going to be fun.

Ninja is on her feet the second class is dismissed. She stuffs her blazer into her backpack, along with her notebook and pen.

"Where are you off to in such a rush?" I ask.

She stops and turns to face me. "Anywhere but here," she says with a smile.

Internally, I grin at her audacity. It should be a turn-off, but fuck if it's not.

"Little Ninja," I call out. This time, she slows but doesn't stop. "There's no escaping."

She doesn't respond as she picks up her pace and bolts for the exit.

The parking lot is a clusterfuck of people and cars. Some are hanging out, and others head to the dorms. I scan the area, looking for the raven-haired rebel. She stands next to her motorcycle. Gunner and Levi come up behind Kade and me.

"Party at my house," Gunner says.

Kade punches him in the arm. "It's Monday, you shit."

"You need to take your Einstein head out of your ass and realize any day is perfect for a party." He takes a joint out of the pocket of his blazer.

Gunner flicks the lighter and sets fire to the tip. He inhales, passes the joint to Levi, and then they start humming the same fucking reggae song. I swear those motherfuckers are always in sync.

Tuning them out, I focus on Ninja. She pulls the band out of her hair. Long black waves fall down her back. I imagine curling my fist around the lush bundle, then pulling it down so that she's forced to look up at me.

I'm yanked from the fantasy as Brielle tucks herself under my arm, draping it over her shoulders.

"Hey, baby, it's been a shitty day, huh?" she whines.

A few of her friends trail after us as we head to my Jeep. Their giggles and nonsensical chatter are annoying as shit.

"Baby, why are you ignoring me?"

I pull my arm away, trying to do just that. She's irritating as hell but puts out whenever I want. Bastard of a reason to keep her around, but it doesn't seem to faze her. She thinks we're destined to be together forever or some shit. The problem with her thinking is that we're not, nor have we ever been, together. Truth be told, there isn't much more between us than her pussy and her mouth.

Brielle follows my gaze and huffs out an exasperated breath when she realizes who has my attention. "And there's the cause of this shitty-ass day in the flesh. The slut can't even afford four wheels." She laughs.

I wish she'd just keep her mouth shut. What money means to her is something very different than what it means to me. The only similarity between my family's wealth and hers is that Brielle's family money has been passed down through generations, growing in size with each reading of a will. I know for a fucking fact that her family's money isn't completely clean, but I'd bet her purse is carrying crisp dollar bills and unstained credit cards, whereas my wallet overflows with tainted hundreds that are laced with dark secrets and sin—in other words, blood money.

"A chick with an engine between her legs is hot as shit," Gunner pipes up.

"Whatever. She's a piece of trash, and she knows it. I bet she's had a lot more between her legs than that."

Levi props his arm on Brielle's shoulder. "Like you haven't, Bri?"

"Shut up!" she spits.

"I've got to go, my girl is waiting for me," Levi says, handing the joint back to his brother.

"That's it, run off to play house," Gunner teases.

Levi flips him off. "Later Edge, Kade."

Brielle tries to intertwine her fingers with mine. I jerk my hand away, tucking my hands into my pockets.

She grabs me by the lapels of my blazer and rises onto her toes. It's like nothing has changed since high school. Why would it? Monarch University is basically the same as Monarch Prep. It has all the same boring people, with the same expectations. Even the campus is the same, just larger. The buildings and dorms are just on the other side of the river, connected by a pedestrian bridge. It's all the same shit. That's one of the reasons why the little Ninja is so intriguing.

With her lips against my ear, Brielle whispers, "Come by my place and I'll have you forgetting all about that piece of trash."

She tries to kiss me, but I turn my head. Her lips brush the underside of my chin. I've never kissed her, nor do I ever plan to. But it never stops her from trying. The sad part is that she's well aware of this, but she still tries, hoping to catch me off guard. That will a thousand percent never happen.

The main problem with Brielle's suggestion is that I don't want to forget about Ninja. I watch over Brielle's head as Ninja unbuttons her shirt. Taking my hands out of my pockets, I remove Brielle's too-long fake claws from my lapels, then move her out of the way to get a better view of the girl stripping near her motorcycle. What in the actual fuck?

Within a few moments, I'm not the only one staring at Ninja. She's got the attention of most of the parking lot as she fucking undresses right there in front of everyone.

Caught between wanting to cover her up to hide her body from the eyes of every other fucking guy here and cheering her on to take it all off, I stay quiet and watch the show.

She isn't stripping for the attention. Fuck, she doesn't even notice that she's the focal point right now. Again, her doesn't-give-a-shit attitude rises to the surface. She slides off her button-down shirt, revealing a white tank top with black bra straps underneath. There's the sexy-as-hell dragon tattoo on her forearm. She said I would never be close enough to her to know what it means, but I'm going to have to disagree with her about that. As dangerous as it is, I have plans for us to get very close.

She stuffs her shirt into her backpack, then she slides down the zipper on her skirt. It falls to the ground, exposing her barely-ass-covering shorts. She bends over to pick up her backpack, shoves her skirt in, zips it up, and hoists it onto her back. She leaves her high socks over her knees. Straddling her motorcycle, she puts on her helmet and starts the engine. Fuck me and my hardening cock. The gasps and whispers around me spread like wildfire. I stay perfectly silent as she backs out of my parking spot. In perfect, fearless form, not giving a shit about what anybody thinks, Ninja pulls out of the parking lot onto the main road and disappears from my view.

Something about her isn't quite right. No one has ever come into Monarch who hasn't been afraid of what's in store for them, having heard rumors about Venom or the Vipers. The new kid always gets shit. Their one job is to win one of us over with their so-called charm or make some kind of offering to make them worthy. Usually, it's their subservience in return for invites and staying off our blacklist. She's made no effort to fit in. And she sure as hell hasn't attempted to play nice. She's done the exact opposite.

At a glance, you could sum her up as a snooty bitch who could fit in perfectly with Brielle and her friends, wearing too much makeup and grinding on every hot guy she sees, either for attention or to get herself off. Up close, though, Ninja is none of those things. Her game is different. She might have fooled everyone else but not me. That girl is after something. And I have a feeling it involves more than getting a degree. I'll find out what she's up to. Keeping her close ensures I remain in control.

And it'll be my pleasure to keep her as close as possible.

8

KINSLEY

DAY ONE... complete.

My only goal at this very moment is to get the fuck out of this place.

I stuff my things in my backpack in such a rush and without a care that the wrinkles may never come out of my uniform. But I can't think of that right now. Edge and Kade weren't far behind me after I bolted out of class, so I know they're nearby. Too close. I put my helmet on, lock down all curiosities, and refrain from seeking him out to steal one last glance at Edge. For some messed-up reason, it's equally difficult to ignore him as it is to feel drawn to him.

"Get a fucking grip, Kinsley." The demand to myself is muffled in my helmet. I start the engine and kick it into gear. Weaving through the parking lot until I reach the open, large iron gates, I don't wait in line to pull out onto the main road. I slip behind the car at the front and pull onto the road without even looking to see if it's clear.

A semi coming up fast behind me blows its throaty horn. I pull hard on the throttle, reeling out the engine before shifting into the next gear. Tearing away, I'm gone before there's ever any real danger. Still, the thrill rockets through me. Adrenaline makes an easy excuse for why my heart is threatening to beat out of my chest.

But if I'm honest with myself, that's all Edge's doing.

Twenty minutes later, I pull into the parking lot of Serpent's Spear Dojo. Through the window, I see my uncle has a class in session. Instead of the usual stench of sweat that usually hits me when I enter, pungent perfumes assault and tickle my nose. The sickly scents of flowers, sweet musk, and fruits blend nauseatingly. My uncle guides the class of older women in a sequence of punches and kicks. Most are kicking serious ass. The ones not kicking ass are busy checking out my uncle. Older guys aren't my thing, but I guess he's good-looking as far as men go.

He glances in my direction, holds up a hand, and indicates a three and a zero, showing how many minutes they have left in the class. Poor guy has another half hour to get eye-fucked.

I toss my backpack on the floor of the office. Luca texted me just as I left school, saying he had to cancel our training today. By all the sad emoji faces, I know he isn't happy about it either. Of all days for him not to show really sucks. I need my best friend today.

I stretch to work out the tension in my shoulders and back that has only knotted more as the day went on. Then I tape my knuckles to minimize the abuse I'm preparing to put them through. My mind keeps wandering to the guy with stormy eyes. He warned me he would become my nightmare. He also made it very clear he won't go easy on me. So far, he's lived up to his word. Shit. Shit. Shit. I refuse to become one of those girls who turns stupid over some guy. I need to keep my head straight.

There's no way to prepare for who I would be going up against, but Venom—in particular, Ledger Hunt—will be more of a challenge than I initially thought. If I'm being honest with myself, I'm not sure what I thought—or if I even thought about it at all. My ego and overall goal to bring them down clouded everything else. Either way, it doesn't matter now. I've committed, and I'm not backing out. I just need to find a way to crack through his asshole exterior.

The collective shout of "Yes, sensei!" and then chatter from the main room signal that the session has ended. I peek around the corner. A few women gather around my uncle, grinning and giggling like schoolgirls. Uncle Trey plays along, then eventually walks the last two to the door, locking it behind them. I come out of the office.

"Hey, you," he says.

"Hey." The word comes off flatter than a day-old can of left-over soda.

"That good, huh?"

I need to show some enthusiasm, even if it's a thread, so I use the teasing approach. "Not as good as your skills with the ladies."

He chuckles. "They're just women trying to stay in shape."

"Cougars is the term you're looking for." The joking takes my mind off some of the shit I endured today.

He laughs as he folds up one of the mats, propping it in the corner. "So, how was your first day?"

There's no way I can give him the full load of my new hell. So, I go with the easy way out: lying. "Yeah, it was good. Met a couple of cool people." I toss Eden in that couple, hoping she'll come around.

"Good. Glad to hear it. I'm sure each day will get easier."

"Yeah." Another lame response and lie. If I listen to any of Edge's warnings, I just lived my easiest day at Monarch University. Rolling my shoulders and neck, I shake off the tension and all thoughts of the asshole.

Uncle Trey picks up his water bottle and takes a long drink. "What's your poison today?"

"I'm going to hit the bag for a while."

He glances around. "Wait, I thought Luca was coming?"

"He had to cancel."

He shakes his head. "That sucks. I'm sorry."

"Yeah, it does."

My uncle waves his arms around the empty space. "Well, it looks like you have the place to yourself. So, have at it."

"Thanks."

As he saunters off to his office, I don't miss his over-the-shoulder glance. I get the sense that he knows I'm lying, which kills me, but I can't let him think I'm having issues already—not on my first day.

I plug in my earbuds and press play on my go-to playlist for practicing. The music thrashes wildly as I pound the bag with my fists and my feet without mercy. A few of my knuckles are bloody from where the tape slipped, and the tops of my feet will have bruises, but I still don't stop. All the shit that happened today, coming face to face with the son of a bitch who may have been the one to kill my father, his lingering stares that make me feel exposed and weak, his warnings, navigating a new school and classes, was more difficult than I imagined it would be. Everything slams into me all at once. With each hit, my mind clears a tiny bit more.

Telling Edge to stay away from me probably wasn't the most brilliant idea, not that he plans to listen, but it was the longest day ever, and I was ready to get out of the Viper's den. I need to get close to Edge and earn his trust. But I'm not sure I trust myself when we're next to one another. The warmth that coursed through my core when he was near me was unlike anything I've felt before.

Even now, just thinking about him, my body reacts, and there's a visceral need for contact. It doesn't help that my mind fucks with me by remembering the titillating way his breath fanned against the side of my neck as he threatened me. If he kept whispering against my sensitive skin, I could have come right there in the hall in front of everyone. That alone is fucked up. Since when did I get off on being someone's submissive? Fuck!

I slam the bag harder, trying to erase any feelings that might hinder my ability to give Venom what they deserve. I'm so caught up in beating the bag that I don't notice my uncle until he taps me on the shoulder. I tap the earbud to pause the music.

"Hey, kiddo, are you almost done? You've been out here for almost an hour."

I deliver another punch and kick before dropping to my hands and knees, out of breath and completely spent. "Has it been that long?"

He leans against one of the thick wooden pillars. "Yeah. Looks like you had a lot to get out. Anything you want to talk about?"

Talking isn't one of my strong points. Despite the thousand things weighing me down, hitting bags and screaming feel more natural lately than talking anything out. What worries me is that if I start screaming, I won't ever be able to stop, and even when I scream until my throat is raw, everything will be the same as it is now. My dad will still be dead, my mom will still be drowning in her loss, and I'll still be hunting down a murderer. I close my eyes, knowing I can't let my rage take over.

When I open them, Uncle Trey still stares at me with sadness and concern. "Are you sure you're all right?"

I nod. "Yeah. Some days are just harder than others." There, finally a truth.

He doesn't say anything to smooth over the hurt or tell me the pain will lessen with time, and he doesn't try to hug me. He simply kneels next to me. We stay there in silence for several minutes. I love him even more for the quiet support.

He and Dad were close once, so I ask him a loaded question that's plagued me since I first saw my father compete in the underground fights. "Do you think he did it for the money?"

With absolute respect, he looks directly into my eyes. "No. I don't." Uncle Trey lets out a deep sigh. "It wasn't the money that got him. He got hooked on the thrill. And it eventually caught up to him."

I'm glad Uncle Trey doesn't believe my father fought for the money. My dad's companies were always successful, so I don't think we needed cash. At least, I never felt that we did. However, in families with considerable wealth, there are often a lot of secrets and greed.

"I never thought it was a good idea for your father to fight in the UG. It's one thing to fight in tournaments and prove your skills there, to be matched and challenged, but it's completely different when you're fighting blind. You don't know what skills or who you're going up against. People betting on you as a sport, like you're some kind of animal..." He shakes his head. "It goes against our training to respect the art of fighting."

He's right. I agree with him. But I snuck into more than one of those underground fights, and the thrilling exhilaration of being surrounded by all the energy intoxicated me. If you let it, it will consume you. My dad was proof of that.

Out of nowhere, Uncle Trey laughs. I jerk my head up to him. What the hell could be funny? "His stage name, the Slayer. It was clever. It was what we called each other growing up."

I smile despite the anger and pain coursing through me. As Uncle Trey gets lost in his memories from long ago, all I can think is that Slayer was slain. The image of his bloodied and helpless body will forever be branded into my brain. I'm not sure if I'm ready to stop talking about what happened with my dad or not. But at least it was an icebreaker with Uncle Trey. The underground fights are a society all of their own, full of secrets, mystery, money, and seduction. I don't know when, but I know that my father's final fight won't be my last. I've given myself no choice but to return to the place where it all started.

"You ready to go home?" Uncle Trey asks.

Clearing my head of those memories and intentions, I nod. "Yeah."

"Pizza tonight?" he suggests.

"Perfect."

The heat of the shower soothes my aching muscles. I pushed too hard tonight, but it was worth it. The pain is real. The pain is a reminder of why I put up with assholes like Edge.

"Stop thinking about him!" Why am I letting him get under my skin?

I don't know, Kins, maybe because he's hot as fuck, and has the same fuck-it-all-to-hell attitude as you?

I growl at my inner self. Telling her to fuck off would be asinine, so I ignore the taunting voice, grab the towel from the hook, and wipe it over the foggy mirror. The black hair still shocks me when I glimpse myself in the streaky reflection. My mom is going to freak out when she sees it. I dry the dark locks with the towel, then wrap it around my body.

My phone buzzes from the bedroom. Luca's handsome face flashes on the screen, wanting to FaceTime.

My thumb is millimeters from the answer button before remembering I can't let him see me like this. "Shit!"

He hasn't seen my hair either. I didn't even tell him what I did. Taking the cowardly path, I deny his chat and call him back instead.

He picks up on the first ring. "What, are you naked or something? I've seen it all, Kins."

"Or—or something," I stammer.

Thankfully, he doesn't push. "How was your day, babe? I want to hear all about it."

I take a deep breath and then let it out in a long sigh.

"That bad, huh?"

"Listen, before we get to my hellish day, I need to tell you something first. You can freak out on me, and then we can try to have a normal conversation, okay?"

His voice suddenly tightens with worry. "What did you do? Are you a mother to a herd of baby ducks? Or plow down a granny crossing the street on your death mobile? Or worse, plow down a herd of baby ducks?"

I can't help but laugh. "First off, I think it's a flock of ducklings, not a herd, and second, my Ninja is not a death mobile."

He ignores my argument. "You're not denying any of those things."

"No, I didn't do any of those things." In his eyes, what I did is way worse.

"Whew. Thank God, 'cause you know—"

"I did another thing!" I blurt out. "You won't like it!" A breath. A sigh.

"Kins..."

Then, without wasting another second, I spew, "I dyed my hair black. Please don't ask why. But I promise to tell you soon, okay? Just not today." The other end of the line is unusually silent. "Luca, are you there?"

"Yeah." Now, it's his turn to let out a long breath. "So let me get this straight. You dyed your gorgeous, natural blonde hair to black, like the color of tar and bat wings, for some secret purpose you can't tell your best friend about?"

I sound like the worst friend ever when he puts it that way. "Um, yeah... kinda," I squeak out.

"There's no kinda about it!" He abruptly hangs up on me.

Shocked, I glance at my phone. Luca has never hung up on me before. A few seconds later, his face flashes on the screen again. There's no getting out of it this time. If I deny him this, he'll make the forty-five-minute drive to see me and give me hell in person. I press the accept button.

The moment the connection is made, he demands, "Take it off!"

Reluctantly, I slide the towel from my damp hair. His eyes bulge out of his head. His mouth opens and closes like a fish, opens once more, and then he covers it with his hand. An ear-splitting shriek threatens to blow out the tiny speaker of my phone.

I run my fingers through the long strands, remaining silent until he calms down from having his freak-out. The background of his room becomes a blur as he paces the length of it back and forth.

I tighten the towel around my breasts, tucking the corner into the top. "Luca—"

"Don't. Just don't speak for a moment…or two …or three."

I clamp my mouth shut as he takes in the change and tries to process why the hell I would ruin my natural blonde hair.

He wipes his brow, then finally speaks. "Kins, I love you. You know this. No matter what your reason is for decimating your hair, I will continue to love you. But why? Just tell me that. Why?"

I can't—not yet. And as much as he's going to hate me, I admit as much. "Okay, since I can't tell you the truth… *yet*, I'm going to lie… I wanted a change."

Luca squeezes his eyes shut. When he opens them, his gaze softens. "Kins, girl, I know you've been through hell these past few months, and I understand some of your decisions in those months haven't been exactly, well, you know… smart. Like when you raced your bike in that chicken fight against that oncoming semi, where you could have died, or when you used your fake I.D. to buy enough booze to die of alcohol poisoning ten times over, just so you could forget, or when—"

"I had to," I interrupt. "This is for a bigger cause—"

"This has to do with your dad, doesn't it? What, to settle a score or something? Retribution?"

I have to look away from the phone. A single tear pools in the corner of my eye. Luca knows me all too well, and hiding the truth from him is too hard. I should have known this would happen.

His voice drops to almost a whisper. "Kins, listen, nothing will bring him back, no matter what you do."

He's right. Deep down, I know that. But I have to make it right—find a way I can live with his death, as selfish as that may be. But for that to happen, someone has to pay.

The rest of our call isn't our usual fun banter and teasing. I give him an undetailed version of my hellish day and training at the dojo. He admits school was boring without me. I miss how things used to be, when everything was so much easier, normal. He would have picked me up this morning for school, had a couple of classes together, ate lunch together, snapped a pic of some passersby, added some bunny ears and fangs, and we'd laugh. There would have been so much laughing. Today, without him, it was the complete opposite.

"Your hair doesn't look terrible. Even though it washes out your tan, it makes your blue eyes pop."

"Thanks." Warmth spreads through my chest. Leave it to Luca to make me feel a little better.

"And for anyone who doesn't know you're a true blonde, keep your panties on."

"Luca!" I pick up my pillow and hit the phone.

His naughty comment breaks the glacier-size ice between us. He laughs without malice. "You know you've got to if you want to keep up your secret agent identity. Plus, that color gives you bad girl vibes." He claws at the screen and growls a purr.

I cringe. "Please, don't do that ever again." Then I shake my head. "I have no plans for getting that close to anyone."

"Better tell me if you do." He fluffs his pillow. "I'm tired. I'll call you tomorrow. Maybe then you'll be ready to let me in on your little mission."

My mission is anything but little. But he doesn't need to know that, not this soon into it, anyway. "Good night. Love you."

"Love you, too."

The screen goes as black as the damp locks falling around my shoulders. As I switch off the light and crawl into bed, my head spins with thoughts of one person. Edge. It's like I'm on one of those whirling rides, and each time I come around, there's his beautiful, haunting face. It's dizzying.

He's proving to be more than just some rich guy who wants to fuck off. He's challenging and curious, which equals danger-ous. It also doesn't help that he's hot as fuck. It's distracting. He's distracting. And I can't afford any distractions. He makes me feel vulnerable in a way that makes me question if I can trust myself with him. Even if I can't accept this truth, I know it's there. I can't let him catch on to it.

If he does, he'll bury me alive.

9

KINSLEY

Day two of the shit show at Monarch.

I debate on whether to be an intentional bitch and take Edge's parking spot again, but I decide not to ask for trouble and find a spot far away from the one Edge has claimed.

"Going to give us another striptease this afternoon?" some random guy asks as he walks by me.

Is that douche talking about me shredding our dreadful uniform yesterday after school? Ignoring him, I continue onward toward my first class. Just inside the main building stand a few guys and a couple of girls I may or may not recognize. This early in the game, everyone looks the same, with only a few who stand out. I won't mention names.

"Maybe today you can take it all off," one guy says. The rest of his friends laugh and agree with crude gestures.

I flash them the finger along with a bored expression as I pass their little group. Fuck them. Maybe I will.

Not a minute passes before I'm confronted again.

"Good morning, sunshine." Bryce's arm wraps around my shoulder.

I let out a small chuckle. "Are you always this happy first thing in the morning? I need to know before I get in too deep."

He looks up to the ceiling as if contemplating an answer as he guides us effortlessly through the crowded hall. "Yeah, you could say that. I'm just naturally an uppity kind of guy."

"Uppity? Is that like your grandma's pet name for you?"

He stops mid-step and turns me with his hands on my shoulders so I'm looking directly at him. "That's not funny. She's dead."

"I'm—"

"Kidding!" He loops his arm through mine and guides us forward. "She calls me Bunny."

I wince. "I don't want to know."

Each time I'm in the presence of Bryce, I feel like I've stepped off the planet Earth and into a different realm where things are happy and everything is right in the world.

He jerks my body against him as his excitement grows. "You should come with me next time I visit her. My grandma would love you. She doesn't take any shit from anyone. Just like you. You guys are like twins."

"Twins, huh?"

"Identical. Boobs and all!"

"What?" I look down at my chest.

"Kidding, kidding!" He looks at my chest. "No, you're right, not identical. Seriously, though, you're fraternal—at least in your badassery."

I shake my head, unable to stop the urge to laugh.

"Listen! I swear, one time when I was shopping with her, she rammed her shopping cart into the back of a guy in the wine aisle because he was yelling at the store clerk for not having his Merlot in stock. Then she proceeded to tell him to go suck a cork and find his damn manners."

Bryce makes it easy to let go of the tension I've held on to lately. The smile on my face feels familiar and natural, like an old friend who decided to visit. I've unintentionally erected a wall so thick I forget to enjoy moments like these—not that there have been that many in the past few months. But right now, here with Bryce, it gives me hope that I haven't lost myself completely.

"Something funny?"

Bryce jerks us to a stop. Damn, that voice! Damn him. Three of the four Vipers, Levi, Kade, and Edge, stand side by side. Their muscled bodies create a barricade across the hallway. Gunner, the missing link, I'm guessing, isn't too far behind.

"Most definitely funny." I force my next laugh, emphasizing the hilarity of the story. "We would share, but it's a private joke." I lightly slap Bryce's arm. "Right, Bryce?"

"Yeah... private," he mutters in a slightly shaky voice.

I wish I could wipe the intimidation off his face. He went from carefree to frozen all in one go. I need to get the poor guy out of here before he shits himself. In the short time I've known Bryce, which includes two morning run-ins and one lunch, I've learned that he enjoys drama but dislikes being at the center of it. If the Vipers are in the mix, drama is inevitable.

It's my turn to loop my arm through Bryce's. "Bye, boys, we're off to see the wizard."

I barrel between Levi and Kade. Throughout the entire exchange, I purposely avoided Edge's face and those dangerous eyes. Getting trapped by those stormy depths is like sliding through wormholes only to find you landed in a place where you lost all control over your own body and common sense. I was caught off guard yesterday. Today, I know better. His beautiful face, even with his well-practiced glare, haunted me until I finally fell asleep last night.

Bryce wipes his forehead with the back of his hand. "How the hell can they induce a sweat attack on command?"

"Come on, Bunny, forget about them." I tug him along, not knowing if his class is in the same direction as mine.

"Will I see you at lunch?" he asks.

"I'll be there."

He unhooks his arm as I push through the large doors leading to the courtyard. "Don't be a coward like me." He wiggles his fingers in a goodbye gesture.

Art is another day of disaster. I have no idea where the hell to begin with my project. I'm almost positive the art professor agrees that I'm a total failure after she tries to help me. There's finally a sliver of peace when Brielle leaves halfway through class and thankfully doesn't return.

"Just so you know, I gave you a ten out of ten for your performance after school yesterday," a familiar flirty voice says.

I look over to see Gunner. His leg is propped up on the stool Brielle vacated. He offers me a cheesy wink while twirling his paintbrush through his fingers. The act wouldn't be complete without his signature grin perfectly in place. I'm not sure if he looks hot or if his flirtatious side has gone a step too far. With his loosely knotted tie and his cuffs rolled to reveal tan forearms, I lean toward the hot side. The cool of his blue eyes grabs my deeper ones.

"Is that going to be a daily occurrence? If it is, just hold off long enough until I get there, okay? We can make some sort of signal to let the other know we're ready."

There's only a grin showing his excitement. He's got to be joking. Right?

I shake my head, not believing this conversation is happening. "Jeez, what is it with you guys? I was just getting comfortable, for fuck's sake. Wearing these stuffy clothes all day, I feel like every cell in my body is being choked out." I scoff. "Besides, if you think that's stripping, then you obviously haven't seen anyone do it right."

He drops his leg to the floor and then leans in my direction.

"Ninja baby, I'm available anytime for you to show me your expertise on the subject."

Fuck me. I need to keep my mouth shut. Closing my eyes, I do my best to ignore him for the few minutes left of class.

"What? You don't give private lessons?"

Ignoring him is useless. He's like a persistent child tugging on your pant leg, begging for just one more piece of candy.

I turn to face him. "Gunner, please shut up."

Shifting back to his canvas, he holds up his hands in defeat. "Fine, I was trying to be friends. But if you don't want to be, fine!"

There's obviously something in the water in this fucked-up, delusional school. Friends? Is he fucking kidding me? Every conversation I have, it feels like I stepped off a cliff and am dangling in mid-air, just waiting to see what I fall into next. Fuck, maybe I need to start drinking the damn water.

The word *happiness* doesn't even begin to cover the relief I feel when class ends.

Hesitating just outside the door, I glance left and right before recognizing the way to biology. I leave the art building, cross the courtyard, and head into the math and science building. Finding the room for biology proves to be more challenging than the classwork itself. Yesterday, I found the room without a hitch. When I turn down a familiar hall, another row of doors confronts me. Guessing, I open the heavy door with the sign *Biology*. It only takes a few seconds to realize I haven't mastered the art of navigating Monarch University, especially when I hear moans from within the dark room.

Curiosity wins over my logic, which screams at me to get the hell out of there. Instead, I let the door close behind me and blink several times, willing my eyes to adjust to the dimly lit room. Why the hell didn't I listen to my freaking gut? The sliver of light from the window creates a line of light down Brielle's bare ass. She's bent over the desk while Edge stands behind her.

His hand rests on her lower back as he pounds his toned body into hers.

I should turn around and leave, but my stunned sense of all sanity has my feet anchored to the floor. Why the fuck am I not disgusted—or even moving in the opposite direction? But I'm too late when Edge's eyes lock on mine. I let those precious few seconds slip by as streaks of heat race down my spine, straight to the center of my core.

The corner of Edge's mouth lifts in a sinful, knowing smirk. By the look on his beautiful face, he likes that he's been caught —caught by me.

"I think she wants to watch," he whispers into the near darkness. I know his words are meant for me alone. Slowing his pace, he moves his hips forward and back in a hypnotic wave of desire, his eyes never leaving mine.

My body is electrified with the building sensations of where he's taking them as he continues to slide into her wetness, intentionally deepening his penetrating thrusts until she calls out in need of more. As much as I hate the girl beneath him, her cries of pleasure only add to the moment's eroticism and the wetness pooling between my legs.

Thoughts of getting out of there clash in the ultimate battle with fiery feelings of wanting to stay until he comes. I want to know the sounds he makes and the way his face shifts from cockiness to euphoria when he has his release.

As I stare into his burning gaze and his heated eyes bore into mine, the throbbing between my legs escalates to an insatiable storm. His merciless grin darkens as if he knows exactly how my body is reacting to him fucking her.

Brielle suddenly looks up and spews a string of curses, snapping me out of my trance. "Are you going to keep watching? Get the fuck out!"

Locating a shard of what's left of my self-respect, I blurt out, "Sorry, I guess this isn't biology?"

Freeing me from his uncompromising hold, Edge says, "More like sex-ed." His deep, throaty chuckle unites with a harsh grunt as he drives back into her.

"Get the fuck out!" Brielle yells again.

I give Edge one last look. I'm unsure what it's saying or even if I'm trying to convey anything as I back out of the door. His scalding slate eyes follow me the entire way until the door slams shut.

I lean against the wall outside the classroom and take several deep breaths. What in the actual fuck just happened? The magnetism in that room between him and me was off the charts. It was like Brielle wasn't even in the room, and she was the one he was fucking. Never have I been so enraptured by someone that I lost all control.

Could my morning start any worse?

I tap my palm against my forehead. The water—it's got to be the fucking water.

Finally finding enough clarity, I ask a random person I pass in the hall where my class is, which I should have done the first time to save that scene from being branded into my skull.

Eden is already there when I plop down next to her.

She says hi without looking at me. Then she sets down her pencil. "What's wrong with you?"

Am I that easy to read? Running my hand over my face, hopefully wiping it clean of any residue of the visual I was just assaulted with, I say, "Nothing. I got a little lost, is all." I walked in on Edge and Brielle fucking, no biggie. "But I'm here now." The tone in my voice is hard to gauge. Even to my ears, I don't know if I sound sarcastic, too happy, or distant, while still lost in how he stared at me.

For the next hour, my head couldn't be further away from the topic of cell division. Eden feverishly takes notes. The only thing I'm looking forward to is alone time in the library, to clear my head of the images that fill every crevice of my skull.

The library is practically empty when I arrive. I set my backpack down on the same table as yesterday and set up the few things I need to work on for biology.

It's come to my attention that all libraries do not smell the same. The one at my other school could have been mistaken for a potpourri factory. Mrs. Feiss, the librarian, had an obsession with everything peach-and berry-scented. Hence, bowls of dried flowers and twigs were on every table. Being a historical castle-turned-library, this one smells like damp stone and ancient secrets. The pages of old books permeate the air. I can't decide which is worse, peaches or history.

Before I contemplate an opinion, another scent tickles my nose—the faint smell of cinnamon. Without turning around, I know Edge stands directly behind me. The carnal need that he awoke earlier is still keyed up and has me begging for release. I shove it back into a dark cave. I'll tend to that need later... alone.

No doubt Edge has come to mock me. He's so close that the heat from his body seeps through my blazer. I refuse to turn around. I can't. If I do, his mouth will be close enough to—

"Did you like what you saw?"

Even with only those few words, that whispered question ignites the embers I'm trying so hard to ignore. I have to grip the chair in front of me to stabilize myself. I close my eyes and inhale.

Breathe in. One-two-three.

Breathe out. One-two-three.

Stealing my resolve, I answer, "Can't wait to do it again tomorrow."

He leans against me, his front against my back, and rests his hands on the back of the chair, caging me in. His fingers brush mine. The light touch creates tiny electric impulses to zap along my skin. "Oh, little Ninja, I'll do it with you anytime." He doesn't give me a moment to react before he continues. "Imagine me bending you over this table, my hands firmly on your waist, holding you exactly where I want you as I slide my hard cock into your dripping cunt."

The deep seduction of his voice lulls me into a visceral trance. As if on their own accord, my eyes close, and I do just like he asked and imagine his words.

"I bet the moans that would fall out of that pretty mouth of yours sound like fucking music." He lets out a sigh. His warm breath fans across my neck.

It's not like me to lose my voice, but fuck him and his torturous imagination. I'm no virgin, but I've never felt this turned on by another guy—and he hasn't even touched me.

Edge drops his hands from the chair and then slowly backs away from me, giving me much-needed breathing room. I look over my shoulder and up at him. The heat in my face is no match for the fire raging between my legs. Thank fuck he can't see that. But from the way he's studying me, there's no denying he can sense it.

His next words are nothing more than a whisper. "I can't think of a better way to break you in and welcome you to Monarch."

And just like that, the balloon of orgasmic bliss bursts. Reality rains down like confetti. And thank God he's back to reminding me of what an asshole he is. I can't ever let him affect me like that again.

Gathering all my senses and making sure they are on the same page, I force myself to focus on the only reason I came to Monarch. It most definitely isn't to get swept off my feet just to be someone's—the enemy's, no less—quick fuck. There's enough distance between us to turn around and face him without the threat of engaging in something I would regret.

When I see his smug, knowing look, anger bubbles to the surface. "You're kidding me, right?"

His stoic expression gives nothing away. "Kidding? No. I am definitely not kidding." He moves a fraction closer to me. "I would bend you over right now and fuck you until you came so hard my name would be the only word you'd ever speak again."

Again, my traitorous body responds to his promise. Threat? Promise? Whatever it is, fuck my hardening nipples straining against my bra and the repeat of the tightness low in my belly. Control, Kinsley. *Get* control of yourself.

I take a deep breath and look him directly in the eyes. "No thanks." I pull out the chair to sit and flip open the book in front of me, opening it to a random chapter because I can't think straight with this muscle-head talking about sex, standing over my shoulder. "I think I'll pass. You and Brielle seem to make the perfect couple."

"Trust me, we are not a couple."

I click my pen and tap it on the open book. "Does she know that?"

Dammit. I mentally slap myself for asking that question. All it does is make me look like I give a shit what their status is. I don't!

"It's an understanding."

For some reason, I don't think it's a *mutual* understanding. "I doubt that."

Why am I even having this conversation? I don't give a fuck what their relationship is. He's got to leave now—right now!—seeing that I turned down his fuck session proposal in the middle of the library or that I have any interest in pursuing this conversation.

He does the exact opposite and pulls out the chair next to me, then proceeds to make himself comfortable. Fuck me to hell. He's so close I can smell the light fragrance of his cologne.

Thankfully, it's only cologne I smell and not the scent of sex on his skin.

He leans into me, his mouth only inches from my cheek. "So, you like to watch?"

I stiffen but refuse to let him bait me. Watching isn't my thing. But at that moment, when I walked in on them, he captured my attention so hard that it was impossible to break free. It was like he was lying in wait, prepared for me to be snagged in his trap. And it had nothing to do with Brielle. It was all him, his alluring eyes, his slow and intentional thrusts, and the way he made it feel like he was fucking me instead of her.

Clearing my throat, I rub my sweating palms over my skirt. "No."

I take a deep breath, hoping the heat in my cheeks has dissipated enough to look him in the eyes and let the lie pass through my lips undetected. I liked watching *him.*

His lips brush the shell of my ear. "I think you're lying. But I'll let it slip… this time."

Chills skitter down my arm. I'm letting him gain control. Take it back, Kins. Abort! Abort! "I'm not lying. And you know, you really shouldn't be so nice. It hinders the asshole persona you got going on."

He settles back in the chair. The grin on his face dismantles a fraction. "Hmm, we'll see."

"Why are you even here? To purposely torment me?" I ask.

He shrugs. "Just like you, I'm here to do some homework."

I jot down a nonsense note to pretend I'm working. When, in fact, I can barely concentrate with him sitting right next to me, talking about sex, reminding me of the way I saw his body move, the rasp in his voice teasing me, suggesting the things he could do to me.

Resting one hand on his thigh and the other near the edge of my book, he says, "I also happen to have a free hour."

Dear Universe, do you hate me?

My internal groan makes its way up my throat until it verbalizes itself.

"Are you silently asking if God hates you?" He chuckles. It's deep and throaty... sexy as fuck.

I place my head on the desk. The cool wood gives me no reprieve from the sadist sitting only inches from me. "Something like that," I mutter.

"Ah, you are capable of telling the truth."

I ignore his sarcastic insight and make a mental note to remind myself to erect my walls higher so the fucker can't read my every thought and emotion.

"Are you going to give the campus another eyeful of your striptease today?"

Apparently, I'm the only one who thinks getting comfortable was a big deal. It's not like I exposed any of my lady bits. I raise my head to look at him. Although the question seems genuine, the corner of his mouth curves up slightly. The wicked smile hiding behind those perfect lips catches my attention. I would blame his ego for noticing, but I've been on Edge's radar since I stole his parking spot.

He doesn't miss the way my grazing eyes fall to his mouth. To prove it and to goad me further, he skims the tip of his tongue over his bottom lip. I tighten my thighs in a desperate effort to ward off the sensations building again. Fuck me into next week. But if I'm being honest with myself, they never entirely went away. He doesn't say anything if he notices the slight movement under the table.

"Did you hear me, little Ninja? Are you going to strip for me today?"

Those words wrench me out of the depths of the dangerous lair I've fallen into. I slide my gaze up to meet his lust-filled eyes, which isn't much of a reprieve from his mouth. I clear my throat. "Trust me, if I were to put on a striptease, you'd know." To say I'm surprised when he doesn't reply is an understatement. He's the opposite of Gunner. I turn my attention back to my book. "What can I say? I like to be comfortable."

He nods, gets up, and politely pushes in his chair. Closer than necessary, he leans down and whispers, "I wouldn't get too comfortable. You won't be here that long."

Then, without another glance my way, he strolls down the center of the library. As if waiting for the king himself, a stumbling guy opens the door from the other side. Edge strolls right on through as though the world is just waiting to bow at his feet.

Obviously, it was a warning of some kind, but I hope he's right. I won't be here that long. There's a good chance that even if I didn't walk in on them fucking like rabbits, he would have made it a point to seek me out.

It isn't as hard to concentrate as I thought after he leaves. Figuring him out is the tricky part. He's hot, cold, then nonchalant, and then quickly transforms again into being an asshole. I might as well take my chances rolling a twelve-sided die to see which side of Edge will appear next. If my luck in the past two days is anything to go on, I'm not sure I have a chance in hell of catching a break.

Tapping the end of my pen against my lips, I wonder if I missed a crucial one-on-one moment to ask him about the underground fights and what he'd be willing to tell me, if anything. Too late now. I take a deep breath as I return to my essay, which is due tomorrow. I've neglected to start it, so I'm thankful I have this free time. I have a feeling this free hour will be a lifesaver, which means I'll have more time to spend on *other* extracurricular activities, like planning my next move.

Then again, I hope Edge doesn't usually spend his free time in the library.

My stomach growls, reminding me it's time for lunch. As I exit the library, Brielle conveniently happens to run into me. I'm able to catch the few books in my hands before they fall to the ground.

"Hey, creeper, did you like what you saw earlier?" She makes a dramatic gesture of wiping the extra gloss from the side of her mouth, even though it's perfectly applied and she knows it.

My immediate thoughts stomp right toward the images he planted in my head only a little while ago. Quickly snapping back to the present, I say, "If you're talking about Edge using you to get off, then I have to go with a no on that one. I've seen better performances on Animal Planet."

Her face is a blast of fury as I bump her shoulder to make my way to the courtyard to meet Bryce and Eden. From behind me, Brielle goes on about how I'm such trash or some other empty and redundant insult.

Once settled against the big oak trunk, I can finally relax a bit. I close my eyes and try to clear my head using the breathing techniques I learned from training. It's more of a challenge than usual with all the shit Edge pumped into my head.

"What's up, bestie?" Bryce plops down beside me.

My eyes pop open. Relax session is officially over. I hold my hand over my eyes to block out the sun. "Not much, Bunny. You?"

I take a protein bar and a sandwich out of my backpack, tear the seam down the center of the bar, and take a bite.

Bryce removes a brown paper bag from his backpack and pours the contents onto the ground. It's the complete opposite of the sushi he ate yesterday.

I glance at the green packaged granola bar, a sleeve of orange crackers smeared with yellow cheese, a squished sandwich, and a browning banana. "Are you responsible for that?" I point to the lunch made for a six-year-old.

"Yep."

"Uh-huh." I pick up his squished sandwich. "What happened to sushi rolls and wasabi?"

"That was courtesy of our housekeeper, Josie." He points to the bagged lunch. "She's out of town. So, I was left to fend for myself. Don't get me wrong, I love a good PB and J, but it doesn't take the place of sushi."

"I hear ya." I take another bite of my unsquished sandwich. "Where's Eden?"

"She had to do some work for the debate club, chess tournament, or some other club she runs. So, it's just you and me today." He bounces his eyebrows.

I toss the corner of my crust at him. "Shut up and eat your squished PB and J."

He laughs. "Did you know she's the chancellor's daughter?"

"Eden?"

"Yeah. That's the reason she attends Monarch University, because of his position."

Interesting. I contemplate my next question, then decide there's no right or wrong way to ask, so I blurt it out. "What's up with Venom? I mean, why are they so popular? What do they have that nobody else does?"

Bryce peels his gooey sandwich out of the folded plastic bag. The jelly seeped through the bread, staining it purple. "Those guys are like gods around here. They've been friends forever. Like, since grade school. Well, at least Edge and Kade, the guy with piercings and tattoos. And by the way, he's wicked smart— like genius worthy."

He's in my psychology class, not a brainiac class, but wicked smart, huh? "What about Edge?" I push, dying for more information.

Bryce swallows his bite of sandwich, then picks up his juice box and takes a swig. "Edge is Ledger Hunt. His dad is some big-time business mogul with his hands in anything that can make him money." He pauses to make a face and glances over his shoulder to see if anyone is listening. Then he continues when he decides the coast is clear. "I've only met Edge's old man once at school near the chancellor's office. He and Mr. Hunt are really close."

I'm soaking up every detail. Who knew Bryce was so in the know?

He points an orange cracker in my direction. "But the weird thing is, Eden says she's never seen them together outside of school, but they're supposedly best friends. It doesn't make sense, right?" He doesn't expect an answer, which is good because I don't know what to say except to agree with him. Searching for a napkin and not finding one, he starts to use his scarf before I hand him one. He wipes the crumbs from his fingers. Shaking his head, he says, "Something doesn't jive, but it's not for me to pry into."

Not caring what the chancellor or Edge's dad does in their free time, I swallow a bite of the tasteless turkey sandwich and try to curve the conversation back to the guy who has been a pain in the ass since the second I stepped foot on campus. "What else do you know about Edge?"

Bryce throws out a mocking right punch. "He's really into MMA stuff."

Now we're getting somewhere. Keep him talking. "Really? How into it? Does he compete?" Damn, that sounded a little too enthusiastic.

He holds up his hands. "Whoa, girl. You just kicked it up a gear."

I shrug, trying to downshift my excitement. "Sorry. It's just something I'm interested in."

"Anyway," he says, "I think so. I've only heard bits of conversation about it, though. It's all a foreign language to me. I don't know shit about that stuff."

Wanting more answers on the subject but not wanting to make it more obvious than I already have, I switch my questioning to a different topic. "So, he and Brielle are like a couple?"

Bryce almost chokes on the granola bar. He waves his hand in the air, his finger oscillating back and forth.

I slap him on the back. "You all right?"

He nods, inhaling a deep breath. I hand him his juice box. He slurps it until its emptiness echoes off its thin cardboard walls. "I'm okay. Thanks for saving me."

"No problem." I laugh and hand him the rest of my water bottle. He takes it and chugs the remaining half down. "Better?"

"Yeah. Thanks." He clears his throat. "So, going back to your question about Brielle and Edge, that's a tricky one. They're like a couple out of convenience, but I'd say that Brielle wants him exclusively. And I'd bet every nickel of my daddy's money that Edge doesn't feel the same way."

That confirms what Edge told me. I keep to myself what I saw them doing earlier. I'm shocked Brielle hasn't told the entire school that I'm a creepy voyeur who gets off on watching her get banged from behind.

"She and her friends create the balance of bitches to the assholes of Venom. The school needs them both to be symmetrical in a way." Bryce shrugs.

His weird reasoning kind of makes sense. There's always a set of popular people who think they're better than the rest. It's part of the hierarchy of being a student in a wealthy school like this—in any school, for that matter.

"Gunner and Levi, they're pretty cool. They're more chill than Edge and Kade, probably because they're surfers. Their dad was a big-time surfer who traveled all over the world. He travels all the time. So, needless to say, Gunner and Levi have some banging parties."

My class is getting ready to start, which interrupts my interrogation. It always baffles me how lunch goes by in a blur, while my classes seem to last for an eternity. I ball up the wrapper of my sandwich. "Thanks for getting me up to speed."

"My pleasure." He gathers his trash and shoves it into the paper bag. "Thanks for not letting me choke to death."

Laughing and shaking my head, I get to my feet. "Glad I could be there to save your life." I gather my backpack and sling it onto my shoulder. "I'll see ya later."

"Hey," he calls after me.

I turn. "Yeah?"

"When you see Eden, tell her she owes me an iced coffee with two pumps of vanilla."

"For what?" It's none of my business, but I ask anyway.

"For not dying."

I shake my head and smile. The guy is definitely a trip. I tell him I'll pass on the message when I see her.

My bed is beckoning me from the moment I walk into the house. I toss my backpack on the floor and obey without a fight. Almost instantly, sleep tows me under.

I watch as my dad gets beaten to death, over and over. I'm completely helpless, unable to stop the beating.

The door to my bedroom bursts open. I'm sitting up, gasping for air as the silhouette of a prominent figure stands in the doorway. The sight steals away the last hints of air from my lungs. They rush in, and then the edge of my bed dips. I'm still confused by the remnants of the nightmare slipping to the surface of my consciousness.

"Kins, breathe... Just breathe... Slow... In... Out..." My uncle's soothing voice matches the gentle circles he rubs on my back.

I try to do as he says. Drag air in through my nose, then slowly release it. I reach up to wipe the dampness from my forehead.

"Are you okay?" he asks.

I go to answer, but my voice cracks. My throat hurts with raw pain from screaming. The nightmare has been on repeat since that tragic night. Every time, it's the same unshakable memory: helplessly watching from outside of the cage, the fight that will forever change my life.

The worst part about the horrific dream is that for the first few seconds after I wake, I think it's just that—a nightmare—one where, when I wake, my family is right back together, and my parents are sleeping just down the hall. Then there's the exact second when it all detonates, the moment when I know it's not as it should be and remember that my dad is gone. That's when the ache becomes all-consuming.

"Yeah, just a bad dream," I croak out.

"I'll get you a glass of water." He leaves to go into the kitchen, giving me a chance to slide on a pair of sweatpants. When he returns, he hands me the glass and sits on the bed's edge again. "You want to talk about it?"

I don't want to talk about it, ever, but it's the only way to get past it. At least that's what the therapist says. But as usual, lies or omissions will have to be woven into my words.

"Just about Dad. I keep seeing him beaten and lying dead on the mat." A memory pops into my head from the dream: Edge standing over my dad's body with that devious grin laced across those full lips. I take a sip of the cool water and will the image of Edge to dissolve.

"Ah, kiddo, it's your brain messing with you. You didn't see him get killed, and it was a closed coffin."

I wish that were the truth. I would do anything to take back what I saw. No one, except Luca, knows I was there the night he was beaten to death. The blow after blow I saw him take, the bruises, the welts, the open gashes on his head and face, all of the blood, the paralyzing shock that took over my body, the guilt of failing to stop it—all of it.

Uncle Trey takes my hand, sadness welling in his eyes. He too lost someone who was like a brother. He just didn't witness the horror of him being beaten to death.

"You lost him in the most horrific way." He sniffs. "I know nothing I say or do can ever bring him back, but I wish there were something I could have done to stop him from climbing into that death trap."

I wipe away the tears streaming down my face. "Me, too."

Then, ever so slowly, my anguish morphs into anger, the fuel that reminds me of what my mission is.

EDGE

GUNNER SLAPS the mat three times. I release him. Sweat coats our bodies, and our breaths come out in pants. He rolls over and rubs the pain out of his arm and neck. I walk over to the table, grab our water bottles, and toss one to him. I take a long, deep drink.

Gunner tests my skills, pushing them to the max every time. Ninety-nine percent of the time, I can take him down and get him into a position that's nearly impossible for him to get out of. But he puts up a fight and challenges me every step of the way.

"Thanks, man," I say once I catch my breath.

He gives me a side-eye glance and takes another swig of his water. "For what?"

"You know, for letting me kick your ass every day."

"Fuck you," he says while huffing out a laugh. After draining his water bottle, he balls it into a plastic ball and tosses it at me. I catch it and send it back in his direction.

"Hey! Knock it off," the sensei hollers from across the gym. "You've got ten more minutes of practice. You better use it."

With his back to the sensei, Gunner rolls his eyes as he climbs to his feet.

"Let's go again," I suggest.

Kade and Levi grapple on the far side of the gym, and our sensei holds the punching bag while Python practices his hooks, grunting each time his fist connects with the bag. His quiet demeanor is almost disturbing. He rarely ever says anything unless spoken to. Python, otherwise known as Alex, is a year older than the rest of us. He also went to Monarch Prep but broke free of the monotony before he was suckered into college. Although we met him at one of the UG fights a few years ago, we knew nothing about him except that he was a great fighter. Because he was a kid at Monarch on a scholarship, it didn't take much for my father to brainwash him to join Venom. He made the deal so sweet that Alex was all but drooling.

Three years later, I bet Alex regrets taking my father's poisonous offer. He's been a different person ever since the night he was instructed to kill Evan West. He had no idea what he was getting into when he signed on with Venom. None of us—not Kade, Gunner, Levi, or I—have talked to him about that night. We act like it never happened. But I know for a fucking fact that night left a scar on each one of us, especially Alex. The five of us have been taught to chug down the bitterness and regret and bury it as deeply as possible. It's what makes us the ruthless fighters we are.

Sensei calls time on our training. Without unwrapping the tape around his hands, Alex grabs his bag and heads for the door. The only reason he still comes to our training sessions is that he doesn't have a choice.

None of us do.

After the guys and I take showers, we drive out to Le Chalet's Subs, a hole-in-the-wall sub shop with the best sandwiches in the world. I expect to have my usual, twelve inches of rare roast beef and all the toppings. What I don't expect is to see my little Ninja, the girl who's been the topic of everyone's conversations since she arrived at Monarch University only a couple of days ago. It seems like she's been here forever, yet she still seems like a shiny new plaything. No matter what I do, I can't get her out of my fucking head. I even tried fucking her out by taking Brielle over the desk. I knew Brielle wouldn't pass up a fuck session. So, getting her to skip class was easy. All it took was a quick text:

Lab 229—10 minutes

Ten minutes later, she showed up in the physics lab, panty-less and ready to fuck. But when none other than my mesmer-izing firecracker of a nightmare walked in on us, all bets were off. My dick had never been so hard.

Ninja sits at a small table in the corner with her books splayed out and a half-eaten sandwich on a plate. She doesn't bother to look up when we come in until Levi asks about the soup of the day. Fucking weirdo. Who eats soup after grappling?

She looks up with a blank expression and then returns to her studies as though we're as insignificant as pissants. She picks up the soda can and takes a sip from the straw. I instantly imagine those lips wrapped around my—

"Dude! What do you want?" Gunner slaps my arm, then points to Val, the owner behind the counter.

I grunt. "The usual, Val. Thanks."

I turn my attention back to Ninja. She obviously finds it far easier to ignore us than for me to ignore her. At least, that's the impression she's giving off.

Gunner taps me on the shoulder. "Isn't that—" He stops mid-sentence as he confirms it for himself. His whole face brightens. The fucker turns it up to full blast, plastering on his come-fuck-me smile. I've watched that work for a hundred other girls. But he's in for a rude awakening because there's no way in hell it'll work on Ninja.

I cross my arms over my chest and prepare to watch him go down in flames.

"Hey, Ninja, what brings you to this lovely establishment?" he asks, adding extra sauce to his voice.

Ninja looks up at him. Her face is unreadable. There's a fifty-fifty chance she'll either laugh and invite him to sit or throat-punch him.

"Lay off, Gun!" Val warns from behind the counter. "Don't you start harassing my customers. Especially that one." She points in Ninja's direction with a large knife. "Kinsley has been coming here a lot longer than you."

I chuckle to myself as Gunner gets reamed out. Then, as Val's words sink in, I'm curious as to why we've never seen her here. At every turn, this little enigma becomes more and more perplexing. It's as thrilling as it is fucking irritating.

"She just moved here. How the hell does she even know about your place?" Gunner asks.

"You know, I'm sitting right here and can hear everything," Ninja says.

Val interjects. "You boys have been regulars for years, but this one here"—she nods toward Ninja as she wipes her hands on a dishrag—"she's like family. So back the hell off."

Gunner grips his heart. "Val, you're wounding me with your harsh words."

"Harsh but true, boy. What can I get you? The usual, too?"

Gunner strolls over to Ninja as if he's getting ready to make a move. She, in turn, looks up at him as if she's already bored.

"How's that art project coming?" he asks.

"It's not," she replies.

Levi sits down across from her. "You want help with that…" —he shifts her book to look at the subject—"biology?"

"No thanks. I think I got it," she says.

"Bro, you couldn't help her if you wanted. You barely made it through biology." Gunner slaps his twin on the back. "Nice try."

Levi knocks Gunner's hand away. "Dude, trust me. I got this."

Ninja pulls her book back into place. "Sure ya do."

"You want me to tell these boys to get lost?" Val asks.

Ninja looks up to Val. "Nah, they'll get bored with me in no time."

As I watch their back and forth, I'd bet my entire trust fund that Ninja will never become boring. Even now, she's doing the most mundane thing, homework, and I'm unable to look away from her as I lean against the glass fridge that's filled with bottles of water and cans of soda. It's not that I don't trust my boys. I trust them with my fucking life. They're like brothers. But I never told any of them I saw her the night of the last fight —the night her father was killed. Hell, I never thought I'd see her again. And for some fucked-up reason, there's this tugging in my gut that has me on alert with *anyone* wanting to get close to her, even my best friends. This invisible need to protect her has grown on its own, and it's getting out of my control.

Levi points to her tattooed forearm. "I got to say, you don't look like the type."

She looks up at him with those icy blue eyes. "You don't know my type."

"Oh, I bet I do." He grins as he squares his shoulders and rolls his neck.

She sets down her pen and settles back in her chair, waiting.

Levi folds his arms on the table. "Let's see. You ride a blacked-out, badass motorcycle. You have a big dragon tattoo, probably hiding more ink under those tight clothes. You got face piercings that Monarch girls never have. And you can climb a rope faster than Edge over there."

He points over his shoulder at me. Ninja follows his gesture, and our eyes capture each other's. She slowly licks her bottom lip and then pulls it between her teeth. I wish it were my teeth biting that lip. Her eyes trail down to my arms to my busted-up knuckles, then back up to my face. In just those few seconds, questions emerge in those ocean-blue eyes.

Levi taps her forearm to get her attention back on him.

"Yeah, so what? You see what everyone else does. That's all obvious stuff. But that sure as hell doesn't mean you know me," she says.

He cocks his hand like a gun, pointing it at her. "That's the thing, they still can't figure you out like I can—who the real Ninja is."

"And, old wise one, what did you come up with?" she inquires.

"Your secret boyfriend is Tarzan. You like the kinky shit, and you're in a motorcycle gang." He smacks the table. "And just like that, I've blown your cover." He points his thumbs back at himself. "That's right! This guy right here!"

Gunner bursts out laughing. Kade even has a grin on his stoic face.

Ninja's lips curl up on one side. "Wow! Are you like Sherlock Holmes's sidekick? Because I must say, that was quite the deduction."

Levi slams his hands on the table again. "See, I knew it. Bam!" He reaches up for a fist bump against his brother's waiting knuckles.

Ninja rolls her eyes and picks up her pen. "Now that you have me all figured out, I'm going to get back to work." Her gaze passes over me once more before she lowers her head, easily dismissing us and giving her full attention back to her books.

Levi stands up and pushes the chair in. He flips her braid from over her shoulder to her back. "Later, Ms. Tarzan."

"See ya in class, Ninja," Gunner says.

The four of us sit at the booth on the other side of the small sub shop. The guys talk about our practice from earlier, but I tune them out. Ninja is the only one in the room I want to focus on. A few minutes later, Val calls out that our food is ready. The guys eat and talk while I take a bite of the sub and continue to stare at Ninja. She doesn't once glance away from her books. I push my sub away. The captivating girl across from me steals my appetite. Her lack of need for attention is, ironically, what's so fucking attractive. The more she retreats, the more I need to know what drives her.

She sets down her pen, then stretches her arms out and up. The exposed cleavage of her firm breasts peeks just over the seam of her tank top. The chair squeaks as she pushes it back to stand. Leaving her books sprawled across the table, she heads down the thin hallway toward the back of the small restaurant. Without thinking, I get up, toss my uneaten sandwich in the garbage, and head in the same direction after her.

On the left side of the narrow hall, there's one dingy bathroom for both men and women. She closes the door in my face just as I come upon it. I tap on it, knowing I'll get rejected in the form of a fuck-off, but I do it anyway. I start to turn away, but to my surprise, she opens it.

Through the restricted opening, she pokes her head out. "What?"

"Do you open the door for anyone or just me?"

"I thought it was Gunner," she taunts.

I brace my hand on the wall next to her. "Sure you did."

"What do you want, Edge?"

Leaning in, I drop my voice. "I just wanted to tell you I don't think you'll make it at Monarch."

In a flat, unworried tone, she asks, "Not that I care what you think, but to pacify my curiosity, why is that?"

"Because you don't play by the rules."

She looks down at her boots, then back up at me. "Yeah, well, I don't see how that's your problem."

119

It's very much my problem—and all of Venom's. Ignoring her response, I ask, "What brought you to Monarch anyway?"

I already know the answer, but I want her to tell me something different. I want to be wrong. This would be so much easier if I were wrong about her motives. Her—me—together—fuck! I don't like where my thoughts are going. Bad fucking idea.

I slightly shake my head, dislodging the seductive images. Ninja and I are dangerous together. I have a thousand secrets I'll protect at any cost. So, I have no choice but to believe she plans to tear through them and destroy them, one at a time. And I can't let her do that. There's too much at risk.

She scans my face before she sneers at me. "None of your business."

"I'm making it my business."

She goes to close the door, but I jut out my foot, forcing it to remain open.

Pasting on a fake smile, she says, "Okay, well, thanks for letting me know you're a creeper and for sharing your insignificant concerns. So, if you would kindly remove your foot so I can pee in peace, that'd be great."

"I'm not done."

"I am." She pushes on the door again, but it doesn't budge. She blows out a frustrated breath.

My head inclines toward her. "I'd bet that you're a good girl, aren't you?" I skim the length of her body. She's wearing those tight-ass short shorts, a black tank top, and her Docs. "Despite that badass front you got going on and your attitude problem, you're a good girl."

"You don't know anything about me."

That fucking scent of perfume and sweat hovers between us. Just a whiff of it is enough to send signals to my dick. I take a deep breath to inhale part of her, to remember it. I want nothing more than to hate her and find something wrong with her besides her defiance and suspicious motives, but I can't. Through her strength, determination, and fearlessness, she firmly stands her ground. She wrestles to keep her demons at bay just like I do. Another reason I need to hate her—she won't back down. I know because she's exactly like me. We're replicas of the same stubborn, fixating mold. But also, because of this very fact, I thoroughly enjoy this game we're having.

Gunner was right. She is my match. She may not be a willing participant, but she's playing my game whether or not she likes it. Not the other way around.

"I know you like to strip in public, and you like to watch people fucking," I taunt.

She opens the door enough to step out. We're only a few inches apart as she looks up with those tantalizing blue eyes. "Well, then it looks like congratulations are in order. You also get a gold star for being an expert on the subject of Kinsley West: lover of kinky shit, Tarzan's girlfriend, stripper, voyeur, biker chick, and despite all that, *probably* a good girl."

I smile as I move in, cutting the space between us in half. "I would go as far as to say that at least three of those presumptions are true. As far as the rest, I'm not an expert yet, but I can assure you I will be."

I back up and move my foot. She doesn't slam the door right away as I expected but stares at me for a beat.

"I don't think that's in our cards." Her voice is calm, seductive, and spiced with a hint of challenge. "But just for the record, I'm anything but good." She steps back into the bathroom and then closes the door. The lock clicks into place.

Fuck. This girl is hot and cold, push and pull, right and all fucking wrong. I bang the wall with my fist. The picture of a dollar bill shudders in the flimsy frame. I fucking want her! In every way and position, I want her. And she's the last thing I should be hungry for. If I'm not careful, she'll destroy me and everything in my fucked-up world.

And I can't let that happen.

11

KINSLEY

IT'S POURING when my uncle drops me off at school with my canvas, otherwise known as my soon-to-be nonmasterpiece. The music grows louder the closer I get to the open door of the art room. At first, I can't determine what type of music it is. As I enter the class, Nirvana's "Smells Like Teen Spirit" becomes clearer. I assume it's Chelsea until I see those unruly locks of mussed hair peak out from between the empty easels. I prop my canvas on the easel.

"I didn't take you for an early-to-class kind of guy," I say to Gunner.

He turns down the music. "Yeah, well, I guess I know you as well as you know me, which, unlike my brother, is not at all. So, let's get to know each other." He waggles his eyebrows.

I can't help but smile. "You're such a joke."

His face is stone-serious. "I wasn't joking." He shakes his head. "Still not kidding. We should start by just fucking. Right here, right now. Get it out of our systems."

I slide my backpack off my shoulders. "That would be a mistake for so many reasons."

He sets down his paintbrush and then crosses his arms over his chest. "Oh yeah? Name one," he challenges.

I prop my hands on my stool and look directly at him. "Because after having me once, I can assure you, it wouldn't be enough."

His leg jerks and bumps his table. He fumbles and catches his paintbrush before it rolls onto the floor. "Girl, you're evil."

I laugh. "Yeah, maybe a little." His artwork has piqued my interest, especially since it motivates him to arrive at class extra early. I point to his canvas. "May I?"

He holds out his hands as an offering.

Moving to stand behind him, I look over his shoulder. His canvas depicts a man standing on the beach, gazing out at the incoming waves with a surfboard under one arm. The colors are incredible. It's only half done and already well on its way to becoming a piece of art that someone would have hanging in their home. "Holy shit! You're amazingly good."

"I know. But you think this is awesome, you should see me—"

"And cocky?" I say, cutting him off before he can finish that sentence.

"Yep, that, too," he agrees with a lazy smile.

Just then, Brielle comes in with her usual attitude that her day isn't going her way or someone pissed her off for something minuscule. "What are you looking at, trash?"

The number of insults gathering on my tongue, ready to spit back at her, almost chokes me. But deciding she's not worth it, I glance away, not giving her the satisfaction with even one word. Luca would be so proud.

On the way to get her project from the closet, she trips over my backpack. "Pick up your shit! I almost fell."

Pursing my lips, I hold in my laughter. "Maybe if you didn't wear six-inch fuck-me pumps— Oh wait. You need those to get over five feet. Never mind."

"Fuck you, trash!"

"Brielle, pipe down back there," Chelsea says as she enters the classroom. "I won't tolerate a dirty mouth. If I hear it again, you might as well not even take out your canvas."

"It's not my fault, Chelsea. She—"

"It's never your fault, Brielle. Now get to work. I do believe, from the looks of your project at the beginning of the week, you're behind."

I don't try to hide the smile on my face. I do love watching that bitch get put in her place.

Knowing that art is far from one of my strengths, I spend the rest of class attempting to draw some semblance of my face. Fail. By the end of another grueling hour, my hope of art class being an easy A has been crushed to merely a long-lost dream.

By the luck of the gods, I managed to find my way to biology without any missteps or unwanted visuals. Eden's not unfriendly when she asks me how I am, but her tone is still stiff.

At the end of class, she slides her notebook toward me. "These are my notes from the beginning of the year. You can use them to copy, then give them back to me tomorrow. I always print them, I find it easier to study."

"Thanks." After only knowing her for a few days, it's obvious she's got something on her mind. "Hey, is everything okay?"

She plays with the hem of her jacket. "Yeah, just got a lot going on."

I nod. "Okay." I thumb through the pages of the notebook. Like everything else about Eden, her handwriting is neat and precise. I slide it into my backpack. "I'll see you later." She's most definitely not okay.

"Yeah, see you."

I head to the library to study. I've pretty much gotten the hang of knowing where everything is, thank freaking God, which means no more walking in on unauthorized sex-ed classes.

Josh catches up to me just as I reach the entrance to the library. "Hey, Kinsley," he says, slightly out of breath.

"Hi, what's up?"

He hands me a small piece of paper. "I didn't have your number, so here's the party's address. I put my number at the bottom so we can hook up. I don't mean hook up like— I mean—"

"Josh, chill, I know what you mean."

His shoulders relax, and he smiles. He has a nice smile. It's a little crooked. The higher side gives way to a dimple. "Yeah. Okay."

We say our goodbyes, and then I go inside. The enormous chandeliers light the windowless building. Plopping down at my usual table near the back, I toss my bag onto the table, pull out the chair, and silently pray Edge has better things to do than harass me today. Lucky me, he never shows up.

As I review Eden's notes, making copies of most of them, I wonder where Edge goes if he doesn't come here. Then I immediately want to kick myself in the ass for even letting that thought through.

Tossing all thoughts of Edge into the imaginary fire in my head, I focus back on Eden's notes. Despite the growling in my stomach, I stay to finish copying the biology notes. An hour later, I'm not nearly done when I pack up. The skies decide to open up as soon as I step into the courtyard.

Running for cover, I take refuge from the downpour in the cafeteria. I have no idea what to expect, but what's in front of me is very familiar. It's set up like my last school, with a fresh salad bar, a grill for burgers and grilled cheese, and a hot buffet line with already prepared food.

Having no idea who sits where or what groups have already staked their claim on the still-empty tables, I head for the salad bar. I figure it's a safe bet, giving me time to get my food while everyone files in and settles into their usual seats.

"Hey, girl." Bryce gives me a toothy grin. It falls as soon as he eyes my salad. "You're one of those, huh?"

"One of what?" I ask.

"One of those healthy bitches who watches her weight, only eating salads and apples. Blah, blah, and boring. Don't lie, I've paid attention."

I laugh. "Actually, no. You have me all wrong. I love cheese-burgers, a loaded deep-dish pizza, and ice cream on all the days of the week."

He props his hands on his popped-out hip. "Okay, spill?"

"Spill what?"

"How do you do it? How the hell do you look as hot as you do and eat all that crap?"

I don't give details but answer, "Exercise. And lots of it."

He glances at the salad and the bottle of water. "So what's up with that?"

I lean into him. "I had no idea where to sit, so I thought I'd keep myself busy until you arrived."

"Girl, I got you." He points to a table in the far corner on the opposite side of the room. "We can sit there. It's by the kitchen, so most everyone stays as far from that one as possible."

"I'll meet you there." I finish putting the dressing on my salad when I hear a commotion. Heads turn in the direction of the noise. Curious like the rest of the gawkers, I make my way over to see what's going on.

"You should know better than to hang out with trash like her. Don't think you're immune just because you're the chancel-lor's daughter. Even your daddy knows he can't protect you from…"

I don't hear the rest of what Brielle says as my blood begins to boil. I can handle the bullying. Maybe Eden can, too, but I'm not waiting to find out. I head in the direction of the crowd to find Brielle and her bitches.

"And trust me when I say, being bald would be better than

this blue shit you got going on." Brielle flips the ends of Eden's hair.

I put my tray on the closest table. The guys sitting there scoff as if I threw a plate of vomit on it. "Get over it," I snap.

Four of them have Eden backed into a corner. Brielle has scissors in one hand and a handful of Eden's blue, cropped hair in the other. Is she fucking kidding me? Who the hell does shit like this? Unable to watch another second, I burst through the slew of ball-less onlookers and grab Brielle's wrist.

"What the—" she barks.

I apply pressure in the precise spot, causing her to drop the scissors. Gasps go viral around me. The entire scene is royally fucked-up. How can these imbeciles do nothing as they watch this abuse like zombies?

"What the fuck is wrong with you?" I ask, still holding her wrist. She lets go of Eden's hair. "I mean, seriously, are you that insecure you need to cut off another girl's hair, or does it give you a major girly hard-on to be a super-bitch?" Still holding her wrist, I drag her closer to me. "So, which is it?"

Her overly made-up face contorts into a mask of rage. "You fucking whore!"

"Hardly. I think all of us here know who the real whore is. And you love playing that part, don't you, Brielle? You love being his little—"

"Let her go." The deep, penetrating voice behind me ruins my playtime. Edge comes up to stand directly behind me. I don't have to turn around to know how close he is. The heat of his body radiates through my shirt.

Brielle pulls hard against my grasp. The second I know it's time, I let her go. She stumbles and falls backward into the lap of an acne-fighting guy. He catches her from falling to the floor. Her skirt flies up, flashing her sheer red thong. His face is as shocked as hers. It would have been better if she had landed on her ass. But I can't be too picky about the landing.

"Get your hands off me," the ungrateful bitch says to the guy who broke her fall.

Edge reaches around me and pulls her to her feet.

"Thanks, baby," she coos. Her sickly, sweet voice makes me want to spew vomit all over the table where I set my tray.

Ignoring her, Edge turns around to face me. His ruthless, slate eyes are full of hunger. "Do we have a problem here?"

I meet his glare. "Not anymore, but you might want to put a leash on your bitch."

As intimidating as he tries to be, he probably thinks I should be quaking. But all I feel is warmth jetting through me as our eyes sear into one another's. The corner of his mouth twitches with the slightest movement. Is he trying to contain a snicker? With practiced control, his mouth resets into his usual lethal thin line.

Brielle brushes off her skirt. "Did you see what she did to me? She has to pay."

Off to the side, Bryce has his arm around Eden.

"Are you all right?" I ask her, and she nods.

"Little Ninja."

I turn my attention back to Edge, who's been in my head more often than I'd like to admit. I don't say anything as I wait for Edge to state his warning. For some sick, unwarranted reason, I look forward to hearing them so I can intentionally disobey him. He has yet to punish me, but I sense he wants to every time I do the opposite of what he says. And on some demented level, I want him to. Maybe put me over his knee?

"Watch yourself."

There it is. With a ghost of a smile, I boldly stand up on the toes of my boots. He stiffens as I move into his personal space. Brielle jerks back. Another gasp erupts from between her painted pink lips. Ignoring the skepticism in his ravenous glare, I lean in until the front of my body lightly skims his. His chest rises and falls with shallow breaths. The friction causes my nipples to harden. I know he feels what he's doing to me, and right now, I like it.

Fanning a light exhale of breath along the edge of his jaw, I whisper, "No."

My terms.

Achingly slow, without breaking our mutual glowers, I lower myself until I'm once again standing beneath his daunting frame. I turn away from him, giving them all my back.

"Ready to eat lunch?" I ask my friends. I return to the table where I set my salad and pick up the tray. It doesn't look as appetizing as it did a few minutes ago.

After a moment, the shuffling of people moving behind me disperses. Although I can still feel one set of blazing eyes on my back. I bet he hasn't taken one step. That feeling doesn't dissipate until I'm on the other side of the cafeteria.

Bryce lets out a long sigh as he drags his hand down his face. "For fuck's sake."

"I miss the courtyard," Eden mutters.

I slide into the booth. "Just another day at Monarch," I mutter.

Eden looks at me, really looks at me. "Thanks, Kinsley."

I had the entire situation under control until Edge stepped in. Was it just a show of his dominance? Or was it to protect his girl from little ol' me? He has no idea what I'm capable of. It's not like he's ever seen me fight. To him, I'm just some new girl who took his parking spot and doesn't take his shit. Little does he know.

"Would she have really cut off your hair?" I ask.

Eden shrugs. "I wouldn't put it past her."

"What a bitch!" I spew.

Stabbing my fork into the heap of lettuce slathered with ranch, Edge lingers in my peripheral. He's taken a seat at the largest round table in the center of the room. The rest of Venom has joined him. Brielle perches on Edge's lap like a poodle. Her arms are dramatically waving around as she talks, no doubt describing to everyone who missed the showdown how she was pushed on her ass and bullied. One of Edge's arms is bent with his elbow on the table. His head is against his hand. His other arm rests on his thigh. A sense of wicked triumph comes over me that he's not consoling her. Hell, he's not even touching her.

Despite the conversations and drama surrounding him, all of his attention is fixed solely on me. Even from across the room, he's found a way to pin me in place like a butterfly trapped under glass. I can only imagine what he sees when he looks at me like that, what he's thinking. A million thoughts bounce around in my head. But I seem to be just an enigma to him like he is to me.

No longer hungry, I set down my fork. Without taking my eyes off his, I pick up the water bottle, unscrew the cap, and sip, but the water does nothing to extinguish the unsatiated fire deep in my core. There's only one way to break the spell. I look away from him. Fuck him and his impenetrable wall. Closing my eyes in defeat, I know I lost this small battle.

There will be a next time.

It's still raining when I get home. Bryce was nice enough to drop me off. I thank him for the ride and rush to the door. My uncle must still be at the dojo when I walk into the empty house. Then I remember that tonight is his late night. He won't be home until after ten.

I grab a bowl of cereal, finish my homework, and shower. The rain is still coming down when I crawl into bed. It's only eight, too early to try to sleep. The nagging in my chest won't let me relax. I don't know if it's from the drama earlier today or the entire week. The loss of my dad? Trying to fit in? No, scratch that. I'm not trying to fit in. I was never good at that. What I want is to stop getting caught in the clutches of Venom, specifically Edge.

My thoughts drift to the party on Saturday. It's probably not in my best interest to go, especially after the shit that went down in the cafeteria today. Not that I'm worried about getting my ass kicked. I'm more concerned about adding to their drama, which would seriously suck.

I hear distant hollering outside my window. Being that it's still pouring, I wonder what's going on. I put on some shorts and go outside. Water pours off the edge of the patio. Since sleep and my nerves are in opposition, I grab the umbrella propped in the corner by the door and walk half a block to the beach. As soon as my feet hit the cool, wet sand, relaxation wraps around me like a blanket. The swelling waves have summoned the surfers like a siren. They call out to each other. Their voices carry back to shore. There's just enough light in the sky to make out their silhouettes rising and falling as they wait to catch the perfect wave. I sit on the beach and pull the hood of my hoodie over my head to block some of the wind.

Edge's warning plays on a loop in my head. *Watch yourself.*

From what? Him? Venom?

He's somehow a key player in Venom, and I don't mean the Venom they portray to be at school, a group of bullies keeping everyone under their thumb. I mean the tight unit of fighters who willingly kill their opponents. It's so obvious. There have been so many concrete tells. The feeling nudging me closer to Edge isn't all heated with desire. The need to know how deeply he's involved with Venom grows daily. If and how he's involved in my father's death. Because I have no doubt he is. I just don't know how yet. Hell, he may be the one who killed him.

I will find out. And when I do, he'll be the one who has to watch his back.

12

KINSLEY

WHEN I CHECK the party's address, I realize it's only a few blocks from my uncle's house. Being that it has been a week from hell, a drink or two might do me good, so I suck it up and go. At least, that's what I tell myself. I'm pretty sure my body has other reasons for wanting to go. Ignoring the tiny tingles of anticipation, I change into my bikini and pull on ripped jeans and a white, cropped, off-the-shoulder T-shirt.

I haven't painted my toes in forever. Luca would have a conniption if he saw me going out like this. But I'm in the I-don't-care mood. After tying my hair up in a messy knot, I grab my lip gloss and phone off the nightstand. There's only twenty percent left on the charge, but oh well, it'll have to do.

I may kill Bryce if he doesn't show. After I told him Josh invited me, he said he knew about it and would probably attempt to go. He was also going to try to get Eden to go, but that would be difficult.

Josh has been riding me all week about the party. So, at least I may have a couple of people I can hang with while I'm putting myself out there.

Luca keeps pushing me to make friends. "Let down your

walls," he says when we chat each night. It's turned into a joke. He knows I don't let my walls down for most people—especially undeserving assholes. Plus, it's not that easy, especially when you have no idea who you can trust.

Uncle Trey is in the kitchen making a drink.

"I didn't know you knew how to make a cocktail."

He turns and smiles. "Vodka with a splash of soda water is hardly a complex cocktail." He swirls the liquid in the glass. "But it does have a lime." He squeezes the juice into the glass and then drops the wedge in. "Tonight, I need something a little stronger than a beer."

"Yeah, you and—" I stop myself before I finish, but my uncle isn't stupid.

He offers a knowing smile. "Listen, I wouldn't blame you. You've been through a lot lately. And just so you know, I was young once, too." He gives me a wink. "I went to my fair share of parties with the iconic red cups—not filled with anything considered alcohol, funnels next to the kegs, and music loud enough to get the cops to show up every damn time."

That brings a smile to my lips. "Well, a party on the beach a few blocks from here will undoubtedly have all. I planned on going with a couple of people I met at school. Are you okay with that?"

"Absolutely. Go have fun." He sets down his drink. "If you need me to drop you off or pick you up, this drink can wait until another time."

"Thanks, but that's okay. I'm just going to walk. It's close enough, and if I have a couple of drinks, I can just walk home."

He eyes me pointedly. "Like I said, if you need me, I'm here. I can be there in a flash."

"Thanks." Wanting to keep the line of trust open, I snap a picture of the address on the paper Josh gave me. "Here's the address. It's right up the beach."

"Well then, if you've got it handled…" He holds up the glass.

"Cheers." Then he takes a sip, the ice clinking against the sides of the glass. "Be careful. Don't take a drink from someone you don't know, don't swallow the pretty pills, and wear a condom!"

"I will. I mean, I won't— I don't plan on—" I slap my hand over my face.

He chuckles through my sputtering. "I'm just kidding. I mean, I'm not. I know you know how to be responsible. At least you look like you do. I'm only trying to be the adult who thinks they should know what to say."

"You do. You sound like my mom," I comment with a sarcastic thumbs-up.

"Great!" He chuckles as we walk out onto the back deck.

"I'll be home before midnight. And I promise to be careful."

He plops down in his favorite chair and kicks up his feet. "Kinsley. Try to enjoy yourself, will ya?"

I turn to look at him before stepping off the last step. "Yeah, thanks."

As soon as my feet sink into the sand, it's not hard to know exactly where the party is. The raging bonfire is the first indication. The second is the music's beats, which can easily be heard from down the beach. The sun hovers just above the ocean. The raging fire complements the melting fiery orange glow as it sinks below the horizon. The closer I get, the clearer the details become. A game of volleyball is going on, a few people are playing Frisbee, and others are tossing a football. It seems like the entire population of Monarch is here.

With so much going on, a small hope sprouts that maybe no one will notice my arrival.

And as fast as that seed takes root, it's killed when an arm wraps around my shoulder.

"You made it!" Josh pulls me tight against him. "Damn! You look hot." His breath reeks with the stench of beer and mustard. This Josh is very different than the cautious and shy one in gym class. "Hey, you want a hot dog? I just had one."

That explains the mustard. "Thanks, but no, I'm good," I say.

"Let's get you a drink," he suggests.

"Great idea."

The second we pivot, I get a full view of what's in store for tonight. And I suddenly want to turn around, head back down the beach, and go home. Then, to sweeten the deal, order a pizza and pop a bag of microwave popcorn while I chill out and watch a movie. Instead, I do the exact opposite. I let Josh guide me toward the house.

The bonfire casts a golden glow over the people surrounding it. Some lounge in beach chairs, while others lie on towels. Most of them are against another body. We make our way around the blaze to the other side. Gunner and one of Brielle's bitch friends are a mess of tangled limbs, groping hands, and fused mouths.

My gaze travels around the curve of the fire. Levi is next in the lineup, lying on a towel. His knees are bent, and a girl is tucked under his arm. The side of his torso is on full display. There's no sign of the snake tattoo. One of them is in the clear. It doesn't mean he isn't involved. He just isn't the one who did the actual killing. All this amateur detective work would be a lot easier if masks weren't mandatory at the UG.

Kade is in a beach chair, eyes closed, and his earbuds are in place as he takes a drag off the joint between his fingers. He's wearing a loose tank that covers any possible ink. There's a girl at his feet, but he's too wrapped up in his happy place to notice or care.

Then there's Edge. His muscular body is splayed out, legs crossed at his ankles. With his head lying on Brielle's stomach, he uses her mostly naked body as a cushion. One of her hands trails up and down his bare chest. With each of her caresses, her overflowing breasts spill out of her triangle top and come intentionally close to his face. He looks uninterested, bored by everything going on around him.

Unable to stop staring at the gorgeous sight of him, I trip on the edge of the deck but quickly regain my balance. His chest is smooth and tan, and his arms are a masterpiece of lean, corded muscles. My attention snags on the black ink curling up the side of his torso, and my mind instantly falters back to the night my father was taken from me. Python had a striking snake tattoo in the same spot. I shift slightly, easing onto the tips of my toes to get a better look. But with Brielle's tits in the way, I can't make out exactly what the tattoo is.

I don't know if I feel more frustration or relief. Am I ready to come face to face with the killer? For the past three months, it's all I've planned for—or at least I thought I did. Now, the situation is more difficult than I thought. What the fuck am I going to do if one of them is my dad's murderer?

Those gray eyes narrow and home in on me. Our eyes catch and hold. Stepping off the edge of a cliff, falling into the abyss, would have been better than to get caught in Edge's snare. My body stiffens. I may be staring right into the eyes of my father's murderer. A flare of intensity flashes over his too-perfect, unshaven face. I dare myself to look away. But I can't find the will as I drink him in. The cursed link we both seem to share doesn't afford either of us a choice in this game of captivation. He looks like he wants to devour me, while I want to drag him through hell. And yet, the silent chant echoing in my head, *murderer, killer, python,* does nothing to ebb the heat coursing through my middle.

"You okay?" Josh asks.

As I'm jerked from the moment, Josh tugs me along, saving me from drowning in Edge's hypnotic gaze. "Uh... yeah... fine." The sadistic side of my curiosity is dying to glance over my shoulder to fall back into those dangerous dark pools. What in the actual fuck is wrong with me?

I walk onto the pool deck under Josh's arm. Not wanting people to get the wrong idea, I gingerly ease out of his embrace. Doing my best to push Edge out of my mind, I focus on the long table lined with every kind of alcohol available. A keg is propped next to the table. Several guys are tapping from it right into their mouths. There's a mad game of beer pong in the corner next to the pool. Whoops and cheers follow the toss of the small white ball.

"What do you drink?" Josh asks.

I wasn't planning on having anything to drink except water. But after almost allowing myself to slip into the clutches of the devil himself, I say, "Tequila."

Josh's red-rimmed eyes question my answer. "Are you sure?"

"Very." At this very second, I've never been so sure of anything in my life.

"Okay then." His gaze falls back to the table, searching for the bottle I already have in sight. "Ah, here it is. Um, there's limes and s—"

"No wheels, I just need a cup." I'm impatient and just want to get the shot, or two, down. By the dazed look in his eyes, he's still not getting it. I dumb it down even further, so there's no mistake. "No ice, no limes. No salt. Just a cup. Just tequila."

Josh, who I'm pretty sure has been drinking for most of the day by the looks of his bloodshot eyes and swaying form, seems to find a sliver of clarity. He hands me a cup, then he uncaps the bottle and pours a small amount in. I take the bottle from him and pour a few shots into the cup.

"Okay then," he says, then clinks his plastic cup against mine. "Cheers."

I down half the tequila. The liquid heats my chest and flows into my empty belly as it seeps its way into my bloodstream. Thank fuck, it won't be long before the effects of it will have all thoughts of Edge and his hot ass out of my head.

"Ninja, baby. You came." Gunner sidles up next to me.

I roll my eyes, unable to help my Gunner-induced grin. "What's up, Gun?"

He throws his arms out, splashing liquid out of his cup.

"We're all here, just enjoying the madness." He pours the remainder of the cup into the grass. His swim shorts hang low on his hips. There's a good possibility they may fall, but by the looks of his drunken status, I don't think he cares. A lot of girls would likely be happy to get an eyeful of the tan surfer.

I glance at his side. No tattoo. His only ink is the small wave on his neck and a tribal sun on his shoulder. The relief I feel is greater than I could have imagined. In some far-off way, I like Gunner. But I have to remind myself that even if he's not the one who took my father from me, he's still somehow involved.

He looks into my cup. "Water? Well, that's quite boring."

Josh speaks up. "Tequila. She's drinking straight tequila." He holds up the bottle of the Blanco tequila for proof.

Gunner grins savagely and wraps his arm around my waist. "A hot biker chick who likes the hard stuff. My dick is twitching as we speak."

I duck out from under his arm. "Gunner, you're drunk."

He raises his cup to his lips. "So close, baby, so close." Realizing his cup is empty, he picks up the bottle of silver tequila. "I bet if I have a shot with you, I'll be one step closer to that sweet goal."

After pouring himself a splash of the clear liquid into his cup, he taps his cup against mine, then takes a drink. Wanting to drink even more now, I do the same, downing the rest of the tequila. I pour another generous amount into my cup.

He squeezes his eyes shut and blows out a puff of potent tequila breath. "Yep, that's going to do it for sure." He puts his arm around me again. "I think we should go find a room."

I pry his arm off me again. "I think I'll pass." I glance over my shoulder. The girl Gunner was lying with gives me a death glare. "I think your date is waiting for you."

"I don't give a shit about her. It's you and me, baby." He clinks his cup against mine. Even though he's drunker than shit, he's still hot with his boyish charm and perfectly muscled body.

I can tell by the way Josh's mouth opens and shuts that he wants to speak up, but he doesn't seem like the type to go up against any of Venom. Not that I was ever attracted to him, but that show of outright hesitation and avoidance would be a serious turn-off if I were. Minus three points for being a pussy.

Gunner leans down to whisper in my ear. But since he's wasted, his voice carries louder than he intends. "Be careful of that one." He points to Josh.

Josh stills as he looks away and takes a drink. There's something else happening between them, but I can't put my finger on it. But then again, maybe I'm reading too much into their weird interaction.

I scoff. "Yeah, I think you're the one I need to be careful of."

Gunner's playful side disappears behind an unsettling veil. His brow dips, and my suspicions only grow. "Maybe," he says, "but if things go south, don't say I didn't warn you." His response leaves me to question what the fuck I've gotten myself into.

And at that, having no idea what the fuck any of his coded warnings mean, I turn to walk away from them. "I'm going to see what's going on inside. Josh, you want to show me around?"

Honestly, I don't want to be with Josh either, but he's the one who invited me, and it's clear he wants to be as far from Gunner as he can get. And at the moment, I want to be as far away from Venom as I can.

"Yeah... sure."

"See ya, Gunner," I say and take off in the opposite direction with Josh.

"Later, Ninja."

I want to go inside because I don't trust myself to confront a shirtless Edge again. If his tattoo is the same as Python's, I'm not sure what I'll do. I can't make a scene in front of most of the school. Besides, I need to be smart when I bring Venom to their knees. I can't allow the sliver of lust for Edge to get in the way.

But that small sliver hopes it's not Edge. I hate the hesitation weeding its way through my emotions.

Why do I even feel anything for him? Because he's hot?

Or because of something else, the way he makes me feel like I never have before? I hate to admit that I like the stirring he produces deep within my core. I like the challenge in his gaze, the absolute control he exerts, and the intensity of him as a whole.

I shake my head to dislodge the madness that has taken over. Because if he is the one, I vow to take him down with everything I have. That was and still is the plan.

I hear my name over the music. Thank fuck, it's Eden and Bryce coming toward me. They each have a cup in their hand.

"I wasn't sure if you'd make it," Bryce says.

I point in the direction of the beach. "I only live a few blocks away, so no big deal."

The party isn't as loud inside, but we still need to raise our voices to be heard over the music. People are spread out on the large sectional. Like around the bonfire, loungers are lying beside each other, passed out or making out.

Eden reaches up and tugs on the end of one of her short blue ponytails. "Want to play pool? Everyone's outside soaking up the last of the daylight before it starts raining."

Just beyond the blue sky, dark clouds hover over the sea. "Sure, a quick one." I want to get home before the storm hits.

We make our way through the house. Just like Eden said, fewer people are in here. The game room is off the main living area. Some people are standing around talking, but the pool table is free.

I set down my cup and pick up a pool stick. "I'm not that good at this game."

"Me neither," Bryce says. "So, what about guys versus girls? You and Eden against me and Josh."

"Sounds good," I agree.

"Besides, if you say you suck, you'll want to have the pool shark on your side." Bryce winks at Eden.

"Eden?"

"What, I don't look like I can kick ass at pool?"

"To be honest, I'm not sure what that kind of person looks like, but if I had to guess, then no."

Bryce laughs as he racks the balls. Eden prepares to make the break.

"What do we have going on in here?" The deep voice resonates in my bones.

I refrain from being hooked by Edge's gray eyes. Eden tenses beside me. Bryce looks away, and Josh mumbles, "Hey," or something and rubs chalk on the tip of his stick. So, I'm the only one left to answer Edge.

"I'm pretty sure it looks like we're getting ready to play pool." I steal a glance at him. Fuck the vanity gods and their talent when they created Ledger Hunt. He looks like he just walked off the set of a photo shoot for the sexiest man alive.

Edge has the audacity to look deliciously fuckable as he folds his arms over his chest and leans against the doorframe. His gaze trails to my mouth as I involuntarily lick my lips. The fraction of a knowing smirk meant just for me. I know I'm staring, but—

"Are you all right, Ninja?" the prick asks.

I scoop up the morsel of self-respect I have left, run the back of my hand over my bottom lip to wipe off any drool that may have escaped, and straighten my posture. "Yep. Great!"

Unfortunately for me, he's taken the liberty of putting on a shirt. The good news is, since I can't gawk at his bronzed, sculpted chest and layers of abs, I at least get to keep that portion of my dignity. The bad news is, I'm still unsure about the tattoo.

Josh burps. He looks like he might be sick. In gym class, he came off so much more confident. Maybe it's the alcohol.

"Want some real competition?" Edge asks.

I bump my hip against Eden's. "Thanks, but I think we already got our teams."

Edge purses his lips.

I move closer to him while the others act like they're busy behind me. I lower my voice. "Don't you have somewhere else you need to be?" I shrug nonchalantly. "Like... I don't know, maybe taking a hit or two from Kade's joint or fondling Brielle so she can return the favor?"

The corner of his mouth lifts. "Those aren't horrible options. But I think I'm fine right here."

I roll my eyes as I turn away from him. "Don't mind the lurker, guys."

Three sets of eyes pop between Edge and me, disbelief written all over their faces with my blatant disrespect for the leader of Venom.

"Eden, break."

She lines up the cue ball and then strikes it hard. It bursts into the group of balls, sending them into a frenzy in different directions. One striped ball and a solid ball each go in a pocket.

"Nice. Looks like I'm on the winning team," I say.

She smiles. "Thanks. We call solids." She lines up her shot and fires away. Again, the targeted ball sinks into the side pocket. She knocks in two more before it's Bryce's turn.

Josh is next. He takes a shot. He makes a solid ball in the corner front pocket.

"Wrong ball, but thanks," Eden says.

It's my turn. I can feel the weight of the stares of the four others in the room. One set of eyes in particular has me especially unbalanced. I ignore Edge as I consider all the impossible shots before me. I make my way to the other end of the table, aiming for the cue ball. The six ball is at the far-end bank in the center. I need it to return and find its home in the left corner pocket by my hip.

"Are you sure you want to do that?" Eden asks.

"No. But here goes nothing. And if I miss, I know you got it and the eight ball on your next turn."

She scoffs in amusement.

I lean over and set up my left hand, easing the stick onto it and lining up the cue with the six. Glancing slightly to my left at the destination pocket, I catch Edge's frozen form standing in the doorway. I pull the stick back and slam it forward into the cue ball. White blurs down the table and hits the six, sending it back my way. I brace myself for the second it takes to sink into the corner pocket.

"Holy shit!" Eden shouts. "That was awesome. I thought you said you sucked?"

"Normally, I do. Maybe I perform better under pressure," I say as I look straight at Edge.

Josh settles in on the dark leather couch. "That was nice, Kinsley."

"Thanks," I answer, still focusing on Edge.

A mischievous gleam flashes in his usually hardened eyes. Before I can decipher what to make of it, he turns and leaves without a word. The pressure in the room immediately dissipates.

"How can one guy cause so much tension?" Bryce asks, visibly relaxing. He shakes his arms, then takes his shot, missing his mark altogether.

I take my next shot and miss. No matter. I made the one I needed to make a point with. Pressure has always been a friend of mine.

Josh misses his turn. The guy is passed out and snoring.

Eden ended up sinking our one ball, then the eight ball, to win us the game.

I go to take a sip of my drink and find it empty. I'm not even feeling buzzed from the alcohol. Damn adrenaline. Damn Edge. Fucking buzzkill. As much as I want to have another one, I don't think it'll do any good, and I'll be just setting myself up for a shitty day tomorrow.

"I'm going to get some water. You guys want anything?" I ask.

Eden and Bryce hold up their cups. "I'm good," they say in unison.

A text sounds on my phone. From my uncle:

Rain's coming hard and fast

Forgetting the water, I quickly return to the poolroom and tell my friends I'm heading home. They try to get me to stay, but the last thing I want is to be stuck in a house with Venom for God knows how long. I say my goodbyes and head to the wall of open sliders leading out to the beach. The sky is nearly black. Not one star is visible.

A throng of slick bodies pushes against me as they rush inside. Flashbacks of the UG erupt in my head. I drive back the onslaught of memories, PTSD striking at the worst possible moment.

"Shit." Determined to get out of there, I weave through the crowd in the living room, hook a right at the pool, and move quickly down the beach. To make even better time, I take off my shoes and run. A scull of wind and rain rips off the ocean. Damn, I still have a couple of blocks to go. The wind and the rain aren't the issue. The lightning striking too close for comfort.

Not wanting to take a chance and get struck, turning into a charred Kinsley, I race to the closest lifeguard stand. Running up the planked boardwalk, I pray the door is open. The padlock hangs loose from the metal loop. Grateful for the small favor, I duck inside and close the door behind me. It's a small, dark room with overriding smells jostling between the rain outside, seaweed, and sunblock. I shiver from the cold rain coating my skin.

When I pull out my phone, the battery light in the top left corner is red, with only two percent left. "Dammit."

I plop into the seat, prop my legs on the wooden edge, and wait for the storm to pass. My eyes are just about to close when the door bursts open. At first, I think it's from the wind, but a tall, lean figure is silhouetted in the doorway. The wind rages behind him, whipping his hair.

"What the—?"

"Fuck," he finishes my sentence for me. His voice has the rough texture of raw sin and dirty sex. He steps in, closing the door behind him. "Is that your first thought?"

I don't know what my immediate thought is, nor do I have time to acknowledge it. All I know is every muscle in my body seizes at the sight of him. My breath catches on the inhale, getting trapped in my lungs. Of all the people to be stuck in the middle of a thunderstorm with, Ledger Hunt is the last one I trust myself to be with.

"Looks like it's just you and me," he says.

I can't see his face, but it's evident by the delight in his tone that he's going to enjoy this.

That makes one of us.

13

EDGE

THE TORRENT of rain has doused most of the raging bonfire. Smoke billows up into the sky like a signal for help. I follow Ninja through the rain. I know it's a bad decision the moment the idea springs into my head, but despite knowing better, I steer in the opposite direction from my friends. Everything in me is telling me not to follow her. Then there's that one flicker that instantly grows into an inferno. Call it curiosity, need, lust, instinct—whatever the fuck you want. But I have to go after her.

I climb the steep boardwalk of the lifeguard stand she darted into, then push open the door. She's sitting in the only chair, staring at her phone. She isn't as startled as she should be to see me. Probably the least of what she was expecting, which was perhaps nobody. Still, even though her body stiffens, I can tell she's not scared. I wonder if haunted houses or horror movies give her the creeps. I consider myself a monster, and I have yet to see her flinch around me. It's almost insulting but impressive all the same.

I rub my hands together. "Yep, it's just you and me," I repeat. "What are you doing here?"

"Same as you, trying to get out of the rain." The answer is too simple to be the complete truth and too obvious to be a complete lie. She has to know I have an ulterior motive. But I don't even know what it is. All I know is my gut, and possibly dick, guided me right to her like a lost boat to a lighthouse.

"Really? You couldn't just follow your friends into the beach house and continue partying there?"

She's right, of course. That would have been the logical thing to do, but where's the fun in that?

I ignore her question. "Where were you going before you ran in here?" I ask instead, sliding down the wall to sit on the floor near the door. I want to call a truce with her, but this game between us, this head-to-head contest of push and pull, cat and mouse, is way more exciting. Even when she never runs, she only challenges me. I want to chase her, see fear in those bright blue eyes, and feel some semblance of control over her. But whenever I'm close, she pushes back a little harder and counters with more angst. And each time she does, I get harder for her.

"Home." She twists the ring in her eyebrow.

Surprised that she answered, I ask, "So you live around here?"

I can tell she wants to let her guard down, but she's wary of me. I don't blame her. She should be. She fidgets with her phone. The screen suddenly goes black, throwing us into complete darkness.

"Shit!" she says, setting the phone on the makeshift desk.

Through the closed shutter, slivers of the amber streetlight stream along the tip of her bare shoulder. She shifts in the wooden chair, trying to get more comfortable.

"You can sit on my lap."

She scoffs. "I'd rather sit on a bed of thorns."

"I doubt that."

Although I can't make out her expression, if I had to guess, she's wearing a scowl that could turn me into stone if she had the power.

"I've got to go." The chair creaks as she stands. She shuffles around for her phone. My eyes have adjusted enough to the dark to watch her shove the useless device into her back pocket.

She should be drunk or at least unsteady on her feet with the amount of tequila she drank. But she's as sober as she was when she arrived at the party. I know because I had my eyes on her from the moment she stepped around the bonfire and came into my line of sight. The fact that she came to meet that asshole Josh pisses me the fuck off. When he brought her to the drink table, I sent Gunner over to ensure that punk didn't spike her drink.

"So, you'd rather take the chance of getting struck by lightning than hang out in here with me until the storm passes?"

"Exactly."

I quickly stand, blocking her escape. Her body bumps against me. The softness of her chest skims the front of my shirt.

"No, you're not getting off that easy," I drawl.

She takes a step back and crosses her arms over her chest. Her tank moves with her movement to reveal the top of her black bikini. "What's your deal, Edge?" She huffs out a frustrated breath. "What do you want? To give me another warning?"

I shrug and shake my head. "Honestly, I don't know. You're a mystery that I want very much to decipher. I have several ideas about what I want to do *with* you, but giving you another warning isn't one of them."

I've realized that my warnings to her are as useless as selling sand at the beach. Her taunting me to give her another one proves that. As much as I want to gaze down at her perfect body, I force myself to remain looking at her face. She's naturally exquisite. But even in the dim lighting of the room, it's easy to see she has her demons. To most, I'd bet she can keep them well hidden, guarded behind her protective wall, under lock and key. I see them, though. I'm all too familiar with them since I keep mine caged in a similar fashion.

She sighs and tries to maneuver around me. "Well, when you think of it, let me know. For now, you can get the fuck out of my way."

"I don't think so." Without thinking, I grab her around the waist and pull her tight against me. The action isn't easy since she's expecting it. Off balance, she grips my biceps and starts to move against me. Fuck, that's the wrong thing for her to do. "Keep moving like that, and we're going to have a bigger problem on our hands that may have to be dealt with."

With her so close, I can easily make out the lines of her face. She looks exasperated as though she's heard it all before, but at least she stops fighting against me.

"Let me go." Her voice is breathy and cautious.

Ninja's damp chest rises and falls against mine as her hands slide down my slick arms. The only images smashing through my head are of ripping her clothes off, pulling her onto my dick, and thrusting as deep as I can into her until her screams drown out the roar of the storm. She's got to feel my cock getting hard, but she doesn't say anything.

"Not until you tell me something," I taunt.

"What?" she says.

Her breaths are short, quick, and tinged with the faint scent of the tequila she drank earlier. It's intoxicating as fuck. I have no idea what I want to ask her, if anything. I'm just not ready to let her go. Instead of asking her anything, I lean down to nuzzle her neck. She smells so fucking good, beach and rain, coconuts and raw lust. She tries to push me away, but her efforts are weak. I know she's not trying nearly as hard as she could. Her feeble nudge gives me an incentive to push further.

"What happened to the fight in you?" I whisper against her

ear. She goes completely still. Her breaths have slowed enough that I barely feel her moving against me, and I already miss it.

"What do you want, Edge?" Her words are low and barely audible above the pounding rain and thunder. The way she says my name is like it belongs to her—like she's said it a thousand times before as her perfect mouth closes around the last sound.

I brush the tip of my thumb over the bare skin of her waist. Goosebumps rise on her cool skin. She shivers against me. Instinctually, I pull her tighter against me. Her body fits perfectly against mine.

"Are you cold?"

"Not at the moment," she answers. Again, there's the honesty I want.

She's almost as sexy when she's not sassing me as when she's telling me to fuck off. Although I have to admit, her scrappy attitude gives my self-control more of a challenge than most guys in the fucking ring.

The temptation to glide my hand up to the center of her back and pull on the string of her bikini, then continue to the one tied at the base of her neck and tug that one loose, is overpowering. But I manage to control myself. Most girls would be begging me to strip them down. Not my little Ninja.

She's been in my grasp for less than a minute, but it's like time has stopped. I glide my lips from her ear around to her cheek, grazing her smooth cheek, stopping only a breath away from her mouth. Her eyes are a convoluted mystery I can't read. Her hands grip my arms tightly, but she isn't pushing me away, and I have no idea why. I thought I would have gotten kneed in the balls by now. I thrive on control, but with her so close, that control is slipping.

Lightning strikes. A current of electricity rips through the small space. There's only a sliver of space between our lips.

Unable to stop myself, I press my mouth to hers. The rain

pounds against the shutters, mimicking my heart's beat in my chest. Her lips are soft and full and maddeningly still.

She doesn't kiss me back. I can tell she wants to by the way her back arches, pressing her body against mine. The exhale of her breath lets me know she's made her decision.

Her hands slide down my arms and drop to her sides. I raise my head. Her eyes search my face in the dark, landing on mine.

"You don't get to touch me," she says. There's no anger or distress in her tone. She simply states the exact opposite of what I want to hear and what her body is begging for.

Then she gently pushes me out of the way. I don't fight her. She whips open the door.

"Where are you going, little Ninja?"

Her heated glare sears into me. The wind tears the loose band out of her hair, freeing it to whip around her. Rain plasters the long, dark stands to her face. "Home."

The storm is one of the worst we've had in a while, but it doesn't stop her as she runs directly into it. Black waves crash angrily against the shore. Thunder cracks as lightning streaks across the sky. Through the thrashing storm, her form gets smaller and smaller the farther she moves away. I stand at the top of the ramp, watching her race down the beach. Lightning strikes down, silhouetting her body in a path of wicked white light.

Then she's gone.

I slam my fist against the wooden wall of the shack and roar into the storm. "Fuck!"

14

KINSLEY

RAIN PELTS MY SKIN. Each droplet feels like a needle stinging my flesh. But somehow, the pain reassures me that I'm still here. For that small moment, I was lost to him. Even though it was brief, it happened. *I* let it happen.

I let him touch me.

I let him kiss me.

What the fuck is wrong with me?

Bolts of jagged white light streak around me. The chaotic ocean carries angry waves crashing against the shore. In bare feet, I make a run for home and don't stop until I burst through the door. My uncle is asleep on the couch and doesn't stir. I head straight for my room to take a hot shower and try to process what in the actual fuck just happened. Or try to forget.

I turn the shower handle to hot. Steam floats around me, warming my freezing skin. Stripping off my wet clothes, I pile them on the tile floor. Still trying to catch my breath, I turn the lever to the center. The water cools just enough that the heat is bearable. I stand under the stream, begging it to wash away more than the sand caking my feet. I want it to erase the past twenty minutes of my life.

Fucking Edge!

I'm just as furious at him as I am at myself. He put me in a vulnerable position. He made me want him. That, more than anything, I hate admitting to myself.

I should have done something to avoid the entire situation—brought my leg around the back of his, then tossed his ass to the floor, or brought up my hands to block his contact. Anything! But I just stood there and let him touch, kiss, and feel me.

Soaping my loofah, I scrub everywhere he touched me: my waist, my neck, my lips, scouring my skin until it's pink and raw. After adjusting the water to a cooler temperature, I slide down the slick wall to the floor. Water cascades down over my head. My black hair falls around my face, hiding my shame from no one.

Hell, he was just fucking Brielle a few days ago, and then I let him kiss me? What the fuck is wrong with me? What was I thinking? Easy...I wasn't.

The worst part is I can still feel his body pressed against mine.

The best part is I can still feel his body pressed against mine.

No amount of water or soap can ever wash those feelings away.

I climb out of the lukewarm water, towel off, and dress for bed. I'm still reeling from the way the night ended. I sit at the desk, open the jar of moisturizer, and apply it to my face, smoothing the cream over my skin. A knock at the door draws me up short of cursing myself more for being so stupid.

"Yeah, come in."

Uncle Trey opens my door and peers in. "Hey, just making sure you made it home okay."

"Yeah, fine."

He walks over to the window and checks the lock. "Quite a storm out there."

"Yeah, I made it home just in time," I lie. The last thing I need is to have him worrying about me.

He takes a moment longer than usual to study my face. I have no idea what he sees—fury, another lie, unshed tears? "All right, we'll talk tomorrow. Good night."

"Good night."

"I'll be just down the hall if you need me."

"Thanks." I scoff. "Hopefully, I'll let both of us sleep through the night."

He smiles warmly and then closes the door.

I crawl into bed. Burying my head in the pillow, I scream until my lungs are on fire.

For such an asshole, Edge was warm and tender as he ran his hands over the bare skin of my arm and waist. As his fingers splayed across my bare skin, the pressure from his touch increased. It felt good, more than good. I hate the fact that I wanted more. I wanted everything he was willing to give—and take. Gentleness was not on his agenda that day with Brielle. But who wants to be treated like a glass flower anyway? The way he grabbed me and held me to his chest, there was nothing gentle about that move. He was taking what he wanted. And my mind went from zero to one hundred, imagining what else those hands were capable of. He knew exactly what he was doing.

Practice, Kinsley. He's had loads of fucking practice. You even witnessed the deed firsthand.

If I let him take complete control, we both would have been in serious trouble. We would both have ravished each other, most likely resulting in the beach having one less lifeguard stand.

I contemplate calling Luca to confess that I'm a complete idiot. He would no doubt agree with me as soon as I told him who I did the kissing with, but then he'd be all about wanting details and pics, and as soon as I told him what Edge looked like and how good his touch felt, he'd be condemning my choice to run.

No! It can never happen again. No touching, no kissing, even no thinking about him, nothing. There should be a morning-after pill for fucking bad decisions—or a spell to forget how he felt, smelled, and the way his lips were pure passion and desire.

Okay, that's it. Enough. I shut Edge and everything about the night out of my head. Closing my eyes, I concentrate on the storm thrashing outside my window.

Tomorrow, I may or may not tell Luca how stupid I am. For tonight, I'm going to fall asleep and dream about witches, fairies, and dragons, anything but Ledger Hunt.

At ten a.m., I pull into the parking lot of the dojo. Luca isn't here yet. I unlock the door, go in, then lock it behind me. After throwing my bag in the corner, I set up the mats for fighting. The sun decided to show its bright, happy face after last night's storm. Its rays stream through the windows over the wooden floor and partially laid out mats.

Stupid storm. Stupid lifeguard stand. Stupid Edge.

Stupid me.

There's a knock on the window as I unfold the last mat. Luca is on the other side of the glass, waving his arms like a madman. "Hurry up," he mouths.

The second I unlock the door, he pushes it open, throws his bag into oblivion, and tackles me to the mat. "God, I missed you."

"Me too. You have no idea." We're wrapped in each other's arms like it's been a hundred years since we last saw each other. It feels like it, anyway.

He raises himself to his elbows. "I think I'm digging the hair." He lifts the bunch that lies over my shoulder on the mat. "Yeah, I'm definitely digging it. You look hot." He smacks a kiss on my cheek.

After everything else this week, I forgot he hadn't seen my hair in person. Either I've gotten used to it, or the drastic change has been replaced with other shit. "Thanks."

His face turns serious. He plays with the loose strands. "So, how are you holding up? And don't say fine."

I shrug, not committing to an answer. I hate it when he worries about me. He doesn't have to, but if he lost one of his parents, I wouldn't be able to help myself either.

"Kins! I'm not messing around. How are you really?"

"Hanging in there," I finally admit. "Being busy with school helps, but it's worse at night. The nightmares come and go. But Uncle Trey has been amazing."

Luca nods. "Thanks for telling me. Your dad was awesome, and I never want you to feel like you have to brush off your feelings about losing him with me." He holds up his hand. "In fact, you better not or I'll kick your ass."

"Thanks."

He rolls off me so that we're lying next to each other. "So how about we kick each other's asses for the next couple of hours, order a pizza, eat in our skivvies, and you tell me all about your week?"

I want to tell him everything, but I'm not sure how much I'm ready to put on the table yet. I definitely can't tell him about the kiss. Or how Edge touched me. What would I tell him? And why do I feel the need to hold back secrets about that asshole from Luca of all people? "Sounds like the perfect plan."

For the next two hours, we stretch, fight, kick each other's asses with weapons, grapple, and beat the ever-loving shit out of each other. I've missed his familiar touch so badly that I haven't even realized I was starving for him.

He spins, throwing out his leg, and swipes my feet out from under me. I go down hard. And lie on the mat, unable to move. He jumps on top of me, straddling me. He's so proud of himself, he can't help the enormous smile turning up his full mouth.

"Why do you have to be gay?" I cry.

He places his hands on my shoulders. "Why do you have to be a girl?"

I squeeze my eyes shut in frustration. "Fair point."

We could be a couple if Luca were straight or I were a guy. There'd be no Edge, no impossible feelings, no difficulties. Life would be so simple. If only.

He grabs his phone out of his bag along with his water bottle. "The usual?"

Our usual consisted of a large pie, extra garlic, all the meats except anchovies, and all the veggies except black olives. "You know it."

We clean up the dojo, putting away the mats and weapons. We throw our last hits as the pizza guy knocks on the door. Luca hands the guy cash, takes the pizza, and thanks him. I'm already on the one mat we purposely left out with our water bottles and napkins.

"Did you ever notice that there's only a small selection of fine pizza delivery boys?" he asks.

I make a point of looking up to the ceiling. "Ah, no, I have failed to notice that tragedy."

He plops down across from me. "And what a tragedy it is."

He sets the pizza on the mat and opens the lid. The steaming pie loaded with meats and veggies smells incredible. He places a bag next to it. I grab for the unexpected treat.

"You better not," Luca warns.

I hold the bag to my chest. "I have to. You're not going to make me suffer, are you?"

"Fine." He picks up a slice of pizza, folds it in half, and then takes a bite. His eyes roll up to the ceiling in delight.

I open the paper bag that has grease staining its bottom. Doused in powdered sugar, the fried dough balls call out to me with their sweet aroma. I take one out of the bag. Holding it between us, I place it in front of his mouth. He swallows the bite of pizza and dives forward for the dough ball, biting it in half.

He gives an exaggerated "Mmmm."

The rest of the goodness melts in my mouth.

"Okay, so spill," he says around a mouthful of food.

My stomach clenches. Here's the moment I've been dreading. In any other universe, I have nothing to hide from Luca. Why can't I just tell him? What if I do? What's the worst that could happen? He wouldn't judge me, but he wouldn't completely support me, either. That's the part that scares me— not having his support. Or worse, if he tries to talk me out of getting my revenge.

Having to give him something, I start with the easy stuff. "I met a couple of people I think I can consider friends. Eden and Bryce. They remind me of us. He's gay. She's an outcast." I shrug.

He grips his chest. "Stop! They sound like our long-lost twins! Our doppelgängers."

We laugh around mouths full of pizza.

"Actually, Eden is the chancellor's daughter. But she's turning out to be cool. She's wound a little tighter than I'm used to, but Bryce evens her out. You would like him."

Luca waggles his eyebrows. "Really? Is he cute?"

I nod. "Yeah, not bad. He dresses like he's strutting the runway every day."

"I love him already."

I hold up my hand. "Hey, wait! What happened to Mr. Blake?"

Luca scoffs. "Girl, please, he is as cold as they come. I was wrong about that one. I don't like to admit it, but I was." He dismisses the conversation with a wave of his wrist. "Enough about me. What else?"

I wipe my mouth, then take a sip of water. "Monarch is a lot like Maylen in most ways but very different in others."

"Like how?"

The first thing that comes to mind is Venom. But I don't start with that. "Their campus is larger than Maylen's. They have dorms. They have meaner girls who are the bottom-feeders of their daddy's wallets and think everyone should bow down to them."

"Uh-oh, what happened?"

I tell him about what Brielle did to Eden in the cafeteria.

He lowers the slice of pizza on the way to his mouth. "Tell me you didn't get in the middle of their drama?" It comes off less as a question than an all-knowing accusation.

"Well, I couldn't just stand back and let the bitch cut off my new friend's hair. I mean, who does that?" I leave out the part about Edge breaking up my fun. Then I also leave out the other part about Edge kissing me and everything about him altogether. Feeling the invisible pressure rising in my chest, I change the subject. "In art class, I have to paint myself on a canvas."

"Kins, you and I know you are no artist."

"Tell me about it. I have no idea what I'm doing. I'm pretty sure the entire canvas will be considered an abstract. Then I'll have to make some crap up about how that's the way I see myself. It'll look like I'm a giant mess of color and squiggly lines that most definitely needs a mental health overhaul. But on the bright side, my professor is cool."

"Still, you'll need all the help you can get."

I smack his arm. "Hey!"

"You know it's true."

I take a bite of pizza. "Yeah, you're right." I think about

Gunner's piece and how amazing it is. If only I had even a small percentage of his talent.

Luca takes a sip of water. "Now, on to the important things. Any hot guys?"

Only all of my enemies. "I guess there are a few, but no one worth mentioning."

He narrows his eyes at me. At first, I don't think he's going to let me off that easily until he does. "Okay, I'm getting vibes that you're not ready to head in that direction, so we'll circle back to that another time. 'Cause you and I both know there's a golden nugget in that topic that I will dig up."

I swallow the bite without choking. One for me—for now.

"How was the party last night?"

I pause, bracing myself to be caught in the lie. "It was like all the rest. Solo cups, drunk idiots, half-naked girls..." I tell him about Josh and, in the same breath, tell him it's nothing to get excited about. Luca's face falls with disappointment. "He's nice and all, too nice, cute, tall, tan, but he's missing something or has too much of something I can't seem to get past, but I can't figure out what it is." Actually, I know what it is, and Edge is to blame for it.

Until it's time to leave, we continue to chat about nothing and everything. He gives me the highs and lows of his week, new gossip floating around Maylen, who's hooked up with who. Except for Luca, none of it makes me wish I were back at Maylen. This week has been hell, but it's been new and challenging. The only thing I miss is seeing my best friend every day. With the pizza more than half gone and the dessert eaten, we doze off for the next couple of hours and wake just in time for the sun to set.

"You know the invitation to come live with me is still open. My parents love you and would love to have you," he says as I lock the dojo's door.

"I know. Thanks, but I'm going to tough it out here for a

while. My uncle seems to like the company, and I love being close to the dojo."

His eyes soften. "For what it's worth, I love your hard-ass attitude. You take down anyone who gets in your way."

That's exactly my plan.

Saying goodbye to Luca is terrible. He's always been my rock, my go-to for anything. It's painful how much I miss not seeing him every day. We hug for a long time before we say our final goodbye.

Even after I took a nap at the dojo, exhaustion slams into me as I pull into the driveway. Falling into bed and sleeping for days sounds like an excellent idea. Sleeping away everything that has to do with death, revenge, Venom, and all thoughts of my enemy, even the way he touched me. It's not lost on me that I separate him from Venom. Something I need to etch into my skull is that they are one and the same. And in twelve short hours, we'll be face to face again.

Uncle Trey is lounging in the Adirondack chair on the back deck. Reggae music plays softly on the portable speaker on the side table next to him. The soft, lazy beats mingle with the waves crashing against the shore in the distance.

"Hey there. Looks like you're enjoying the night."

He glances up at me. "Life does not get better than this."

"Paradise," I say.

He lets out a long sigh. "Yep, paradise."

"Thanks for letting us use the dojo. It's all locked up."

"My pleasure. I'm glad the place gets used even on a day off."

As peaceful as the night is, I turn to leave. "I'm tired, and my body is sore, so I'm gonna take a long bath, finish some home-work, and then go to bed."

"Sounds good. Hey, there's leftover Chinese food in the fridge if you want some."

"Thanks, but Luca and I ordered pizza."

I drop my bag on the floor of my bedroom. Before peeling

off my clothes, I turn on the water for the bath. When the temperature is hot enough, I pour a generous amount of lavender-scented Epson salt to soothe my muscles. With exhaustion riding my ass like a hellcat, I sink into the steaming water. Thoughts of Edge and Venom plague the stillness and quiet I long for. Knowing they fight, they have to train. Where is their dojo? Tomorrow, I'm going to find out. I could just ask, but I doubt they would tell me. Besides, asking them outright could raise unwanted suspicion.

Just before the water cools completely, I get out and get ready for bed. I prop my pillow against my headboard and grab my phone. I should study, but my brain may explode if I try to comprehend biology or psychology right now. I check my social media sites, respond and like a few pics of people I follow, when a text pops up on my screen from a number I don't recognize:

Venom's bite is deadly. Back the fuck off. 🐍

Only two people would send this. The image of them fucking pops into my head. Brielle and Edge. And neither of them has my number.

That's not how I want to end my day. I slam my fist against the bed. Was I wrong not to tell Luca what I'm up against?

Fuck off!

Is all I respond to the text.

Tomorrow is Monday. I'll deal with all of them then. I turn my light off, along with my phone.

After what happened in the lifeguard stand, I assume Edge will be waiting for me.

15

KINSLEY

MORNING COMES WAY TOO SOON. Streams of light fall along my comforter at my feet. I stretch out my screaming muscles. Luca did a number on my body yesterday. At least it was mutual. He'll be waking up just as sore as me.

Remembering the text from the night before, I'm reluctant to turn on my phone. When I do, I regret it the second the screen comes on. Nine more texts from the same unknown number. The last one says:

Don't be late!

I don't bother reading the others before I erase them. However, after a few minutes, when the anger, confusion, and frustration lessen, I wish I had read them. But whoever it is doesn't seem like they're going to let up any time soon, so I'm sure I'll be privy to more of their electronic abuse soon enough.

I take a quick shower before getting ready. After saying a hasty good morning and goodbye to my uncle, I hop on my motorcycle to drive to hell.

Monarch is the usual bustle in the morning. When I take off

my helmet, I notice not only students sipping their lattes as they talk about their weekend but they're pointing at me as they do it. Their whispers thread through the morning air like a poison fog.

Okay, I'm being way too judgy for the first thing in the morning. I mean, shit, I used to be that girl. I give myself a mental slap. By the sounds of some of the conversations I pass, the party seems to have been a big hit, especially after I left and everyone moved inside during the storm.

Doing my best to ignore the peculiar stares, I head for art. If it wasn't evident that they were talking about me, it becomes very apparent when I pass the tenth or so group of people in the hall with their tight-lipped mouths and trailing eyes. With only hearing slivers of conversations on the way to class, I construct what the gossip is all about: I disappeared from Saturday night's party *with Edge*. We snuck away during the storm, and then he was the only one to return to the party house two hours later. What the fuck?

If he spread rumors about me opening my legs for him, I'm going to fucking kill him. I should be able to get something out of Gunner. He likes to talk it up, so I shouldn't even have to ask. He'll be the first to ask me how fucking his best friend was.

I stop at the vending machine before heading to class. The protein bar falls to the well as Brielle comes straight toward me. Her frown is so deep it's gouging into her Botox treatments.

"So, you are a whore?"

What I want to do is grab her shiny blonde hair and smash her pretty bitch face into the glass of the vending machine. Instead, I adult, take a deep breath, and ask myself if I should hear her out or completely ignore her and walk away. Since she's in my first class, I don't think ignoring her is an option, so I might as well get the suffering out of the way.

I plaster a sickly sweet smile on my face. "Yes, Your Gracious Highness, what can I do for you on this lovely Monday morning?" Then, to top it off, I do a little bow. Patiently waiting for her to say something, I maintain a fake smile as I pull my hair over my shoulder.

Her lips peel back over her straight, unnaturally white teeth. "You fucked Edge, and you're going to pay."

I unwrap the protein bar. "Wow. That's news to me. Thanks for letting me know."

"Don't fucking lie about it, slut."

"Where did you get this insane information about my fucking habits from?" I ask. I know she has no intention of telling me, but it's worth a try to ask.

"Venom is taken."

"By you? All of them?" I laugh because she makes it hard to take her sorry ass seriously. I've seen the way each of them treats her, and she must be one delusional hoe to think she's with any of them. Her face turns red like the Corvette I blew by on my motorcycle this morning. "So, can I assume you're the mystery person who's been blowing up my phone with empty, dumbass threats?"

She takes in a deep breath, then pulls back her shoulders in her all-mighty bitch posture. "Trust me, they're anything but empty."

"Bring it on." Happy to have the mystery solved, I slap a smile on my face and take a bite of the chocolate bar. Pointing it at her and looking up to the ceiling as if contemplating something, I say, "Tell me something, since I don't remember, do you know if I enjoyed fucking your boyfriend?"

She snarls as fury blazes in her narrowing eyes. "Stay the fuck away."

Remaining in complete control, I take one step so that my face is within inches of hers. Her friends step back a couple of feet, their heels clicking in sync. Smart of them. Lowering my voice to a growl, I say, "I have no idea what the fuck you're talking about. After I saw him drilling into you last week, I wouldn't want his putrefied dick anywhere near me."

I back away. Her face drops a fraction as if the relief of knowing I'm telling the truth sets in. I take another bite of the bar even though I've lost my appetite.

"Maybe if you're not getting fucked, I'll see you in class." I turn and head toward art.

I toss the rest of the uneaten bar in the garbage. Even though what I said is true, I went to sleep last night thinking about Edge and his body, including his man parts. But we won't go there with Brielle. That's nothing she needs to know about. I want to know who started the rumor. I have a few guesses in mind but none that I'm entirely sure about. If it was Edge, what would he have to gain by spreading a lie about fucking me? He has nothing to benefit from it. The guy can have any girl in this school he wants—well, except for me.

Someone behind me calls my name and rushes up to me before I can answer. Josh's expression is stricken with regret and hurt.

"What's up?" I ask.

"I wanted to apologize for Saturday night, passing out like I did. It had been a long day of drinking and sun, and it kicked my ass earlier than I wanted."

"No problem. It started storming, and I went home."

"Home?" His face etches into confusion.

I immediately stop in the middle of the hall to face him. A few huffs and curses follow as I disrupt the flow of traffic. "Yes, home, Josh. In contrast to the rumor floating around about me. I went home... alone."

His tense shoulders visibly relax. "Good," he breathes out. "I mean, if that's what you wanted to do, then..."

Knowing where he's going with this and deciding to save him, I say, "Yeah, it's what I wanted to do."

I hate to give him the sense of any hope between us, but

there it is, unintentional hope. I'll have to steer that ship away from my shore another way and another day. Today's missions are to shut down the rumor about me hooking up with Edge and find out where Venom trains.

"I have to get to class. I'll see you later."

"Yeah, see you—"

I'm gone before I hear him finish his sentence.

Gunner isn't in class when I arrive. Dammit, I was hoping to get him alone or hear his sarcastic comments or teasing before class got started so that I can set the record straight.

Waiting at my easel is a used condom. Oh, joy. And here I thought my Monday would be boring, with sleuthing on Venom and trying to find their dojo. I guess the joke is on me. My face flushes as anger swells inside me. I lightly touch the scar on the left side of my stomach. It grounds me, reminding me why I'm here at Monarch. Taking a deep breath, I use a pen to remove the disgusting item and toss it in the trash.

Eden pops her head in class as I'm setting up my canvas. "Hey, Kinsley."

"Hi."

"Where did you go Saturday night?"

Even my new friend is curious, and I can't blame her. "Home. I went home."

I leave out the part about the pitstop in the lifeguard stand and the unfortunate events that I was trapped in. Besides, what happened there is irrelevant to the rumors being spread. They aren't about me being shacked up with Edge to get out of the storm but straight up fucking him.

"Oh."

"Yeah, oh. I think there's something I need to clear up today. Maybe the fact that I fucked Edge isn't true."

"So, you've heard."

"It was news to me that I slept with Edge." My gaze finds its way to the ceiling. "And yeah, it was obvious when the stares and finger-pointing started the second I got off my bike that something was up. Then I was confronted by Brielle."

She, like Josh, lets her shoulders drop in relief. "Your mornings really suck."

Her remark pulls a smile from me. "Yeah, since I moved here, you're right."

Gunner takes that exact moment to enter the class. His eyes gravitate right to me. The grin on his face widens like the great divide. Seriously?

"I'll catch you in biology," Eden says as Gunner passes her on his way into class.

He glances over his shoulder. "You know, tapping the chancellor's daughter doesn't seem like it would be too bad. She's kind of growing on me. She has funky hair like mine and is smart like me. We might have more in common than I thought."

Eden wouldn't give him the time of day if someone paid her. But I don't say this. As selfish as it is, I'm keeping this moment all about me.

He glides onto his stool. "So, you and Edge, huh?"

I act like I have no idea what he's talking about. "Where'd you hear that?" My innocence is pretty convincing if I'm judging my performance. I shuffle around with the tubes of paint.

"Partying, storming, lightning, thundering, fucking... sound familiar?"

Nonchalance plays in my lies. "The partying, storming, lightning, and thundering all sound very familiar, but about that last thing you listed, I have no idea what you're talking about."

As I squeeze a few colors onto the palette, he's across the room and next to me without me realizing it. Reaching into the closet, he grabs his canvas. His breath feathers along my neck. "Oh, come on, just give me one little detail."

I turn. Our faces are mere inches apart. "There's nothing to tell. But if there were, I suggest you look elsewhere. I never kiss and tell. Or, in this case, fuck and tell."

His smile only grows more devious. He backs away. "Well, my boy won't spill, and you're tight-lipped, so how am I supposed to get the nasty details?"

"I hate to break it to you, Gunner, but there are no juicy or nasty details to share. I never slept with *your boy*, as you call him." I place my hands on my hips. "What I would like to know is where you heard that little rumor?"

He only winks, then fills one of the cups with water in the sink behind us. "Both of us can play this game."

So much for Gunner being helpful. I guess I'll have to go right to the source, my so-called fuck buddy.

On to the next item on my checklist. "So, where do you guys train? What dojo?"

Gunner pauses, the brush hovering above the blob of blue paint as he lifts his eyes to me. Without any of his usual humor, he says, "It's a private establishment."

Feeling like I've just been dismissed, I drop the subject. I guess I'll have to find that out another way, too.

A few days pass without a word about Edge and me hooking up. It's weird, like everyone suddenly found something new to talk about, and just like that, our imagined fuck session is old news.

Edge ignores me the entire week and barely even looks in my direction. Since the rumors stopped, I haven't initiated any conversation either. I don't think it's as easy to think I've become old news, and he's given up on trying to make me another scratch on his scorecard. At this point, it doesn't matter who started the rumor. But I can only assume he was the one to put it to rest. I still don't know what his game is—if he even has one. It's been almost two weeks since I started at Monarch, and I've let things stagnate long enough. It's time to act. I thought about following them after our last class, but things could escalate to dangerous levels if they catch me.

Eden plops down next to me under our tree. There are no words for her hair. It's an out-of-control, frizzy mess. It looks like someone got hold of a fine comb and a can of hairspray.

Trying to keep my eyes from falling out of my head, I take out my turkey wrap. "What happened? Did you blow yourself up in a science experiment or something?"

"No. I was trying to get pics for the website from the rooftop."

I look at her like she's lost her damn mind. "Why the roof?"

"I was trying to get different angles of the school and the football field. The dancers were practicing, and I thought I'd try something new."

"And that explains your hair how?"

She blows out a puff of air, sending chin-length blue tendrils flying upward, only to land back across her eye. "The AC kicked on, and the giant-ass fan was behind me." She points to her hair. "Result."

With my wrap gripped in my hand, I fall to my side, laughing.

"Stop laughing," she gripes as she starts laughing, too.

Both of us are rolling with belly laughs when Bryce comes up.

"What did I miss? What the fuck happened to you, girl? It looks like you got attacked by an angry mob or a flock of birds." He kneels next to Eden. From his backpack, he tosses his squished brown lunch bag next to him, then takes out a comb. He gestures for her to sit in front of him. She does. "If this doesn't work, we're going to have to shave it." Being the best

171

friend he is, he proceeds to brush out the whirlwind of her tangles.

"Thanks." She glides her hand over her untangled hair.

"You know, Bryce, you could have left it like that. Could be a new style for the psychos at this school," I suggest.

Eden throws a carrot at me. "Hey!"

I catch the veggie stick in mid-air and take a bite off the end of it. "You could have dipped it in hummus first."

It's nice to have friends to laugh with. I've been so caught up with other shit that I forgot how to enjoy other things, normal things.

It's almost time for our next class when Bryce finishes combing Eden's hair into her usual smooth bob.

Eden and I head for the north wing of campus when Josh strolls up next to us.

"Hey, Kinsley, you got a second?"

Eden eyes me, and I motion for her to go on without me. "I'll see you in class."

"I wanted to ask you something. I know our last— Well, the last time we made plans to meet at the party, it didn't go so great. I wanted to make it up to you."

I can already feel the rejection forming on my tongue, but I let him continue. "It was fine," I assure him, hopefully derailing him from asking me out again. "Honestly, I'm not much of a partier anyway."

"You could have fooled me the way you can down tequila like that."

I chuckle. Yeah, but adrenaline had a way of drowning the alcohol. As did certain people.

He shifts from his left to his right foot. Then he adjusts the stack of books in the crook of his arm. My phone dings with a text. Glancing at it, I notice I only have a minute before class starts. With such a short amount of time, whatever proposal he planned will need to be postponed.

It's not. And he carries on as if he didn't hear anything. "Anyway, I wanted to know if you want to go to the Halloween party with me."

Not wanting to give him an answer, I use the time as an excuse to duck out of it. "I've got to get to class. I'll let you know. I'm not sure what I'm doing yet."

"Okay... sure." He backs away, running his free hand through his hair, looking much younger than he is and very vulnerable.

Maybe Eden and Bryce can save me from this commitment, and the three of us can go together, if that's something they're into. A Halloween party doesn't seem like the kind of thing Bryce would miss.

"Josh, huh?"

I look over my shoulder to see Edge. He hasn't spoken to me all week, and now he's confronting me about Josh. What gives? I start to walk backward toward my class as I stare at him. His form and stature are the complete opposite of Josh's. Edge is fearless, unfriendly, and threatening.

"I don't see how that's any of your concern."

Narrowing his eyes, he doesn't respond. But it's not the end of the conversation.

16

EDGE

I PURPOSELY IGNORED Ninja all week. It's been hard as hell. I can't get her out of my fucking head. I have to say, she hurt my ego a bit by not kissing me back. I know it was a ruse. She wanted to, but she wasn't about to let her walls down—not yet. I have no idea who started the rumor about us fucking, but I sure as hell put a stop to it as soon as I heard the whispers. Although, if I were smart, I would have let everyone talk shit about us. Then maybe at least half the guys would stop fucking staring at her like she's their next hookup.

Ninja's bike is still in the parking lot when the guys and I leave for my house to train. There's a fight coming up soon, and this time, I'll be the one in the cage. A lot is on the line: large bets, big-name players, and very few rules.

Later, after practice, when I drive Kade back to school to get his car, Ninja's bike is still in the parking lot. Like at the party when I saw her take off, I resist the urge to listen to my gut and leave her alone.

It's almost eight at night, but several people are still in the library. No one looks up as I enter. As focused as these students are, it'll take a hell of a lot more than someone walking by their table to snag their attention. I walk down the center aisle, glancing left and right until I spot my little Ninja. I call myself out for what I am becoming, a fucking stalker. She's sitting at the far table in the corner, her usual table. Books and notebooks are scattered over it. Anyone paying attention would notice her head bobbing slightly to the beat filtering through her earbuds. I want to know what she's listening to.

Just like in the lifeguard stand, I have no idea what my intentions are. But after the other day, when I questioned her about Josh and her smug response, I couldn't let it go. The top several buttons of her dress shirt are undone. Her tie is loose. The knot rests on the smooth skin between her breasts.

I pull out the chair in front of her and unapologetically sit down. Her eyes pop up to me and then slowly narrow. She doesn't bother to acknowledge me further as she looks back at her notes. With my intrusion, I know she's not seeing her books, her notes, or anything else anymore. Her head is consumed with me. I reach over and pluck one of her earbuds out. The music blares from the tiny speaker. It's an alternative rock band I can't place.

"Don't you have better things to do on a Friday night than hang out in the library?"

"Don't you?" she retorts. She reaches across the table to grab her earbud back, but I yank it out of her reach.

"Yeah, like keeping you away from that asshole Josh."

"And you're not an asshole?" she snaps. She starts to pack her shit, then pauses.

I inwardly laugh. "Oh, I am an asshole, all right. I just don't try to hide it."

"At least you're honest." She closes her book and then opens it again. "You know what? I came here to study, so I won't be the one to leave. You will."

"Nah, not yet. I was thinking of studying myself."

She looks around me, then at the floor. "Kind of hard to study when you don't have anything to study with."

"My studies require less bookwork and more observation." And in my quick observations, I notice her plaid uniform skirt peeking out of her backpack. Fuck me. I run my fingers through my hair. This girl does not play fair.

She pushes back her chair and stands. I get up, too, following her down the main walkway to the back of the library. Her untucked shirt falls just below her ass, making it look like she's not wearing anything underneath it. But I know she has on those tiny, tight-ass shorts underneath. I don't stop at her ass but continue to trace the back of her body. Down the back of her tan thighs, then toned calves, all the way to her boots. Fuck... I rub my hand over my smooth jaw.

Turning down the science aisle, she peruses, or pretends to, the spines. As I glance at the titles, I notice we're in the biology section, so maybe she does need a book, and she's not just trying to avoid me. She pauses and pulls a book off the shelf. Still holding onto her earbud, I shake it in my palm like a pair of dice, then tuck it into my front pocket.

When she tries to pass, I block her way. It's a move she's familiar with, so she turns to go in the opposite direction. I grab her wrist and spin her back toward me. Her hand darts up to jab me in my side. Catching me off guard, I let out a grunt and a harsh breath.

"What the hell was that for?"

"I warned you not to touch me on my first day of school."

"You didn't seem to complain when we were in the lifeguard stand."

She looks away from me and attempts to pull her wrist free.

"Calm down, I just want to talk," I say. She stills, but her eyes are fixed on me with fire. "See, that wasn't so bad, was it?"

The lights in the library dim, signaling that it's closing soon.

The light over our section conveniently darkens to a shadowy glow. The emergency bulb is the only one to stay lit.

"Let me go," she demands in a low, breathy growl.

"No."

She goes for another hit, but I block it. The book falls from her grasp with a light thud, not loud enough to draw attention from anyone. I grab her other wrist and pull it behind her, gripping them both in one hand. She stops trying to move or fight. I'm guessing if she wanted to, she would. For some fucked-up reason, I enjoy taking her free will, making her work for it.

"What do you want, Edge? Another rumor floating around about how I fucked you in the library?"

"I didn't start that shit," I tell her.

Her eyes are like mesmerizing blue pools. I can't look anywhere but at her sublime face. I tuck strands of her hair behind her ear. Her body is rigid against mine, but for a brief moment, she closes her eyes before her gaze locks with mine again. She's not used to being controlled. With me, I think she internally battles against relenting and keeping up her tough girl act. There's a part of her that wants to taste this uncharted territory.

A part of me enjoys watching her struggle against what she should do and what she wants. For her, they are very different things. For me, they are one and the same. I want her to run so I can chase her. And I want her exactly where I have her, in the clutches of my depraved and devious grasp.

"Then who did?" she asks.

"I don't know, but I shut it down the second I heard about it."

Her eyes fall a little, and her face relaxes. I can tell she's grateful, but she'll never tell me as much. And I don't expect her to.

Like in the lifeguard stand, I want to kiss her again, but this time, I want her to kiss me back. Fuck, do I want her to kiss me back. I lean in. She doesn't turn her head, so I continue to push her out of her comfort zone until our lips are only centimeters apart. Her light breaths are like whispers over my mouth while her eyes are full of apprehension.

"I'm going to kiss you," I warn her, giving her a chance to turn away, reject me, knee me in the balls, even jerk her hands free to punch the shit out of me, something.

But she doesn't move.

Her breasts rise and fall against my chest as I hold her hands tight behind her. The knot of her tie has moved, leaving me a perfect view of the valley between her breasts. I lick my bottom lip. Her lips part.

Is that an invitation? Maybe, maybe not. Either way, I take it as one and close the small distance until my lips are on hers. Her sapphire eyes close in response, but her mouth doesn't move. I press my tongue along her lips and lick the seam of her supple mouth, tasting the sweetness of her lip gloss. But fuck if I don't want more. I tilt my head and press her harder against the bookshelf. My knuckles press against her tight ass as I grip her hands behind her. Afraid she'll run if I let go, I hold her, forgoing the need to grab a handful and squeeze. Her fists tighten into balls in my hand, but still, she's not fighting. Her mouth opens another fraction but not enough for me to enter without forcing my way in.

Her mouth moves slightly, a small movement, but enough for me to know how hard she's fighting this. I back away to look down into her conflicted eyes. Want and lust battle for dominance over the will to deny me. I'll make the decision easy for her; hence, I won't give her one.

I brush my lips over hers. "Fucking kiss me," I demand against her mouth.

Her voice is as quiet as a breeze. "You're going to regret it."

I pull harder on her hands. Her head falls back as she lets out a small cry. "I don't give a fuck. Open your mouth for me."

Her lips part, and I eagerly plunge into her sweet, promised sea of regret. With every sweep of her tongue, I know I've never in my life experienced something so fucking incredible and never will again. And it's just a kiss.

My head races along paths to get her naked beneath me. Her mouth moves with mine in a rhythmic dance created by the force of attraction neither one of us can deny. With my free hand, I smooth my fingers up her jaw until I cup her face. She moans into my mouth. My dick hardens. Her tongue effortlessly entangles with mine in an easy banter for dominance and pleasure. I deepen the kiss, wanting to devour this unruly girl. I grip her wrists tighter and force her arms lower. Her body is taut against mine. It would be impossible not to feel her body craving my touch.

She pulls slightly back, severing the irresistible contact between us. Her gaze slowly rolls up to meet mine. Lust swirled with regret and lack of trust is written all over her flushed face. It takes several seconds for her to catch her breath.

"Let me go," she whispers.

I can tell that's the last thing she wants. But my hand slowly slides off her cheek. Reluctantly, I take a step back, releasing her wrists as I do. She licks her bottom lip, and fuck, if it doesn't take everything for me not to grab hold of her body and take her right here. She doesn't move for a long moment. Like a skilled dancer, without taking her eyes off me, she bends straight down, my dick nearly touching her mouth as she picks up the dropped book from the floor, then rises back to her feet.

"I have to go." She glides the edge of her thumb just under her bottom lip, wiping away the thin line of wetness. Lowering her gaze, she starts to walk away from me.

"Little Ninja," I say. She pauses and looks over her shoulder, gracing me with only half her beautiful face. "You're not going anywhere with Josh."

She shifts around to look directly at me. Her voice isn't argumentative, loud, or defensive. It's flat and to the point. "I will go anywhere with anyone I choose. And while we're making things crystal clear, you do not own me, Edge. I will talk to, kiss, and fuck who I want and when I want." Then she turns and walks away.

I let her go like I did in the storm when she ran away from me. I may not be able to tell her who she can talk to, but I'm going to make damn sure I'm the only one she chooses to fuck. The moment I laid eyes on her, I knew she would be mine. She just doesn't know it yet.

17

KINSLEY

It's early when I head down to the beach. The shore is empty even though it's beautiful out. The waves quietly crest the shore. A couple of people are on surfboards, despite there being not a single wave to surf. I assume they're here admiring the sunrise from the water and watching the dolphins swim around the pier, hoping for a handout.

I pull off my tank and slide my shorts off. Wading out into the cool water just beyond the rolling of the waves, I fall into the clear water. My muscles ache from working them so hard this week at the dojo. On top of all the studying, I've made a point to beat my frustration along with everything else out of me... Including my sexual dissatisfaction that Edge has managed to work into me. As hard as I try to keep him at bay or away from my thoughts, he still manages to worm his way into them at no fault of my own.

Wait, that's a complete lie. It feels like I'm lying to everyone right now, and I can't start lying to myself, too.

I did let him get close—too close. I not only let him kiss me but I kissed him back this time. And fuck, if I didn't want more. With his impressive hard length against me, I knew he did as well. If it were anyone else, I might have let him take me right then and there in the freaking science section of the library. He was rough and handled me in a fashion I could get used to. Which I won't.

So I keep telling myself.

The water caresses me. I lie back, letting the soft waves control my body, holding me in their gentle embrace. The flow of the water moves me as it rolls toward shore, then back out to sea. I touch my wet fingers to my lips, remembering how Edge's mouth felt against mine. The way his possessive lips and tongue dominated me as he explored my mouth and invited me to take part in the dance he led.

I lick my lips as the warm water grazes my bare skin. The taste of the salty water has me instantly imagining the taste of his cum. A surge of energy shoots straight between my legs. Instead of pushing the fantasy as far away as possible, I revel in the sensations loitering in my torturous mind.

"Ninja, is that you?"

I flail around, trying to get to my feet. The ocean floor is too deep for me to touch. I floated farther away from shore than I realized. I kick my feet, spinning around in the water as a surfer straddling their board comes up alongside me. I hold my hand over my eyes to block the sun. Wild hair is silhouetted as rays of sunshine filter through the unruly strands. "Gunner?"

"Yours truly." He drifts on his board next to me. "So, what's your reason for escaping to the beach this lovely morning?"

"Just clearing my head. You?" I lie and leave out the part about how I'm working on a plan to follow them to their dojo without being caught or how I'd like to find a way to get his best friend out of my head for good. He probably knows that Edge and I kissed, but I'm not about to say anything to verify it.

He points to the ocean. "I have to come out here when it's this beautiful. It calls to my soul." He holds out his arms as if giving himself over to a sacrifice.

It sounds like me training at the dojo. I don't have to be fighting, just need to be in my special space, which gives me peace.

"I don't even have to surf. I just need to be in the water frolicking with the dolphins."

"Frolicking?" I can't help but laugh at his word choice.

"Great word, right?" He rolls his head to the side to look at me. "I didn't know you lived around here. I mean, I heard you walked home from the party last week, but I didn't think much about it."

"Yeah, I live up there a half-block east." I point to the nearly covered path behind him.

He glances over his shoulder and then back at me. "You come here often?"

"Yeah, whenever I get the chance between the dojo and homework." Shit! I didn't mean to say that out loud.

"Dojo, huh?"

I start to swim toward shore. He follows me, paddling until it's too shallow, then gets to his feet and tucks his board under his arm. "Something like that."

"So, your nickname, Ninja, fits more than just the one you ride?"

I smile without answering. Treading through breaking waves, I make my way back to my clothes. Sand cakes my wet feet. Plopping down on the sand, I lie back. It's still cool and damp in the early morning. A shadow falls over me, blocking the sun.

Gunner lays his board on the sand next to me and then makes himself comfortable. "No dojo talk. Okay, I get it."

"You weren't forthcoming when I asked about your dojo."

"True. Our—my training—"

"You don't have to act like Kade, Edge, and your brother aren't into fighting as well. I saw you guys in the gym practicing headlocks and submission positions."

"You got me. So, yeah, we are all into MMA shit."

"And?" I press.

"We don't have an actual dojo per se. Edge has a full gym at his house, so that's where we mostly train."

Edge's house—interesting. I want to ask him a thousand more questions but hesitate, not wanting to push too hard. Plus, he shared, so now it's my turn. "I train at the Serpent's Spear."

"I've heard of that place. No offense, but it doesn't seem like a place for *real* fighters."

Offense taken. "It *is* a place for real fighters who want to train the way authentic martial arts was meant to be used—for self-defence and discipline."

He holds up his hands. "Sorry. I guess we have different opinions about our pastimes."

Before I can stop myself, I say, "I think MMA is more than just a pastime for Venom."

Gunner doesn't miss my insinuation. "I guess you can say we're committed to the arts more competitively."

Like illegal high-stake betting and murder.

"That's some scar," he comments as he trails his finger along the puckered skin of the knife wound.

"Yeah." I grab my tank top to cover it. Three and a half months and seventeen stitches later, the darkened pink skin still looks angry. The moment the doctor told me the knife hadn't hit anything vital, I knew I got lucky. Although grateful, I still hate how ugly it looks and the constant reminder of that horrid night.

My mind strays to how dazed I was when I woke in the hospital, covered in blood, with my mother and Luca standing over me. Question after question from police, doctors, and my mom about what happened. I couldn't tell any of them the truth.

No, I don't have any enemies. No, I don't think I was targeted. No, I've never been to an illegal fight before. No, I didn't know my dad was fighting. Lies. Lies. Lies.

"I'll take it that topic is off-limits," Gunner says.

"It's not something I like to talk about."

He claps his hands and then slides them together. "Next question. How is it you've managed to gain the attention of everyone at Monarch without even trying?"

I scoff. "Trust me, it wasn't intentional. My goal is the exact opposite."

Gunner clutches his muscular chest and laughs, full-on hysterical laughs.

Baffled, I ask, "What the fuck is so funny?"

"Girl, the second you climbed off that motorcycle, you never had a chance in hell of staying invisible." He laughs again. "Fuck! I think I answered my own question." He shakes his head in amusement.

His laughter quiets down until we only hear the tide lapping the shore.

"You know, for being part of Venom, you don't seem so tough."

He chuckles. "I've taken my share of being a dick. Mostly, I've learned to save it for the octagon. But if the need serves, then I'm all in. Mainly, though, I'm just along for the ride."

I can see that about him. "What about the rest of your friends? Is that the way they feel?"

"Nah. Edge does a good job keeping us shitheads in line. He may be an asshole, but he's as loyal as they come. Since my brother has been re-pussy-whipped, he's ducked out of a lot of shit."

"Re-pussy-whipped?" I question.

"Yeah, in love with the same girl, she leaves, then moves back, they get back together. So yeah, re-pussy-whipped."

"Thanks for the vocabulary lesson." I chuckle. "And Kade?"

"As for Kade, he's just Kade. Nothing gets past him. He's the one who decides who can sell pot and who can't at Monarch. He only likes the good stuff, so all the others get waitlisted until they can get the good shit. If he needs to get involved, he does. Otherwise, his presence alone scares people shitless."

That's the exact impression I got on the first day.

Gunner glances sideways at me. The sun shines on his tan, scruffy face. "You know you're almost as scary as him. You with your tattoos and piercings and badass attitude."

"I don't have an..." I stop before I tell another lie. If and when I'm going to lie, it won't be over something so obvious. "I only have the one tattoo."

"And two *visible* piercings," he adds.

"Visible?"

His eyes fall over my body. "Yeah, you know you could have your—"

"Drop it!"

"I was hoping you were going to say your—"

"Gunner," I warn.

He holds his hands up, surrendering all hope on the topic. "Fine, I'll assume you're boring everywhere else!"

I can't help but laugh. "Yeah, let's assume that."

Seagulls fly overhead. Their sights scan the sand for breakfast.

"If you could be anything, what would you be?" he asks.

The question is so random it catches me off guard. And even if I did know, I'm not sure I trust him enough to tell him. His friendship with Edge throws a giant wrench into things. But this time, I don't have to lie. "I'm not sure."

"Well, I wouldn't suggest you be an artist. You'd give new meaning to 'starving artist.'"

Instinctively, I reach out and slap his arm. "That wasn't nice."

"Oww!" He laughs and rubs the spot where I hit him. "I'm just being real. You're terrible."

"Well, in my defense, it was the only class available when I signed up so late in the year." Curious, I ask, "What about you?"

He sits up, crosses his legs at his ankles, and rests his arms on his bent knees. "I want to be exactly that. Well, an artist or a pro surfer. Or fuck, both. Why the hell not?"

I've only known him for a few weeks, but I can see that. "Not a professional MMA fighter?"

"Nah. It's fun and all, but I'm not a lifer like Edge or Kade."

Lifer? Like Python? Python fought with the ferocity of a killer, not someone who's in it just for fun. This conversation just keeps getting more interesting by the topic.

Speaking of Edge, I want to ask where he is this morning or what he did this weekend. And I hate myself for wanting to know. He's supposed to be the one I *use* to get close to Venom as a whole, to bring them down, not actually get close to *him* in the process.

Since my curiosity has a way of taking over, I try to ask nonchalantly and hope Gunner doesn't catch on. "Where are your friends while you're out here?"

He shrugs. "Probably home passed out. There was a party at some guy's house last night. Kade drank more than I have ever seen him drink before, my brother was with Estelle, and Edge was off somewhere getting high and fucking the bitch, Brielle."

The bottom of my stomach sinks into a trench as deep as the Mariana. I feel like I'm falling through the sand for an unknown amount of time. I can't seem to stop until the imagined quick-sand is replaced with nausea. I clear my throat. Where the fuck did all those dreaded feelings rise from? Forcing myself to stay situated on the sand to hear what else he has to say instead of bolting up to go home, I rest my hand over my stomach and close my eyes, still wondering what the hell kind of reaction that was. Thankfully, Gunner doesn't seem to notice.

"Listen, I have a proposal for you," he says.

Instantly on red alert, I open one eye and look at him. "What kind of proposal?"

"Give me your hand."

Reluctantly, I do. He pulls me up into a sitting position. His gaze travels over my breasts when my shirt falls away, then travels up to meet my eyes. He shakes his head as if coming out of a trance. "Unfortunately, those— You are off-limits." He wags his finger in my direction. "But if they weren't..." He claws his hands down his face.

"Off-limits? What's that supposed to—"

He doesn't let me finish. Coming again to his senses, he asks, "So want to hear it—my proposal?"

He looks at me as if nothing he said is out of the ordinary and incredibly fucked-up. Not that I want to hook up with Gunner, but who decided to take my boobies—and me—off the market? Hearing him tell me that an alien ship just landed behind me would be weirder.

Stunned, I say, "No, I would like to return to your previous bewildering statement, please."

Gunner is shaking his head before I finish my sentence. "Nope. No. And no. We are not going there. I'm blaming that slip on the extra good weed I smoked last night. It was an after-effect."

"You can't be serious."

"Dead." He grabs an invisible noose from around his neck and tugs it. His tongue lolls to the side as his eyes roll into his head.

My mind is still whirling through that coded sentence, but his loose lips have magically turned into a vault. Like a dried-up well, he won't reveal anything else.

I sigh dramatically. "Fine, what's this proposal?"

He smears a section of the damp sand with his hand, smoothing it over, then picks up a broken shell. With the tip of it, he draws a circle in the sand, then adds details. I can tell immediately it's a girl with long strands of hair fanning over one side of her face in an imaginary breeze.

"What if I help you with your art project?"

I glance from his sand art to his face. "Really?" Then I jerk my thoughts to where this is going. That sounds great, but he has his own agenda. "Wait, what do you want in return?"

He uses another shell and a piece of small driftwood to finish his quick but very impressive sand girl. Discarding the random objects, he looks at me. "By spring break, I want you to tell me why you're *really* at Monarch."

I wasn't expecting him to want *that*—the one thing I can't give. But damn, if I don't need help with my art project. "Why that?"

"Because you're full of secrets, Kinsley 'Ninja' West." He wipes his hands together, dusting off the granules of sand.

He's certainly not wrong. "And?" I push, sensing there's more.

"And I want to know your biggest one."

I force a soft laugh. "Dealing in secrets now?" Wanting nothing more than to avoid his eyes, I look away in fear of giving in to the truth of his accusations.

"Stop trying to conjure a lie. I want the truth." He bumps my shoulder. "We all have them. But yours"—he taps the tip of my nose—"I'm sensing yours are big."

Maybe all of this will be over before the time comes when I have to tell him. I can only hope. If not, I'll tell him the truth in one word—without details—*revenge*. "Fine," I agree.

He holds out his hand, and all his fingers are folded except his pinky.

This time, I do laugh. "You want to pinky-swear?"

He feigned shock. "Is there anything more binding?"

I loop my pinky around his. "Deal."

With our fingers still looped, he stands, pulling me up with him.

"Are you going to tell Edge you saw me here?" I wipe the sand off my butt.

"Do you want me to?"

I shake my head. "I don't care."

"Yeah, you do, but I won't." He offers a small smile. "It's our secret." He picks up his board. "But, Ninja, just know...I bet he knows more about you than you think."

Every muscle in my body stiffens, and it's obvious he notices the change in my posture when he tilts his head down.

"He's Ledger Hunt, a rich asshole, son to a bigger asshole, who has people—who have their people. Once you enter Venom's den, there's no hiding." He tucks the surfboard under his arm.

And here I thought I was the clever one.

"Want another tiny piece of insight? Edge would have come after you even if you hadn't parked in his spot." The corner of his mouth lifts to one side. "He's been my best friend since I can remember, but I haven't seen the before-Ninja Edge in a long time, not since you arrived and stepped into our little world."

"I haven't stepped into anything," I argue.

Gunner scoffs. "No? Are you sure about that?"

No, I'm not sure at all. It seems that Edge is full of secrets, especially dark ones that he keeps in the shadows about the ones closest to him. "What's he got on you?" I ask.

"Nothing that another soul will ever know about."

"That's not an answer."

He shrugs and gives me a lopsided grin. "Sorry, Ninja." He turns an imaginary key over his lips and then pretends to eat it.

I don't push him further. He already told me more than I expected. I'm not that much of an idiot to think he'd be more loyal to me than his friends he's known forever. Besides, who am I to judge? I have my own deep, dark, dirty secrets.

"Tomorrow, be in the art room at seven," he says.

I nod, still off-kilter by the turn in our conversation. "Yeah, okay."

He takes a few steps toward the ocean, then whips back around, holding up his finger. "Oh, and, Ninja."

I pause with only one leg in my shorts. "Yeah?"

He runs his hand over his golden hair. "Let's keep up my badass persona. Ya know, for fun."

I tug an invisible zipper across my mouth. "For fun."

He offers me a salute and then runs into the breaking waves.

Secrets layered with more secrets. There's a chance I may drown in them soon.

18

KINSLEY

THIS EARLY IN THE MORNING, Monarch's campus is a ghost town. I wonder if Gunner is even here. Only a few cars are in the parking lot. No Jeep. I'm not sure whether that's good or bad. Either way, I make my way toward art.

True to his word, Gunner is already at his easel when I get to class.

"I thought you might have reconsidered. Maybe your secret is bigger than you're willing to share," he taunts.

Oh, it is. "I guess you'll have to wait to find out if this was all really worth it."

"It is. You're too badass for it not to be."

"Your confidence in me is quite high."

For the next half hour, he helps me with the basic lines of my portrait and then explains how to blend colors. Applying them with certain styles of brush strokes and the amount of paint to use is the tricky part. How does any of this come so naturally to people? Gunner has an image in his head he's working toward, so that's what I'm aiming for.

By the end of class, I feel more confident about what I need to do to pass. I put the almost-empty tubes in my backpack to run by the store to match the colors of the ones I need to replace. Thanking Gunner, I breeze past Brielle. She spews some regurgitated comment that I ignore as I head for biology.

The rest of the day drifts by on a lazy current. I can't wait to hit the dojo after school to release this pent-up energy. It's only been a day, and my muscles aren't nearly recovered, but I already decided by the time my last class is over. I head straight for the parking lot. It's gorgeous out. On days like this, Luca and I would skip and make the two-hour drive up the coast to an old dojo. The owners, friends of my uncle and dad, are great. They loved it when we joined their classes on those rare days. Damn, I miss those times.

I slide off the suffocating blazer, then unbutton my collared shirt. Metallic waves of heat glisten off the black asphalt. I pick up my pace when I notice a group of people hovering around where I'm parked. When I come upon them, their chatter ceases.

"What's going on?" I ask.

None of them answer. They separate, making a thin path for me to get to my bike. I abruptly jerk to a stop when I see my motorcycle. The word Ninja is X'd out with what looks like pink nail polish. Next to it is the word "Slut" along with a crude drawing of an open mouth next to a dick, hairy balls and all.

"Oh, hell no," I seethe.

Anger instantly fuels my blood as my heart pounds and my veins sizzle with fury. I glance around at the faces surrounding me. They go straight-faced, trying to hide their giggles, but it's useless. I roll up my sleeves and tie the tails of my shirt around my waist. That'll have to be as good as it gets today. I get on my motorcycle, insert the key, and then rev the engine. Without putting on my helmet, I back out of the spot. Brielle and her friends stand with Edge and the rest of Venom by his Jeep. They each look smug like they've made their point and have had the final say.

Well, fuck them. This shit just got real.

Unable to help myself, I forget all of my training to control my rage and drive right up to them. I come so close to Brielle that she squeaks and jerks back to avoid her toes getting crushed. Her back slams into the oversized tire of the Jeep. Stopping in front of their group, I stare longer than I need to at Edge. Fury and something else I can't read are smeared across his face. But I'm too angry to try to figure it out.

Gunner gives me his usual salute along with a rare, solemn look on his face.

I plaster on a disgusted smile for Brielle. "Hi, Brielle."

She juts out her hip and slides her arm through Edge's. He doesn't move. "Nice bicycle, trash. New paint job? Looks like art class and your private lessons with Gunner are really paying off."

I don't miss the jerk of Edge's head twisting in Gunner's direction. Ready to breathe fire, I ignore whatever it may mean, refocusing on the bitch in front of me.

"Oh no, Brielle…" I swish my wrist forward and roll my eyes dramatically. "I can't take all the credit. I bet you're way more creative than I am."

She laughs along with the rest of her friends. "Don't you know it?"

I've always been taught never to lower yourself to your enemy's level, but this whore strips me down until my worst pours out of me in buckets of hateful sludge. Though, it'll be fun to fuck with her at her own game.

"I do, actually. Though, thanks to Gunner, he's been showing me all kinds of artsy tricks. I'll have to show you. See all of you assholes tomorrow. I have to go practice my paint blending technique."

"Have fun with that." Brielle breaks out in brazen laughter and looks at Edge for approval.

Those slate eyes fix on me.

Like switching off a neon sign, I let my facade fall. "Have a colorful ride home, Brielle."

"Fuck you," she spits.

On their own accord, my eyes slide to Edge for one brief moment. His dark expression is unchanged. I back out from the confines of their group. Driving slowly through the parking lot, I pull up beside Brielle's red convertible Mercedes. Why wouldn't she have the top down on such a gorgeous day?

Did I also mention the convenience it offers me?

I slide my backpack around to my front and pull the almost-empty paint tubes from my backpack: Ruby Red, Jet Black, Midnight Blue, and Royal Purple. Unscrewing the caps, I squeeze what's left through the opening. The blobs of paint plop onto her white leather seats. I use the end of one of the tubes to smear the colors around, swirling them just the way Gunner showed me. I'm such a good student. Then, practicing my brush strokes, I use my finger to draw a smiley face in the paint.

She's behind me, screaming like a banshee as she runs toward me. "What the fuck are you doing?"

"I told you I'd show you my new skills. Enjoy your ride home," I call over my shoulder and toss the empty tubes in her car before I take off. Serves the bitch right.

The rawness of rage feels slightly healed. It shouldn't, but it does.

On the way to the dojo, I make a quick stop at the local hardware store. Grabbing a can of black matte spray paint off the shelf, I pay, then head back out to my motorcycle. The person sitting in the yellow Ferrari next to my bike is the last person I would have ever expected.

Kade places his arm on the ledge of the open window.

"This car seems a little flashy for your dark and silent type. Don't you think?"

"I like yellow, and I like fast cars."

I shrug. "Then who the fuck am I to judge?"

He takes a drag from the joint pinched between his fingers. Holds his inhale.

I nod at the hardware store behind me. "You planning on buying a rope or a hammer? Maybe a nail gun or a drill?" I cross my arms over my chest. "Or did you follow *me?*"

He exhales long, the sweet stench of weed wafting out of the open window. "That was a shitty thing Brielle did to your bike."

I kick a pebble near my foot. "Yeah, well, I'm sure it'll cost a hell of a lot less to fix than to replace her seats."

Is that a tiny smile I see before he folds his tongue, tapping the metal bar against his teeth? "You're probably right."

"Why are you here, Kade?"

He doesn't look at me as he takes another hit. "Edge asked me to check on you."

Fueled by shock and another bout of fury, I pop off the top of the spray can. "If he wanted to know, he should have done it himself. Besides, I don't need to be checked up on. I can handle myself just fine."

He barely nods. "I figured as much."

I shake the can, the little metal ball inside bouncing off the sides.

Kade's expression is impassive as he revs his engine and puts the car in gear. "Hey, Ninja. We should race."

I don't try to hide the grin spreading across my face. Flutters of excitement blossom in my chest at the idea of racing him. "Yeah, we should."

He pulls out of the parking lot. I turn back to my bike and spray over the pink graffiti, mumbling all sorts of things that should never come out of a lady's mouth. Good thing I'm not a lady. Even more in the mood to kick the shit out of something, I drive to the dojo a couple of blocks away and park under the tree at the far end of the parking lot.

"Hey, kiddo, I wasn't expecting you today," Uncle Trey says.

"Today's a good day to let off steam."

He nods. "Have at it. The place is yours until seven."

Two hours later, sweat runs down the side of my face and my back. I take a short break before practicing with my favorite weapon, the bo. By the time I finish, I'm beyond exhausted to care about what Brielle did or why Edge had Kade check on me.

It's almost seven when I leave the dojo. I tell my uncle bye as his next class prepares to start. The cool night air feels refreshing against my heated skin. The couple of lights in the parking lot are too dim to light up the spot where I parked. That wasn't too smart on my part. A dark parking lot and a single lone girl equals a perfect setup for very bad things. The sky is clear with an almost full moon, so at least I have that going for me.

I put on my backpack, freeing my arms in case I need to defend myself. I know I'm being melodramatic. Nothing ever happens in this part of town. But fuck me if today hasn't screwed with me enough.

I'm almost to my motorcycle when a figure steps out from behind the large oak.

"Isn't it a little dangerous for you to be out here all by yourself?" Edge asks.

I take off my backpack and lay it by the wheel of my bike. "Like I told Kade, I can handle myself just fine." I pull the band from my hair and put it on my wrist.

"I don't doubt it for a second, but I'd still like to see you try." His voice is low, menacing, challenging.

He steps toward me. The moon streaks his smooth face with pale light. The adrenaline from training still pumps hard through my veins, and the thrill of his challenge amps up my anticipation of giving him what he wants. That and the anger I still feel, more toward myself than him, have me wanting to kick his ass even more. He kissed me, I let him, and he went back to fuck Brielle. I have no claim over him, nor do I want one, but fuck if it still doesn't make me want to drop-kick him, then beat the shit out of him. And who knows what involvement he had in having my bike vandalized.

He runs his hand through his hair.

Wanting to erase the way those hands touched me and the way his lips claimed mine, I busy myself with finding the ignition key. "What? Kade checking up on me wasn't good enough for you?" I reach for my helmet. "I don't know why you even care." I sound like a jealous girlfriend, and it pisses me off even more.

He places his hand over mine. "I had to see for myself."

Without effort, my eyes find his in the near darkness. A sea of torment and defiance swirls through my thoughts. The frustration and confusion on his face, the lust and carnal need simmering in his stormy eyes. It's as if I'm staring in the mirror.

What the fuck is going on between us? I've had stupid crushes on guys. That feeling of giddiness when it builds, knowing you're going to run into them in the hall, the jumble of nerves when they notice you staring, or the excitement mixed with tension when a friend tells you they heard "crush guy" likes you back.

Whatever is happening between Edge and me is on another level. A level so high I can no longer see the ground. I feel as though I'm floating and fading all at once. That's the scary part —the slice of this infatuation. It's dangerous for all parties involved. All the other stuff is kids' play. The constant thoughts about him are messing with me.

By the way he's studying me, he hates—or he's confused by—this confliction, too. But it doesn't seem like either of us can stop. I have no idea what his story is or why a collage of mistrust, resentment, and torment is painted on his beautiful face. I have a million reasons not to get involved with Ledger Hunt. Yet my body goes rogue from all rational thought, and the desperation for him to touch me when he's this close is almost unbearable.

I don't look away as I straddle my motorcycle. "As you can see, I'm fine. So, why don't you go stalk Brielle?"

A deafening silence lapses between us before he answers, and when he does, need and dominance weave through his hushed words. "She's not the one I want."

I tell myself the chill skating across my skin is from the light breeze drifting by.

But I know better.

19

EDGE

HER BLUE EYES, almost black in the near darkness, are still locked on mine. There's no escaping her penetrating glare and the heat stirring within it. Nothing could tear me away. She reaches for her helmet, but I grab it first, needing anything to tether her to me, even for this brief moment. I'm not ready to let her go yet.

She drops her hand, not giving in to my childish antics. "I'm not in the mood for your games, Edge."

"I'm not playing." I hold her helmet just out of her reach as I take another step closer to her.

She studies me, likely not sure if I'm fucking with her or not. I wish to hell I was and that I didn't give a fuck. But without even trying, this girl has found a way to slip under my radar and burrow beneath my skin.

Her motorcycle is leaning toward me on its kickstand. Her right leg is bent, with her foot resting on the pedal. The other foot, the one closest to me, is settled on the ground. As hard as she tries to keep herself closed off from me, I don't believe she intentionally opened her legs as an offering to me. It's simply a habit. It doesn't matter. I can't help but take something I crave that's so close.

So, without thinking, I move into that void between her leg and the engine. The only evidence of annoyance, or maybe uncertainty, is the jerky inhale of her next breath. I don't give her a chance to do or say anything before I slide my hand onto her leg just above her knee. Ninja doesn't move. Her skin is chilled and slightly slick with sweat. I nudge her leg, spreading it farther to nestle in the small space closer to her. There's nowhere for her to go without a fight.

Goosebumps race along her leg. She doesn't jerk away or push my hand off. She only continues to stare at me with that steely, unrelenting glare, daring me to move farther up her thigh. Wanting more, as I always do with her, I can't help but push those limits.

I unhurriedly slide my hand up her bare leg. My thumb grazes her inner thigh. Her eyes are like liquid pools filled with equal amounts of warning and wanting. I toss her helmet onto the grass behind me. The gradual speed my hand moves toward her sweet spot is agonizing. Just as I reach the edge of her extremely short shorts, she places her hand over mine. The worn white tape, still wrapped around her hand, scrapes the tops of my knuckles. It reminds me that I'm not dealing with just any girl.

I trap her pinky finger under my thumb, holding her hand there with mine, and lean into her. My mouth waters as if preparing to taste a decadent dessert.

Finally, she looks away, down to her hand resting on mine, dangerously close to her sex. "You wanted to check on me. You can see that I'm fine, so I think you should go now."

I ignore her as I take her chin between my thumb and fore-finger, guiding her face to look back at me. "Does fighting get you wet, Ninja?"

Her hand twitches over mine. But still, there's no struggle

from her. It's as if she's been spellbound to remain captivated and calm for me. I lean in and lightly press a kiss to the corner of her full, pouty lips.

"I bet it does," I say against her mouth. I release my hold on her chin. My hand glides down the length of her neck. The beating of her pulse thumps wildly under my fingers. As I continue down to her chest, her breath picks up the pace.

She consciously tries to slow them, dragging in deeper and longer streams of air. The effort is noticeable only because I'm doing the same to control my breathing, a technique we were both taught to use when fighting. The deeper she inhales, the higher her breasts rise. I slide my gaze down, appreciating the sight of the smooth swells of her creamy skin. Unable to stop myself, I pause just long enough to graze my thumb over the edge of her sports bra and bare skin.

Fuuuck.

I should have kept my eyes on hers and my hand moving. When I'm with her, it's a constant battle of wanting to take as much as I can, as much as she'll allow, and wanting to take my time, soaking up every second and letting myself drown in every touch, every movement, no matter how small or insignificant. I don't want to miss or forget a fucking thing when we're together. I need these memories because the moment I get home, I'll rewind the feel of her, remember the exact way she looked at me, as I grip my hard cock in my hand and imagine it's her hand wrapped around it.

When I look back at her face, her eyes are still fixed on mine. I move my hand between her breasts, grazing her erect nipples with my knuckles. Her hand tightens on mine as she lets out a small gasp.

The languid movements torture my dick as it hardens against my jeans.

I press my mouth to hers. Like the first time in the lifeguard stand, she doesn't kiss me back. I take her bottom lip between my teeth and bite hard enough to evoke a small whimper. The sound is like a siren pulling me under the waves, deeper and deeper, into her dangerous embrace.

Her body tenses as if remembering that she should be hating my hands and mouth and teeth on her. I sense with every fiber of her being, she wants to—and should—push me away, but like mine, her body is running the show, orchestrating an all-consuming and intoxicating dance that can only end up badly for both of us. The torments and suffering she's endured must make it hard for her to trust. And I'm the last person she would want. So, in the end, I'm no fool to think there's a happily ever after waiting. There is no happy ending for people like us.

I just need a taste of her before she realizes who and what I am.

My hand strolls lower, sliding across her bare stomach and resting on her ribs. Despite the heat emanating from her, her skin remains cool. She opens her mouth just enough for the tip of her tongue to ease out and lick the spot where I bit. Each second that passes intensifies my craving for her.

"Edge." Her voice is filled with as much hate as it is fueled by pure lust.

Again, my name. Still liking the sound of it on her lips. "Hmm?" The simple word vibrates against her mouth.

"Why me?"

I don't back away from her, keeping my mouth only a breath away from hers. There are as many answers to that question as there are none. I simply shake my head. The tips of our noses rub together. "I can't explain it."

Most girls would push me to keep going *faster*. Unlike most girls, she isn't and doesn't.

Too far in to stop now, I try to kiss her again. Her lips hesitantly move against mine. *Fucking finally*. Using what little restraint I have, I refrain from devouring her, afraid of scaring her off. The kiss remains light and innocent.

Innocent is not a word I want to use when she's in my grasp like this. I highly doubt she's a virgin, but she's far from being the type to give herself over to just any guy—especially me. But all I want to do is dirty her up with my hands and mouth, just for me, until I'm the only one she begs for.

I trace my hand back up through the valley of her chest, to her shoulder, pushing her hair away to reveal the sensitive skin of her neck. Resting my hand on the back of her neck, I gently tilt her head, trailing my mouth from her lips to kiss the curve at the base of her neck, letting my warm breath fan across the delicate skin as I follow the line of her collarbone up to her ear and push her hair off her shoulder. Her pulse is racing. I lick the sensitive skin, tasting salt and remnants of her perfume.

My other hand presses more firmly into her inner thigh, my fingers threatening to leave marks.

The moment is going fucking perfect until Ninja wraps her fingers around mine, stopping my hand from furthering its progression to her pussy. "Is this the way Brielle likes you to touch her?"

The question fucking freezes me in place. I lift my head from her neck but keep my lips desperately close to hers. "I don't give a shit about Brielle," I breathe out onto her lips. The blood streaming through my veins picks up speed but not for the reason I aim for.

She moves our hands off her inner thigh, then releases mine. "It didn't look like that today after she fucked up my bike, or in the cafeteria, or when you had her bent over the desk."

Her tone is so calm, she could as easily be telling me what she's planning to eat for dinner. Her lack of emotion is curious, and I'm unsure what to make of it. I know this physical attraction between us isn't just one-sided. I feel her nerves hum every time we're in the same vicinity of each other. I don't defend or deny what she's saying. I would be even more of a prick if I did, because that's exactly what she saw each time. At least that's what it looked like.

But Ninja is far from being an idiot or unperceptive. She knows the truth... Brielle is convenient, and this is Ninja's way of saving herself from falling too deep into this moment.

Instead of releasing my gentle grasp from around her neck, I tighten it. "You're as stubborn as I am." I crush my lips against hers, then pull back just as fast, letting my hand slide down the length of her back before falling away completely.

She rubs the back of her hand over her mouth. A sickly sweet yet seductive smile is left in its wake. "It's not a matter of being stubborn. I won't ever play anyone's second." Her fierce gaze drops from mine. She turns the key in the ignition and starts the engine.

Relenting for now, I pick up her helmet and then hold it out to her. She slowly takes it, likely unsure if I'm playing with her or not. I can't fucking blame her, considering what Brielle did to her motorcycle, then I let the bitch cozy up to me right in front of Ninja and I didn't say a fucking word like I didn't give a shit. I did give a shit. But being the asshole that I am, I wanted to see what my little Ninja was going to do to retaliate. She didn't disappoint.

She puts on her helmet, the visor still raised. "Bye, Edge." She puts the bike into gear and drives away, leaving me to watch her go.

That time, I don't like my name on her lips. I shove my hands into my pockets, wishing things were different. Kinsley West is proving to be more challenging to penetrate than I thought. She's stubborn as fuck and doesn't take shit from anyone, and she can also kick some serious ass. I watched her train for the past two hours through the large storefront windows. What I wouldn't give not only to fuck her into the next century but also to go hand-to-hand with her on the mat.

I run my fingers through my hair. Fuck me to hell. I don't

think she could take me, but that's only because I have my size going for me. But fuck, if she wouldn't give me a run for my money and make it fun as hell. Most of her moves are old school, her weapon skills are like nothing I've seen before, and her focus is unwavering.

I knew who she was the moment I confronted her on her first day at Monarch. But if I didn't, after I crept up on her tonight and studied her moves, as well as admired the lines of her body when she delivered each strike with deliberate precision, I would have known right away. Only one other fighter I know fought like that, and he's dead.

She's been trained by one of the best, and her skills are fire on so many levels. I have no doubt she could kick most of the fighters' asses I know. Even with their cunning ways, her skills would no doubt have them on their knees, begging for mercy and tapping out.

Her father didn't deserve what he got. It kills me every time I look into those sad blue eyes and see her pain shining through them like a beacon. She thinks it's invisible, but she can no more hide her anguish than I can hide my regret for what happened that night. My little Ninja just hasn't figured that out yet.

20

KINSLEY

TWO DAYS LATER, during biology my phone vibrates with a string of texts. A name I haven't heard from in weeks flashes across the screen. Adam. He's my insider to the UG fights. After what happened at the last one, I wasn't sure if I'd ever hear from him again. I texted him last week to see if he knew anything coming up, but he never responded. I don't blame him. Hell, he probably thought I lost my damn mind.

Unable to wait until the end of class, I read the messages and freeze.

Adam:

UG coming

That's all it says and all I need to know... for now. I'm hoping when he knows more, he'll tell me—like when and where the fight will be. Because I'll be there.

This tiny piece of insight leaves my head in the clouds for the rest of class.

I wish that were the only reason for my lack of focus. Since I pulled out of the dojo's parking lot, I've barely been able to concentrate on anything or anyone that isn't Edge. My thoughts have found little reprieve from the way his warm mouth felt on my neck, his rough hand sliding up my thigh, or his breath against my skin. Since then, he's made a point of ignoring me. Conflicted feelings come and go as frequently as the tide. That kind of attention from him is the last thing I need. But when I try getting my body on board, she wants to bitch slap my head into next week.

Now, I need to be patient until I hear from Adam. Yeah, my focus is shot.

Brielle has been especially distant. None of her friends have even looked my way. I guess I'm not as easy a target as they expected. Unfortunately, it took my motorcycle and her car seat to make that point clear.

All in all, the week has been relatively quiet. When the day's last class comes to an end, Eden says bye and that she'll call me later. This is a new development. She'll either call to go over homework or text me something random she thinks I'll find funny or interesting. I must admit, I like having a girl in my corner. For so long, it's just been Luca, who I wouldn't trade for the world, but a girl sees things differently.

I pack up my books and head for the gym. Taking a shortcut down a nearly deserted hall toward the locker room, I hear footsteps fast approaching. Out of habit from my training, I turn and raise my arms in defense.

Josh immediately throws his arms up as he backs down. "Hey, it's just me."

I lower my arms. "Sorry. I'm a little on edge."

My choice of words only proves to be a reminder of my nightmare. Insisting that there's nothing more to my word choice than anxiety over the text from Adam and having nothing to do with the fact that Edge is on my mind, I shove the obsessive part of my brain back into the shadows.

Josh is waving his hand in front of my face. "Earth to Kinsley."

I shake off the Edge-induced fog. "Sorry... again." Do something normal, Kins. I tuck my hair behind my ear and force a smile. "What's up?"

"Have you decided to go with me to the Halloween party?"

I don't answer right away as a figure pauses behind Josh. Levi, Gunner's twin, raises his finger to his lips. My stomach clenches with dread. His girlfriend, Estelle, isn't at his side. Christ, what now?

I look back at Josh. Needing to get him to get moving along so I can find out why Levi is now stalking me, I blurt out, "Yeah. Sure."

The guy's face splits into a grin, and then he swoops in for a kiss.

I jerk my head and lift my hand to stop him. "Whoa, there. Too fast!"

He grabs the ends of his short hair. "Yeah. Yeah, sorry."

The silent twin behind Josh narrows his eyes. If there's something I should know, I wish he'd spill it already. Instead, he's creeping in the background, waiting to pounce.

"I'll see you in class." Josh hikes up his backpack on his shoulder and walks past me toward the guy's locker room.

Levi shakes his head as he steps out of the darkened hallway. "I thought you were smarter than that, Ninja."

"What are you talking about?"

He, too, walks past me, going in the same direction as Josh. "Ask your friends about him."

What the hell is that about? With so much to deal with, I have no time to think about Josh, Halloween, or Levi's coded warning. I rush to the locker room to change before class starts. After shoving my crap in the locker, I change as quickly as possible and head out to the gym. Since it's raining out, some of the teams have decided to move practice indoors, including the cheer team.

The place is crowded as shit, but it's still easy to spot Edge and the boys playing basketball. Gunner tosses the ball into the basket from a reasonable distance. It's simultaneously weird to watch them do something so ordinary and impressive. Are they bad at anything?

A group of people surrounds them, primarily girls. Some giggle. Others try the sexy approach with their hip kicked out, arms crossed over the chest to push up their tits, and the perfect pouty expression on their overly made-up faces. None of the attention they're vying for is thrown their way. Edge and his boys are too enthralled in the game to notice or care about their fawning fan club.

The coach blows his whistle. When our class gathers around him, he instructs everyone to run four laps around the gym. I'm one of the first to take off. The sooner I start, the sooner I can cross the finish line.

When we finish and gather back in the same location, he throws a bunch of basketballs out. "Grab the rope, head to the weight training room, anything. Just keep moving."

He's giving us busy work for gym class. If I'd have known this, I would have skipped today. I grab a ball.

Josh catches my eye and starts to make his way over, but then he notices Gunner and Levi closing in on me. Josh smiles, then changes his mind and returns to his friends.

Perceptive Gunner notices the exchange of what just happened. His grin is too proud and cocky as hell. "Stay over there with the rest of your pussy friends," he calls out to Josh. "Fucker," he mumbles more to himself. Then, as if nothing happened, his playful smile is back in place right before he knocks the ball out of my hand and dribbles it as he runs around me. "Want to play?"

There's something I'm missing between Josh and these Vipers, but fuck if I know what it is.

I glance over Gunner's shoulder at Edge, who shoots baskets alone. "What, are Edge and Kade too good for running and doing what the coach asks?"

Levi shrugs as he dribbles the ball. "Nah, Coach lets Edge slide because he's trying to get him to join the basketball team. But he's wasting his fucking time." He jerks his head to Kade, who's sitting on the bleachers. I swear it looks like he's rolling a blunt. "Kade doesn't do anything he doesn't want to," Levi explains.

For the next twenty minutes, we play a chaotic game of basketball. I have no idea what I'm doing except knowing the ball needs to go into the net, but Gunner and Levi make it fun. Asshole Edge ignores me the entire time. I'm not even shocked anymore. The guy is a mixed bag of crazy and hotness. Neither of which I know what to do with. One second, I want to fuck him. The next, I want to knock him upside the head. Who's the fucked up one, Kins? Shut up, I silently tell the demons fighting on my shoulder. One is terrible, and the other is worse. No angels, just corrupt little devils.

The coach blows the whistle, signaling the end of class. We rack the balls and head for the locker room. My phone lights up with a text from Bryc:

> Meet Eden and me at the coffee house after school-my Treat!

In the next text, he sends me the address.

I respond right away that I'll be there. It'll be the perfect time and place to ask them about Josh.

I slide on my skirt and pull my button-down over my sports bra. I toss everything else into my backpack. As I'm heading out into the hall, my phone dings again. I expect it to be Bryce, but it's a notification that biology has been canceled. My boots hit the ground with determination to get the fuck out of Monarch.

To my pleasant surprise, the rain has stopped for now. Hopefully, it'll hold out until I get to the coffee house. That's the one thing about having a bike, it sucks to drive in the rain or cold.

I tie the button-down shirt around my waist. "Fucking uniform," I mumble to myself.

"There she goes again," someone says while his friends laugh.

"Back the fuck off." Another voice dominates the first.

I close my eyes and pray it's not who I think. But that deep baritone is undeniable, and it's exactly who I think it is when I glance up. The guys who blabbed shit are scurrying off in the opposite direction.

Edge is at my side in only a few strides. His gaze scans me slowly from my boots to my face. "Are you avoiding me, Ninja?"

"You're kidding me, right?" I scoff and shake my head. "And here I thought I was the one who was being ignored—not that I'm pining for your attention." I don't bother saying he was the one who acted like I was invisible while I played basketball with his friends. The two, I believe, are innocent of murdering my dad. Edge... the jury is still out on him.

It's his turn to scoff. "You don't pine—"

"At least we agree on something," I interject as I pull on the straps of my backpack, tightening them on my back.

"You don't pine, you tease."

"Tease? You're full of shit." I don't give him a chance to answer. "Just because I'm not falling at your feet like every other girl around here doesn't mean I'm a tease. It means I don't have the time or patience for your fucking games."

His jaw ticks. And that twinge of excitement dances on my ego in knowing I can rile him up with only a few words. He steps closer, invading my personal space like he does when he's going to touch me. I tense, ready for the heat of his hands to trail along my skin.

This time, though, he keeps his hands to himself. He only leans down to whisper in my ear. "Are you still wet?"

It's then I shift my stance to look at him. I don't give him the satisfaction of an answer. Because I am, and I have been since his fingers glided toward my very aroused pussy and his talented mouth trailed along my neck. I shake the images out of my head, but not before he notices the changes in my demeanor or the fucking way I slowly close my eyes, only to open them to him staring at me with his deep penetrating steel gaze boring into mine.

He grins knowingly. "I'm going to take that as a yes."

Shit me!

"You should let me get you naked to know exactly what my mouth…my tongue…my hands feel like when I can really take my time before I fuck you."

Even if I wasn't wet before, he's taken care of that with his taunting. How could I have let myself be so easy to read?

Erecting my walls again, I take a step back. "I have to go."

"Where?"

I throw my leg across my bike. "None of your fucking business."

"Levi said you're going to the Halloween party with Josh."

"Yeah, so?"

"He's not the sweet, innocent guy you think he is."

I look directly at him and grin. "Who says I'm looking for a guy that's sweet and innocent?"

That statement is directed at him until I can prove he had nothing to do with killing my father. But I'll let him believe it's intended for sexual purposes. It's way more fun that way and safer.

The muscle in his jaw ticks again. "Don't push me, little Ninja."

Using my helmet to break our eye contact, I pull it over my head. "We've already been over this. And something you should know about me: I hate reruns." I kick up the kickstand and back out of the spot. Putting the bike in first, I lower my visor and take off. My heartbeat matches the high RPMs of my motor-cycle as I wind out the gear.

I need to accept that there's no escaping my encounters with Ledger Hunt as long as I'm in his world. Or at least until my dad's murderer is behind bars or dead. Only then will I be completely free.

I'm the first one to arrive at the coffee house. It's only a block away from the dojo. I've passed it a hundred times but never paid enough attention to notice it for what it is. I sit down at one of the tables near the window. Bryce and Eden pull up and park just outside the window. He's yelling at her as they get out. Eden slams the door and hollers something unintelligible back. Within the next thirty seconds or so, they're hugging, and then he opens the door to the coffee house for her, laughing as he does so.

I raise my brows. "Did you guys just have a major powwow, then make up in less than half a minute?"

They glance at each other and grin. "Yeah," Bryce says and shrugs. "That's just what we do. I hate her unfriendly ecosystem gas guzzler, and she hates me telling her every time she drives us somewhere."

I glance out the window at the antique convertible gold Cadillac. It's the complete opposite of the Tesla Bryce drives. They usually take his car, but I guess she insisted on driving today.

Bryce asks what we want, then goes to the counter to order our coffees.

"Hey, why don't you guys come by my uncle's dojo one of these coming weekends? You can meet my best friend, Luca, and see where I train."

"You mean kick ass," Eden says.

I laugh. "Sure, if that's what you want to call it. But really, I've told Luca all about you guys, and he wants to meet you."

"Is he hot and gay?" Bryce asks as he slides into the booth.

I laugh again. "Actually, yes and yes. If he were straight, I would have claimed Luca a long time ago."

Bryce raises his hands and slaps them on the table. "Hell yes, I'm in. Sign me up to get my ass kicked."

Eden shoves him. "You're too easy."

The barista calls out Bryce's name. He jumps up from the table to retrieve our drinks. "Be right back."

I twist a paper napkin around my finger, debating whether to ask Eden about Josh. I decide to bite the bullet. "Hey, what do you know about Josh Carter? When we were playing pool at the party, it didn't seem like you guys had a problem with him. I mean, is he an okay guy?" I don't tell them about the warnings from Edge or Levi.

Eden's eyes do a funny thing before darting left, then right. Finally, they land on the packets of sugar. She takes one out of the holder.

"What's that silent-ignoring-the-question thing you just did?" I wave my hand in front of her. "What do you know? You'd tell me if it was anything bad, right?"

She rips the packet and pours the sugar into a small mound on the table. "I think Josh is all right. I mean, I never had any issue with him, but—"

Bryce returns to the table with a tray of coffee. He studies us before setting it down.

"But what?" Bryce sits down at the table, not missing much today, and places our coffees in front of us. "Who are we talking about?"

I let out a resigned sigh. "Josh Carter."

"Ohhh, Josh again. Are you sure about him? I mean, he doesn't seem like your type." Bryce eyes the smeared pile of sugar in front of Eden.

"No, I'm not sure about him, but he's nice. Wait, what's that supposed to mean, my type? What's my type?"

Bryce looks up from the sugar to Eden. Is he searching her face for confirmation or permission?

I tap my fingers on the table. "I'm waiting. Please explain."

Through some best friend's telepathic link, they decide Eden is the one who should speak up. "We just think Josh might not be the best fit for you."

"I'm not trying on clothes. What are you talking about?" I have no idea why they're being so cryptic. In their lengthy pause to give me a straight answer, I blurt out, "Well, he asked me to the Halloween party that everyone is talking about, and I said yes."

"So, you like him?" Bryce asks.

Definitely no. But he's a distraction from my deliciously hot, egotistical nemesis.

I shrug. "Not really, but he seems all right." Since they're not giving anything up, I try a different tactic and tell them what I know. "Look, Venom and Josh are in my gym class. Levi overheard Josh asking me about the party, and then he warned me about Josh. And then, just today, Edge said he wasn't a nice guy. And before you guys start in on me about how Venom probably isn't the best judge, I just think it's weird, that's all. So I'm not taking what they say at face value. That's why I'm asking you guys." I throw out my arms toward them.

They look at each other again, both of them opting to use that exact moment to take a sip of their coffee. Their delay tactic won't work for much longer.

"Come on, guys, spill it." I lean back and take a sip of the sweet coffee, waiting. The caramel dances on my tongue while the whipped cream tickles my lip. I lick off the sweet goodness, still waiting.

Finally, after a full minute of staring at each other, Bryce sets his cup on the table. "At the end of junior year, Josh was accused of raping a freshman."

My mouth falls open. This wasn't what I was expecting to hear. Josh... rape. I would have never guessed those two words fit into the same sentence. "And what happened?"

"There was an investigation, but nothing ever came of it," Bryce says. "A couple of weeks after the charges were filed, they were all suddenly dropped. It's like nothing ever happened." He pauses to take a sip of coffee.

"I heard his parents have deep pockets and friends who are well-connected," Eden adds.

I sit up, leaning my elbows on the table. I have so many questions. "Nothing? He just got away with it?"

Bryce spins the coffee sleeve around his cup. "There wasn't proof."

"What about the girl? What happened to her?" I ask.

Eden draws a circle in the spilled sugar on the table. She answers without looking up. "The girl left Monarch Prep and started attending some all-girls Catholic school."

"Do you guys think he did it, or was the girl just trying to get attention?" I ask, hoping for the latter.

Eden finally looks up at me. The look in her eyes is too somber for the story to have a happy ending. "We'll never know. She committed suicide shortly after she left Monarch." She pauses to swallow before continuing. "They found her body in the girls' bathroom at school in one of the stalls. Her head was resting on the toilet seat with an empty bottle of pills next to her."

My eyes widen with disbelief. I cover my mouth with my hand. "Oh my God."

Bryce takes a sip of coffee, then sets it on the table and studies the uninteresting sleeve on his cup.

"That's not all, is it?" I ask.

He slowly shakes his head, and when he speaks, his voice drops. "No."

I glance at Eden, and she's looking at Bryce, clearly hopeful he'll be the one who tells me the main punchline of the story.

Getting the hint, Bryce looks up at me. "The girl was Ashton Kade's little sister."

My mouth drops open, but I have no response to that bomb drop. Badass, silent Kade. No wonder the guys warned me. They believe it to be completely true. And why wouldn't they? Who would commit suicide over a lie?

A more critical question is, why wouldn't they kill him for what he did?

It's impossible to fall asleep. One thousand and one thoughts slamming against the side of my skull are enough to make me want to drive a stake through it. The one that keeps playing over and over is the rape Josh was accused of and by whom—Kade's little sister. I want to ask Gunner or Edge, but it's not my place. Should I find a way to get out of going with Josh, tell him I can't go, give him some bullshit excuse? I could ask him straight up about it. But what's going to keep him from lying to me? Nothing.

I shouldn't worry about it. I have enough on my plate. But what if he did do it and tries to rape another girl? Being the vigilante I'm becoming, I almost want him to try it with me, then I could teach his sorry ass a lesson. My muscles tense at the thought of doing just that.

I glance at my phone and remember Adam's texts. "Shit!" Finding out when the next fight is should be at the forefront of my mind.

I send him a quick text back:

> Do you know the venue yet?

His reply comes fast with a thumbs-up emoji.

Maybe the pieces are starting to line up. Now, I just need to make sure I'm playing the right game.

Sending my last text for the night, I reply:

> Get me in

KINSLEY

MORE PEOPLE ARE in the library than usual. Bryce catches me this morning, asking me if I'm still considering going to the Halloween party with Josh. After what he and Eden shared with me yesterday, I'm not sure. Being the good friend he's turning out to be, Bryce gives me an out and tells me I could tag with Eden and him if I want. I tell him I'd let them know. And I need to let Josh know soon since the party is only a little more than a week away. Hell, I don't even have a costume yet and haven't even thought about what I'm going to go as. If I go at all. Staying home sounds so much easier.

I set my bag in the chair and then begin my search for the biology research book I used last time. Someone wrote a shit-load of side notes in the margins, which proved more helpful than the assigned textbook. In the far back corner of the library, rustling and low-spoken words grab my attention. It doesn't sound like people are getting it on. God knows I don't need another eyeful of another live-action sex session.

Deciding to check it out, I follow the noises. When I turn the corner around the bookshelf, a couple of guys back a younger-looking guy against the wall. Unable to keep to my own business, especially when someone is being bullied, I quietly close in on them, stealthy like a panther. I should walk away and mind my own fucking business. But the second I catch a glimpse of the fear on the guy's face, I can't turn my back. Please don't let him piss himself. I may regret my stupid decision to get involved.

"Your brother owes me money for the weed I sold him last week. He hasn't been around, so it's up to you to pay."

Great, petty drug lords. Here goes nothing. Conjuring my sexy voice up from the deep, I say, "Hi, sorry to interrupt, but can you guys help me find a book?"

The bully, holding the guy's jacket lapels, drops him. His eyes seethe with fury. His friend, a preppy blond, smiles at me as if he isn't on the verge of plowing the poor guy's face in.

"Do you want to watch? Get the fuck out of here!"

I shake my head. "Sorry, I can't do that. I really need that book."

He slowly closes in on me. I let him. The other jerk catches his friend's drift and decides he wants in on the action.

The dark-haired guy presses his forefinger and thumb to his chin as if he's debating how to handle me. "Yeah, think you can take on two of us?"

"I don't know. Maybe." I grin shyly.

"Let's find out," the blond asshole says as he waggles his eyebrows.

Sizing them up, I say, "I don't think I'll have a problem taking on the two of you." Even though my meaning differs significantly from his, I don't verbally correct him. Instead, I decide to show him.

They eye each other, grinning like the idiots they are. I swear their small cocks would high-five each other if they could. The blond moves in closer, and the dark-haired guy closes in on my other side, sandwiching me.

That's when I strike.

I knee the blond in the balls, and he goes down like a fucking rock. The dark-haired guy reaches for my wrist, but I yank it away before he can get a grip. Grabbing a handful of his hair, I jerk back his head. He reaches up for my hand as I spin him around and shove him face-first into the brick wall. He hits it hard enough to be dazed as he tries to get his balance. He fails and slumps to the ground on his knees.

I take a quick second to find the wide-eyed guy still frozen against the wall. Jerking my head, I say, "Here's your chance to get lost. What are you waiting for?"

Without a second thought, he takes off.

The blond finds the strength to stand. "You bitch," he rasps. "You just cost me two hundred bucks."

"Yeah, well, you just caused me to break a nail. So I'd say we're even." I go in with an uppercut.

His dark-haired friend watches him go down. His shit-colored eyes widen as he tries to catch his breath.

"You got a little something there." I point to the dark-haired guy. A thin trickle of blood seeps from his forehead down between his eyes. Propping my hands on my jutted-out hip, I wait to see what he'll do next. "Are you done, or do you want more?"

He decides to come at me again. His knuckles are white as rage thunders through him. Growling, he throws a punch. I dodge it and come up beside him, elbowing his kidney. Then, while he's paying attention to that pain, I pinch the pressure point at his neck. He slumps to the floor next to his friend, unconscious.

"Assholes," I mumble and consider what to do next. I never played with dolls when I was young, but I feel like I may have missed out. I undo each of their belts, then place their hands respectively over the other's dick. I wipe my hands down the front of my skirt and giggle as I turn away.

My soft laugh dies in my throat when I see Edge standing at

the end of the aisle. His expression could be construed as "Nice job, Ninja." or "What the fuck?" I'm not sure I want either one from him. This would be the perfect chance for him to turn me in and end my time here at Monarch.

"Oh, shit," I hiss. "Hey. Just a…" I throw my thumb over my shoulder to the assholes. "Just…" Still, nothing comes out of my mouth as he makes his way straight for me.

22

EDGE

"We have to stop meeting like this," I say.

"Trust me, it's not intentional." There's less feistiness in her tone than usual. I have a feeling it's the shock of seeing me that has her tongue.

Even after kicking the two douchebags' asses, she's not even breaking a sweat or out of breath. She takes a step away from me.

I peer over her shoulder. "Did you kill them, then set them up as fuck buddies?"

"No, I didn't kill them." She hesitates. "They were getting ready to pound the shit out of someone, so I stepped in and... helped." She crosses her arms over her chest. "Since you're a bully yourself, you wouldn't understand."

I laugh. "Yeah, maybe. But from what I saw, you handled it just fine." I glance around. No one else is here. "Is the guy okay?"

She looks surprised that I would ask but says, "Yeah, he ran off." She knits her brows in contemplation. "I want to ask you something."

Oh shit. Here we go. "What?"

"How come, with all of your warnings, you never told me what Josh did to get on your shit list?"

"It was none of your business."

"Nice." Shaking her head, she starts to walk away.

I grab her arm and bring her face very close to mine. "Look, Kade doesn't like talking about it."

She pulls her arm away. "Well, for your information, I don't like the idea of being raped."

It's a stupid comeback because she and I both know Josh would never be able to get that far with her, even if he had a couple of his sick friends helping him. She'd tear them apart like the two dicks on the floor behind us. And if Josh did hurt her, no one could stop me from fucking killing him then.

She looks away from me, then folds her arms over her chest again.

"He would never get anywhere with you. You know it, and so do I."

She returns her gaze to mine. "How come you guys haven't served him up what he has coming?"

I shake my head. "It's not that easy. Believe me, I fucking wish it was."

"Too much red tape and money involved?"

Nodding, I say, "Yeah, that's most of it."

Giving her credit, she doesn't ask me anymore.

I pull her shirt. She unfolds her arms and tries to pull free, but I grab her hand before she can protest too much.

"Come on," I say. If watching her fight doesn't get me hard as fuck, nothing will. And if she's anything like me, fighting gets her fucking worked up.

She resists less than I thought she would. "Where are we going?"

I don't answer as I continue to lead her to the back of the library. A couple are already making out in the corner I aimed for. I clear my throat. The guy looks up, grabs the hand of the girl, and then, without a word, they scurry away in search of another place to try to make it to second base.

I pull Ninja into the dark spot they just vacated. Tilting her chin up to look at me, I ask, "Why are you so fucking stubborn?"

"I'm not stubborn. I just know what I want and what I don't." Her voice is tender but stern, as if trying to convince herself of her own words.

"Little Ninja, you and I are so similar, but you don't even see it, do you?" I slide my hand down to her waist. She doesn't move or protest. I move it lower to her mid-thigh, just below the hem of her skirt. Her smooth, bare skin is warm against my hand. She shudders but tries to cover her reaction by shifting from her left to her right foot.

"I don't think you're going to get any studying done today." I pull on her tie, loosening the knot away from her neck. The top few buttons of her shirt are already unfastened. I push the thin fabric away from her throat.

Bending my head to hers, I brush my lips over hers as I move in for her sweet-tasting neck. The light scent of her perfume is inviting all on its own. I nuzzle her in the soft crevice where her shoulder swoops up. Her head falls slightly to the side. It's enough for me to suck the tender flesh at the base of her throat. She moans before cutting it short as if to act like she's not enjoying my touch.

"Tell me to stop and I will," I whisper against her flawless skin.

She doesn't.

My hand slides up higher along her thigh, then slips around to her ass, cupping one firm, perfect handful in my grip. My fingers dig between her ass cheeks.

"Fuck," I growl against her skin.

Her unsteady breath fans over my face. She lifts onto her

toes. The shift provides me with even more access to her body. I slide my free hand down her arm, intertwining her fingers with mine.

Her other hand grips my bicep. "Edge, we can't do this."

"Why?"

"I'm not really who you want."

"You're exactly who I want. And right fucking now," I growl against her neck.

I squeeze her ass harder before releasing my grip. Sliding my hand down to the back of her thigh, I gently pull up, raising it so that her leg is high enough for me to graze her most sensitive area with my fingertips. Her wet heat soaks through her short-ass boy shorts. She tenses, and her grip tightens on my arm. But then she lets out a long breath as her head falls back and rests against the wall behind her. Adding more pressure against her hot cunt, I rub from her center up to her clit. Her mouth opens, releasing a soft moan.

Needing to see her face, I lift my head from her neck. Her eyes are closed, and her bottom lip is trapped between her teeth. The long, dark strands of her hair rest over her chest as it rises and falls with each of her seductive breaths.

As much as I want to fucking take her right now, I'm not about to rush anything, especially in the dimly lit corner of the library. When I finally have her, I plan to take my sweet time with her body. And no matter how long I have to wait, it'll be fucking worth it.

With every ounce of willpower I've ever had to gather, I release her thigh. It slowly slides down my leg. As if waking from a dream, she languidly opens her eyes and releases her lip. I raise my fingers to my nose and inhale, praying her scent is there. Thank fuck it is. But hell, having her scent on me without actually having her is pure fucking torture.

"I can't wait to taste you," I say against her mouth.

She licks her bottom lip, the sweet, plump flesh glistening. I grind against her. Her breathy sigh feathers across my face. In a ghost-like touch, I glide my mouth against hers. Then I back away and take in the sight of her. The only difference in her appearance now from before I touched her is the lust swarming in those bright blue eyes. She can try to fight the magnetism between us, but it's no fucking use.

"I was right," I boast.

"Right about what?"

"You're just like me. Fighting turns you on." I slide my hand down her arm to take her hand, pulling her out from the dark corner. Needing to feel her one last time, I trace her cheek with my knuckles, then follow the touch with a kiss. I place another on the corner of her mouth. Not once does she fight me. I'd say that's progress. Hand in hand, I guide her back to the empty table where her bag sits on the chair.

I lower my voice. "Don't worry about those guys. If anyone says anything, I'll take care of it."

"I can take—"

I place my finger over her mouth. "I know you can. But you don't always have to take care of everything by yourself."

Surprisingly, she doesn't say anything, only nods.

I trace her top lip and around to her bottom lip. Her mouth opens just enough for me to feel her exhale on my finger. I want to slide it into her sweet mouth. Instead, I drop my hand and lean into her.

"I'd like to see you try and concentrate now, little Ninja." I swipe my forefinger under her chin.

With excruciating effort, I turn from her and walk toward the exit. I glance over my shoulder to get one last look at her. As if on instinct, her eyes lift to mine. The minute hand officially stops. My pace slows. The guy to my left, who was just studying his pencil a second ago, disappears. It's only her I see. Her usual icy blue stare blazes with heated desire. Bringing my fingers to my nose, I inhale. The intoxicating scent of her pussy invades and awakens every cell in my body. I force myself to look away from those pouty lips and mesmerizing eyes. My cock twitches as I push through the doors and head to the cafeteria.

Fuck if I know what I'm getting myself into but fuck if I can stop it.

KINSLEY

"Shit! Shit! Shit!"

I don't bother going to the usual spot to have lunch with Bryce and Eden. They'll be able to read my face and know something happened in the library that I can't explain. I can't let anyone know.

This isn't part of the plan. Getting close to him—yes. Getting him to trust me—check. But letting him feel me up—hell no! *And* wanting more of it?

Absolutely fucking not.

I stay in the library. Edge is right. I'm unable to concentrate on anything other than the feeling and the memory of him touching me, inducing sensations that make it impossible to think straight. All I want to do is touch myself, imagining my hand is his, and finish what he started. I consider going to the bathroom to do just that when I stop myself, refusing to be that desperate. Instead, I crush my thighs together and ignore the pulsing between my legs.

I skipped out on the rest of my classes, staying in the library to *try* and study. When my head feels like it's going to explode, I pack my stuff and head for my bike. I'm zipping my backpack when I look up to see Venom and their groupies standing no more than five feet away. My shitty timing sucks lately. My steps slow when the onslaught of them forms a wall between where I am and where I want to go.

The clicks of too-high heels and the heavy footfalls of boots echo off the corridor's stone walls. Seeing Brielle standing next to Edge twists my insides. Option one, I can take this chance to show the jealousy that has slithered into my chest, or option two, I can beat the shit out of Brielle, or option three, I can turn and walk away. Option three is the most responsible and mature approach, but it's also the least fun and unsatisfying. Option two would most definitely make me feel better. And after how Edge left me in the library, I already feel very unsatisfied.

After dismissing the other options, I create a new one. I let my backpack slide down my shoulder. It thumps on the floor by my feet. Without moving my eyes from Edge's, I take off my blazer, then slide down my skirt, kick it off, catch the flying fabric with the toe of my boot, and shove them into my bag. I unbutton my shirt, slide it off, then tie it around my waist. Picking up my backpack, I hang the strap over my shoulder.

"You are such a nasty slut. No matter how many clothes you take off, no one will ever want your stank ass," Brielle snaps.

I smile at Brielle. "You're welcome."

She sneers. "Welcome for what?"

For not taking option two, I say to myself. To her, I say, "For priming him."

"What the fuck are you talking about?"

I glance over her head to meet Edge's eyes. He's biting the corner of his lip as he gives me a simple wink meant for no one else. I move my gaze back to her. Then I take a step forward, with the only intention of letting her know she can't get to me.

"What, you want to fight, biker girl?" Brielle tries to provoke me as she starts toward me.

Edge places his hand on her shoulder. "Bri, I wouldn't if I were you."

She places her hand over his. He slides his out from underneath it. "What, you don't want me to break a nail over this piece of trash?"

Gunner laughs. Even I crack a smile.

Edge grumbles, "Oh, trust me, you'll have more than that broken."

Brielle ignores him. Her enraged glare is still on me.

"Keep your panties on, Brielle. I'm not fighting you." But shit me if I don't feel tingles down my spine at the idea of kicking her ass.

Catching Kade's eyes, I ask, "When's that race?"

He flicks his tongue bar. "Soon."

I smile and nod. "Looking forward to it."

"What fucking race?" the rest of them ask behind me as I walk away.

The clouds are heavy with the threat of afternoon rain. They're like a mirror image of the thoughts and feelings thrashing in my head and heart. I put on my helmet, lower my visor, and race out of the parking lot. Just because I can, I lift the front of the bike up into a wheelie.

A light rain begins to fall as I pull onto my street. I make it onto my driveway just as the heavy downpour starts. It's not the getting wet that sucks. It's the needle-like pinpricks as each drop splatters against my already-sensitive skin. I feel like it's on fire, unable to cool down from Edge's touch. I throw my bag under the porch's overhang and walk out into the rain.

I ache to have every emotion washed away, to cleanse every tear of pain, every memory of his touch. I can't have him being a distraction. I can't afford to feel something for him, but damn, he isn't backing off. And fuck if I don't want him to.

An engine revs, grabbing my attention. I open my eyes and lower my arms.

Kade idles in his Ferrari in front of my house. He lowers his window enough to shout, "Want to go for a ride?"

I've only driven in a Ferrari once. It was with one of my dad's work buddies. He took me around the neighborhood at a snail's pace. It was cool but not the way a Ferrari should be driven. My dad was more into luxury cars like Bentleys and Rolls-Royces, not fast cars. So, any chance I got to speed, I was all in.

"Give me a second. Let me change."

Taking only a couple of minutes, I pull off my wet clothes, quickly dry off with the towel I threw on my bed this morning, put on a dry tank, and slide on leggings. Grabbing a sweatshirt, dry socks, and my boots, I race out the door.

Curiosity, more than anything, has me agreeing to go with him. He barely speaks to me, much less offers me rides in his car. I'm hoping this little side gig will clear Kade from my dad's murder.

I close the door. The inside is sleek, the dash full of gauges. Unsurprisingly, there's the slight scent of weed.

"So, I know Edge didn't send you."

He shakes his head. "No, not this time."

There's a very good chance that I just got into the car with a murderer, but something in my gut tells me to trust Kade. It may be because of what I know about his sister, his loss. Could he take another life after one was taken from him?

I wait for a beat, but he doesn't elaborate as to why he followed me home. So, I guess. "Is this about your sister?"

He doesn't look at me as he explains. "He raped her. She's dead because no one believed her except me. And I wasn't enough to keep her alive." His eyes never leave the road, not even when we stop at the red light.

Holy shit, that's a heavy admission.

"Why are you telling me this?"

He shrugs. "The madness needs to end sometime."

Those words could mean a million different things, but I take them to mean two in particular: his sister needs justice and I'm possibly the one to deliver it. The delicate exchange between us opens up much more than I bargained for. Do I want to be involved with getting revenge for Venom's demons? The same guys I swore to take my own revenge on? But then another thought haunts me, is there another girl out there who might have the same fate as Kade's little sister?

"Kade." My voice sounds small and unsure.

"Yeah?" His reply is thick with sadness and anguish.

"Why hasn't Venom done anything?" I hope to get a different answer than Edge told me. I understand the red tape and financial excuses, but I need more than that. This is about rape and girl's. life

He answers without looking at me. "We can't. A few days before she was found dead, a Venom meeting was called to order. We were given strict orders, forbidden from touching the asshole." He takes a breath. "I can still see the look on Edge's face. He was on the verge of committing murder. We all were. But if they found out we even laid a finger on the fucker, it would be our asses they would have taken out. Josh's daddy knows too many other assholes in high places." He shrugs. "The day after we were warned, all the evidence disappeared. That's when my sister lost it. After everything she was dragged through, tests, questioning, the humiliation, all of it, she lost the one thing that kept us from going to the dark side. She lost hope. Hope that she would be believed or vindicated for what happened to her."

He shakes his head as his foot presses harder on the gas pedal. I grip the armrest as I look at the speedometer. Eighty-seven. I like speed, but we're approaching a red light.

"That's what killed her," he says over the roar of the engine. His knuckles are white on the steering wheel. "The next day, she took her own life. There was nothing I could do to help her."

The light changes green seconds before we blow through the intersection. I let out a breath of relief. It's like Kade either knew his timing was perfect or didn't give a shit if he killed us both.

"It doesn't sound like there was much you could have done to help her."

The engine whines just before he presses down on the clutch. He shifts up again. "I saw the exact moment Abigail decided to take her life. And there wasn't anything I could do. I was just a stupid kid. There was nothing left, just a small shell of a girl." Kade rubs his chin, lost in some faraway, hopeless memory. He shakes his head. "Her will to live died. Then, the next day, she really did. In a fucking bathroom. She was that desperate to die."

Nothing is said for several miles until he pulls into a gas station with a Quick Mart. "Every day, I'm haunted by her. I know she would have forgiven me, but I'll never forgive myself. Not fucking ever."

I wonder who he was before she died, before he blamed himself for something out of his control. "What was her name?"

He puts the car into neutral. "Abigail." He huffs a humorless laugh. "She hated it when people called her Abby." The metal bar in his mouth clicks against his teeth. "When she was in a mood, she wouldn't answer to anything but her middle name, Rose."

"Rose?" The delicate word comes out like a question. "Rose is my middle name, too."

He steals a glance at me as if to say, *Of course it is.* His nod is confirmation of something I can't pin down. "Named after your grandmother?"

I nod. "Yeah, on my mom's side."

"Same. She was a snooty old bitch." He shakes his head. "Not Abby Rose, though."

"Sounds like I would have liked her."

He scoffs. "Everyone did."

235

KELA MARQ

The pained look on his face is awful to look at. So I turn my gaze to look out the window.

"I called her Abby Rose just to be a dick. She hated it." A faint, faraway smile blossoms over his mouth. "She always answered, though."

Could this conversation be any more heart-wrenching?

His eyes have since moved from me to looking through the windshield at the convenience store. There's a long moment of silence. "Want to drive?"

The mood in the car is as heavy as a freight train. It takes longer than usual for me to answer. The topic shift happens way too fast for my head.

"Yeah, sure," I finally say. For some reason, I can tell it would please him if I did. I'm still asking why the hell I want to please Ashton Kade after the answer has already slipped out of my mouth. But the real reason is I can't bring myself to deny him after his painful disclosure.

"I'll be right back." He goes for the handle of the door.

I lay my hand over the one still gripping the steering wheel. "I'm sorry, Kade. I won't say it's not your fault or that there was nothing you could do. I'm sure you've heard those things a thousand times." He closes his eyes and then slowly opens them. "I'll only say this... I'll do whatever I can to make sure it doesn't happen to anyone else."

And there it is, sprouting up like a new little budding flower, all on its own. A promise I didn't intend to make.

He finally looks in my direction. "Be careful, Ninja." He opens the door and climbs out of the car, closing it behind him.

I slide over the center console and into the driver's seat.

Yesterday passed in a blur. I'm just happy it's Saturday, and I get to see Luca. He's taking me to pick out a Halloween costume. I'm still very unsure what in the actual fuck I'm doing, but it doesn't seem like I'm thinking too clearly about anything these days. I wear my usual Docs, cut-off jean shorts, and an unimpressive self-made half-shirt. When he pulls up to my house, I climb into his car.

I lean over and give him the biggest hug I can manage in the small space. "Hey, you!"

We untangle. His disapproving eyes roam over my outfit. "Girl, I see you dressed up for me."

"What? I'm wearing panties. What else do you want?"

He rolls his eyes as he puts the car in drive. "So, I'm thinking something masquerade-y."

"Masquerade-y? Is that even a thing?"

He touches his chest. "Hell yes, it's a thing. I'll paint on your mask so you won't have to worry about taking it off and putting it on a million times. That's a pain in the ass."

For the entire ride to the mall, he talks about how he'll do my makeup and dress me. He spares no details on what he has planned.

Ugh... the mall. I used to love the place, but now I can't stand it. Only because it's Luca, I get out of the car. He waits for me and holds out his hand for me to take.

"I'm picturing a hot two-piece black dress that shows off your defined abs. Short skirt in the front and longer in the back, layers of sheer, delicate fabric, and heels to kill for. You're going to be smashing." He squeals like we already shopped and acquired all of those things.

"Sounds like you're going to dress me up like a gag-me Barbie." I follow him around the stores like a puppy wanting a treat and act halfway excited. The truth is, I just want to find something so we can leave and get meatball subs.

"Oh my God, there it is!"

The only dress I see in the large display window that fits his Barbie description doesn't leave much to the imagination. But I have to admit, it is gorgeous.

I gasp and cover my mouth. "OMG, right! That's exactly what I was thinking. Very masquerade-y," I tease.

"I don't think that's a word, but let's go with it, anyway." He grabs my hand, drags me into the store, and tracks down a salesperson. She barely has a word out before he points to the window and says, "I need that dress in a size two."

When I go outside to look at the black two-piece dress on the mannequin again, four figures come toward me.

"Dammit all to hell," I mutter to myself. I hook my thumbs into the loops of my shorts and drop my head in hopes they don't recognize me as I duck back into the store.

Luca is busy talking with the sales lady by the dressing room. "Come on, what are you waiting for?"

Hurrying to his side, I jump into the dressing room and slide the drape closed. I pray Venom is long past this boutique when I come out. Taking longer than necessary, I slowly change into the dress.

Luca slides the drape aside enough to peek in and hands me a pair of strappy heels. "Take off those damn boots and put these on."

I try to peer around him to see if certain someones are lurking, but I can't see anyone past Luca's tall frame without looking like a completely crazy person. I pull the drape closed. It's hard to think about anything else with them here. Don't they have better things to do than wander the mall?

Finally, I tell Luca I'm done. He pushes the curtain to the side. His mouth drops open. "Kins, baby, you just turned me into a straight boy."

I laugh. He takes my hand and gently coaxes me out of the small, enclosed space into the open where everyone in the store can see. Turning, I face the mirror. The black, beaded halter top leaves a couple of inches of bare skin to the skirt's waistband. Aside from a three-inch band just above my waist, my entire back is exposed. The sheer layered skirt is short in the front, resting above my mid-thigh, then gradually gets longer until the back rests just short of the floor with the three-inch heels. I touch my scar hidden beneath the fabric and sigh in relief that it can't be seen.

My best friend comes up behind me, taking my hair and piling it into a messy bun on my head. He pulls some strands out, letting them fall around my face. "Now imagine a painted lace mask, lower on one side than the other, dusted with blue glitter to bring out your gorgeous eyes. We'll incorporate your eyebrow piercings..." He draws the imaginary mask on my face as he explains his plans for the intricate design.

When I look up and see Edge staring back at me in the mirror, Luca's words fade into a string of distant, incoherent chatter.

Luca snaps his fingers next to my head, jerking me out of my trance. "Kins, are you listening to me?"

"Yeah... yeah, I'm listening."

"You know that I know when you're lying... right?" He follows where my attention has strayed and stiffens behind me. "Please tell me he's gay," he whispers, still loud enough for anyone around us to hear.

I shake my head. "I don't think so," I rasp. My voice doesn't sound like my own.

Luca shifts to the side as Edge closes the distance between us. The others in the dressing area have all gone quiet. I don't have to look around to know they're staring at the man behind me. He's quite something to take in.

Edge reaches for my hand and wordlessly pulls me away from the small group of other customers trying on clothes. He still doesn't say anything when he glances over his shoulder at me. The look in his eyes is unreadable. Disapproval, distrust, lust, a combination of all three. He stops in between the displays of clothing and turns.

There's a small effort on my part that fights against him as he pulls me to him. It's not enough to make any difference. Before I know it, my body is flush against his, my breasts pressed against his chest. He takes notice of where our bodies are touching, his gaze lingering on the swell of my breasts. A deep, hungry growl crawls up his throat. He swallows it down and slowly raises his eyes to meet mine. For a long moment, he just studies my face. I find myself lost in the storm of his gray eyes, riding the waves of a tsunami brewing in his mysterious gaze.

He skates his fingertips up my arm. Chills follow in the wake of his feather-like touch. I close my eyes and let my head fall forward from the sweet, torturous sensation. As if tracing the roads on a map, he makes a trail with the tip of his finger over my shoulder, up the side of my neck, over the curve of my jaw, and pauses just under my chin. He tilts my face up. I open my eyes and am swept away again by the searing heat in his untamed eyes. I couldn't move if I wanted to.

He pinches strands of my hair between his thumb and finger, then slides them down until he's close to the ends. Then he curls them around his finger. With gentle force, he pulls the wrapped curl. My head follows the movement, exposing the side of my neck. He bends down and inhales. The rest of the world falls away as his lips brush against my ear, sending shivers of blazing heat over my skin. My breath catches, and I don't dare breathe.

"One day soon, I'm going to fuck you with that dress on." His voice is loud enough for only me to hear. It's desperate and raw, tender and dangerous. Already, I'm replaying his promise in my head. Fluttering sensations settle low in my belly, and moisture settles between my legs.

His mouth glides along my jawline until our lips are almost

touching. I wet my dry lips. His mouth skims over mine. Still holding my hand, he tightens his grip. I don't know if he's aware or not. I, on the other hand, am aware of every one of my nerve endings that ache for more of his touch.

He releases my hand and slides it along the bare skin of my waist until it settles on my lower back. "I'm going to assume sweet and gentle is not the way you want it." He jerks his hand, pulling my hair, which is still wrapped around his finger, to make his point. "Is it?"

I whimper in response. The fact that he knows me in this way is as disturbing as it is arousing. I hate myself for reacting to him, his touch, his words, like I'm a lovesick girl. It's the last thing I am, but fuck, if it doesn't take effort not to collapse against him.

"No," I whisper.

He lightly kisses the hollow space between my shoulder and neck. Slowly moving his mouth to my ear, he plants a soft kiss just beneath it. His hand squeezes my waist. To anyone looking on, we appear to be a couple, or at the very least, we seem to like each other. And he's telling me a secret. For me, though, he's too close, dangerously close. A threat of the worst kind. Skillfully seductive. I still don't know what his motives are, but he's found a way to infiltrate all of my boundaries and take control of my body before I can escape.

His lips brush the shell of my ear with each word he whispers. "The next time you touch yourself, I want you to imagine my tongue trailing up the inside of your thigh to your throbbing clit."

He kisses my neck. I'm frozen in his embrace and his taunting words. My lips are the only thing to move, parting as I visualize the seductive image. As if making good on his promise, his lips part against my neck, and his teeth graze the tender flesh, nipping, then stop just short of piercing the skin.

I jerk at the sudden ignited pain. He holds me tight against him as his tongue soothes the bite. Shivers of need course through my body. My breaths quicken into shallow gasps. I swear I can feel him between my legs.

"As you're rubbing your clit and pushing your fingers deeper into your wet pussy, imagine it's my tongue sliding through your slick folds and my fingers curling up into that sweet spot until you're coming harder than you ever have in your life."

It's with those final words that my knees weaken, and his grip on me tightens, holding me upright.

"That's right, hold on, Ninja baby." He takes my lower lip between his teeth, biting it hard enough to create delicious pain throughout my entire body. Then, achingly slow, he glides his tongue along the tender flesh. "What I wouldn't give to slide my fingers inside of you right now to see how wet you are for me." He places a delicate kiss on my swollen lips. "I would bet my life that you're fucking drenched."

Holy fucking hell.

He's not wrong.

"Until then…little Ninja." He uncoils my hair. The ringlet falls against my cheek. His hand drops from my waist. Relaxing his lustful gaze, he frees me from his mesmerizing hold. It seems like hours have passed as if I were transported to another time and dimension.

In a daze, I make my way back to the dressing room. Luca doesn't say a word as he slides the drape closed after me. Taking a minute to regain my composure, I sit on the round, pink, cushioned seat in the corner. Each time Edge touches me, the pull drawing me to him intensifies. It's electric and captivating as fuck. I'm drowning in the intoxicating ocean of Ledger Hunt.

I change out of the dress and hand it to Luca through the open seam of the curtain. After the few moments it takes for my breath to return to normal and for me to change back into my shorts, I join Luca at the counter.

The sales lady arranges the dress on the hanger, places it in a garment bag, and then hands me a bag containing the shoes.

"How much is the total?" I ask.

"You're all set, dear."

I look at Luca, then back at her. "But I haven't—"

"The handsome gentleman who was in here a few minutes ago paid for your purchase. He took care of it while you were changing." She hands me a small piece of paper. "He also asked me to give you this."

I unfold the note. Written in neat handwriting is a phone number.

The second we leave the store, I look up and down the mall for Edge. He's already gone. I'm not sure if I'm relieved or disappointed.

Luca spins me toward him. "Girl, you listen here. You are buying me a big, fat, dripping mozzarella meatball sub and telling me everything there is to know about Prince Charming."

Absentmindedly, I nod. The first thing Luca needs to know about Edge is that he's neither Prince Charming nor a knight in shining armor.

He's a poisonous viper, prepared to strike at any moment, and he doesn't pretend to be anything else.

24

KINSLEY

AFTER MY CONVERSATION WITH KADE, I decided to go to the Halloween party with Josh. If he does try something, I'll be ready. As I did last time, I tell Josh I'll meet him at the party. Needing to stay in control of the situation, I don't want him to pick me up.

Luca is on his way to do my makeup when I get a text from Adam. It's short and sweet:

1127.10p269sw10s

I've been to enough UG fights to decode the string of letters and numbers: November 27th at 10:00 p.m., at 269 SW 10th Street.

He's done his first part by getting me the fight's time and location. Now, he needs to get me in so I can do my part. Even though I'm still trying to figure out what that is. I know Venom will be there. The venue might change, but the gamblers and murderers are guaranteed to come out and play. After all, the UG is their game.

I take the dress out of the garment bag. It's more stunning

than I remember. The images Edge planted in my head at the dress shop have haunted me all week. When I got home from the mall, I texted a simple thank-you to the number on the piece of paper the woman at the dress shop gave to me. I had to assume it was Edge's number. When the response came back, I had all the confirmation I needed... *One day soon.*

As usual, Luca doesn't knock when he arrives. He waltzes right into my bedroom and sets down his makeup bag on my desk. "Kins, you are going to have the hottest costume there." He kisses both of my cheeks. Luca is never flamboyant until he starts talking or shopping for clothes or makeup—the two things I suck at. "I'm going to assume you're clean because of the towel on your head."

I smell my armpit. "Don't I smell clean?"

He waves me off, ignoring my question, and takes the towel off my head. "I'm going to do your hair, then makeup, then put you in that beautiful gown."

"Most guys try to get girls out of their dresses," I tease.

"Girl, I've already seen you naked more times than I care to count. And as perfect as your little body is, it does nothing for me, babe. Sorry. Besides, you already have a taker in that department. And if he's not the one, that come-fuck-me dress is a calling card for any guy you have your eye on tonight." He taps the tip of my nose. "And don't try to hide it. You know as well as I do that is what every straight guy is going to be thinking when they see you tonight."

"Luca!" I spin in the chair to look at him. "You know that's not the goal here."

"Whatever." He brushes my comment away with the flick of his wrist.

Over meatball subs, I told him about Edge. At least the trivial details: he drives a Jeep, is popular, and is in a couple of my classes. I wanted to say to him more, but it wasn't time yet. Luca's only advice was to wear a condom. So, I especially didn't tell him that Edge said he wanted to fuck me with the dress on, but that was obvious enough in the dress shop.

What my best friend did share was his thoughts about me backing down, to leave my dad's death alone, and wanting me to believe what the rest of the world was told, that his death was an accident. I know Luca doesn't believe this. It's just his way of trying to keep me safe.

Luca taps his phone screen, chooses a hip-hop playlist, and then gets to work. Almost two hours later, he's done. Thank fuck! I'm not one for being pampered. The prodding and poking —not my thing. But if I complained or fought Luca about it, he would have tortured me by making the process three hours.

He places his hand on the back of the chair. "When I turn you around and you see all of my glamorous and hard-as-hell work, you're going to love it. If you hate it, bitch, you better lie straight to my face."

I laugh. "I can't imagine I'll hate it. I just might not be as comfortable looking as glamorous as you want me to be."

He puffs out a breath. "Don't go there." Luca covers his mouth as if haunted by a thought. His eyes widen to the size of beach balls. "Oh, Jesus on wheels! Please tell me you're not riding that crotch rocket to the party."

"Of course not. Eden is coming to pick me up. Now, can I please see your masterpiece?"

"Oh, thank fuck for small gifts." He lets out a relieved sigh. "Okay, here we go, the reveal. Ready?"

"Yes!" He turns the desk chair to face the mirror. My breath hitches. "Luca, I look... I look... Holy hell. Amazing. I mean, I'm not trying to get all cocky and brag on myself, but damn. I'm bragging on you. Look what you did."

He tosses his head to the side and fans his face in all his glory. "I know, I'm a goddess. But I have to give you credit, too. You give me a beautiful canvas to start with."

The intricate lines of the lace mask look so real. My blue

eyes are brighter than usual with the ombre of royal to light blue colors. My hair is in a sophisticated, loose bun with long tendrils curling on either side of my face. I have no words. The girl in the mirror looks so refined and sophisticated. I pucker my pale pink lips. I can't stop staring at myself.

"There's only one rule," he says, holding up a poised finger.

"Do I have to be home by midnight?"

"Girl, as hot as I made you, you better not come home at all."

I most definitely have intentions of coming home... alone. "Then what's the rule?"

"Do not touch your face. I put a finishing spray on it to help it stay in place, but don't rub your eyes, itch your cheek, or let those hot lips of Mr. Edge trail across the mask in any way. He must know he has boundaries. Stay to the areas of lips, neck, breasts..." He gives a dismissive wave. "You know the places."

"If you could see my face, I'm turning red."

"Yeah, right. The last time you blushed in front of me was with anger when I kicked your ass and made you tap out." He gives me a knowing look. "Listen, I know you can't stop staring at your stunning self, but let's get the dress and heels on. Then you can admire the entire costume."

Twenty minutes later, the doorbell rings. I open it to find Eden in jeans and a sweatshirt. I give myself another quick once-over. "Shit! I am waaay overdressed."

She doesn't speak, then stammers, "No—no. You look amazing."

Luca steps up behind me. "That would be all me."

I look over my shoulder and smile. "Eden, this is Luca. Luca, Eden."

"Kins has told me all about you and your bestie. It's nice to finally meet you," he says, extending his hand.

She shakes it. "Thanks. You, too."

"Can we be any more formal?" I roll my eyes.

"Please forgive her. She isn't the most polite creature," Luca says. "Especially when she's all dolled up."

"Ready to go?" I ask Eden.

"What are you?" Luca taps his lip, checking Eden out. "Wait —let me guess. An angry college student on the verge of rebelling against uniforms."

She laughs. "My costume is in the car. Bryce and I are going as an avocado. Each of us is a half. I'm the one with the pit."

"Very clever," Luca says.

I kiss him on the cheek. "Will you be here when I get home?"

"I told you not to come home."

I give him the dumb face. "And I told you to come, but you'd rather spend your evening with Trey, eat pizza, and watch old Bruce Lee movies."

"You won't watch them with me."

"You're right." I'm jealous of his simple, laid-back plans. "I'll see you later then."

"Call me if you need a ride home." He rubs his hands together as if concocting a wicked plan. "Hopefully, you won't," he sings.

"Thanks, Luca. Love you."

"Love you back," he says. "And I want every effing dirty detail of the night."

I follow Eden down the driveway. "Bye, Luca."

"Wait!" Luca hollers from behind me. He races after us and hands his phone to Eden. "I need a pic! Do you mind?"

We pose as she takes a few pictures. "Thanks," Luca and I say as she hands him back his phone.

He gives me one last hug. "If you need me, I'm here," he whispers into my ear.

"Love you." I release him.

"Me, too."

"Send those to me," I call over my shoulder to him and climb into Eden's boat of a car. Thankfully, it's not a small car with the layers of fabric I need to tuck inside. "Thanks for picking me up. I didn't want Josh to. If I meet him there, it's technically not a date, right?"

"Absolutely right."

Bryce is standing outside the large, modern beach style house when we arrive. Most everyone is dressed up. There are funny costumes, sexy ones, scary and clever ones, like Eden's and Bryce's.

"Holy shit! You look amazing, Kinsley," he says.

"Thanks. But I may not make it the whole night in these shoes."

Josh sees me just as I see him and hurries over.

"He's been looking for you since I got here," Bryce says.

"Yay me," I say flatly.

"Hey, Kinsley. Wow! I mean, whoa. Your costume is awesome. You look gorgeous."

He's dressed as the Phantom of the Opera. I didn't think I mentioned what I would be, but ironically, we kind of fit together. He reaches for my hand, but before he can take hold of it, I slip it away, pretending to adjust my hair. Nausea becomes a swirling entity in my gut when I look at him now. Before, it was just that I wasn't that into him. But now, after Kade told me about his sister, there's a yucky writhing sensation I have a hard time ignoring. I want to ask him straight up, but I'm not sure tonight's the night.

"A lot of people are inside," Bryce says.

"I heard there's a hedge maze in the backyard," Josh says.

"Of course, there is. We're at Mikayla Winward's house," Eden says as she points to a group of girls. "There's the guest of honor, sexy Medusa."

The name doesn't jostle any faces in my memory until I see Brielle draped on her arm like an accessory to her costume. Oh, that Mikayla, one of Venom's groupies.

"This is considered a mansion," Bryce corrects.

Josh nudges my arm. "I'm thinking we should hit it before it gets busy."

I don't look forward to going in there with him, but I still agree, hoping he'll forget. "Yeah, sure."

Carved pumpkins line the steps up to the front doors. Walking through the entrance is like walking into another place entirely, a haunted house, to be precise. Hundreds of black lights flicker, flashing against large, gruesome figures and monsters. Spider webbing streams across the stair banisters to high chandeliers. Either the Winwards are professional holiday decorators or they hired one. The place looks amazing.

A smorgasbord of sweets is splayed over the landscape of the massive dining room table. Bowls, dishes, and silver serving trays are layered with chocolate and candy of every flavor imaginable.

Straight through the house, toward the back, more lights and decorations surround the pool area and yard. A wooden dance floor is set up behind the pool's waterfall. To one side of the dance floor are round tables with black tablecloths and ghostly decorations, and to the left, tables overflow with finger food and drinks. Several bars and carnival candy booths are also set up on their sprawling lawn.

"Why don't you grab us a table and I'll get us drinks?" Josh suggests.

I take Eden's hand and pull her along with me. "Let's sit over there."

Only twenty minutes have passed, and as much as there is to see, I'm bored out of my mind. If it wasn't for Bryce and Eden, I would have ditched already. More people have arrived, and several are dancing. Finally, the music is loud enough that you have to yell to be heard over it. It's beginning to feel like a party.

"Want to dance?" Josh asks.

"Sure." I'm not the best dancer. I move my hips and sway, adding a little bounce or jumping occasionally, depending on the song's beat. Not that it matters. Dancing isn't what I came here to do.

He follows me out to the dance floor. As I begin to move, he steps in closer and goes to reach around my waist, but I dance away, creating much-needed space between us. I bump into the person behind me.

"I'm sorry—" I begin, then turn to see it's Brielle and cut off my apology. Peyton and Mikayla are standing with her.

Brielle's eyes narrow, then widen when she recognizes me. "Your costume is... interesting. Didn't anyone tell you it's a Halloween party, not a masquerade ball?"

Looking her up and down, taking in her devil horns, skimpy low-cut red leotard, wicked pointed tail, and pitchfork, I laugh. "Since you dressed as yourself, I could ask you the same thing."

She takes a step forward, then sways as she retreats. "You're not worth it."

I could probably catch a buzz from the potent stench of alcohol on her breath. I don't respond, nor is there a chance to, before Venom comes up behind her.

She sees my shift and turns around, laying her hand on Edge's chest. "Hey, baby." Glancing over her shoulder at me, she gives me a bright smile. "Trash here didn't get the memo that it's a Halloween party, not a masquerade."

The four guys who make up Venom are all dressed in dark pants and black shirts, each wearing a different creepy clown mask. Even with the mask, it's easy to tell them apart. I wish I had the same sense when they were in the cage and my dad was killed. Then all of this bullshit would be over.

Edge removes Brielle's hand from his chest as his eyes stay fixed on me. I look around for Josh, who found a friend to talk with. So much for using him as a distraction. Without a word, I make my exit from the clown and devil group, weaving through the crowd of gyrating bodies, not bothering to tell Josh where I'm going. Hell, I don't even know. Even though I'm outside, I feel like I need some fresh air. In the far side of the yard, under an oak tree, is a popcorn machine and a cotton candy machine.

"Hey, where are you going?" Josh calls after me.

I keep walking as I call out an answer to my so-called date. "Saw you were talking with your friend and thought I'd get a snack. Brielle's presence makes me want to throw up and run in the opposite direction." I mumble the last part to myself.

He picks up his pace and is next to me as I order popcorn and cotton candy. "How are you supposed to eat both at the same time?"

I stick out my tongue into the popcorn bag, a piece of popcorn sticking to its tip.

"Nice." He looks at the server. "I'll take the same."

He thanks the guy. Together, we walk to one of the benches under the lit tree. He pulls off a piece of candy and tries to feed it to me.

"I have my own, thanks."

Deflated, he lowers his hand. He's trying way too hard. Or maybe I'm trying too hard to avoid him touching me in any way.

"Why don't we go check out the maze after we finish these?" he suggests as he holds up his popcorn and cotton candy.

"Sure."

I hate the fact that I decide to go only to see if he'll try anything with me. And I know I don't owe Kade anything, but if Josh did rape his sister, then I bet there have been others, and there will be more.

The anticipation has small doses of adrenaline starting to course through my veins. Maybe Brielle sparked the need for me to pick a fight and get physical. "Let's go now."

"Yeah?" He licks his lips as the smile on his face grows. He gets up, takes my treats, and tosses them in the nearby trash can. This time, when he reaches for my hand, I let him take it.

A familiar silhouette stands near the pool. Our eyes lock with one another. Edge dangles the string of his mask from his fingers as he watches me go into the maze. His glare is as dangerous and dark as the storm at the beach a couple of weeks ago, those dark clouds threatening to overtake my blue sky. A small red bead of light ignites as he inhales from a joint. Smoke seeps out between those perfect lips like a thick layer of fog rising into the night air. For some unknown and incomprehensible reason, knowing that he's watching me and who I'm with brings a sliver of comfort.

As we near the maze, distant laughs and screams come from somewhere within. It's exciting and creepy.

"Ready?" he asks. The smile on his face is cunning instead of his usual innocent boyish one. "Come on, it'll be fun."

I follow his lead as we head into the maze. We twist and turn through the narrow path, hitting a dead end, then laugh as we maneuver back the way we came. The farther into the maze we go, the darker it gets. Something isn't right about this. Uneasiness begins to spread through me. The creepy sensation prickles at the base of my neck, slithering down my spine. I have to stay on the balls of my feet to avoid my heels from sinking into the dirt.

Josh suddenly stops. I bump into his back. Abruptly, he whips around to face me. Our mouths are mere inches apart. "What are you doing?"

"Giving you what you want. You've been playing with me since you started school. Flirting with me, playing hard to get like the cockteaser you are."

And here we are, folks, introducing the *real* Josh Carter.

All of the distant giggles and teasing have ceased. Only the music from the house can be heard.

He grabs hold of me, wrenching me flush against him.

I try to give him fair warning. "You don't want to do this."

"Yes, I fucking do. You think you're all mysterious and quiet, but I know your type. You can't wait for a guy like me to take control and fuck you senseless."

I push him back, but he barely moves. I warn him again before I let loose. "Josh, you don't want to do this. From what I've heard, you've already gotten into trouble for pulling this. Didn't a girl die or something?"

"I didn't fucking kill her. I was just the one who gave her what she asked for, then she decided it was a mistake or some bullshit."

There it is, his disgusting and sardonic confession.

"I was hoping those rumors about you were lies. I trusted you," I plead as I gag on my own words. "I don't want you to hurt me."

He holds me close as I pretend to put up a fight by twisting back and forth. Luca's warning about not smearing my makeup pops into my head. Granted, it comes at a very inopportune time. But there it is nonetheless. My best friend is going to kill me. He wanted me to get laid, not get into a fight.

"Trust me, it won't hurt a bit," Josh purrs.

I go completely still. He relaxes a fraction, believing I've caved and he's won the right to rape me.

Time's up.

"Well, I can't promise the same," I growl as I grab his arm from behind my waist, pulling it hard as I spin away from him and slip around to his back. When I yank his arm behind him, he howls in pain. He ducks under, out of my grasp. I lose my footing and stumble back. *Fucking heels!* I'm going to kill Luca later for making me wear them instead of my boots.

I lightly punch him in the chest. My way of letting him think he has the upper hand. We're face to face when he comes at me again.

"Come on, baby. That's right. Give me a little fight to keep it interesting."

"You seriously need help." I thrust my hand up into his nose.

Not hard enough to kill him, but enough pressure to cause blood to gush out.

He touches his nose. Blood coats his fingers. "You bitch!"

"Yeah, I've been called that before by assholes like you." I kick out my leg and catch the back of his. He goes down on his knees. Before he has a chance to get to his feet, I serve a kick to the side of his head. The short front of the dress makes the maneuver easier than I imagined. He falls onto his stomach. I manage to stay on my feet. The spikes of my heels sink into the soft dirt, grounding me in place. Maybe not kill Luca, just wound him a little.

Josh flounders a bit as he tries to get to his feet again. I round on him, then shove at his back before he can stand. Bending down, I grasp him around his neck in a chokehold that only those who have had training could get out of. From the way his body is starting to go limp from lack of oxygen, it's easy to guess that he's not one of them.

I loosen my hold so he doesn't lose consciousness. "Looks like you fucked with the wrong girl this time, huh?"

"You cunt!"

I tsk. "Is that all you got?" Without tightening my hold, I jerk his head back farther. He grunts in pain. The blood from his nose smears the bottom half of his face and drips onto my arm. Uselessly, he uses both hands to pry my arm away from his neck. "Josh, listen very carefully. You will turn yourself in, or I will do it for you. I have the means and the connections to make your life a living hell. So, you will admit to raping Abigail Kade and anyone else you raped. Then, when your ass is in prison, you'll get yours. Just like you deserve."

"No fucking way. I didn't do shit."

I tighten my hold. In the near darkness, I watch as his face swells from the lack of oxygen. "Let's try this again. The desperate feeling you feel right now, the god-please-don't-let-me-die feeling, the feeling of being helpless, paralyzed, desperate for a gasp of air, all of those feelings are nothing compared to the pain I can cause you. With only my bare hands, I could hurt you beyond repair, worse than anything your sick imagination can conceive."

One of his hands, slick with his blood, loses its grip on my arm. "Fine," he growls.

"Great! I'm glad we had this little chat." I apply just the right amount of pressure to his airway. His body goes limp under me. I'm not convinced he'll confess, but at least it's a start. I stand up, smoothing down my dress. Without thinking, I flip Josh's limp body over and kick him as hard as I can in the balls. "Fucker."

I go to wipe my face, then stop. Luca's words ring in my head. I still need to go back to the party, and I don't want to look like I was just in a fighting match with a rapist.

Clapping from behind me has me jerking around to see my audience. Edge and Kade stand at the bend in the maze. I make my way to them, remembering to walk on the balls of my feet to keep my heels from sinking into the dirt.

Kade pulls me into his arms, hugging me tight to his chest. "Just seeing him get the shit beat out of him puts a smile on my face. I owe you. It's not all he deserves, but I'll be able to help with that." He holds up his phone to show he caught the whole thing on video.

I pull away. "The only thing you owe me is a race."

For the first time, he delivers a genuine, complete smile. He gives Edge a fist bump before heading out of the maze.

"How did no one come and see any of that?"

"Kade and I had the area blocked. You guys were at a dead end, so it made it easy. Besides, most people are already drunk."

Without a word, Edge takes me into his arms. I lean against his chest for a beat before he takes my hand and leads me farther into the maze, deeper into the darkness.

EDGE

MY EYES NEVER LEAVE NINJA. I trail after her as she slips through the crowd into the darkness. I wonder where she's going by herself but refrain from following until I notice Josh follow her out.

She's up to something, and I want to know what it is. Plus, I'm not about to let Josh lay a finger on her. If I'm being completely honest, I also have the menacing hope to get him in a dark place—despite my orders—to kick the fucking shit out of his pussy ass.

I jerk my chin at Kade. He gets up and walks in the direction I indicate. After peeling Brielle's hands off me, I push her drunken ass back into the chair. "Stay the fuck away from me, Brielle."

"Come on, baby. Don't leave me. Dance with me." She tries to stand but falls over. Her friends catch her before she lands on the ground.

I follow Kade outside. He pauses at the entrance of the maze. A few people run out, cheering that they found the exit. We blindly walk through the tall hedges until we hear Josh's faint voice. He's laughing and making stupid-ass jokes. I don't hear my little Ninja, but she's with him. I can smell the faint scent of her perfume.

Kade peers around the corner before walking right up on Josh as he starts to manhandle and grope Ninja. The shit he says to her has my blood fucking boiling. Kade starts to step in, but I grab his shirt sleeve and shake my head. He looks at me like I've lost my damn mind. I want to kill the fucker, just like I've imagined a thousand times in a hundred different ways. I swore if he ever touched Ninja, I would end him. But like always, she has the situation under control.

"What the fuck?" Kade mouths.

"She's got this," I whisper back.

He does as I ask, but I know it's killing him not to jump in and break Josh's face himself. He's had his sights on Josh Carter for two years. And now, here's his chance to take him down and save the girl. It's the perfect excuse to get revenge for what he did to Abigail.

Josh and Ninja go back and forth. I can tell she's playing with him. She's the hunter, and he's her prey. He doesn't see it that way, but I have no doubt he will. And soon.

Steam practically comes out of Kade's head. He starts forward again, and again, I grip his sleeve to stop him.

Ninja lets Josh make his first move. He grabs her, a sloppy hold she easily maneuvers out of. Then she delivers her first strike just above his ear.

Josh swipes at the side of his head. "That wasn't very nice."

"Maybe it has something to do with you trying to take something I'm not giving."

"Oooh, looks like you enjoy playing rough. This is going to be fun." Josh starts for her again. His hands reach out and yank her forearm.

I hold my stance. My fist is pressed to my mouth as I try to remain calm.

She spins out of his hold. As she comes to face him again, the lines of her face are smooth with determination and anger. I've been dancing in the cage and on the mat long enough to know what that look of fire means. She's done playing. The next time he starts for her, Ninja doesn't waste time. She punches him in his face. Bones crack, and blood spurts from his nose.

"You bitch!" Josh wipes his upper lip on the sleeve of his shirt.

Kade watches the entire scene in awe. He glances my way a couple of times, but otherwise, his eyes are glued to the action, like mine. Watching her fight is the hottest fucking thing I've ever seen in my entire life. She's in a sexy as fuck dress, kicking the shit out of a rapist, avenging a girl she's never met, and doing it all in fucking high heels.

In a futile attempt, Josh grabs the layers of fabric of Ninja's dress—the dress I fucking bought her. I swear to fuck, if he tears even a thread, I'll jump in and help her. But as I watch the very one-sided match, my little Ninja has everything under control.

With Josh's grip on the fabric, she closes the distance between them and maneuvers him right where she wants him, lining up his body in perfect order with hers, his front to her back. She throws back her elbow, slamming him in the face again. The prick falls back on his ass. His hands are covering his banged-up, bloodied face.

I tilt my head, listening for the cries of pain. I don't hear anything. When I look back at them, she's choking out the fucker. Ninja's words are low, but I hear something to the effect that he needs to make things right. Then, within seconds, Josh Carter is nothing more than a limp heap on the dirt.

Ninja delivers a final, unnecessary blow, a swift kick to his dick. It's hard enough to make me wince and cringe in imagined pain. If the asshole were conscious, his cries would have been heard a mile away.

"Better than any MMA fight you've seen?" I ask Kade, already knowing his answer.

"Holy fucking shit," he says under his breath. "What the fuck just happened?"

I don't say anything. I don't have to.

I didn't know what she was up to. I only knew whatever it was, she would be able to handle it. The only thing she hasn't been able to handle is her feelings for me. I'm the unruly kink in her well-orchestrated chain. And I like it that way very much.

Miraculously, her painted mask is still perfect. Her hair is a little messed up, but fuck me if I want to yank the rest of it out of that hair clip, pull the shit out of it until she's staring up and seeing only me.

Kade can't help but start clapping.

Ninja jerks her head in our direction. The shocked look on her face at seeing us is priceless. She lets out a deep breath. Her eyes meet Kade's before they catch mine.

Conveniently, my best friend brought a bottle of water. After he hugs her and they exchange a few words, he opens the bottle and pours some on her arm to wash away the asshole's blood. I hate that even specks of the fucker's blood mark her skin. Kade pulls off his T-shirt and wipes away the filth. She scans Kade's body, paying particular attention to his side. Something in her posture visibly relaxes.

After Kade helps her clean up a bit, I go to her. They've had their sweet moment. Now it's time for me and her to have ours. She falls against my chest, all of the emotions no doubt catching up to her. She's a fucking badass, but there's a soft girl under that hardened fighter exterior, and I want that sweet side right now more than I've wanted anything in a very long time.

"It's okay. I got you," I murmur, and her body relaxes against me. "After what you just threw at him, he'll be out for a while."

She nods. "I hope the asshole doesn't wake up for a long time."

"When he does, he's going to be instantly reminded you

kicked him in the nuts when they're double their size and painful even to look at."

She chuckles. "Fuck, I hope so."

I slide my hand down her arm, which is still slick with water, and link our fingers together. "Come on." I lead her to the darkest part, only the moon lighting our way.

"How did you know?" she asks.

"I saw him follow you to get cotton candy, then into the maze. I wasn't sure he would try anything, but I knew you'd be ready if he did." I shrug. "And I wanted front row to the show." I was also there for backup in case things got too intense, but I don't tell her that.

"Is Kade okay?"

I smile. "I don't think he's been this okay in a long time."

I sit on a bench in another dead-end corner and pull her onto my lap. Sliding the pins from her hair, I toss them on the ground. Her hair falls loosely around her face. "You look amazing."

She smiles coyly. "Thank you for the dress."

"I wanted you to have something from me. And something I can take off anytime I want."

She gently hits my chest. I grab her hand, keeping it there. She has to feel my heart beating wildly under her palm. I slide my hand into my pocket and take out the earbud I stole from her at the library.

"I was wondering where it was."

"You can have it back after."

"After...?"

Pressing play on my phone, I place the earbud into her ear. The first beats of "Under Your Scars" by Godsmack filter through the tiny speaker, playing only for her.

I tilt her head so that she's facing me. Her eyes are blue flames of scorching heat. "Come here."

Gently, I cup the back of her neck, then draw her to me. For once, she doesn't hesitate as her lips press against mine. They open, and she slowly eases the tip of her tongue between my lips. I know she's on a fucking high from the fight. The adrenaline is still coursing through her veins. And I'm taking complete advantage of the situation. But I don't fucking care. I deepen the kiss. There's never going to be enough time on this planet that I'll get sick of the feeling of her against me.

"I want you," I say against her swollen lips.

I grab her waist and ease her up. I turn her around so her back is to my chest and angle her head so she's looking up at me. Kissing her, I run my hand over her bare stomach.

I whisper in her ear without the earbud, "Do you remember what I said the last time I saw you in this dress?"

Breathily, she whispers, "Yes."

"Did you make yourself come when you got home, imagining it was me touching you like this?" I slide the tips of my fingers into the band of her skirt.

Her breath hitches against my mouth. "Yes."

I love her unashamed answer. She reaches her arm around the back of my neck. I slide my hand in deeper until I feel the edge of her silk panties. She sucks my bottom lip into her mouth.

"Fuck, baby," I groan.

The thin band across her hip exposes more skin than her usual boy shorts. The silky, barely there thong she's wearing has only been in my fucking dreams until now. Desperate to feel her, I inch lower until I'm cupping her hot sex. She moans against my mouth. My dick threatens to rip the seam of my jeans. But tonight isn't about me.

"I know you want to hate me, but you can't. Can you?" I kiss a trail down her neck until I reach the path of her collarbone. I sink my teeth into the delicate flesh. She cries from the sensual pleasure of my bite. Stopping just before breaking the skin, I suck the tender area, soothing it with my tongue. "I also know you want to fight against me touching you like this, but you want it too bad. Don't you?"

Her thighs slightly relax. Working my hand under the edge of her panties, I feel the smooth skin of her slick folds. Fucking hell. Her pussy is searing. I glide one finger down the center to her dripping opening, then back up, trailing her wetness over her swollen clit.

"Fuck." She moans the word as if it's a sinful prayer to beg for mercy.

Mercy is the last thing I'll give tonight. I've waited too fucking long to feel her writhe against me. Achingly slow, I slip through her sex, back and forth, until she's moving against my hand. Unable to wait anymore, I slip a finger inside. She's so fucking tight as I push in a second one. She rises onto her toes. Her nails dig into the base of my neck. Her other hand is layered over mine at her waist.

Sliding my fingers out, I use her wetness to sweep my thumb over her clit. Her mouth pulls away from mine.

"Look at me," I demand, craving to see the desire in those blue eyes as I take control of her. With effort, she does. "I want you to see only my face when you come for me."

Her hips slowly rock to the rhythm of my hand.

Fuck, if my dick isn't as hard as a rock. I press it against her lower back. "Fuck, Ninja."

Her thighs tense. She's getting close. I work my fingers in and out of her as I rub her clit harder. She begins pulsing against my hand. With the layers of the dress between us, she covers my hand with her own, holding it exactly where she wants it. Her body has no choice but to heed the orgasm consuming her. The only thing I wish is that I were fucking inside of her right now, riding out the hard pulsating waves with her, spilling inside her, claiming her.

"Holy fuck," she pants as the final spasms rake through her.

She collapses forward. I fold my arm around her and remove

my fingers from her wetness, holding her as I turn her toward me. I sit back down on the bench and pull her onto my lap again. Her legs rest on either side, facing me. My cock is nestled beneath her. I can feel the heat through my jeans, and it's pure agony of the best kind.

She's still catching her breath as I take the fingers I used to get her off and place them in my mouth. She tastes better than I ever could imagine. And fuck me if I don't think about it a lot. I've jerked off to this exact moment more times than I can count. Tonight will be no exception.

"The next time I taste you, it'll be from the source." I whisper the promise against the shell of her ear.

She doesn't say anything in response. I don't care or expect her to. All I know is that if I can make her come that hard with just my fingers, I can't wait to see the pleasure spill from her as she writhes against my mouth.

She squirms on my lap, rubbing against my cock. I know she could easily go again and then again, coming for me until she's too exhausted to move. One day.

I pull out the earbud and place it on her palm. "So, is this what your motorcycle feels like when you straddle it?"

She laughs and closes her hand around it, thoughtfully looks up, contemplating, then says, "Almost. But my seat is softer than your cock under my ass, and I bet you're not nearly as fast."

"Want to try me?" She lightly chuckles. I push strands of her hair away from her face. She leans into the light touch. "So I was right," I say.

"About what?"

"You being fucking drenched." I wrap her hair around my hand, then pull her mouth to mine. I brush my lips against hers. "Someday soon, I will fuck you in that dress," I promise again, not wanting her to forget. Her eyes look deep in thought. "What's wrong?"

"The song you played, *Under Your Scars*. Why?"

We all have scars. Some are deeper and more jagged than others. Without her scars of anguish and loss, I wouldn't be with her right now. From the moment I saw her, I wanted her. I claimed her as mine. I don't know how long I'll get to keep her, so all I want to do is sink into this moment and live under her scars.

"It fits us," I say, then bite her lower lip, dragging it between my teeth until it slips free. "It just fits us."

26

KINSLEY

"WHERE DID YOU GO LAST NIGHT?" Eden asks.

Hmm… let's see. I kicked a rapist's ass, then I got off by the leader of Venom—who may or may not be a killer.

After Edge and I went our separate ways Saturday night, I called Luca to pick me up and take me home. I wasn't sure where I stood with Edge—if anywhere. It's not like we have anything else except this crazy strong attraction to each other. He wanted to drive me home, but that would have been a very bad idea. The trust issue I'm developing with myself is becoming unhealthy. Which, by the way, I had to tell myself over and over that I deserved that mind-blowing orgasm after kicking the shit out of a rapist. Then I screamed into my pillow for half an hour, telling myself how stupid and weak I was for wanting it so bad.

Aside from the not-so-regretful mind-blowing orgasm, I found out Kade did not kill my dad. I'm not sure how obvious my perusal of his torso was, but I wasn't about to let the opportunity pass without catching a glimpse of his shirtless body. Hence, the only one left of Venom, who I'm not sure is a killer or not, is the one who masterfully summoned the otherworldly epic orgasm out of me.

What if they're all innocent? The idea never occurred to me. What if I've had this whole thing wrong from the beginning? No, there are too many coincidences, too many tells... right?

Eden and Bryce came by the dojo to check it out. Luca showed up a little after they did. He began showing Bryce a few entry positions and moves. By the looks and laughs from each of them, both seem pretty happy to be dom and sub—I mean, the teacher and student. I catch Luca's expression a couple of times, and he has a huge smile each time. His eyes also have a glint that may or may not be naughty.

"Want to walk across the street and get a couple of subs?" I pull Eden to her feet from the mat.

"Sure." She's not nearly as invested or excited about learning martial arts as Bryce. But if I had to guess, I bet Luca has a lot to do with that.

"We'll be back. Going to Val's," I call over to Luca. "You want the usual?"

"Yeah," he grunts as he holds Bryce in a submissive position and proceeds to teach him how to maneuver his way out of it.

As we walk out, a guy with dark hair and a toned fighter's build comes in. "I'm looking for Trey Mitchell."

"Yeah, he's in the back. I'll get him," I say.

My uncle is sitting at his desk doing paperwork.

"Hey, there's some guy here to see you. He looks very MMA-like."

He sets down his pen and removes his glasses. There's a long sigh as he gets up and goes out into the main room of the dojo. "Can I help you?"

"Yeah, I want you to train me."

My uncle slips his hands into the pockets of his joggers. "I'm sorry. I can't help you."

He turns away and goes to walk back into his office when

the guy grabs his arm. Uncle Trey's eyes light with disbelief and fire as they intersect the stranger's.

The guy instantly drops his arm. "Sorry, man. Listen, I heard you're the best around here and—"

"I don't train fighters who fight for money," my uncle interrupts.

The steroid juice or whatever he's taken has him reaching his next level of anger fast. I want to ask him where he's fought, but I don't want to give anything away to any of the other company in the room.

"It's not for—"

"Please leave," Uncle Trey cuts him off.

The guy glances around the room, stopping his gaze on me. "Do I know you?"

He may, but I deny him the answer he's looking for. I may have seen him in one of the underground fights, but there's no way he would recognize me. I used to have blonde hair and always wore a mask with a hoodie. "No, I don't think so."

Mr. MMA huffs, then storms off. His fists are as tight as iron. He pushes the door open hard enough that it slams against the concrete wall.

Without a word, my uncle returns to his office.

I follow him. "What was that all about?"

"He's just a guy who thinks he can win a few bucks beating someone else at the game. It's not about that. There's no respect in what they do."

I'm quiet for a moment as he picks up his pen and continues to do whatever he was before I interrupted him. "Eden and I are going to Val's. Do you want anything?"

"Sure, I'll take a piece of her pie. Doesn't matter what kind."

"You got it."

He looks up. "Kinsley, you know why I said no to him, right?"

"Yeah, I get it." I know we're both thinking about my dad, the position he put himself in in that cage, and what it ultimately led to. I sweep a tear away before it builds enough momentum to fall.

He nods solemnly. "I'm sorry." There's so much sorrow and genuine regret in those two words.

"Me too."

Eden is waiting for me by the door.

"Everything okay?" Luca asks.

"Yeah." I pull on my baggy boho pants and slip my bare feet into my boots.

Eden holds the door open for me as I pass through. "So, are you going to tell me?"

I still haven't answered her about where I went last night. I'm not ready to tell her about Edge. But I want her to trust me, so I need to give her something. And I like Eden. She's a good person. I just have to be careful with my words.

"I went into the maze with Josh."

She grabs my arm, jerking me to a stop. "Was that you who beat the shit out of him?" When I say nothing, that's enough of an answer. Her eyes bug. "What happened?"

I close my eyes and shut out the pain of all the girls he hurt who couldn't defend themselves. When I open them, Eden is staring at me with empathetic kindness. Her eyes are soft, but her face is filled with concern.

I give her a half-shrug. "He tried to take something that wasn't being offered, something he thought he was entitled to. And unfortunately for him, he went up against someone who could take care of herself."

Edge and I left before the maze was supposed to get busy. I wasn't about to hang around to see what happened when Josh came to.

"Holy shit!" Her voice drops a little. "So what happened to that girl was true?"

I don't have to confirm what she already knows.

Very unlike the Eden I've come to know, she wraps her arm around my shoulder as we continue walking. "You know, I knew I liked you from day one."

We both burst out laughing at her blatant lie.

"I'm pretty sure you couldn't stand me for at least a week."

"Nah, not the whole week. I knew you were good people the moment you had my back in the cafeteria. I just misjudged and misunderstood you."

As honest as we're being, I leave out the intimate moment between Edge and me. There's a part of me that wants to tell her —to tell someone, for fuck's sake. But I can't. I have no idea what he and I are or what the hell is even going on between us. All I know is I keep telling myself to keep my distance emotionally. But my betraying body has plans of her own.

Although I can't deny our attraction for each other, I have to stay on course with my plan to take Venom down. As sure as I am that they're involved in my father's murder, I'm beginning to think someone else is pulling the strings behind the scenes. Edge is the only one who I haven't discounted as being the murderer. Figuring out who did it and making that person pay is the only thing that matters. There is no other option. If using him in the process also has orgasmic benefits, so be it.

Val has a few customers waiting who already placed their orders. "Hey, Kins! How are you, sweetie?"

Eden's head jerks toward me. "I'm guessing you come here a lot?"

"Yeah, at least once a week." I turn back to Val.

"You and Luca want your usual?"

"Yes, please. Also, Trey wants a piece of today's pie."

She writes the order on a small pad. "It's key lime. And for you?" she asks Eden.

I tune them out as Eden orders for her and Bryce. The bell on the door jingles, catching my attention. I look over my shoulder as Gunner, Levi, and Kade stroll into the place like they own it. They're in compression spats with baggy shorts and tight shirts—clothes designed for grappling. Where's Edge? Then I notice one of the waiting customers moves closer to the wall. Another tightens themselves against the condiment counter. I silently laugh and shake my head. Fucking Venom and their scare tactics.

I refrain from asking about their missing friend. It's none of my business. And besides, I probably don't want to know where he is as Brielle's face pops rudely into my thoughts.

"Look who we have here. If it isn't the masked beauty," Gunner says.

I smirk. "The one and only."

Kade catches my eye and jerks his head to the back of the sandwich shop.

"I'll be right back," I tell Eden. I give Gunner and Levi a look of warning. "Be nice."

They both hold up their hands in unison. "Promise," Levi says.

I head toward Kade. Once we're in the back, Kade lowers his voice. "Josh told the police he was jumped last night, but he didn't see who did it."

"And?"

"Nothing. That was it."

I fold my arms over my chest. "So, basically, what you're telling me is that he needs a reminder?"

His lips curve up into an almost half-smile. "Something like that."

I nod. "I'll take care of it."

I can't bring myself to ask him where Edge is, but the question must be evident on my face because he says, "He's with his father."

For some reason, I never pictured Edge and his father doing stuff together—like father and son shit. I relax and try not to let my relief show.

KELA MARQ

But I'm not as smooth as I think because Kade says, "He didn't go home with anyone last night."

I shrug one shoulder and bite the tip of my thumbnail. "Yeah, if he did, it isn't any of my business."

He's quiet until I finally look up at him. His stare is set dead on my face. "Yeah, it is."

"Why do you say that?"

He rubs his hand over his shaven head. "I've known Edge almost my entire life, and since you walked into our lives, he's been distracted."

"So? That doesn't mean anything."

"It does to him."

I'm still not sure what he's getting at, so I keep my mouth shut. But he and Gunner have said similar things about him now.

"Ninja, all I'm saying is don't break him. He's been broken enough." And with that, Kade pats me on the head like a puppy, then joins his friends in their usual booth. That guy's tone never changes. He could tell you the worst news possible or the best news ever, and he would deliver both in the same deep, unemotional voice.

I'm not sure what to do with the information he just told me. I'm still conflicted with my feelings toward Edge, but I don't like that someone hurt him to the breaking point. He, of all people, seems to be indestructible, invincible even. I wonder who's capable of such a thing. Then I think of myself and what I'm fighting for. I could be that person who brings him to his knees. I silently hope that Edge is innocent.

Because if he isn't, I'll have no choice but to do just that: break him.

After practice, me and Luca head back to my house to chill before he has to head home.

"It's your birthday next week, and we are going out. I won't take no for an answer." Luca lies back on my bed and folds his arms behind his head.

"Fine! Putt-Putt and milkshakes." We plan to celebrate my birthday next Friday, Luca style. I make him promise to keep it simple and that there will be no shopping, no heels, and no exotic makeup involved.

"Fine!" he yells back, then laughs. "You know birthdays are a big deal."

I curl up on the bed next to him. "These days, not much seems like a big deal."

He wraps his arm around me. I lie against his chest. "Your dad loved life so much. It would kill him to see you *not* living and enjoying yours."

"This is the first one he's ever missed." A tear falls from the corner of my eye and drips onto his shirt. I can't hold it back, no matter how hard I try. I'm overdue to have a good cry. It's been several weeks since I really let it all loose. Holding it all in, trying to handle all the bullshit coming at me lately, only allowing myself to let a tear fall here and there, isn't nearly the release I need. There's another pressure that I can no longer take. The weight of it is suffocating me.

I sit up and face my best friend. "Luca, there are some things I need to tell you." I can barely look at him as I prepare to release more than just tears. "I didn't tell you before because I didn't want you to worry and..."

He gently lifts my chin so I can look at his kind face. "You didn't want me to stop you."

I shake my head. The unpreventable tears begin their descent. "I'm so sorry."

"Hey, Kins, it's me." His voice is as supportive and compassionate as ever. I wonder why it took me so long to get to this point. "I'm here, so tell me now. No matter what it is, I promise I'm not going anywhere." He plays with the few strands of hair that have fallen away from my messy updo.

For the next two hours, I tell him everything, from sneaking into the underground fights to watching my father die, the real reason I wanted to attend Monarch University, my vow to destroy Venom, kicking Josh the Rapist's ass, my nightmares, and finally, Edge and the tangled mess I've gotten myself wrapped up in.

Luca listens, asks a few questions, and listens some more. He takes in every detail, sentence, and syllable as I lay out all of my spiraling feelings of pain, fury, confusion, lust, all of it. I try to explain how Edge makes me feel, how he consumes my thoughts and all of my senses, physically and emotionally. The hardest part to explain is the perplexity of my heated desire that constantly collides with the fear that he's guilty, equaling a massive clusterfuck at its finest.

"You know what pisses me off the most?"

"Um, everything you just told me?" he teases.

I laugh. "Yeah, that. And the fact that Edge is an entirely different breed from all the standard dicks. The way he let me handle Josh. He wasn't there for a show. He was there if I needed him. He trusted me to carry out the punishment, had faith that I could do it, and that alone shows respect. He's more intuitive than most, and that's the part that does me in. But what I hate most is that I'm unable to hide from him. He knows exactly what he does to me, how I can't seem to resist him no matter how hard I try. He senses what I want, what I'm thinking, or what I need, then carries it out perfectly. We won't talk about the times when he left my lady bits screaming for more of his touch." I slam my fist against the pillow and groan. "What is wrong with me?"

"Absolutely nothing."

"That doesn't help." I snuggle closer to Luca. "I just need to try harder to force all of that shit back. Stuff it into a corner in the back of my mind where the cobwebs can grow over it. He's part of a fighting crew that kills for sport. I have a feeling his dad has something to do with Venom. It was the way Kade told me he was with his dad yesterday. It felt off. So, what then? What if Edge turns out to be the son of a killer who I intend to pay back for what he took from me? And if he goes down with his dad, then—"

Luca presses a finger to my mouth. "Don't finish that sentence. You may regret it."

That's the only advice he offers, those few words of wisdom. I love that he never tells me comforting lies. This conversation was long overdue, but Luca isn't mad. Luca is Luca, my best friend.

I'm suddenly exhausted. My night of confessions spent more energy than twelve rounds in the cage. Luca holds me until I finally drift off to sleep.

When I wake, cool empty covers are next to me. Luca must have left before the sun rose. I'm so grateful to have him in my life. He stayed with me, knowing I needed him here, even though he had to rush home early to get ready for school. As I become more coherent, I hear rain splattering against the window.

"Shit!" I don't want to wake my uncle.

I reach for my phone to text Bryce since he lives closer than Eden. My phone dings with a text as my thumbs hover over the keyboard. I crawl out from between my warm sheets. I assume it's a text from Luca. But the text isn't from Luca. It's from Edge:

Be ready in 20

KINSLEY

EXACTLY TWENTY MINUTES LATER, a sleek matte-gray BMW pulls up in front of my house. The window slides down. Edge is sitting in the driver's seat. He looks hot as fuck without even trying. I can only see his white button-down, the Viper tie hanging loosely around his neck, and a dark, expectant expression. It's the opposite of inviting, more like daring me to challenge him.

"Are you going to stand there staring and continue to get soaked, or are you going to get your ass in the car?"

Those words are enough to snap me out of my trance. I open the car, then slide in. The door closes with a swoosh of finality. He's got me in a car with him. I'm trapped, doomed.

You're so stupid.

What's worse is I'm not looking for a way out. I wipe the raindrops from my face with the sleeve of my blazer. I haven't even looked at him yet, and already this has *bad idea* written all over it. I pull the seat belt over my chest, then click it into place.

He tenderly touches my damp cheek. I look over at him. Slowly, he glides his finger down the side of my face through drops of rain I missed.

"Why do you look like this is a bad idea?" He doesn't give me a chance to respond before he answers his own question. "Because you wouldn't be wrong." Those few words have so many layers, I don't even know where to begin to decipher them.

Am I that transparent or does he feel the same way? "It is," I agree. "A very bad idea."

He leans over the console and grips my chin between his thumb and forefinger. In the small confines, there's very little distance to cover. He tilts his head and brushes his lips with mine. The lightest touch sends shivers down every one of my nerve endings. He's gone too soon when he settles back into the driver's seat. His rolled cuff exposes his tan, lean forearm as he grasps the steering wheel. He pulls away from the curb.

My eyes follow the seductive movement of his mouth. He bites the corner of his bottom lip, and I don't think he knows how sexy it is. But then again, this is Edge. He's very aware of everything he does.

He gently lays his hand on my thigh. His thumb lazily glides back and forth on my bare skin. My back is warm, and I realize the seat heater is on. Fuck, I do not need any added heat right now. The sensations stirring low in my core have nothing to do with the heater toasting my ass. Edge has personally taken care of that detail with that tender kiss.

"I think you should let me take you somewhere and get you out of the wet clothes," he suggests.

The pressure of his touch on my leg increases. I rest my head against the headrest and close my eyes. Bad idea. Bad idea. Bad idea.

He continues with the fantasy I can too easily imagine. "Then, when you're thoroughly dry, except for the wetness pooling between your legs, you let me taste you properly." Just from the deep sensual suggestion of his tone, I could fucking come. He traces the seam of my panties with a featherlike touch.

"Edge." My voice is raspy and pleading. It's too much. I place my hand over his to stop the rush of sensation of what he's promising. My pussy screams at volume ten that I've lost my damn mind. "We can't."

Dejected, he asks, "Tell me, why not?"

I roll my head to the left to look at him. "Because we…" I don't even know what a reasonable argument is, except I can't dive any deeper into whatever this is until I know for sure that he didn't have anything to do with my dad's murder.

His slate eyes catch on mine. I feel raw and exposed, as if he just stripped me of all my defenses.

His face turns stoic. "You have secrets, Ninja. We all do. But something tells me yours are going to fuck up whatever this is."

He doesn't have to indicate what *this* is. *This* is us. An invisible link between two people, drawn together, each wanting nothing more than to give in to their animalistic desires—rip each other's clothes to shreds, then fuck like it's the last day on earth until we're completely spent and sore.

He moves his hand from my thigh, resting his elbow on the center console.

I don't trust myself to say anything, so I stay quiet. It's safe here—at least for a little bit. But my silence only does one thing, confirm his accusations. It dawns on me that he didn't call me little Ninja, just Ninja. I wonder if I graduated to some unknown level or if he's trying to be less condescending.

We drive in silence for several minutes. Low music I can't make out fills in as muted background noise.

"Thank you for picking me up."

He nods once. "You're welcome."

I'm not usually one to fill silence with meaningless small talk, but the moment is too heavy. Without thinking, I stick with a generic topic. "Are you doing anything over Thanksgiving break?"

"Probably dinner. You?"

Something else seems to have his attention, but he's trying.

"Same, dinner with my uncle." The conversation is so normal. There's no challenge in his tone or fight in mine. It's easy.

"Nice." He sounds genuine, but hints of jealousy cling to the simple word, and I wonder what triggers it. "You don't spend Thanksgiving with any other family?"

"No." I shake my head. "Not this year. My mom is away, and my dad is..." I glance out the window, watching the rain form perforated streams along the glass. "He passed away a few months ago." The words just kind of tumble out. I didn't ever plan on talking about my dad's death with Edge, unless it was to confront him.

He glances at me. "I'm sorry."

Most people who heard that would ask what happened to my dad. Edge doesn't. I'm thankful for this, but it also spikes the needle on my skepticism meter. Maybe he doesn't ask because he knows exactly what happened to him. Since I'm still figuring all this out, I simply reply, "Thanks."

It's quiet again for the next few miles. If I don't say something to derail my instant sadness, my mind will ride on the carousel of grief for the rest of the day. "I might drive my motorcycle up the coast."

His gaze slides to mine, then slowly returns to the road. "What... or who is there?"

Is that jealousy I detect? For some fucked-up reason, that gives me a sliver of joy. "Shark teeth."

His hand loosens around the steering wheel, a pink hue returning to his white knuckles. "Shark teeth?"

"Yeah. I like to sift for them."

Edge's stiff posture relaxes against his seat. He angles himself to look at me. "Shark teeth?"

"Yeah. They're not great white or Megalodon size. They're tiny black fossil teeth." For whatever reason, I feel brave and comfortable telling him more. So I do. "The beach is my happy place. It's one of the only places, besides the mat, where my mind doesn't wander off into dark and deserted corners."

He doesn't respond, and I think I may have given too much away. I fold my hands in my lap and look out the passenger window again.

"I know how that feels," he finally says. "It's exhausting."

He places his hand over mine in my lap. Even though the heat settles in my core with his touch, it's a gesture meant for comfort, not sexual. He stops at a red light and then glances over to me. He seems so lost in thought, as if something is consuming him from the inside. I know I shouldn't, but I lace our fingers together. His mouth softens, but his eyes remain hard and focused on me.

The light changes, but he doesn't take his foot off the brake.

"The light is green."

He slowly shakes his head. "I don't care."

He glides his hand from mine, up my arm to my shoulder, under my hair, then gently rests it on the back of my neck. He guides me closer to him as he once again closes the distance between us. Pressing his lips against mine, he lightly draws his tongue over the seam of my lips. I open them a fraction.

A car blares its horn behind us. Edge doesn't flinch or rush to move away from me. He pulls back a few inches to look at me, then gently kisses me again before returning to his side of the car. He presses down on the gas, propelling us forward.

We don't speak another word until we pull into his self-appointed parking spot at school.

"I miss this parking spot," I tease.

His chuckle is deep and sexy. "You can have it."

I shake my head. "Nah, you might lose credibility, and people might start to think you're nice."

"I would park on the other side of town just to watch you get off that Ninja motorcycle."

I laugh. "Yeah? The other side of town, huh?"

"Every damn day," he confirms.

I turn to look at him. "Thanks for the ride."

His windows are so dark that no one can see in. I'm still conscious of people seeing us together. I don't need any more shit stirred up after I finally got free of Brielle's claws. Not that I can't handle her, but I don't need to give her another reason to start her petty shit with me again.

"I think it's best if you go back to ignoring me," I suggest.

His expression tightens, then relaxes. It's only a quick change, but I see it. "As you wish. But you might want to be careful in the library." The devious grin presents itself, then dashes right back behind the curtain again, only a brief preview of what's in store for me.

That's only three hours from now. What the fuck is this guy doing to me? Just with those few words of warning and teasing, heat stirs low in my center. I keep telling myself that as long as I stay focused on the main goal, I can have a little fun along the way, right? It's just knowing when to stop.

Fuck me to hell. That's the part where I'm not sure where to draw the line anymore. I'm allowing Ledger Hunt to slither his way under my skin like a fucking snake. It doesn't matter how much I try to fight against it because fuck if it doesn't feel all warm and fuzzy for now. But it's the bite that's coming that scares the shit out of me.

"I'll get a ride home from Eden or Bryce." I spin the hoop in my eyebrow. It's a habit I used to do more frequently.

He nods, and I'm grateful he doesn't try to pull his macho bullshit, insisting on taking me home.

I'm not sure if we should talk about Saturday and what it means or leave it alone. I want to know what's going through his head. I want to know what the fuck is going through my head and try to make some sense of it.

One confusing thought keeps circling in my mind. I might

not know where I stand with him or even where I *want* to stand, but I need to know how deeply he's involved with Venom and the illegal fights.

Pulling the reins on my thoughts, I reach for the door handle.

Edge presses the lock button. "Listen, I don't know what the fuck is happening here." As always, he knows exactly where my thoughts are. "I know you have a shitload of secrets that you're not ready to share, but I have to tell you that it pisses me off how bad I fucking want you."

There's a long silence after his admission. He runs his hand through his hair. It's like the words he was only thinking decided to free themselves, and now he's not quite sure what to do with them. The radio is no longer playing. The heat in the car is rising too fast with the ignition shut off. My blood begins to pound through my veins as my heart wants to beat out of my chest.

"I'm not sure what to say to all that." Another long pause passes before I continue. "I mean, I don't know what or if there is anything between us—"

"Are you fucking kidding me!" he cuts me off.

Needing to diffuse his anger without giving him more to feel heated about, I place my hand over his. "Listen, I have no idea what I want. I've lost a lot in the last couple of months. My dad. My home. My mom is off somewhere playing house. And most of my shit is in boxes in some storage unit. The only things I know and have for sure right now are my motorcycle, my generous uncle, the dojo, and my best friend, Luca, the guy you saw me with in the dress shop. Those are the staples in my life right now. I mean, I have no idea about you and Brielle. On again, off again. The way she touches you, she thinks you're hers. Hell, maybe you are. I have no fucking idea."

And then there are the million reasons why we can't continue down this dangerous path.

"What else?" he pushes.

I hate the fact that he doesn't deny being Brielle's, but I continue with new vigor. "Like you. I hate the way you make me feel. I'm not used to feeling like I'm subordinate or weak or vulnerable. It's not in my nature to feel helpless." With all my energy spent explaining, I crash. In a hushed voice, I admit, "With you, I do. I feel all of those things—like I'm at your mercy."

His jaw ticks with anger. What the hell does he have to be so mad about? Now, I'm the one getting pissed.

"You never denied that you and Brielle are an item." Jealousy is not a thing I've ever known. But with him, I want to peel the skin off Brielle's face when I see her touch him, which is the last thing I have the right to feel. The worst part is that she knows it and so does he. No matter how hard I try to conceal those feelings in front of her and even him, I know they see through my mask of indifference. I've never been that great of an actress. Hell, I even failed drama class in ninth grade. Pretending has never been one of my strong suits.

He looks at me. "I shouldn't have to deny or confirm anything with her. I thought I made how I feel about you pretty obvious."

I don't know what to say to that. My emotions are jostling around like a beach ball at a pool party. I reach for the door handle again.

"Ninja, I haven't touched her since you walked in on us. And even then, it was you I imagined I was fucking, not her."

Fuck! None of this was supposed to happen. No feelings. No touching. And especially no heat blossoming low in my core as he confesses shit like this.

My hand rests on the cool metal. I tilt my head down so he can't read my face. I close my eyes and try to erase how they looked together. It was in his eyes that day that he already told me everything I should know. The image and the feeling that I wished I were the one with him that day hit me like a boulder.

He grabs my wrist and pulls me to him. "Stop fucking denying this."

He's anything but gentle as his mouth slams against mine. The want and need for him override every rational thought. His tongue sweeps over my lips, and he forces his way through the tiny slit, taking possession and all of my control with it.

He pulls back, both of us breathing heavily. "Just so you know, Ninja, I'm done ignoring you. In front of others, I'll respect your request. But when we're alone, you're mine." He bites my bottom lip, dragging it through his teeth, then licks the tender flesh. "Mine," he repeats.

My breath catches in my throat. Deep inside me, an unfamiliar spark ignites with his possessive claim over me. It should piss me off, but it does the exact opposite.

Mine. His claim over me doesn't escape my mind the entire day. *You're mine. You're mine. You're mine.* It's on repeat, reverberating against my skull. Concentration is not a very good friend today. Thankfully, Edge gave me more space than I assumed he would after his declaration.

The relief when my final class is over is substantial. I head to the parking lot toward Eden's Cadillac. While fumbling with my jacket, I don't notice Josh until he's right in front of me.

"A word, please." His tone suggests it's more of a command than a pleasant request.

I lower my voice to a growl. "I heard you didn't do as I told you."

"Like I would go to prison for those sluts wanting to be fucked. They should be thanking me. I was nice enough to give it to them—and good, I might add." A sick slash of satisfaction settles over his mouth. His pride and ego are clearly running the show. His self-righteous confidence makes me want to throw my gloves down right here.

"You keep telling yourself those fucked-up lies. Because it's those lies that are going to have you begging on your knees for forgiveness."

"Yeah, right," he says. Laughing, he throws up his hands. "And there's not a damn thing you can do to make that happen."

I take a step closer to him, then lean in. "You should know, the other night was just a taste of what I could do to you. I could bring so much pain down on your ass that you may never walk again, or worse, you'd never be able to get your fucking dick up again." I tap my finger against my lips as he snarls. Grinning, I add, "Hmmm, yeah, that might not be a bad idea. One less rapist in the world sounds good."

He tries to take a step back, but I grab his wrist. "Get your hands off me, or I'll sue you. You know my dad—"

"Is a piece of shit like you, yeah, so I've heard. It seems you guys like twinning it. You're both dick-less and think women are yours to do whatever you want. I'm here to remind you that they're not!"

He jerks his hand away. "You can't prove anything," he spits.

"Josh, listen carefully. I know what you intended to do to me, what you were planning. You thought you knew exactly what I wanted, and you were going to be the one who gave it to me nice and good. So there's that, my word against yours. But this is the part you'll want to pay close attention to." I grab him again, digging my nails into his forearm. Wetness pools under my fingers. He tries to pull away. I tighten my hold as I loop my boot around the back of his leg, planting it at the heel of his loafer. "Not only could I kick your ass into tomorrow, but there's shit on you now—a video of you in action. And I think that alone will be enough to dig up every shred of evidence your daddy buried to keep his sorry-ass son out of prison. Then your ass would really be in a sling before you even have a chance to get your dick up."

His face turns a few shades lighter with that little detail. I drop his wrist. Blood is smeared across his skin and my fingers.

I look at my hand in disgust. "I'm getting tired of having your blood on me." I wipe my hand down the front of his white shirt. Stunned, he looks at his arm, then at his shirt. The idiot's eyes widen when he sees the blood. "This is the part when you say, 'Okay, I'll go make things right.'"

He growls with rage as he storms off. He knows I've got him by the balls. This time, he can't run.

Eden comes up next to me. "What the hell was that all about?" She unlocks the door and climbs into her car, slamming the heavy door behind her.

I climb into the passenger side. "Josh is being difficult. I told him to turn himself in, and he was an asshole about it." I shrug. "So I had to up my game. I can't let him get away with what he tried to do to me or what he's already done to others or will do in the future."

"You're a hero." She turns the key. The engine roars to life.

I scoff. "Yeah, don't go that far."

"You are!" she argues.

She might retract that statement and her friendship if she only knew what I plan.

KINSLEY

"Birthday time!" Luca bursts into the kitchen holding a bouquet of at least twenty balloons, a cookie cake, and a small, wrapped gift. "I see you counting. There are twenty-one, to be exact. Nineteen, for obvious reasons, plus one for good luck. And the giant birthday one because it was a must-have." He hands the balloons to me as he sets the cookie cake on the island.

"Luca, you're making me look bad," my uncle says when he enters the kitchen, eyes wide. "My gourmet breakfast of an omelet, bacon, and toast is flying right out the window."

I tie the balloons around the dining room chair. Then I hug my uncle around the waist. "Breakfast was amazing!" My eyes shift to Luca. "As for you, this is way overdoing it."

"What, a guy can't spoil his best friend?"

"Of course you can." I hug him. "Thank you!"

He hands me the wrapped present. "Here, open it."

"This can't be better than what Uncle Trey gave me," I challenge.

Luca's face falls as if it were a real competition. "What did he give you?"

"A free lifetime membership to the Serpent's Spear Dojo," my uncle says proudly.

I bump his shoulder. "That and a trip to Venice Beach. Well, a hotel room for the weekend whenever I want to use it," I add.

Luca looks at my uncle. "Nice one, sensei."

"Now, let's see what's in here." I pull the ribbon off the small package. My fingers slide under the purple foil paper, exposing a black jewelry box. Usually, I'd be nervous to open a present like this. You never know if you're going to like it or not. All the while, the person who gave it to you thought it would be the best gift on the planet for you. But I must admit, I never feel that way when Luca gives me something. He knows me too well. Plus, he usually has better taste than I do.

I slide off the lid. A silver chain with a lotus flower pendant lies on the soft velvet pillow. "Luca, it's beautiful." I take out the delicate piece of jewelry and hold it up to the light.

"Want me to put it on?" he asks.

I hand it to him. Turning around, I move my hair over my shoulder.

"There," he says.

I walk into the den to look at the mirror and smile as a grateful tear runs down my cheek. He comes to stand behind me.

"I love it," I say to his reflection.

"I knew you would. As full of badassery as you are, you're still my fragile and beautiful flower," he says. I turn and hug him fiercely. He pulls back. "Okay, enough with all the sappiness, let's go have some fun."

"Yeah." I look at the mirror one more time. The pendant is cool as I touch the flower. "It's perfect."

Luca kisses the side of my head. "Like you, my little mud flower."

"Hey!" I slap his shoulder. "That's not nice."

"Actually, it is. Lotus flowers grow in mud." He takes my

hand. "Also, we have to grow through the mud to reach the sun. And I think you're almost touching that golden light. I know you're going through a lot right now. Just know that I got you. We'll get through it all together."

Tears fill my eyes. "I hope you're right."

He nudges my arm. "Did you forget that I'm always right?"

I laugh and push him back. "Yeah. Yeah." We head back to the kitchen. "Uncle Trey, you want to go play Putt-Putt?"

"I wish I could, kiddo, but my women's class is at eight."

"Don't they have anything better to do than learn to fight on a Friday night?" I ask.

"I think this is something they look forward to," Luca says as he winks.

"Ugh!" I mock a gag, putting my finger in my mouth. I kiss my uncle on the cheek. "I won't be too late."

"Have fun!" he calls after us.

On our way to the car, Luca says, "I have another surprise for you. I invited a couple of your friends, so don't be mad."

My heart jumps in my chest. Edge pops into my head. The image of him playing something as simple as Putt-Putt makes me laugh. Even though his declaration that I'm his scared the shit out of me, my excitement grows all the same. "Who?"

"Eden and Bryce. They're meeting us there."

The disappointment in my chest weighs heavier than I imagined it would. But fuck, did I really expect Luca to invite the king of Venom to play Putt-Putt? "Great," I say, trying to sound thrilled—which I am. Bryce and Eden are good people.

"Yeah, I thought you'd have more fun than if it was just us."

I get into his car and slam the door shut. "Luca, that is the biggest freaking lie you have yet to tell me. Because first off, we have a wicked good time all on our own, no matter what we're doing. And second, you hate when I beat you at Putt-Putt, so I know you wouldn't want an audience. Finally, the real reason you invited *my* friends is more for your sake than mine—maybe your *and* Bryce's sake, to be exact."

He holds his hand over his heart. "Kins, you wound me with your words." Starting the car, he says under his breath, "But you might be right, even though I will forever plead the fifth and say you have no idea what you're talking about."

I roll my eyes. "This has everything to do with you being sweet on Bryce, and this is the perfect opportunity for you to see him again. So, shut up, and let's go so I can kick your ass in front of your boyfriend." He goes to protest, but I hold up my hand before he can say anything. "But I think it'll be a blast, and I'm glad you thought to invite them."

He smacks his lips. "Damn, girl! Fine, I admit it! You're right. Is that what you want to hear?"

"Yep, that'll do." I flash him a wide smile for the win.

He backs out of the driveway. It's probably better that he didn't invite Edge. God knows what would have happened. I don't need any of my friends forced to witness our make-out sessions.

Although I can visualize in detail what would happen in the cave, behind the waterfall, on the way to the ninth hole…

Shame on me.

KINSLEY

THE RIDE UP the coast is beautiful. I packed a towel, my strainer, a Ziploc baggy for the teeth, a few snacks, and a bottle of water. Today's trip will be a quick turnaround, rather than staying here overnight. With my motorcycle, it's easy to find a spot close to the stairs leading down to the beach. The sky is blue, the air is only slightly cool, and the waves are as low as they'll get this time of year. It's the perfect day for hunting for shark teeth. The beach is slightly crowded due to the holiday, but there are still plenty of spots to claim and look for teeth.

The past few weeks have gone by in a blur between classes, homework, training at the dojo, and seeing Luca on the weekends. This week, his family took their usual vacation to the east coast of Florida to visit his grandparents. They spend the entire week there, so for me, that sucks. I was invited, but I didn't want to leave my uncle on Thanksgiving.

Edge has been hit and miss. I watch as he avoids Brielle. Brielle tries to avoid me. I mind my own business while only talking to Eden and Bryce. So, all is right at Monarch University.

At least, that's the way it looks on the outside.

More than once, Edge found me in the library and made up for ignoring me in front of others. He's also kept his promise about staking his claim on me when we're alone. It seems we're both taking what we want while still trying to figure out what we need from each other. It's complicated.

To make it even more complicated, I plan to attend the fight in a couple of days to see what Venom is up to. On the night of the last fight, six guys stood off to the side of the fighting cage, and there was the fighter inside the cage. He remains a mystery. I haven't been able to rule out Edge. He has a mysterious tattoo on the same side as Python. He's aggressive, dominant, and the leader of Venom. I just don't know who else is involved.

I've gone over every intention Edge could have for being the bad guy. More so, I've made a ton of excuses for him to be innocent. I need to see his tattoo. With Python's etched in my mind, I'll know in an instant if Edge is the one who killed my father. And if he didn't, what role did he play in his death? If any?

I strip off my shirt and shorts, then retrieve my strainer from my pack and dip it into the water, dredging it through the sand. Sitting on a cluster of rocks, I sift the pile of sand and shells in the water until most of the sand has been washed away. A little black shark tooth lies among the few broken shells.

One for one. I place the tooth in the baggy tucked into my bathing suit bottoms. Then I repeat the process at least a hundred more times. Without a cloud, the sun has crossed the vast blue sky and started its descent. I head back to where I left my stuff.

"Funny seeing you here."

I whip around to a guy who looks vaguely familiar.

"Remember me?" he asks.

Then it hits me, the MMA fighter who came into my uncle's dojo. "Um… yeah, the dojo."

"It's like I've seen you before." He's trying this angle again.

"You did… at the dojo."

"Yeah, I mean before that. But it's been a while."

I take a scrutinizing look at his face. It's the scar trailing along the line of his jaw that's familiar. I don't remember his name, but I may have seen him fight at the UG. From what I recall, he isn't bad, but he tends to lean toward the cruder side of fighting. His mask was ripped off during the fight. He was right to come to my uncle for training—if my uncle would train a guy like him. Trey would help him clean up his kicks and punches, move with more finesse, and show him how to use more intention in martial arts instead of reacting on impulse. But it looks like he'll have to find that somewhere else. It's odd, though, how he thinks he remembers seeing me. It has to be someplace else.

"Yeah, that guy was a real asshole."

I ignore his comment without mentioning the asshole is my uncle. Instead, I ask, "Where do you fight?"

"How about a name?" he counters.

"Kinsley."

"I'm Dylan 'Dark Warrior' Shane." He holds out his hand.

"Nice to meet you, Dark Warrior." I shake his scarred, callused hand. "So, where do you fight?"

He hesitates, and I know immediately that *all* his fights are illegal. My uncle called it on this one. "All over," he responds.

All over, technically, isn't a lie. The UG moves locations all the time. "Underground?" I guess.

His eyes widen, then slowly narrow into questioning slits. A slow grin slides over his mouth. He might be good-looking if it weren't for his arrogant attitude. Plus his puffy cauliflower ears.

"Sometimes," he admits as he shrugs. "That's where the money is."

I can't blame him. If you're good enough and willing to risk your life, you can make a good living. "So I've heard."

"Do you fight?" he asks.

I nod. "Yeah, but not in the underground scene. I used to compete in tournaments but not anymore."

"You any good?"

I shrug one shoulder. "I can hold my own."

A loud whistle comes from down the beach. Dylan glances over his shoulder at a group of people waving him over. "Listen, I've got to get back to my friends, but maybe I'll see ya around sometime."

"Yeah, see ya."

He stops mid-jog and shuffles backward to me. "Maybe I can get your number, and we can tumble some time."

I raise an eyebrow. "Tumble?"

He combs his fingers through his light brown hair. "Yeah, maybe you can show me some of your moves, and I can show you mine. Come on, it's not like I'm asking for a date or anything." He shrugs, a grin growing across his face. "Seriously, I'm not even going to go there. You'll probably kick my ass." His friends call for him again. He holds up his hand with his middle finger pointed skyward. "How about I give you my number instead?"

I squat down to get my phone from my bag. "Okay, what is it?"

He tells me his number, and I save it to my contacts.

"I've got to go. Call me sometime and we'll tumble." He smiles and takes off toward his friends.

How ironic to see him here, of all places. It's over an hour away from the dojo. I wonder if he knows about the underground fight that's happening in two days. I bet he does. And I wouldn't be surprised if he's one of the fighters on the card.

EDGE

WHAT I WOULDN'T GIVE to know where my little Ninja is right now. Wherever it is, I'd rather be with her than spend another minute with my father.

It's Thanksgiving, and he called me away from our guests to have a one-on-one. He only wants to discuss money and fighting with me. He never asks about my classes or if I'm seeing anyone. He doesn't care about any of that shit. Winning the next fight is all he's concerned with.

We're behind closed doors in his dark cigar room. The humidor box rests on the side table next to the black leather club chair currently occupied by my father.

Taking out a cigar, he closes the lid, brings it to his nose, and breathes in the expensive scent of the tobacco. "There's nothing like a fine cigar."

I watch his deliberate movements from just inside the doorway. My hands are tucked deep into my pants pockets. I wish he would get to the real reason he brought me in here without all the fucking theatrics. Then we can get on with the conversation leading up to our inevitable fight and return to our guests.

He cuts the tip of the cigar, flicks his lighter open, then lights it. Smoke billows around him as he puffs on the end. The fiery-red and orange tip sears brighter as he brings the flame to life.

"As you know, you're on the card to fight tomorrow night."

"I know." The last time I fought, I knocked the guy down and out. With the instruction from my manager, a.k.a. good old dad, I delivered a final blow to my opponent that didn't kill him, but he won't be fighting for a while.

Father picks up his brandy and takes a sip. "I have no doubt you're ready. However, I did speak with your sensei earlier to confirm. The size of the bets is already quite impressive. I suspect it'll be a high six- or seven-figure night."

I don't need to respond. He isn't expecting me to.

He takes another hit from the cigar. "There's another matter I want to discuss with you."

I know exactly what the other matter he's referring to, and she's the last topic I want to discuss with him. I force myself to remain in place because I know as soon as he speaks her name, I'll want to lunge for his throat.

"On top of that short list is the subject of Kinsley West."

There it is. The second after her name falls casually from his dry lips, he sips the brandy. He somehow knows she attends Monarch. I can only guess he's had one of his henchmen trailing her since he set his sights on her. It also helps to have the chancellor as one of your high betters.

"What about her?" I cross my arms over my chest. It's a defensive position, and I know he notices, but I don't care.

"Don't fuck with me, boy." He slams the glass of brandy down. The dark liquid sloshes onto the mahogany table.

His heated warnings are nothing new. Fortunately, they haven't been backed with a punch or some other painful contact for the past couple of years. Maybe he finally realized I can easily kick his ass—kill him even. He should know. He's the one who made me into who I am.

If I don't give him something, he'll plan to make moves of his own without me. So, if I can keep her somewhat secluded from his plans—as safe as I can—I need to stay involved for now. "She's still training at the dojo almost every day. She looks stronger and more in touch with her skills than ever."

He nods with approval. His slick smile disappears behind the cigar as he brings it to his mouth. "Excellent."

I turn to leave.

"Have you fucked her yet? Gotten her to trust you? In case you forgot, that's still our plan."

I close my eyes and take a deep breath. How the fuck do you forget something like that? That's all I've thought about since the second she took off that damn helmet when she stole my parking spot. But I don't want to be with her to use her the way he expects. I've come to need her in ways I never dreamed of. I want her for myself.

Besides, little does he know that getting Ninja to cave isn't an easy job. She's not like other girls who drop to their knees at the snap of my fingers. And caging her is the last thing I want to do. Nor do I want her to give in or submit. Where would the fun be in that?

I turn back around to face him. "No, I haven't forgotten. Nin — Kinsley." I catch myself before I reveal her nickname. "She keeps to herself and pushes away anyone who tries to get close."

He takes another sip, then sets the tumbler roughly onto the table. "Oh, come on, son. Getting a bitch on her back doesn't require trust. It's about the plays in the game, the manipulation, and empty promises. Most women will believe anything if you wave something flashy and expensive in their face."

Knowing my mother is in the next room, entertaining our guests as her husband talks about women as if they're nothing but a way to get off and do your bidding, fucking kills me. He's a piece of shit who wants nothing more than for me to hone my skills at fighting, make him richer than he already is, and be exactly like him—a greedy bastard. He'll only see one of those things happen. And honing my fighting skills won't be for him.

He raises his glass into the air. "You need to make her yours. Play with her, fuck her, buy her fucking flowers for all I care, whatever it takes. After you've had your fill, I'll gladly take her off your hands. Just make sure you don't break her too badly because that's when the real fun begins. That's when it's my turn to play."

The sick grin spreading over his lips is enough to make the few appetizers I ate roil in my stomach. I want to pick him up by his collar and slam his weak body into the glass shelves behind him, over and over, until he doesn't even remember who I am. Tensing to the point of nearly shattering, I force my muscles to relax. If he glimpses any weakness I have for her, my little Ninja is as good as—

The old man continues. "She walked right into our hands. Who knew she would transfer to Monarch? It's a fucking blessing. It's all coming together. And now that her father is out of the way, that girl and her fighting skills can lead the path right to Venom's very lucrative future." His greedy, repulsing smile flashes as he brings his glass to his lips again.

Just before her father's death, I learned that Ninja was always the end goal. It was never about her dad. His death was just a way to get him out of the way of Venom's real prize. But as long as I'm alive, I'll never hand the girl I'm falling hard for over to the devil himself. I may have started as a player in his depraved game, but things have changed. And he doesn't need to know that right now. So, there's nothing else for me to do but nod.

My hand is on the door handle when he says, "We have less than three months. Don't fuck it up."

I close the door behind me without responding.

As soon as I walk out of my father's study, still reeling from our little father-son chat, Brielle loops her arm through mine. "Hey, baby, I've been looking for you."

I slide her arm out from mine. "Not now, Brielle."

Her lips turn down as my mom saves the day. "Oh, Ledger, there you are."

My mom, the good woman she is, places herself between me and Brielle. Brielle's mom comes up behind her. My mom kisses me on the cheek. Unlike my dad, her touch is gentle and loving. The only reason I don't pack her bags and send her off to a place he could never find her is that she's very capable of taking care of herself. She knows exactly the kind of asshole my father has become. I've watched her closely over the past several years, and I have nothing to worry about regarding my mother. Thank fuck for that.

My and Brielle's parents have been friends for as long as I can remember. It's mostly been business between our fathers, but my mom has been a good sport at entertaining his wife.

Mrs. Young says, "I haven't seen you and Brielle together lately." She rests her hand on top of my forearm and squeezes. She makes an effort to contort her Botox-filled face into a sad smile. But the gesture fails when her lips can't quite make the frown. She doesn't need to know that Brielle and I were never an actual couple. Her daughter let me use her for sex while she used me to get off and boost her popularity status.

Brielle starts to speak, no doubt to begin spewing nonsense, but I interject, "With school and other extracurricular activities, I haven't had much free time."

Flames dance in Brielle's eyes. She knows precisely what—or rather who—my extracurricular activities involve. Mrs. Young's already pouty lips protrude grotesquely.

Brielle goes to argue, but my mom cuts her off. "My boy has been as busy as ever." She picks up a fork from the tray of a passing server, clinks it against her wineglass, and announces that the first course of dinner is ready to be served. With grace, she smiles and guides our company into the dining room. She tucks her arm through mine. Lowering her voice, she says, "Oh, honey, I'm sorry. I had no idea, or I would have never put you in that position."

"It's fine."

"You know, I must say I'm delighted to hear that. I never did like that girl."

I snicker. "Me either."

"Let's eat, shall we?" she says.

I sit as far away from Brielle as I can manage. Course after course is brought out. It's rare, but I don't have an appetite. I blame my father for that. He's perfected his gift for bringing out the worst in me. I eat everything that's placed in front of me out of respect for my mom and what the day means. I'm more privileged than most, but I'd rather be poor as fuck than have a father like mine. I wonder what everyone at this table would think if they knew the dinner they're eating was paid for with blood.

I eat in silence unless spoken to. And even then, I give short, one-word answers if possible. Mostly it's my parents' friends drilling me on school and other bullshit. I nod and agree until I can put an end to this hellish night. As the last course is served before coffee and dessert, I set my napkin on the table and stand. Rounding the table, I kiss my mom's cheek.

"Love you," I whisper.

She gives my hand that's resting on her shoulder a tight squeeze. Without looking in my father's direction, I excuse myself. There's only one person I want to see right now. She's the only one who can temporarily erase the hate.

KINSLEY

AFTER I STUFF myself with turkey, green bean casserole, and mashed potatoes drenched in homemade gravy, my belly screams at me to stop. Scraping the last little bit off my plate, I can't help but take one more bite. I lay down my fork in surrender. "Oh my God, I can't breathe."

Uncle Trey is leaning back in his seat, rubbing his stomach. "You and me both, kid."

After a few minutes of resting, I start to clear the table. Uncle Trey gets up with me, reaching for the platter in the center of the table. The kitchen looks as if we cooked for twenty people, not two. The warm bread and roasted turkey don't smell as good as they did about thirty minutes ago.

There's a knock on the door as we put the food away and wash dishes.

"I got it." Grabbing a dish towel, I wipe the soapsuds off my hands.

When I open it, Edge is standing on the porch. I'm not only confused but downright shocked. One hand is tucked into his pressed pants while the other hangs at his side, holding his keys.

"Hi," I say. The simple word is like a loaded gun exploding in my head. What the hell is he doing here?

"Hey." His tone is laced with nervous tension as if he doesn't know what he's doing or how he ended up on my doorstep.

Edge fidgets with his key ring. He looks completely out of his element. I narrow my eyes. "Everything okay?"

"Yeah, I just thought I'd stop by to say Happy Thanksgiving."

"Um… thanks." I tuck a few loose strands of hair behind my ear. "Happy Thanksgiving to you, too." There's definitely more to why he just showed up on my doorstep. I want to push, but something in his vulnerable expression has me hesitating.

He stands there, shifting his attention from me to the ground. "Listen, you want to go for a ride or something?"

I look over my shoulder toward the kitchen. The sound of pots and pans clattering together comes from inside the house. "Maybe after I help my uncle clean up. There's still a ton of dishes to wash. And we haven't had dessert yet." I open the door wider for him to come in. "You're welcome to join us if you want."

He spins the key ring around once. Twice. "Yeah, okay."

He steps over the threshold. As he enters the small foyer, his face is a mask of confusion. When he looks off to the right into the living room, I can't help but laugh, covering my mouth with my hand. He jerks his head in my direction.

"I'm sorry. You look like you've never been in a house this small, and you're not quite sure what to do with yourself."

"Actually, I have, and I'm fine," he assures me as a rare smile forms on his lips. "I'm just taking it all in."

I nod. "Okay then."

It seems like something is wrong, but maybe he's just nervous. That thought alone makes me want to laugh again. Edge, nervous? If that's the case, then something happened that he had no control over. I haven't known him very long, but control is the one thing he likes. I would even go as far as to say he needs to have it at any cost.

"What's that smell? It smells like a campfire."

I spin away from him on my heels. "That would be the very toasted marshmallows on the sweet potatoes." I lead the way into the kitchen. My uncle has his back to us. I point at the charred heap in the garbage. "That's what you smell."

Edge chuckles. "Your doing?"

I place my hands on my hips. "Actually, no. My uncle is responsible for charring the tiny puffs of sweetness."

Uncle Trey turns around, soapsuds falling off his hands.

"Uncle Trey, this is Edge. Ledger Hunt, this is Trey Mitchell." I toss the dish towel to my uncle.

He wipes his hands, then juts out his hand to Edge. "Hey, Edge. How's it going? I haven't seen you in a while."

A while? Do they know each other? What in the actual…?

"Good. Happy Thanksgiving." Edge's posture seems to relax slightly.

"How's your father? I assume he's doing well." There's a slight edge to my uncle's tone that wasn't there before.

Edge nods. His voice tightens as he answers, "Yes, sir. He's well."

Sir? Who is this equally delicious replica of the Edge standing in my kitchen? I'm a million percent sure I stepped into a different realm. I have no idea what the hell is going on, but I hope I get to keep this Edge for a bit longer.

I break my awkward ogling and stupidly state the obvious. "We were just cleaning up from dinner."

"Yeah, Kins isn't the most organized cook." Uncle Trey laughs and then tosses the dish towel back at me.

I catch it. "Hey! You helped make this mess, marshmallow murderer."

My uncle looks around the kitchen and raises his hands in

surrender. "I take full responsibility for that." His wandering gaze lands on the flour-dusted countertop. "And that, since I made the apple pie."

I toss the dishrag over my shoulder. "That you did, and it better be good since that's my favorite."

Uncle Trey nods in the direction of the dining room. "I got this. Why don't you set out the dessert?"

"Sure, and I'll start some coffee," I say.

"I'd normally have some with dessert, but I'm enjoying this wine." My uncle holds up his glass in a mock toast, then takes a sip.

"Want some help?" Edge asks.

Help? Something isn't right. With my uncle's focus on the dishes, I pull Edge into the other room. The second we're out of sight and earshot, I ask, "Who are you?"

"What are you talking about?" His voice drops to a whisper-yell to match mine.

"You're, like, being nice and polite."

Wickedly, his full lips tilt up on one side. "And? Is that a crime?"

I cross my arms over my chest. "It might be for Ledger Hunt."

He laughs. "Not quite."

His playful expression sobers as his gaze strolls down the length of my body. "You're wearing a dress, so I could ask you the same question. Where's my badass girl and her boots?"

My badass girl. I let his possessive words slide through the moment without comment. Their meaning and intent still warm my core. I glance down at the simple slim waist, short dress, and flats. "You've seen me in a dress before."

Grasping my hand, he pulls me farther down the hallway. Long shadows coat the walls, darkening the small space. My dress rises as his hand glides up my bare thigh to settle on my hip. The thin line of my panties is my only barrier against the warmth of his palm. A low growl rumbles from deep in his throat. He never takes his eyes off mine as he leans down to kiss me.

"Mine," he whispers against my mouth. His lips barely brush mine.

Now, this control freak of a person is the Edge I know. My body instantly reacts to the carnal need in his heated gaze. Without hesitation, he crashes his mouth to mine. His insatiable hunger is unmistakable with every swipe of his tongue. Dominance intertwines with fevered passion as he claims me. His hand tightens on my waist, threatening to bruise my skin. This kiss is different than the other times. This one is all-consuming, like the night chasing away the sun, the dark swallowing the light. The swirl of his tongue around mine sends vibrations to every one of my cells.

His other arm curls around my lower back, pulling me to him until I'm firmly pressed against his hard body. He clings to me as if he's taking precisely what he needs to get him through to the next moment. My hands follow the lines of his rigid muscles as I glide them up his arms until they settle around his neck. He moans into my mouth. Tremors dance low in my belly even as he slows his rhythm.

Simmering heat leaves me dizzy as he breaks the kiss. Our breaths come out in low gasps as we try to catch our breath. I lower my hands to his waist.

He touches his forehead against mine. "I had to see you," he confesses.

Those simple words have guilt stampeding over my complicated feelings for this man. As I stand in the dimly lit hallway, fully content with being in Edge's arms, I can't help but think that our possible beginning or our end is right under my fingertips. Only a thin layer of fabric separates his innocence or his punishment. Wanting to stop the torture this man is putting my heart through and needing to know the truth once and for all,

I'm seconds away from asking him to lift his shirt to see his tattoo when my uncle calls out for me.

"Be right there," I answer. I hate and cherish the relief I'm spared to still have the possibility of the truth.

Edge's stormy eyes never stop penetrating me with need and desire. I tilt my head when I notice more than the blazing heat in his stare. There's familiarity. I don't want to see it, but it's there. In that tiny moment, a fraction of time, I realize that we are the same. Like me, he has demons haunting him. My only question is if they're as arresting and monstrous as mine.

"Kinsley..."

I wait for him to whisper more, but he doesn't. He says only my name. Not Ninja, *my* name.

I trace my fingers over the smooth line of his jaw, lightly skimming his swollen lips with my thumb. His mouth parts. Soft, warm breaths curl around the tips of my fingers.

"What do you want?" I don't know what possessed me to ask him such a personal or open-ended question. Maybe it's the vulnerability I sense. It's as if his walls are crumbling, and this is my only moment to claim a fragile truth.

He doesn't hesitate to answer. "You." Delicately, he kisses the pad of my thumb. "Only you."

My hand slides from his mouth, down his throat, to rest on his chest. The beating of his heart pulses against my palm. His simple answer drives away the rest of my curiosity... at least for tonight. I reach up onto my toes and tenderly kiss him. I don't give him a response. He doesn't need or want one. His naked truth of wanting me says everything. Him being here is proof of that. Taking his hand in mine, I guide him back to the dining room.

The drive never happens. Edge seems happy just hanging out and eating apple pie and pumpkin pie with Uncle Trey and me. The conversation is easy, and the company is nice. He sits next to me at the table. His hand gently rests on my thigh. He doesn't try to move it. Fleeting hopes of him being naughty tease my imagination, but despite my cravings for his touch, he stays respectful with my uncle sitting directly across from us.

He and my uncle seem to be more familiar with each other than I thought. There are a few conversations I don't have anything to add to: past events they both attended, tournaments, and competitors. But the UG never comes up in conversation. I almost ask about it, then decide not to. I'm not ready to show that hand yet. Not only that but Edge is relaxed with no one to impress or kick the shit out of. He's just being who I can only assume is normal, low-key Edge. And fuck me, do I like this Edge—a lot.

He's making my mission anything but easy.

3 2

KINSLEY

THE DAY OF THE FIGHT, I dress in black from head to toe: jeans, tank top, hoodie, boots, and my mask. Adam texted me earlier, giving me the entry word. I'm officially all set. The venue is in an abandoned warehouse near Airport Road. Cars are parked along both sides of the street. Most are everyday cars, with a few luxury models scattered among them. Some cost more than my college tuition. Those belong to the big betters. The shit boxes usually belong to the fighters, the ones who risk their lives to entertain these rich assholes.

I park my bike behind a green rusting dumpster, then put on my mask. It does nothing to tame the stench of garbage. I brought nothing with me, no money, no ID, not even my phone. The only item on me is my motorcycle key, which I slide down into my boot. I lower the mask over my face and lift my hood over my head, then I head for the side door. Gravel crunches under my boots.

The bouncer is the same guy at every fight. Even though he wears a mask, it does nothing to hide his protruding belly and thinning, uncombed hair. If that didn't give him away, his bland personality would. Monotone doesn't even begin to describe him. This time, though, he's wearing a different rock band T-shirt. Usually, it's AC/DC, but tonight it's Ozzy Osbourne.

I step up to him. He just looks at me without saying a word.

"Ninja," I say as I internally cringe, giving him the entry password.

The unease that crept up my spine when I read the text from Adam had me questioning if tonight was safe to come. And since Venom is the one running the show, the word is either a coincidence or a shout-out to yours truly. When Edge came to Thanksgiving, he knew my uncle, so I can only assume he figured out who I am. And telling him my dad died a few months ago was a huge hint. It's not like the world of MMA, especially the UG, is a very big one. Everyone knows everyone.

Mr. Boring unhooks the rope, allowing me to enter. I'm not sure how I expect to feel when I walk in and am hit with the visual of the cage, but fuck me, I feel like I've been slammed up against a concrete wall as the breath whooshes from my chest. The octagon cage at the center of the vast room sends a nasty, unwelcoming chill skating up my spine. The hairs on the back of my neck stand on end. The unpleasant surge of tingling is like tiny spikes of fear. My heart pounds in my chest with so many horrid images flooding me all at once. Coming here used to evoke feelings of excitement and thrill, but the death of my dad overshadows all that used to be. The thrill and excitement have given way to anxiety and dread.

With people coming in behind me, I move out of their way toward the back of the room. I rub my side where the scar from the knife wound is. Maybe coming here isn't such a good idea.

Taking a deep breath, I slowly let it out. Get your shit together, Kins! You're just here to gather information.

The card has four fights on it for tonight: two lightweights, one middleweight, and one heavyweight. I scan the names and freeze. *Viper vs. Python* will fight in the heavyweight challenge. I don't know who Viper is, but I guarantee that with a stage name in the reptile family, he's part of Venom. Edge is known as *the* Viper at school, but that's only because of the mascot and his status, right?

As for Python, I don't know who he is, but I sure as fuck know what he's capable of. If Edge is Viper and he's fighting Python, that has to mean he isn't the one who killed my dad.

My head is spinning too fast to comprehend everything and try to fit all the pieces together. I take another deep breath to calm myself, then work my way around the room to see if there's anyone I recognize.

Even though everyone is wearing a mask, they're still easy to identify. But if this place were to get overrun with cops, no one wants to have to be the snitch. And if you did, with the money and connections involved, your ass would be dead the moment they find out it was you.

There's a crisp feel to the air tonight, but with the number of people pouring in, it won't last long. Sticky heat will soon suffocate us all. I do what I can to push all of my feelings aside. Tonight is a night of truths. I can only hope I'm ready for them.

Music begins to thump throughout the warehouse. I can't hear shit unless I'm right on the person. So, eavesdropping is going to be an issue.

Keeping my distance from the majority of spectators, I try to look inconspicuous. My hair is tied up and hidden under the hood of my hoodie. My mask covers most of my face except my eyes. The volume of the music drops until the hard beat has ceased. Everyone in the place goes completely quiet as a guy in a black sports jacket, who looks like all the other big betters here, steps into the cage. He taps the cordless mic. The loud knocking rocks through the surrounding speakers.

"Let's get our first fight started, shall we?" He looks over to his left. A brooding man with arms crossed over his chest nods at the announcer. The announcer says, "Looks like we're ready to start."

That's code for all bets have been made.

My gaze travels from one masked figure to the next, searching for one specific person. Even with a mask, Edge would be easy to recognize. At least, that's what I tell myself. The Venom boys have distinct body types for MMA fighters. In likeness, they have very defined muscles on every inch of their body. The difference they possess is their muscle mass, and they're several inches taller. It also helps that I've memorized Edge's form, ripped to perfection with an intimidating posture. He won't be able to hide from me behind his mask.

The first lightweight fighter steps into the cage. The announcer drones on about the fighter's stats and experience. His opponent is next. Although curious to see their skills, I stay focused on my task of scanning the room.

I don't see anyone I recognize before the first fight ends. There should be a Venom mask somewhere in the crowd. Where the hell are they? They're the reason I'm here.

The second lightweight fight is very similar to the first. Although I don't pay much attention, I can guess the defender is trying to work his way up the ranks. The newcomer thought he could easily remove his opponent but royally underestimated the standing champion.

The middleweight fight is the same as the first two. After the announcer calls the winner, the crowd begins to chant, not for the winners of the lower-class fights but for the one coming up. It's the real moneymaker. A shit ton of money is on the line. And there's a chance the winner will move up in the ranks and receive a higher payout. Popularity equals a fatter wallet. To some fighters, it doesn't matter if they don't get any credit in the real world. To them, this *is* the real world. They get to do what they love, and they get paid to do it. Win-win.

Unease races up my spine. I stand near the back of the crowd, avoiding whatever attention I can while continuing to look for Edge or any of the other guys. Just as the announcer calls the first fighter of the heavyweights to enter the cage, I see Venom. Five of them huddle on the other side of the octagon. By the looks of their physiques, I determine that they are Gunner, Levi, and Kade. The man in the suit may be a manager or an investor. But from where I'm standing, I can't be sure. He shakes hands with one of the organizers, who's wearing a jacket with a snake logo on the pocket.

I don't see Edge standing with them. My imagination jumps to places I don't want it to go. I hug my arms around my stomach. The leftover mashed potatoes I ate before coming here threaten to make an appearance of their own.

The announcer stands in the center of the octagon. "Are we ready for the big boys? First, we have our champion, PYTHON!"

The room explodes. Their fists pump in the air as they scream and chant for the murderer himself. Bile rises in my throat. I cover my mouth and force myself to swallow it down.

"Hey, what are you doing back here? You won't be able to see the fight." Some guy in a Joker mask grabs my attention.

"I'm fine."

"Why don't you come over and hang with me and my friends?" he insists.

Even as badly as I want to see the fight, I'm not going with this guy. "I said I'm fine."

Not taking no for an answer, he tries to grab my arm. "We're just right over here."

His heaving breath smells like stale beer. I refrain from gagging. "Get the fuck off me," I growl, tearing my arm away from his grip. Trying to avoid a scene, I take off in the opposite direction. I can't take the chance of Edge or Venom seeing me.

"Bitch," he calls out as he walks back to his friends.

God, what is it with that guy? And how did he know I'm a girl? Asshole! They come to these fights, and as soon as they cross the threshold, they think they're instant MMA fighters and invincible, that they can do whatever the fuck they want and to whom.

Piled against the back wall are empty pallets. Since the octagon is in the center of the room, I should be able to see the fight from there. I use an abandoned chair to climb onto the pallets. Once on top of them, I balance to avoid crashing to the ground and creating a huge scene.

I'm so focused on the fighter who killed my dad that I tune out what the announcer says. Python's snake tattoo slithers down his side as a sick and crippling reminder of what he's capable of. His oversized gold champion belt rests on his shoulder like a badge of honor. Bile rises in the back of my throat. The killer opens his arms open wide, absorbing all the energy and testosterone the assholes around me exude.

Behind Python, in the shadows, the other fighter shakes his arms to loosen his muscles. He bounces lightly from foot to foot as he rolls his neck. My heart threatens to jump out of my chest. Afraid for the opponent, I wonder if he knows what he signed up for. I bite the tip of my thumbnail and tamp my hand over my bouncing leg.

Someone is going to die tonight. And I can't bear witness again to the looming horror.

I climb down the pallets when the other fighter comes out of the shadows. The moment he steps into the spotlight, I don't need the announcer to introduce him to know who it is.

Edge.

I freeze my descent, barely able to hang on to the pile of wood. A tsunami of dread rips through my entire being. I'm trapped between confusion and unadulterated shock as the onslaught of unwanted emotions shreds me into a million pieces. My right leg hovers without finding purchase. I'm unable to breathe freely with the mask, and my quickening, heated breaths are stifling—suffocating me. My grip tightens around the wood. Splinters pierce my palm. The pallets teeter beneath my weight. None of that matters. All of my resolve to leave is instantly forgotten.

In that sliver of time, everything stops as I pick up the shattered pieces of a distorted and fucked-up puzzle and try to put them into place. *Viper.* Mask or no mask, I know that Viper and Edge are the same person. It isn't Edge's ripped body, the corded muscular arms, the same arms that have held me more times than I can count, that gives him away. Hell, I've only ever once seen him without a shirt once, and bitch Brielle was draped across his chest, covering most of it. It isn't his rigid posture as he crosses his arms over his chest.

I know it's Edge from how intensely he scans the crowd. Rage brews behind those gray eyes. They bore into every soul surrounding the cage.

Who or what is he looking for?

Before Edge can locate what or who he's looking for, he focuses on his opponent. If I didn't know him as I do, I would have missed the almost imperceptible tells of his uneasiness. The center of the cage is the last place he wants to be. Reluctantly renewing his resolve, he walks right up to face off with Python.

The announcer's words battle to be heard above the blood pounding in my ears. His mouth moves as he bellows into the microphone in his hand, but I can barely hear a syllable with the roaring in my head. I've been to enough of these that I don't need to hear what he's saying to know he's doing his job, announcing the two men in the cage.

"Fighting against Python is Viper!"

The crowd erupts.

The two fighters face each other as the ref goes over the rules. Rules. What a joke. Maybe tonight he won't turn a blind eye. They nod to each other, and then both back away, retreating to opposite sides of the cage.

The million thoughts and feelings that have clouded my

judgment for the past couple of months surface. I've put so much on the line. The chances I took, the feelings I let develop and emerge, the way I couldn't control myself with him. Staying in control was the only thing I had to do, yet I failed miserably. Do I feel relief Edge didn't kill my dad?

Yes!

Edge isn't Python. Edge isn't the one who killed my father. Relief is like a living thing as the repetitive thought fills me with reassurance. Just yesterday, it was me he wanted. He held me in his arms and told me as much. *I only want you.*

But fuck! What if Edge had turned out to be the killer? There's still a very good chance he had something to do with getting my father killed. I shove down the possibility and take another deep breath.

"Edge didn't kill my dad. Edge didn't kill my dad. Edge didn't kill my dad," I repeat over and over until the tension begins to melt away.

Now that I have my answer, I have no reason to stay. Surveying the room, I locate the exit and start to climb down again. Just as I'm about to drop to the ground, I pause. I should leave. Staying should be the last thing I want to do. But I can't leave knowing Edge is in the cage with a murderer.

"Holy fucking shit! This can't be happening—again." It's like the threat just fell from the fucking sky.

I gingerly ease back onto the pallets and pull my legs into my chest. Resting my forehead on my knees, I lift my mask just enough to uncover my mouth and nose, then drag in long, deep breaths. The slamming of my heart against my ribs begins to slow. I raise my head, sliding the mask back into place.

Feeling the need to be wrapped in a cocoon of comfort and safety, I wrap my arms around myself and nervously wait for the bell to signal the start of the first round. It's the best I can do in this fucked-up situation. The last thing I want to do is watch them beat the shit out of each other. But there's no way I'll be able to peel my gaze away from them.

The bell signals the start of the first round. Numbness overtakes me as the roar of the crowd goes ballistic. Once again, I'm rooted in place. I can't move or even scream. Another person I care about is about to face off with a murderer.

Edge's familiar stormy gray eyes are laser-focused on Python. Until now, his tattoo has been a mystery. I have a full view of it when he turns to the side. It's beautiful. From the top of his ribs to his hip bone is an inked black feral snake intertwined with a fierce Chinese dragon.

Doing my best to turn off all emotions, I try to switch to my fighter brain. Python riles the crowd by shuffling back and forth on the balls of his feet as he pounds his chest. Edge takes the opposite approach. His arms hang limply at his sides. His usual confident demeanor is a hundredfold as he studies his opponent. Both have similar heights and builds, but Edge's body is more defined. They're both agile and strong.

Python makes the first move. His left fist misses Edge's face by a breath. Edge retaliates quickly, not giving Python the time to set up for another strike, slamming a sloppy punch across Python's jaw. They're evenly matched. But the more I watch, the more I see that something seems off. Edge is faster and more precise, his footing is more versatile and sure, and his punches, although powerful, aren't as direct as Python's. It's almost as if Edge is coddling Python. By the boos coming from the crowd, they see the same thing.

Their moves are too similar, which is interesting and unusual. Most fighters have different techniques. They're known for certain moves or takedowns. The same sensei likely trained these two fighters. I've seen firsthand what Python is capable of, and Edge should try to take him down as fast as possible. Python only needs to get the nod, and he turns into a killing machine. My nightmare is morphing into a horrific reality. I press my hands together and whisper a prayer to the universe.

Then, like a switch has been flipped, Edge doesn't hesitate for another second. He punches Python with an uppercut to his face. It's fast, forceful, and with perfect precision. Python falls back against the fencing. Edge wraps his arms around his waist and tackles him to the ground. They each get in a couple of kicks and punches before Edge can wrap his arm around Python's throat. He spins so Python's back is to his front. Python turns his head so his airway is in the crease of Edge's elbow. The chokehold is so tight, the thin stream of air he's getting won't be able to sustain him for long. The jiu-jitsu submission Edge has Python in is a favorite of the crowd.

I lift my leg and rest my chin on my knee. The pallets creak beneath me. My nerves are heating my body to dangerous levels. I'm dying to take off my sweatshirt, but I don't dare. I glance at Edge one more time.

For a split second, his concentration breaks from Python. I follow his gaze to the man in the suit just outside the cage. Is that who he was looking for earlier? The man nods at Edge, giving him some sort of signal. I count in my head the number of seconds going by. Eyes glued to the fucked-up scene in front of me, I wonder if the nod means the same command that Python was given to kill my dad. When I reach ten, Edge tightens his hold on Python.

As my eyes lock onto Edge, the happiness of knowing he's innocent of murder doesn't completely diminish. Fear still taints my suspicion with the fact that he's a major player of Venom. I just witnessed how connected he is when he took the command from the guy in the expensive suit. He and Python may be adversaries on that stage, but they are on the same team, Venom.

If Edge were the one in the cage with my father, he would

have taken the order and been the one to kill him just as easily as Python did. I know this with every fiber of my being.

I wanted to believe he truly cared about me. Fuck, in some demented way, I still do. What he told me might be true. I really may be all he wants. But I'm not sure any of that matters now. He's shown me tonight who he truly is: Viper, a fighter who fights without honor and takes orders from bloodthirsty, greedy men.

I jump down from the pallets with disgust swirling in my gut. Swallowing down the nausea, I make my way to the exit. The action in the cage has the crowd's full attention. Just before I touch the door handle, someone grabs my arm and pulls me in the opposite direction. I bend down, using my body weight to strain against them. They grab my other arm. I kick out my leg to trip them, but they're ready for the move.

"Let me go!"

"Stop fighting me," says a deep voice.

They use their strength and size to pull me into a dark corner of the warehouse. A few people are near, but no one pays us any attention. I jerk my wrist free of the asshole's grasp. Distracting him by pretending I'm rubbing the pain from my wrist, I reach up and grab his mask. It slides over his head, revealing his face.

"Levi? What the fuck?"

"Hey, Ninja."

"How did you know it was me?" I lift the fabric of my mask to rest it on my forehead.

Levi shrugs. "Easy, you're the only chick crazy enough to find her way into an illegal underground fight."

He has me there. "You know you could have just said, 'Hey, it's me, Levi. Can I talk to you for a sec?' instead of kidnapping me and dragging me into a dark corner."

"This is hardly kidnapping."

"At least you don't deny the dragging me into a dark corner

part. Anyway, what do you want?" I glance over his shoulder to the fighting ring.

Levi looks toward the cage. "Don't worry, your boy can handle himself."

I follow his gaze to see Python barely able to tap out. Blood covers the floor under his face. The crowd roars, sounding pleased to be leaving a little bit richer.

"See, I told you," Levi says.

I scoff and turn back to him. "First off, no one in that cage is *my* boy. Second, I don't give a shit."

He chuckles as he shakes his head. "I'm going to call your bluff on both counts."

"Call whatever you want. I'm going home."

He grabs the sleeve of my hoodie as I turn to leave. "Not yet, little Ninja." He glances at the silver ring and the bar through my eyebrow. "Why did you come here tonight?"

"Answer my question first. Why did you want to get me alone?" The crowd amps up. It takes all of my will not to turn around to see what's got them riled up.

"I wanted to make sure you were safe."

I cross my arms over my chest. "What a crock of shit."

He shrugs. "It's the truth." Leveling his gaze on me as if searching for my truth, he narrows his eyes. "Now it's your turn."

I try to look anywhere but at him. "It's personal."

Using his thumb, he twirls the ring on his middle finger around. "Does your reason relate to what happened to a certain fighter not too long ago?"

Of course, he's talking about the night of the fight that forever changed my life. I don't want to discuss that night with him or any of Venom—not yet. "No."

He looks up from his silver rings. His expression turns somber. "You really shouldn't lie."

My patience is thinning. "What do you want?"

I'm curious to see how Edge takes the win. But I already know. If I turned around to look at him, he would give nothing away that he was happy. His body language would be as cloaked as his face behind his mask. He'd show the crowd only what he wants them to see: a fierce, cold-blooded fighter as the ref holds his hand in the air, declaring him the winner.

"We didn't kill your father."

The words are like a muffled declaration trying to be heard over a freight train. I *must* have misheard him. I *had* to have misheard him. I can only stare at Levi as the announcer declares the winner. *Viper.*

Regaining my composure, I say, "I know who killed my father. Edge just took him down in the cage. He's part of Venom, just like you. Python is wearing the same mask Venom wears, exactly like the one you're wearing now and the one Edge has on his face." I wave my arms around like a crazy person. "You're all Venom. So, yeah, you did kill my dad!" I don't care that I'm basically yelling, "Murderers!" in front of hundreds of people.

Levi shifts his attention from me to something or someone over my shoulder. I close my eyes, having a horrible feeling about what's getting ready to go down. I was so close—seconds away from getting out of here—so fucking close to fleeing. The instant the hand grips my waist, I know it's too late. My lungs deflate as the trapped air swooshes out in a harsh breath.

Levi purses his lips, then nods to Edge. "I'll let him explain it."

I smack Edge's hand away as I turn to face him. "What's there to explain? I think it's pretty fucking simple. Venom killed my father."

Edge doesn't even blink. "It's not that simple."

Frustration ebbs into fury. The edges of my vision darken, shadows closing in on either side of me. "I saw Python kill my father with his bare hands. My father was down, unconscious, and still, he kept beating him, slamming his fists into his face and body." My voice cracks. "Venom gave Python the order or permission or whatever the fuck you want to call it. I watched it all happen with my own eyes. Python could have refused, but he didn't."

Levi slides his mask from my hand. Slipping it over his head and down his face, he backs away, disappearing into the crowd behind us.

Edge's dangerous gaze is unwavering behind his mask. "Like I said, it's more complicated than that."

"I don't give a fuck how complicated it is! My father is dead because of you!" My voice is rising, but I don't care who hears me. I start in the direction of the exit. Foolish me glances at the octagon one last time. Over the crowd, Python is being dragged away. His body is bloodied and broken. *Not again.*

My hand covers my mouth. "No. No. No—" I whisper.

Regurgitated feelings claw up my throat. I can't watch another person die in the cage. As much as I hate Python for what he did, and as much as I want him to pay, I don't want it to be Edge to do it. Edge, the guy I'm falling for, the one who wasn't the one who killed my dad. He can't be as bad as the rest of them. Can he?

Warm fingers slide under my chin. Gently, Edge tilts my face back to his. "I didn't kill him."

Does he want a badge of honor or something? Python can't even stand. All of his dignity was ripped away by the guy standing in front of me. I slowly shake my head in disbelief. Wet streams of tears fall down my cheeks. I can't be near him for another second. People start moving toward the exit. I jerk away from Edge and follow them.

"Ninja," Edge calls after me. I slow just enough to hear him warn, "Be careful."

I pull my mask down over my face and slip into the crowd.

33

KINSLEY

THE HOUSES and trees blur by as I drive through the dark, empty streets. It's after two in the morning when I finally pull into my driveway. My thoughts are on the carousel of hell. I'm constantly wondering how deep Edge's involvement is with Venom. He obviously supports them and their ways, or he wouldn't be a part of them, right? The hardest part to swallow is that I have no reason to believe he wasn't there the night my father was killed, that he didn't watch him get beaten to death like I did. It physically pains me to imagine he had anything to do with my dad's murder.

I shed my clothes and collapse into bed, too lazy to get back up and close the drapes. The shadows of the palm trees outside my window sway on my wall and ceiling. The few hours before dawn slowly drain away, taking the night with them as I try to fall asleep.

For the next two days, I ignore all of Edge's texts and calls. I spend most of that time at the dojo. It's closed for the holiday weekend, so I have the place to myself. I swear, a couple of times, I glance out the window and see a figure standing under the oak tree. But it could also be my imagination, because, unfortunately for me, Edge and Venom took my thoughts hostage, leaving me consumed with what-ifs and memories I'm not ready to let go of yet.

There has to be a way to penetrate Venom's nucleus or find out who's in charge. But shit me if I can figure out how to do that. I have a strong feeling that Edge is high up on Venom's hierarchy list. Hell, maybe he's in with the guy in the suit outside the ring. Edge could be the one calling the shots from the sidelines when he's not fighting. My stomach twists with dread. I hate sounding so naïve, but the hope in my chest that he isn't so heavily invested was crushed when Python was dragged away.

I'm furious for allowing myself to spiral so far down into the dangerous depths of his touch and charm. I have no one to blame but myself that I fucking let him touch me, kiss me. Thank God we haven't fucked. He was never supposed to see the feelings I held tightly. But he knew exactly how to draw them out of me until he peeled away my toughest layers. He found a way to my core, revealing my vulnerable side that I rarely show anyone.

The admission of my weakness to him is in every punch and kick I throw at the bag. I've given my body no time to recuperate or heal after pushing it to the limits for the past couple of days.

Exhausted, I drop to my knees on the mat.

There's no turning back the clock for everything that has happened between us. But I can stop it from here on out.

Edge's last message from this morning is a verbal collage of all the others. *We need to talk, I'm sorry.* Blah, blah, blah. This time, though, there's the puzzling warning to be careful. Those were his final words to me at the UG: *Be careful.* What the fuck does that even mean? Be careful of whom? Him? Venom?

I'm so fucking tired.

I vowed to avenge my father's death and for how they wrecked my world. But as much as I hate to admit it, I feel lost and defeated. I feel the exact opposite of how I felt when I started all of this.

I fall forward, stretching my arms in front of me. My head rests on the mat, and my body relaxes into the yoga position child's pose, allowing my back, neck, and other muscles to unwind. I breathe in and out, slowing my breath until most of the tension melts away. My head clears enough to rid the poison that Venom has flooded my bloodstream and every thought with, drugged me to the point that I lost focus. The sad part is I thought I was immune.

I'm not.

There is a silver lining to all of this. I learned that keeping your enemies close isn't always the wisest approach. The antidote is to refocus and keep my distance from Edge and the rest of them. I can't and won't give up on what I set out to do.

New strength and vigor slowly seep back into my tired body. There must be a way to learn more about this fight team. It's been less than two months since I started at Monarch. The few things I know for sure: who the four players are that make up Venom at school, Edge is considered their leader, Python is part of them but older, and there is most definitely someone higher than Edge who oversees them. As for who that may be, I have no idea. Kade said something about Edge's dad. Could it be him?

My Sherlock Holmes brain starts kicking around some ideas. The one that sticks out is Python. He was forced to lose the other night after he was forced to win over my father. Why? He might be the key to all of this.

It's already five in the afternoon on Sunday, the last day of the break, and we have to be back at school. Avoiding Edge for the next several hours shouldn't be that difficult. Tomorrow at school, I won't get off so easily.

After I take a shower and settle into bed, I call Luca.

He answers on the first ring. "Hey, Kins, what's wrong?"

"Why does something have to be wrong?"

He sighs. "It doesn't, but I know you. So give it up." Leave it to Luca to cut right to the chase.

I heave out a breath. "Everything, actually. But right now, I need a way to get to Python. Find out who he is, where he lives, if he goes to school—"

"Kins, stop!"

"What?" Impatience eats me alive from the inside. As difficult as it'll be, talking to him is the next step. That is, if I don't kill him first.

"Do you even hear yourself?"

"Of course."

My phone dings. I accept the FaceTime call with Luca. Flames from the fireplace dance behind him. I would much rather be hanging out with him on the couch than playing detective and finding ways to plot revenge.

"That's better," he says. "Now I can see the full-on attack of the maniacal invasion of my best friend."

"Luca! I'm serious. I don't see another way."

He drops his head to his chest. Even though I can no longer see his face, I can perfectly imagine the disappointment and defeat of being unable to talk me out of my insane plan.

Letting him have his moment, I wait a few beats before pulling him back. "Luca, please," I say in a soft voice.

He takes a sip from the glass he's holding. The glow of the fire intensifies the color of the amber liquid. Knowing Luca, it's probably from the most expensive bottle of bourbon his dad owns. He lowers the glass from view. "Let me get this straight. You want to *talk*"—he makes quotes with his free hand—"to the fighter that killed your father? Kins, baby, I know you better than your own mother, even yourself. And there's no way in hell you won't wrap your hands around the guy's throat the second you come face to face with him."

I huff out an impatient breath. "I— Well, I can control myself. Besides, I don't have a choice. It's the only way to find out what's really going on in Venom."

Looking back at the camera, he says, "Kinsley West, you know that I have always been—and I will continue to be—by your side, no matter how crazy your asinine ideas are, but this is insane." He wipes the front of his pants, closes his eyes, takes a deep breath, and then lets it all out in one long sigh. Opening his eyes, he zones in on me, studying me like a weird new species. "So please, just tell me that you're fucking with me and this is one big joke."

I slowly shake my head. "I'm not joking." I was going to avoid telling him about the fights the other night, but I don't see another way around that either. "I went to the fight the other night." The confession slips through my lips, leaving no room to back out.

I wince as he spills his drink on his lap. "Oh shit!" He abruptly pushes off the lounger, ice cubes falling from his sweatpants. He throws his hands in the air. "Jesus, fuck, Kins! Are you trying to get yourself killed? Getting stabbed wasn't enough?"

"Python was carried out of the cage. He couldn't even stand after the... the other fighter got done with him. He was the one on the receiving end this time. Why?" I leave out the details of the other fighter. That's a whole other level of fucked-up. "Luca, something seriously dark is happening, and more fighters will step into the octagon, and they may end up like my dad. I believe Venom is at the heart of this, and they need to be stopped."

"And you're going to be the one to stop them? To put an end to this corruption?"

All I see for the next several seconds is the fire swaying and jerking in the background as the camera swings back and forth. I picture him scrubbing his hand over his face and head, cursing silently, and finally biting his pinky nail. When he lifts the camera to his face, the tip of his pinky is between his teeth. He knows me as well as I know him. There's comfort in that.

"I know I've done some stupid shit. And this probably tops it all. But I need to do this."

He hastily shakes his head. "None of this feels right. You and a killer, meeting face to face in some dark back alley—"

"It's not going to be in a dark alley. It'll be a coffee house or... something." I have no idea where the meeting will take place, but I'll do what I can to avoid anywhere too private. "Besides, you and I know I can take him down if I have to."

"Girl, you know I'm not underestimating your skills. But he's a killer. Your dad's murderer. He took down Slayer! And nothing is stopping him from filling the space in the ground next to your father."

"I know." The words come out in a breathy whisper.

"It doesn't matter what I say. You're going to meet him, aren't you?"

I close my eyes. A welling tear falls as I nod. "Yeah." I swipe it away and look directly at him. "I have to." He knows I'm not looking for his permission. I want his support. And he's never not given it to me. Until now.

We talk for a bit longer after we drop the Python conversation altogether. Luca is hoping for a miracle that I'll somehow get over my new plan and change my mind. I won't.

Since I can't trust Edge to tell me anything, maybe the guy

who got the shit beat out of him by someone from his own team will.

After we hang up, I take a huge leap and text Kade. Since I helped with the Josh situation, maybe he'll return the favor by setting up a meeting with Python. I hate testing his loyalty to his friends, but I need this meeting to happen. And he's the only one I trust enough to make that happen. After I press the send button, all I can do is find a way to be patient.

Nothing is working out as I thought. It's not like I had a perfect plan, but I was going to destroy Venom. Expose them, fight them, find a way to prove them guilty for what they did. *Something*. Get close enough to them, learn their secrets, and use them against themselves. But none of that is happening. All I know is I've gotten myself in deep. The only way out is to slither out of the hole I crawled into or come out fighting.

Fighting seems like a way better option.

34

KINSLEY

Some days, I feel like I have all my shit under control. Those perfect days when the sun warms my face with its invisible caress or when I deliver a flawless high kick to my opponent's head or even paint the perfect, elegant line in art class.

Today isn't going to be one of those days.

I'm anticipating today will be the kind that seizes me by my soul and shakes me like a rabid dog until I'm battered and bruised.

When I pull into the parking lot, two cop cars are near the entrance. The door opens, and Josh comes out between two officers with handcuffs on. I don't know what he's saying, but it looks like he's cursing them out and spewing empty threats. Good riddance.

Maybe this day won't be so bad after all. Then, as soon as I think that's a possibility, I see Edge. With his arms crossed over his chest, Edge is waiting for me near the parking spot I claimed as mine since day two at Monarch. I let out a long breath as he walks toward me. His predatory strides are as menacing as they are graceful. I should look away, not in fear or shame but to avoid being spellbound by those mesmerizing eyes.

The second I remove my helmet, I know there's no escaping Edge or his wrath. He's on me before I turn off the engine of my motorcycle.

"What the fuck is going on?"

I don't want to look at him, but he's making it very difficult. "What are you talking about? Nothing. It's Monday." Every cell in my body is furious with him, but I can't let any of that show. I need him to back off until I learn more about the UG.

"I know it's fucking Monday." The sneer on his face says he's not in the mood to be fucked with. "Let's go, we need to talk," he demands.

I turn off the engine and put down the kickstand. "I don't think so. I'm going to class."

He reaches for me, but I slink away just out of his reach. His eyes are a mass of gray fury swirled with torment.

"What's with all the avoidance, ignoring my calls and texts? What the fuck happened that you didn't already know about?"

That one question stops the world around me. There's only me and Edge in our vast universe as we stare at one another, taking the other in as if our very lives and our next breath depend on it. I feel like I'm catching glimpses of him I just noticed for the first time. Another mask or facade—no, his expression is raw with genuine confusion and hurt.

Does he think I knew he was a key fighter for Venom? Granted, I suspected and even knew he had something to do with Venom. But not enough clout to jump out of the ring to come for me after almost killing someone. I've spent more time making empty excuses about how he couldn't be involved that deeply with the enemy. I let myself become so immersed with him that I even found a way to distort and twist the truth to my liking.

Stupid. Stupid girl.

Deciding not to admit my clouded judgment, I say, "I can't do this anymore."

It's a cop-out of the worst kind, but it's all I have right now. I've never seen his face contort with so much anger. It's a hundred times fiercer than when he went up against Python. His fists are balled at his sides, and his breaths are shallow pants as I turn away from him and walk toward the school. I close my eyes for a long moment, open them, take several deep breaths, and then carry on. It's so much harder than I thought it would be. There's a crumbling ache in my chest that physically hurts. The sting of tears burns the corners of my eyes as they threaten to fall. I do everything in my power to hold them back, at least until I'm out of his sight.

Show no weakness.

Eden joins me as I cross the courtyard toward the arts building. The good friend she has become, after one quick look at my face, she doesn't pry or ask me a thing. She stops at the large wooden doors with me. As I reach for the handle, she gently sets her hand on my shoulder. "If you need me, I'm here."

I give her a weak smile. "Thanks."

Thankfully, Brielle couldn't find the time to make it to class. She's the last irritating little stone in my shoe I want to deal with right now.

Levi had to have told his twin brother he saw me at the fight. And the second our gazes lock, it's all over his face. For the first time since I transferred to Monarch, Gunner completely ignores me. He was probably instructed to do so.

It's almost the end of class, and I can't take the silence anymore. "Why didn't you guys tell me you were going to the fight?" I blurt out.

He ignores my question as he paints a few brush strokes on his canvas.

"Gunner..."

He swishes the saturated tip in the cup of water before setting the brush down. I wait for him to look at me. When he finally does, I hate the sadness and disappointment in his eyes.

"I could ask you the same thing, little Ninja." His voice lacks the light and fun tone I've grown used to.

He's right. I don't know what to say. Trying to defend his counter-question will only make the situation hurt worse. Over the past couple of months, a slow-growing connection has developed between me and each of the boys, an understanding and an unspoken trust. But with all of the secrets between us, there was never any chance of true friendship or trust.

Chelsea announces that it's time to clean up our supplies.

Gunner is locked up as tightly as I am. I'm both relieved that I don't have to answer and irritated because he's the easy one to talk to, the one who can't wait to spill all the juicy details. Not today.

Going through the motions, I barely remember anything said or explained in biology. Like a zombie, I write illegible notes that may or may not make sense when I need them.

I keep my head low on the way to the library, the place where Edge and I had several intense and uninhibited moments. These moments I relived in my imagination more than once. I briefly look up to see the four of them standing just outside the massive wooden doors. Shit! I turn to make a one-eighty and practically run into the group of people I didn't notice. Apologizing, I maneuver and spin around, only to land directly into the arms of Venom.

"I just want to talk," Edge says. He's a hell of a lot calmer than he was this morning. I'm not sure if this new demeanor is good or bad, or what his angle is. By talking, does he want to confess shit, or does he want information from me? If it's the former, he already told me he wasn't the one who killed my dad. He also said it was complicated.

I glance at the others behind him. Kade catches my attention first and gives me an inconspicuous nod as if he's letting me know it's okay. It's all going to be okay. I can trust them.

Can I, though?

Edge is staring at me when I turn my focus on him.

"What about?"

He reaches out his hand for me to take. "The past."

35

EDGE

RELUCTANTLY, Ninja nods but doesn't take my hand. Gunner, Levi, and Kade stay behind as I guide her away from the library. Tension mixed with relief coils in my gut. The combination is virtually impossible to conquer as I try to keep my cool. I've had days to think about what I would say to her, how much I would tell her, or if I should tell her anything. The smartest thing I could do is leave her the fuck alone, but then she'd be in even more danger than she is now. No one has ever been able to tear down my steel walls, but she managed to find a way to get under my skin and burrow her way into my life. I can't leave her to fend for herself against wolves she has no way to defend herself against.

The courtyard is empty. Side by side, we walk to the stone bench in silence. She sits down without glancing in my direction. I do the opposite. I straddle the bench so I can look directly at her. Even with the hurt, fury, and confusion streaking across her face, she's the most beautiful woman I've ever seen. It takes more power and self-control not to reach out to touch her than it does to take down a beast of a man in the cage. I wind my hands around each other to keep them from drifting toward her. The last thing I want to do is freak her out. If she runs from me, then I can't protect her.

I need to figure out what's going on in that pretty little head of hers. Talking to her and getting her to open up won't be easy unless I'm willing to give her something in return. Where she is in all this, what her intentions are, and how dangerous those intentions are to Venom. And, in turn, how much she's putting herself in danger.

She plays with the ring in her eyebrow as she impatiently waits for me to start the conversation.

The first time I ever saw her, despite the pure agony splayed across her face as she watched her father brutally murdered, I knew, one way or another, she would be the one who could end the madness. She's been marked by Venom for over a year. I can't blame them. A powerful and fierce fighter lives in that perfect body and could bring millions to the table. What they didn't bank on was for their new plaything to make her own agenda after what they took from her. They also haven't figured into their plan that their all-star fighter would fall for her. I wish I could change our circumstances, but there's not a goddamn thing I can do about that now.

"What do you want, Edge?" Exhaustion, above all else, settles into that question.

"Why are you ignoring me? We—we had—are—"

She lets out a small laugh, but there's no humor in it. "There's not even a name for what we *had*. And now, we're nothing." She shrugs. "It's as simple as that."

As much as her words sting, I can't focus on the label of what we were or still are. It doesn't matter right now. I just want to get to the bottom of what made her shift. "Tell me, why the hell are you so mad at me? The last thing I knew, we were eating apple pie, and then nothing. Friday morning, you were a ghost, then after I saw you at the fight—" I run my hand over my head. "Fuck!"

I expect her gaze to still be distant when I look at her, but she's looking at me. Light glints off the silver bar above her tired eyes.

"What? Why are you looking at me like that?"

She shakes her head. "Don't play stupid. Did you honestly think I wouldn't find out that you fight for Venom?"

With my frustration rising to dangerous heights, it's taking everything I have to stay calm. Losing it will only push her further away. "You knew I was part of Venom."

"I knew you were part of the Venom that was feared at school, the part of Venom who fought and trained in a secret dojo, not the part of the Venom who are murderers," she says, and I wince at her selected word. "I didn't want to believe you were part of the money-hungry scoundrels who kill innocent men." She closes her eyes and tries to catch her breath. "That's what I'm trying to say. I *hoped* you weren't part of them."

Hope. What a fucked-up notion. When what you're hoping for is still possible, all is still right in the world. But when that *hope* comes crashing down, there's no pain like that kind of devastating loss.

"I couldn't watch as you delivered your final blow to Python." She turns to look at me. "I knew it would be like watching my father murdered all over again. I saw you glance at your manager. A nod was given, and you followed the order, carrying out your strike... just like a viper." Her face is a mask of pain and betrayal. Slowly, she reaches up and lightly skims the line of my jaw. "Etched in the lines of your face was a hate and fury so palpable and intense it chilled me to my core. I've been around fighters my entire life. I know that look all too well. It's the one worn when more than just pain is intended to be inflicted. It's the same one Python wore when he killed my father."

She drops her hand. Her shoulders hunch forward in defeat.

All of the energy seems to have been sucked out of her with that one admission.

I take the chance and rest my hand on her lower back. The pressure in my chest eases when she doesn't jerk away or recoil from my touch. Her hazy blue gaze shifts to look at me.

"Kinsley, I told you it's complicated."

Her tense muscles relax a little under my fingers. She lets out a breath and closes her eyes. "Complicated isn't an excuse for murder."

She's right. My hand slides from her back to the cool stone bench. I keep replaying what she saw, and aside from the pain I caused—opening her barely healed wound of losing her dad—the thought of my girl at the UG makes me want to punch the shit out of something.

My girl. I drag my fingers through my hair again. The UG is the last place I ever wanted her to be—again. My world slowly closes in around me as everything settles into place. I knew this day would fucking come. I just wasn't ready for it this soon.

"I never wanted you to see me like that," I admit.

She looks at me then. "Like what? A murderer?"

It's my turn to duck my head. Python—fuck! Things got way out of control the night her father was murdered. I felt as though I was possessed by the assholes running the show. I did things that night that would haunt me forever. "I wasn't the one who killed your father."

"But you would have!" she lashes out. "If you were in that cage that night instead of Python, you would have taken the orders just as easily as he did. Just as easily as you did Friday night."

I don't say anything for fear of what I'll lie about, who I'll make excuses for, or worse, because she's not wrong. She has every right to hate me.

"After you pinned Python, I saw how you looked at Venom to

see what your next move should be." She blows out a harsh breath. "Python did the exact thing right before he killed my dad. He waited for some kind of fucked-up command or something."

She's right again, and we both know it. My father controls me and the rest of us. The worst fucking part is the girl I'm falling hard for is the key to all of it. Ninja is who he really wants. She has been all along. Killing her father was only to get to her. This is something I can no more admit to her without implicating my father or, worse, giving her the perfect out to never speak to me again. I can't face that—not when I know what she fucking tastes like, the feel of her next to me, the pure passion she exudes. Fuck!

And worse still, what will she do with that information? I planned to shut it down before now, but there's no stopping Venom when the stakes are raised to immeasurable heights. If Ninja were a fighter for Venom, she would bring in millions. And that's the problem.

Fuck. Fuck. Fuck. There's no way out of this unless I put both our lives on the line, and I'm not sure I'm ready to do that yet.

"I know you watched your father die in the most horrific way."

In that single nod lives a thousand reasons why she went to the UG on Friday. Strands of her black hair fall against her face as she bows her head. I brush her hair away from her damp cheeks and tuck it behind her ear.

In a hushed voice, she says, "You knew it was me the whole time." With her head lowered, she waits for me to respond.

"I'll admit the black hair threw me at first, but the second I saw your fearless blue eyes, I knew you were the girl with blonde hair I saw at the fight that night. Then, in gym class, your tattoo confirmed it. It's the same one your father had, except yours has cherry blossoms."

"It was you that night at the fight? You told me to leave."

I purse my lips before giving her the truth she already knows. "Yes."

She tilts her face just enough to look at me. I hate the betrayal dwelling in her eyes. "You stabbed me."

I jerk at her accusation. "What? No! I would never." She looks like she believes me, though it's another half-truth on my part. With utter shame, I close my eyes and whisper, "It wasn't me, but I know who did."

When I open my eyes, she's staring at me with absolute horror etched into her face. "You know who stabbed me?"

"I tried to get there in time, but—"

"Are you fucking kidding me right now?" She bursts up from the bench.

I grab her arm before she runs off. "Kinsley, I know you hate me right now, and you don't owe me shit, but I need you to hear me out."

She shoves my hand off. The hatred in her eyes could set fire to a forest. "You're right. I don't owe you anything. My father is dead because of—"

"Mine!"

"What?"

"Mine," I repeat in a softer voice. "My father had your dad killed." There, I fucking said it. The release should make me feel better, but it doesn't. "Please sit back down. Please."

"All for money?"

I shake my head. "Mostly, yeah, but it's more than that."

She slowly sits back down. Her ass is barely on the stone bench as if she's ready to bolt at the first second she gets.

The girl next to me has been through hell. It's obvious Ninja came to Monarch University with the intention of revenge. Her need to avenge her father has not only gone unfulfilled but has also been pressed and compromised into something more dangerous and formidable than she knows.

"Hey." I guide her face toward mine using the lightest touch.

"Whatever you're planning, I want in." As calm as my voice is, it's the opposite of the storm raging through my body.

She doesn't deny my accusation that she's up to something. Her face is still a mask of pain and confusion. Slowly, she shakes her head. "No. It goes against everything you stand for." Her voice is even. Her tone is ominous.

It makes complete sense that she would believe that.

"I can help," I insist.

She shakes her head violently. "Not with this, you can't. And even if you could, I don't want your help. I don't trust you."

"I'm not letting you go that easily."

She drops her head as she laughs mercilessly. "You can't let go of something you never had."

I want to scream at her, shake her until she stops spewing shit about us. I take a deep breath and slowly release it. As calmly as I can, I say, "You can tell that shit to yourself all fucking day, but you know goddam well you were and still are mine." I know I'm being a controlling and relentless asshole, but I don't give a fuck. I move closer to her and wrap my arms around her waist. "Let me in, Ninja."

She slowly shakes her head. "I can't."

I lift her chin so she's looking at me. "You know I'm not fucking going anywhere. And whatever you have planned, I can help. I don't want this fucked-up life anymore. I want you."

Relenting, she rests her hand against my chest. "You don't know what you're asking for."

I smooth my hand over her cheek. She lays her head against my hand. Wetness coats my palm.

"Yes, I do. I want to bring him down just as much as you do. I've lived with this shit my entire life, and I'm done."

When everything comes crashing down, one of us, or both, won't make it out of this unscathed. But I'll do everything in my power to keep her safe. I just wished she believed me.

KINSLEY

I want to hate Edge.

I need to hate Edge.

Everything would be easier if he hated me. He has no idea what he's asking. The only problem is that he may be playing me as much as I'm playing him. So our dance isn't so different. It's the same song and steps. The only difference is I know how this ends.

My trust, pain, anger, and hate toward Venom have grown into a tsunami of fury. I'm scared of what this rage will do to me, who I will become when I carry out my revenge. The stakes are higher than I thought.

Am I willing to die to avenge my father?

He would never forgive me. But instantly, the answer is clear. He's worth that risk, and so are all the other fighters who are killed for sport.

Next to me, my phone buzzes in my bag. I slide it from my pocket and glance at the screen. There's a text from Kade.

Python agreed to meet with you

I put the phone into the side sleeve of my bag before Edge has a chance to see the message.

Edge reaches up and tucks loose strands of my hair behind my ear. "I want you to know you can trust me, Ninja."

What he wants—what he's asking—for me to trust him after everything that happened, I can't possibly give him that one thing that may save me in the end.

I stroke the lotus pendant at the base of my throat for strength. Not only do I have trust issues with the guy I'm falling for, a murderer to meet, and a new plan of attack to devise—preferably one that won't get me killed—I need to keep my emotions in check. I can't allow Edge to break me down into nothing but a pile of sappy feelings.

As I look up at him, I can't focus anywhere but on his exquisite face. His dark and dangerous eyes penetrate me in ways that make me want to crumble and give in to him, but I won't allow myself to shatter that easily. I owe it to my father and to myself. With everything he told me, I have a lot to process, but I know one thing for sure. The last UG was my final one as being just a spectator.

"When's the next fight?"

He drops his head into his hands. "Please, Kinsley, don't do this."

I stand and drape my backpack over my shoulder. "It's the only way."

"It's not safe."

"It never was." Offering a dry laugh, I add, "I have the scars to prove that."

There's nothing he can say to counter the truth.

"I'll find out for myself. And, I assume I'll see you there." It pains me to turn my back on the only guy I've ever felt this deeply for. Something I've learned from my past: most things suck shit before the light can shine through. And something tells me whatever we have between us is no different. If we break, then it was never meant to be. If we survive, that'll be the real challenge.

CONTINUE KINSLEY AND EDGE'S STORY IN...

Poison Kiss

Read FREE with Kindle Unlimited

ALSO BY KELA MARQ

Monarch Vipers - Vengeance

Poison Touch

Poison Kiss

Poison Bite

Forbidden Poison, Levi and Estelle's second-chance HEA story, is available for FREE

Download it HERE

ABOUT THE AUTHOR

The fantastical world of fiction is like oxygen to Kela Marq. Reading and writing stories filled with forbidden love, morally gray men, badass heroines, angsty tension, and romance releases a surge of endorphins, transporting her to her happy place.

She lives where it's warm and sunny year-round. Her three daughters, four black cats, and practicing Pilates keep her busy when she isn't reading or writing.

Visit Kelamarq.com

www.ingramcontent.com/pod-product-compliance
Lightning Source LLC
Chambersburg PA
CBHW051946240626
47153CB00005B/1645